BECAUSE FAT GIRL

Lauren Marie Fleming

BECAUSE FAT GIRL

This book is a work of fiction. Names, characters, places, and incidents are the product of the author's imagination or are used fictitiously. Any resemblance to actual events, locales, or persons, living or dead, is coincidental.

Entangled Publishing, LLC
644 Shrewsbury Commons Ave., STE 181
Shrewsbury, PA 17361
rights@entangledpublishing.com

Amara is an imprint of Entangled Publishing, LLC.

Visit our website at www.entangledpublishing.com.

Edited by Yezanira Venecia and Madison Pelletier
Cover design by Elizabeth Turner Stokes
Stock art by durantelallera/Shutterstock, Denys Drozd/Shutterstock
Interior design by Britt Marczak

Paperback ISBN 978-1-64937-691-6
Ebook ISBN 978-1-64937-622-0

Manufactured in the United States of America

First Edition October 2024

10 9 8 7 6 5 4 3 2 1

Other Books by Lauren Marie Fleming

Bawdy Love: 10 Steps to Profoundly Loving Your Body

Because Fat Girl is a larger than life romantic comedy about making space for yourself, your art, and maybe even a little someone special in your heart. Nonetheless, this love story contains elements that may not be enjoyable for all readers. Mentions of past sexual assault, disordered eating in a minor character, grief and death by cancer, and men…tal health struggles (including talk of suicidal ideation and past self harm) are all present in the text. This novel addresses systemic biases, including fatphobia, homophobia, biphobia, transphobia, racism, sex worker discrimination, and the right of all people to exist—and thrive—in the skin they're in. Readers who may be sensitive to these elements, please take note. Now sharpen your eyeliner, button your cuffs, and get ready to bet on your dreams!

For Kylee Singh
I'm so glad that our grandparents were best friends, so our dads could be best friends, so we could be best friends. Thanks for being my first and biggest fan.

Chapter One

By the time I heard the giggles, it was already too late. A junior clerk had my arm in a grip and was pulling me behind a mannequin.

"Is it true?" she asked.

"Is what true?" I replied.

"Is Chris Stanson really in the store today?" Her voice was a conspiratorial whisper.

"God, I hope not," I said.

"Do you need any help with him, Diana? I know he has a reputation for being very particular." Another clerk—Tim, or maybe it was Jim—sidled up to me like I was his best friend. He was the only one I'd ever talked to before this, all of them new recruits in a department far removed from where I worked.

"I'm sure we'll be able to handle whatever or whomever the day brings us," I said, extracting myself from the group and walking toward the Personal Shopper department where I worked.

"I'm in shoes today if you need anything," said Tim or Jim, but there was no way any of them were getting a call from me. They'd already proven they couldn't handle someone like Mr. Stanson, and we couldn't afford another Marie incident.

I hurried over to the staff room, glancing at the large stack of inventory paperwork that would be ignored again today, much to the chagrin of accounting. Putting my purse and phone into our new lockbox, I adjusted my clothes, reapplied my lipstick, and headed out onto the floor. My colleague Emmy was waiting for me, giving the gawking junior clerks a steely glare that made them all scatter.

"Is he here yet?" I asked.

Emmy didn't answer, just pulled back the privacy curtain and gave me a "see for yourself" look.

Opening the dressing room door, I was greeted by a tall, white, sandy-blond heartthrob with a set of mesmerizing blue eyes and the kind of smile that could charm your clothes right off.

"Emmy, my love," Chris Stanson said, getting up and walking right past me to kiss her on the cheeks. "It's been far too long."

"You were here last month," Emmy pointed out.

"Like I said, far too long." Mr. Stanson laid on the charm.

Chris Stanson was a child star turned leading man and Hollywood's latest obsession, starring in multiple box office hits that summer with a couple more planned for the fall. With his success came press junkets, galas, award shows, and society events, each of which needed a uniquely different yet similarly dashing ensemble. That's where we came in. Or Emmy, I should say, since people like Chris Stanson never gave me the time of day.

We were technically equals at work, but Emmy's supermodel stature granted her an access to megastars that I didn't have. Emmy, a flawless fashionista with impeccable taste, hadn't gotten her job on looks alone, and the ensembles she put together were truly inspiring. Her personality, however, was rather cold, which made it hard to get to know her as a colleague, but it somehow drew celebrities to her even more. Some came with their stylists, some came alone, but all came to see Emmy.

Unless it was to or about a client, Emmy rarely spoke to anyone, including me, opting instead to stand and silently evaluate. I wasn't sure if she was a snob or shy, but she'd never been outright rude to me, and she was always good about sharing commissions when I helped her, which was the definition of considerate at a high-end, often cutthroat store like Roussard's. I was pretty sure she was queer, like me, but even that I hadn't nailed down over our seven years working together. All I really knew about Emmy was she loved every little detail concerning fashion.

She'd texted me the night before to see if I could come in early to help her with a client, and I'd begrudgingly agreed, weighing the potential commission against the anger our accounting department would aim at me for putting inventory off for another day.

Marie, our newest junior clerk, usually helped Emmy with fittings, but she'd been fired recently for sending her friend a photo of action star Drew Williams shopping in gray sweatpants. The photo made its rounds on the internet, causing a scandal that ended in a new store policy: locking cell phones in a box during our shifts.

Now, I wish I'd thought to ask who we'd be dressing. I might have said I was too busy, even booked another client, if I'd known I'd be starting my day with this guy.

Here's the thing about Chris Stanson: he was even more gorgeous in person than on screen and taller than you'd expect. More often than not, movie stars were uglier and shorter in person, a fact that made me feel more comfortable near them. But not Chris Stanson. He was an Adonis, and he knew it, which made him even more insufferable to work with and made me even more aware of my status as a mere mortal.

Today was no different. Mr. Stanson was going on and on about this dinner party he was throwing, telling Emmy she should come, name-dropping pop star Kali and action star Drew Williams, as if that would draw Emmy in. She worked with celebrities all the time; Kali even used to come into the shop to get dressed by Emmy. If Chris Stanson was trying to impress her, it wasn't working.

"This suit would be great for your dinner party," Emmy said, holding up a dark gray Armani.

"Actually, I'm here for another event." Mr. Stanson went on to explain he was hosting a fundraiser for the Los Angeles County Museum of Art (or LACMA as the locals called it) at his house in a few weeks, requiring him to break free from his usual classic black or navy and go for something a little flashier.

"None of these will do." Mr. Stanson pointed to the suits Emmy had laid out. "I need to *pop*."

Anyone else would have been flustered by the game change, but if Emmy was bothered, she didn't show it. She simply excused herself to go pull other options, leaving Mr. Stanson and me alone in the room.

"Would you like some Flamingo Estate cold brew?" I asked to fill the awkward silence. Emmy had preordered the famous pink cans—his file said it was his drink of choice—from the notoriously bougie L.A. lifestyle company and put one in his room on ice. Just the kind of touch a place like Roussard's was known for.

"Sure." He grinned. I could tell by the way he smiled that he was used to it having an alluring effect on people, and I could see why. The way his lips curved seductively, the intensity of his eyes when he fixed them on me.

But Chris Stanson did nothing for me. Not in that fake way girls in Hollywood say celebrities don't affect them, pretending they're used to walking in the presence of the gods, acting like they're blind to the disparity between us and them. It's precisely because I was acutely aware of our differences that Chris Stanson didn't faze me. I studied Greek tragedies; I knew what happened to mortals who consorted with gods. I wanted no part in that.

It was one of the reasons I excelled at my job. A lack of fawning over the rich and famous was a unique asset in this town. Celebrities came to Roussard's to work with Emmy. Desperate people came to work with me. Awkward rich kids were my bread and butter, especially fat girls and gender nonconforming queers whose mothers were exasperated with trying to dress them "in a manner appropriate for the occasion." Their size, style, sexuality, and gender presentation were all seen as a personal fault, a rebellion against their families' wishes for them to be thin, pretty, straight, and cis. I was a last resort, and the parents often came to me exhausted and looking for a miracle.

The key to my success was not settling for the small selection of clothes we kept in the store, but helping the person dream about finding an outfit that actually made them feel confident, beautiful, sexy even—something fat, queer, and trans people don't really get to experience like thin, straight, cis people do. I'd grown up belittled for my weight, bullied for being gay, and generally miserable in my body. It wasn't until I found plus-size fashion that I truly connected with myself, and I saw it as my job at Roussard's to help others feel the same.

But while I loved fashion, dressing people was not my dream. Like a typical L.A. cliché, I moved to Hollywood because I wanted to make movies. I longed to write, direct, and star in the kinds of films that transformed audiences, ones full of characters that looked and acted like me and my friends, the people pushed to the margins of society: femmes, queers, people of color, gender nonconforming folks, and bodies of all different shapes and abilities.

You needed money to make movies, though, so I stayed at Roussard's and lived with my sister and her kids in the suburbs, trying to save up as much as I could, working tirelessly on scripts during my days off, hustling my way to a big break.

I was starry-eyed but not naive, and I knew that break wouldn't come from someone like Chris Stanson. He was him, I was me, and there was no bridging the gap society placed between us. So while most of America would love to be sitting in a room alone with *People* magazine's "Sexiest Man Alive," I was itching to get out of there and back to my own clients.

"If you don't need anything else, I'll go help Emmy," I said after pouring his coffee.

"Sure, yeah, great," he replied, texting on his phone, not bothering to look up at me as he spoke.

I left the customer lounge and headed straight for the bright coral Kiton cashmere jacket we'd gotten in the day before, the suit I'd been thinking of ever since Mr. Stanson said he needed something that "popped." I grabbed a bright white pocket square, white pants, and a white shirt with light orange stripes to complement it. No tie, I decided. This was an artsy event; he'd want to be less formal.

"What do you think?" I showed the pairing to Emmy.

"He's basic," she said dismissively.

"Can I still take it back to see?" I asked, knowing better than to present something to her client without her approval.

She agreed that it was worth a shot. "If only for contrast."

Emmy pulled an additional pocket square and cream pants for my jacket, and together we headed back with our bounty. Chris Stanson was busy talking on his phone, so we displayed the items on various pegs around the dressing room while we waited for him to finish sweet-talking whoever was on the other line. Without hanging up, Mr. Stanson pointed to his now-empty coffee cup, then at me, and mouthed, "More." Emmy looked at me expectantly, and with a sigh, I left for the stock room where she kept extra.

It's not that I was above getting someone coffee. I got coffee without complaint for the first year I worked in Personal Shopper, and I'd happily grab coffee for a friend. But there was something about a man telling me to pour him coffee that riled my feminist brain. It always brought up images of old men in suits sitting around large mahogany desks, the only woman in the room pouring them drinks while they admired her ass and called her "toots." Or the stories I'd heard from women executives in corporate jobs who were still expected to order everyone coffee, take notes, and clean up the men's messes while guys their junior sat back and relaxed.

I wondered if Chris Stanson ever got coffee for anyone else, if he ever even noticed how his coffee got to him, or if he took for granted its appearance in his hand. As I grabbed another can of the overpriced drink, I thought for the millionth time about what life would be like if women quit catering to men.

What would we wear?

What would we say?

What would we weigh?

Coffee acquired, I walked back into the fitting room to find Emmy and Mr. Stanson laughing together as he stood on the pedestal wearing the outfit I'd picked out for him, neither of them acknowledging my reappearance.

"I love it," he said, fake posing for photos in the mirror. "I never would have thought to wear something like this, but I love it. What's this color called?"

"Coral," Emmy replied.

"Coral," he repeated, trying the word on like a piece of clothing, seeing if it fit. "I guess I like the color coral. Thank you, Emmy."

"It was Diana's pick," she corrected, acknowledging me as I poured more coffee into his mug. "She gets the credit."

"Thanks, Coffee Girl." He was smiling like I should be grateful for his attention.

I wanted to punch him in that cocky, dimpled face of his, but instead I dismissed myself to go downstairs and find shoes for his outfit. Hoping to vent, I searched for my best friend, Janelle, who also worked at Roussard's, but she was on a break. I grabbed a pair of Gucci loafers patterned with coral and green *G*'s and a gold buckle on them. Tim or Jim offered to help bring them up to the dressing room for me, but I made him stay away. Though the shoes were a bit outrageous, they paired well with the coral jacket, and Mr. Stanson loved them.

"I feel like a different person." He strutted around the

dressing room. “It’s not too flamboyant, is it?”

“It’s perfect for LACMA,” Emmy stated in her matter-of-fact way that left no room for discussion.

“If you can’t make it to dinner, you should come to the LACMA fundraiser,” Chris said to her. “See the suit in action.”

“I’m busy,” Emmy declined, taking the shoes from him and putting them back in their box.

“I’ll have Bradley bring over an invitation for you anyways, just in case,” Chris insisted, coming out of the dressing room and handing Emmy his credit card. “As a thanks for finding me this suit.”

“Diana found the outfit,” Emmy reminded him, ringing up his purchase. “She should be the one to go.”

Chris Stanson glanced at me, then back at Emmy. “Then I’ll have Bradley bring over two invitations, one for you, one for Coffee Girl.”

“Fine. Here you go.” Emmy handed him the bag with his shoes and pocket square. He said his goodbyes and invited her to dinner one last time before he left, saying nothing to me.

“Are you going to the party?” I asked on our way to clean up the dressing room.

“No,” she said, gathering the suits Chris had passed on. “You?”

“Normally I’d veer far away from that guy… but I really love LACMA, and it could be a chance to meet some interesting artists.”

“Both tickets are yours, then,” Emmy said as I walked over to the table and picked up Chris Stanson’s coffee from where it sat, untouched.

Chapter Two

My best friend scoffed when I said I was going to wear a simple black GANNI dress and Tory Burch flats to the LACMA party. She sat across from me in the booth at our favorite Thai restaurant the next day, vetoing all the options I showed her. "You cannot roll up to Chris Stanson's house looking basic."

Janelle Zenon and I met as incoming freshmen at UCLA film school, the two queer kids in a sea of geeky white dudes who all thought they were going to be the next Tarantino. It was Janelle who got me the job at Roussard's when I was struggling to make rent and pay for my senior thesis film. They were hiring extra help for the holidays, and she'd dragged me to the job interview, promising it would be an easy way to pay the bills.

She was right; it was easy money. A little too easy. Instead of pursuing the shitty-paying director's assistant roles my fellow graduates had taken, I worked my way up the Roussard's ladder, enticed by the high-paying commissions I made from selling clothes I couldn't fit in or afford. It was fine in the beginning, when I had the time and energy to work at Roussard's and hustle for film gigs on the side, but then my brother died and took my ambition with him. These days, the closest I got to making movies was watching Emmy dress the stars of them.

Janelle hadn't let Roussard's consume her like I had. A talented cinematographer, she was the best director of photography to come out of our program, yet she always seemed to lose the big jobs to people "with more experience" and "a style closer to what the director was seeking"—a.k.a. straight, white, and male. Those same "more experienced" cinematographers, however, would have to hire Janelle to come in and consult on scenes involving Black actors, which they had little to no practice in lighting. That sums up white privilege right there: the world is lit up for your skin tone.

Despite our setbacks, neither of us had abandoned the dream of making a movie together, and with Janelle's encouragement, I'd started writing scripts and putting myself out there again.

"This party is our ticket to network with the big dogs," Janelle said as we ordered our lunch. "We have to go all-out. Make a statement. Think Cinderella going to the ball."

"Except we don't have a fairy godmother to come bibbidi-bobbidi-boo us some gowns and a carriage."

"No, but we have connections at Roussard's," she replied. "And your film fund."

"Which I refuse to tap into for an outfit to a random party."

"This isn't just some party! This is exactly the kind of event you've been saving for," Janelle argued as a waiter dropped off our food. "It will be years before you make enough money to fund a film on your own. Even if you want to make an indie film, you'll still need five hundred thousand dollars bare minimum. And I know you don't have close to that much saved. So you're still going to need investors. This is the kind of party where you can meet them! But you're not going to attract anyone looking like you're going to a funeral."

I sighed, resigned to the fact that she was right. "What do you suggest?"

"I thought you'd never ask." Janelle grabbed her phone and opened up JIBRI's latest collection, a designer whose outfits I'd drooled over for years. The clothes were gorgeous, fashionable, and colorful—total showstoppers.

"We aren't Emmy," she said, grabbing a spring roll. "We don't get invited to Hollywood parties every week. This is your opportunity to hobnob with the elitest of the elite here in town. You've got one chance to shine like the star I know you are. Wear something so bright that they can't help but notice your brilliance."

"These are from the spicy curry." I motioned to my tears, the ones that had pooled during her pep talk.

"Sure they are." Janelle winked.

"I have only one problem." I pointed down at the JIBRI site still up on her phone.

"What?" Janelle asked.

"How do I choose which fabulous skirt to buy?" I laughed, scanning the assortment of colorful options.

By the end of our meal, we had our whole outfits planned. "We can get our hair and nails done at that salon around the corner, the fancy one with the blue awning. I know someone who can get us a discount on services."

"You mean the owner that you slept with?" I smirked, counting out my cash as the bill came.

"Those details don't matter right now." She placed down her credit card. "What matters is that we're going to get a discount on our brow wax before Julio in cosmetics does our makeup for us. I'm thinking high femme, full face for you, and a subtle stud vibe for me."

Janelle continued to plan everything, never pausing to see if I agreed with her ideas. Her enthusiasm was contagious, though, and soon I was chiming in, both of us acting like we were celebrities headed to the Oscars, which we someday soon would be.

• • •

By the time the big night arrived a few weeks later, we looked like we belonged on a red carpet.

"Damn, I look good." Janelle posed in front of me, fully dressed and ready to party. She wore a white suit with black trim on the lapel and a very light pink shirt underneath. Her pants were white skinny cut, paired with her favorite crushed velvet Gucci shoes and matching bow tie.

"We clean up well," I said, glowing in my JIBRI atomic tangerine skirt and sunshine yellow shirt with large structured sleeves and an open back, both items accentuating my curvy, hourglass figure. I was worried the colors wouldn't work with my olive skin, but Janelle assured me they would pop, and she was right; I looked like I'd walked out of a Mondrian or Lichtenstein painting. To complete the look, I added a Kate Spade x Darcel pop art clutch that I'd gotten years ago in a rare splurge moment, and the whole thing felt perfect for a modern art museum gala.

My collarbone-length, dark-brown hair was parted in the middle and slicked back into a low twist at the nape of my neck, showing off the large sparkling hoops that had cost a hell of a lot, considering they were Swarovski crystals, not diamonds. I planned on taking them back immediately tomorrow. I hated being that client who bought something and returned it after an event, but they were way out of my budget, even with the film fund's help.

"We're fine as hell," Janelle said as we preened ourselves in her full-length mirror, a ritual we'd had since college. We never left for a party without stopping to stare at our reflections and shower each other with confidence-boosting compliments.

"And sexy as fuck." I stared at the glowing image reflected back at me. This was the kind of outfit I'd always wanted but never let myself splurge on. I tried to forget about the cost and instead focus on how it made me feel like a bright star who deserved to be in a room full of A-listers. Because tonight, I was.

"People are lucky to share space with us," Janelle said.

"They should pay us to be in their presence."

"Damn right," Janelle agreed.

"Damn right," I repeated. "Tonight, we are the works of art."

"It's charity simply showing up and letting them get a glance of our grandeur," Janelle replied.

"Now, let's go do our good deed for the week and share our greatness with the world." I grabbed my clutch, Janelle looped her arm in mine, and together we headed downstairs to hop in a cab.

Our driver was chatty, pointing out celebrity homes and tourist attractions as we wound our way up into Beverly Hills. Janelle mentioned we were locals, but he didn't care, taking his role of tour guide for the evening very seriously. He seemed impressed as he let us out next to limos and Lamborghinis, and we tipped him extra after he wished us a fun night being rich and famous.

It wasn't hard to tell which house was Chris Stanson's, with bright lights and even flashier people surrounding it. I was grateful for my cute yet comfortable Sarto flats as we hiked our way up a steep entrance to a security checkpoint where a very large guard asked for our invitations and IDs.

"These are made out to Emmy and Coffee Girl," the guard said, glancing at our documents, then back at us. "Neither of those names match your IDs."

I took the invitations back to inspect them, and sure enough, they were made out to Emmy and Coffee Girl. I wanted to punch Chris in the face for it, but mostly I kicked myself for not checking this sooner.

"Yes, well, that's what Chris Stanson calls us." I pointed at Janelle, then at me. "Emmy and Coffee Girl."

The security guard looked down at our IDs again, over to our invitation, and back to a list he was holding. "I'm sorry," he said, handing us back our stuff. "I can't let you in."

A very chic and pretentious couple behind us snorted as they pushed me aside to hand their paperwork to the guard, sure in the knowledge that they were cool enough to be on that list. Not me, though. I was just some Coffee Girl to Chris Stanson. Why had I been so stupid to think he would let me into his home?

"I can't believe I spent so much money on this outfit just to wear it in a cab!" I cried.

"Our driver did make a big deal out of how fabulous you looked," Janelle pointed out. "That's something."

"At least someone noticed me tonight," I replied as more

people filed past us and into the event.

"There's got to be a way to get in." Janelle refused defeat. "Can you call Emmy? I guarantee you at some point Chris Stanson has given her his number. Maybe she could call him?"

"Wait, you're brilliant." I took out my phone.

"You're calling Emmy?" Janelle asked.

"No, even better," I said, shooting a rapid text. A few minutes later, a smiling twentysomething wearing a tuxedo and an earpiece came running our way. "Bradley!"

"Diana!" he said, giving me a very quick hug. "You look amazing! I'm so sorry about this mix-up."

"Are they with you, sir?" the guard asked Bradley.

"Yes, John, they're good to go inside," Bradley replied. "Their names should be changed now on the list."

The security guard pulled up a list on his tablet, double-checked it, then moved aside to let us in. "Enjoy your evening."

"Thank you so much!" I said to Bradley as we made our way past security.

"Oh, of course, and I'm sorry about that—Chris thought it was funny calling you Coffee Girl," he explained.

"It's not," I said.

"That's what I told him, but he's Chris." Bradley rolled his eyes. "Anyways, I gotta run, but it was nice to see you again, Diana. Let's get coffee sometime. Or wait, no more coffee. Chris ruined coffee. Let's get tea."

We hugged goodbye, and Bradley ran off to put out another one of Chris Stanson's fires.

"Who was that?" Janelle asked.

"I'm so sorry. I should have introduced you," I apologized. "That was Bradley, Chris's assistant. He comes in to pick things up for Chris, and we chat. He's a good guy."

"That whole making-friends-with-everyone-you-meet thing sure does pay off."

"Us peasants gotta stick together," I said, looping my arm through hers and taking a deep breath as we approached the large, black, open front door. "Ready?"

"Born ready," Janelle said as we gathered all the confidence we had and strutted into Chris Stanson's home like we belonged there.

Chapter Three

Immediately, I was impressed. Which was probably the point of hanging a massive Jackson Pollock painting in the foyer.

"Holy shit," I swore, taking in the masterpiece.

"No big deal," Janelle said. "I've got a Warhol in my entryway."

"The postcard I sent you from MoMA doesn't count."

We passed under a mobile hanging from the ceiling that was very likely an Alexander Calder.

"It's got sentimental value, ups the price," she insisted as we made our way into a large, open living room. Chris's subtle black-and-white furniture allowed the modern art covering the walls to be the center of attention, each piece perfectly lit and framed.

"I'll be damned," I blurted, looking around. "Chris Stanson has taste."

"Or his decorator does," Janelle countered, grabbing two champagne flutes off a passing tray.

"Salud!" We clinked our glasses together as Mindy Kaling walked by.

"Was that...?" Janelle asked.

"Yep," I replied.

"I'm gonna need a stiffer drink." Janelle walked toward the bar.

"And some food," I called out, following a waiter with a tray going in the opposite direction.

When we met back up, Janelle was carrying two tumblers of bourbon, and I had a couple small white spoons with some kind of liquid inside of them. She looked at my findings, disappointed.

"This was the closest thing to food I could find," I said as we awkwardly tried to hand each other our bounty.

"Bottoms up!" Janelle downed her spoonful of broth in one gulp. "Dammit, that just made me hungrier."

"I should have known there would be no real food at an event full of actors," I said between bites of the side of olives Janelle had convinced the bartender to give us.

"Is that why this party is so boring?" Janelle asked as she leaned against the railing of an upper patio.

"Even the celebrities are hungry." I pointed to some familiar faces gathered around a waiter, whose tray was rapidly emptying. "That's how you know there isn't enough food."

"I feel stupid for not eating beforehand," Janelle said.

"I feel stupid for choosing fashion over the ability to carry snacks," I added, lifting my tiny Kate Spade clutch that adorably looked like a monster but sadly had very little room inside.

"Rookie mistakes." Janelle sipped her bourbon. "We'll do better next time."

"Here," I said, biting my last olive in half and handing it to her.

"Aww, you shared your last olive with me!"

"Ride or die."

"Which might come sooner than we think if we don't distract my body from eating me alive," Janelle replied, her stomach growling.

"Let's play I Spy," I offered as a distraction. "It always keeps the kids busy when they're cranky. We can do it adult style—you've gotta take a drink if you guess wrong."

"I'm in." Janelle perked up.

"I spy with my little eye," I said, looking around for someone we'd both recognize, "an action star with a nice ass."

"Hmm." Janelle scanned the room. "Tom Holland?"

"Does he have a nice ass?"

"I think so."

"That's not who I meant, so drink!"

Janelle took a sip of her bourbon and returned to scanning the room. "Ooh, Drew Williams!"

"Ding, ding, ding!" I clinked my cup with hers, both of us drinking.

"This could get dangerous," I said, observing how low my drink had gotten and remembering our lack of food.

"Here." Janelle reached into her coat pocket and pulled out a box of some super-fancy electrolyte water the celebrities were all drinking right now. "I grabbed these off a waiter earlier. Much safer, still fun."

"Brilliant," I said, opening it up like a milk carton. "Now, your turn."

"I spy with my little eye," Janelle said, scanning the room once again, "someone whose ex-wife will be there for you when the rain starts to pour."

"That might've been harder if you hadn't practically sung

the *Friends* theme song when you said it." I pointed to Brad Pitt down by the infinity pool.

He was standing next to rock star Kali and Broadway and film star Beanie Feldstein—two queer women I'd admired for years and longed to befriend—apparently saying something hilarious because they were all laughing. There seemed to be a stratum of fame at this party, and we were stuck on the nobody level. Still, it was fun to look out onto the garden below and see some of my idols.

"I spy with my little eye..."

"Some real food!" Janelle shouted, grabbing my shoulder and dragging me toward a waiter with a tray of sushi. We pounced on the poor woman, taking all that we could before she ran away.

With our bellies somewhat appeased, we made our way toward the silent auction area to see if there was anything good to buy.

"What kind of event starts bids at one thousand dollars?" I asked, glancing at overflowing gift baskets and magazine-quality photos of potential prizes.

"Ones that offer things like courtside seats to the Lakers with Leonardo DiCaprio," Janelle read off the sheets. "Or staying at Robert Downey Jr.'s home in Aspen."

"Or afternoon tea with Meryl Streep!" I squealed, way too excited at the idea of sipping tea with my hero to keep my cool.

"Girl, you gotta!" Janelle grabbed a pen and wrote my name and number down for three thousand dollars.

"I cannot afford to spend three thousand on tea!" I protested.

"If you win, we'll figure it out. Host a GoFundMe or some shit."

"I'm going to cross it out." I grabbed the pen from her hands.

"Hear me out first," Janelle said, pulling me away from the table. "You're probably going to be outbid, and if not, you can tell them it was a mistake and not pay. But this is Meryl Streep we're talking about. You've idolized her since film school. Putting your name down on that sheet of paper tells the universe and your brain that you're the kind of person who bids on your own dreams."

"That's some hippy-woo shit," I said.

"You know I'm right."

"Okay." I sighed. "But if I win, you're paying."

"I can't. I'll be too broke from my ten-thousand-dollar tennis lesson with Serena Williams."

"Bourbon makes you reckless." I pulled her away from the tables. "Let's get out of here before you bankrupt us both."

I steered Janelle toward the bar, where I ordered us fancy pink non-alcoholic cocktails and two more boxes of water, knowing that neither of us should have more booze tonight.

"I spy with my little eye," I said, picking up our game from earlier, "someone who tripped and fell getting golden."

"Jennifer Aniston," Janelle said.

"Drink!"

"I meant Jennifer Lawrence!"

"Too late, you already said Jennifer Aniston, drink!"

"Dammit, I meant J-Law. I know J-Law! I *love* J-Law! Why did I say Aniston?" Janelle said.

"Probably because she's speaking to Brad Pitt," a voice next to us said.

I turned around to see who it was and rammed right into him, spilling the frilly pink drink in my hand all over my brand-new designer clothes.

"Shit!" I cried, looking down at the mess on my shirt.

"I'm so sorry." The man pulled a handkerchief out of his lapel pocket. "Here."

"We're going to need more than that," Janelle assessed, heading toward the bar and returning with a handful of napkins and some club soda.

"I hope it doesn't stain," he said, standing there awkwardly.

"It's definitely going to stain," I replied, blotting my top, praying I was wrong. I tried to remember it was just an outfit, but my eyes started watering anyway.

"We'll get it out," Janelle tried reassuring me as she patted club soda on my shirt.

"How are you spotless, wearing all white, and I've got pink drink all over me?" I asked her.

"Blame me," the man said. "This was all my fault—I snuck up on you. I'm really sorry about that."

"It's fine," I lied, not wanting to admit to a total stranger that he'd just ruined the most expensive thing I owned.

"Hi, I'm Andy." The man extended his arm to me.

I looked up from blotting my shirt to shake the offered hand, only to realize it belonged to Drew Williams. Great, not only did I ruin my very expensive outfit, but I just made an ass out of myself in front of the man whose face I saw every time I drove down Sunset Boulevard, a man who was famously best friends with Chris Stanson and probably as big of an asshole as he was.

"Hi, I'm Andy?" I mimicked, suddenly very annoyed and angry. "Like, no big deal. I'm Andy."

"Hi, Andy." Janelle shook the hand he'd extended to me and glared my way. "Nice to meet you."

"What's wrong with my name?" he asked me.

"Nothing," I said. "It's just, you're a celebrity. Everyone knows you're Drew Williams. Why introduce yourself as Andy?"

"I was striving for humility."

"Pretending you're not famous isn't humility. It's like rich people pretending they're poor. It's insulting."

"I'm sorry," Janelle said, stepping between us. "Usually she has better manners than this. You must forgive her. She's hangry."

"I'll be back," he said, leaving us alone.

"What's with that guy?" I glared at his receding back.

"What's with *you*?" Janelle shot back. "Why are you being an asshole to one of the biggest stars in Hollywood?"

"He ruined my shirt!" I cried, pointing down at the stain that hadn't come out.

"It's a fucking shirt." Janelle grabbed me by the shoulders. "Don't ruin our chance to network with one of Hollywood's biggest stars over an item of clothing!"

"Famous people are overrated." I pouted.

"I know this look. You're crashing. We gotta get food in you, stat."

As if on cue, Drew Williams showed back up, guiding two waiters carrying trays full of food our way. "All I could find was shrimp and sushi. I hope you eat fish."

"You're a lifesaver!" Janelle grabbed some sushi for both of us.

Within a few bites, I instantly felt better.

"I'm sorry," I said, looking up at the famously fit celebrity watching me eat. "I kind of get mean when I'm hungry. No offense meant."

"None taken." Drew Williams smiled. "My mom is the same."

"Do people really call you Andy?" I asked, but before he could answer, Chris Stanson appeared at his side. He looked gorgeous in his coral suit, the colors perfect for the tone of the party, and I felt a burst of pride at having picked it out for him.

"I heard you were assaulting some of my waiters," Chris said.

"You really should have more food here," Drew replied.

"The key to a successful fundraiser is providing enough food that the attendees don't barf on the art, but not enough that they sober up before spending godawful amounts of money on shit they don't need at the auction."

"That's your idea of a good party?" Janelle scoffed. "No wonder everyone looks bored and miserable."

"I have a question for you," Drew directed at Chris. "What's the name you have for me in your phone?"

"Cocksucker," Chris replied.

"Inside joke," Drew explained, looking at us.

"Sure it is," Janelle said.

"If we were across a room full of nuns," Drew continued, "and you were shouting for me to come over to you, what name would you use?"

"Drew," Chris said.

I looked up at him, smirking.

"Okay, but what does my mom call me?" Drew prodded further.

"Andy," Chris replied.

"See!" Drew smugly shot a look at me.

"My mom calls me sweetie, but I don't introduce myself as that," I retorted.

"What do other people call you?" Drew asked.

"She's Coffee Girl," Chris said before I could answer. "She works for Emmy at Roussard's."

"I have a name. And I work *with* Emmy," I corrected, shocked Chris remembered me but annoyed he only saw me as the person who got his coffee. I turned back to Drew. "I actually chose your friend's outfit here for tonight."

"Nice look," Drew said. "Very not Chris."

"I'll take that as a compliment." I beamed.

"Hey, Coffee Girl, where's Emmy?" Chris asked.

"Tragically, her cat has fleas, so she couldn't make it," I said, mockingly serious. "But lucky for all here, I brought with me the award-winning cinematographer Janelle Zenon."

"Nice to meet you, Janelle." Drew shook her hand again while Chris scanned the crowd, probably looking for someone more interesting to talk to than two shopgirls.

"And you are?" Drew said, turning back to me.

"You don't know Diana Smith?" Janelle chastised, her voice in outraged shock. "I'm very surprised you haven't heard of her. She's quite an accomplished writer, director, *and* actress."

"A triple threat, huh?" Drew's eyebrows perked up.

"Hey, Kali's downstairs," Chris interrupted, grabbing his friend's elbow and giving him a pointed look, probably trying to convey how not worth his time us lowly servants were. "And she needs our help with something."

Drew turned back to us. "Duty calls. But it was nice meeting you both."

"Nice to meet you, too," I said as Chris dragged Drew away to hang out with the rock star I'd idolized since I was a kid. I watched the duo go down a set of stairs off the kitchen that was blocked by a bodyguard and sighed. "And they're off to go hang out with someone way more fun than us."

"Look around you." Janelle pointed her finger out into the milling crowd. "See anyone more fun than us? No. We're the best."

I didn't feel very confident, having once again been put in my place by Chris Stanson and still wearing a bright pink stain down my shirt, but I decided to borrow some of Janelle's cocky flare and rally my self-esteem, even if I had to fake it. "So what you're saying is we're the coolest people at a party full of cool people?"

"Was there ever any doubt we would be?" Janelle smirked.

"There was that one moment when a drink spilled all over my shirt, but then I realized it adds to my mystique."

"Oh yeah, now that shirt is officially one of a kind," Janelle said, looping her arms through mine. "Just like you."

"That's a cheesy line," I shot back, squeezing her into me.

"Mmm, cheese."

"Come on." I pulled her back toward the living room. "Let's go see if we can steal something edible off the auction table."

We weaved our way through crowds of polite chatter, everyone looking as bored and hungry as we were. Chris Stanson, it turned out, took the fun out of fundraiser. It was kind of nice knowing he wasn't perfect.

"Sad news." Janelle directed my attention to tea with Meryl Streep. "You've been outbid."

"Is it wrong that I'm disappointed?" I asked, looking down at the $9,800 most recent offer. I hadn't expected to win, couldn't afford it even if I had, but still, I felt weirdly heartbroken at having lost the chance to talk with my hero.

"You hoping to have tea with Meryl?" Drew Williams probed, sidling up next to us at the auction table.

“Oh, hey there, Mr. Andy,” Janelle said. “Chris let you mingle with us common folk again?”

“I wanted to check on the bids before they close.” He pointed to a gift basket touting rare, high-end wines down the table.

“This stuff is so ridiculous,” I said, more to Janelle than to him. “Spend an afternoon on a yacht with Kim Kardashian—do you even get to go anywhere, or do you just sit there looking pretty?”

“If you’re looking for a more active outing,” Janelle said, “you could go for surfing lessons from Chris Hemsworth.”

“Can he even surf?” I asked.

“He’s Australian. Don’t they all surf?” Janelle replied.

“We could find out for eight grand,” I said. “Or we could pay $5,800 for this one here. Play a round of golf with…” I stopped, seeing the name on the prize.

“Drew Williams,” he finished for me.

“I’m sure it’ll be a great time,” I lied, trying not to show the embarrassment on my face. “If only I had an extra six grand.”

“If only.” Janelle sighed dramatically as Channing Tatum pushed past her. She turned to me, wide-eyed. “This place is surreal.”

“Surreal, but nice.” I nodded.

“That’s from *Notting Hill*, right?” Drew smiled.

“What can I say”—I shrugged—“I’m a sucker for a good rom-com.”

“Wait.” Drew stopped, recognition dawning on his face. “Are you *the* Diana Smith from *Lalo’s Lament*?”

“How do you know my movie?” I asked, completely shocked that someone as famous as Drew Williams had seen my short film, much less remembered my name from it.

"I saw it at the L.A. Film Festival years ago and loved it."

"Ah, the L.A. Film Festival, may it rest in peace." Janelle bowed her head in mock mourning.

"RIP." I placed a hand on my heart in reverence. "It died after our film was featured."

Just like my brother and my career, I thought, my heart aching.

"That shot of Lalo stepping onto the stage to finally sing," Drew said, "Breathtaking."

"That was all Janelle's cinematography." I smiled, proudly motioning to my best friend. "She makes me look good."

"Not only on film," she replied, pointing to my outfit.

"I actually had my agent try to set up a meeting with you after watching it, but you were swamped with other offers," Drew said. "What are you working on now?"

I looked at him, stunned, not knowing what to say. Henry died right after *Lalo's Lament* came out, and I fell into a deep depression, unable to answer any calls, especially from my agent. She told everyone I was swamped with offers, when really I was crying on my sister's sofa.

Buying myself time before answering Drew, I reached up to fix a strand of loose hair and realized my left ear was naked.

"W-where's m-my earring?" I stammered, patting my shoulder, hoping it was stuck in my shirt.

"Shit." Janelle looked at the floor around us. "When did you last see it?"

"Your house," I said, desperation in my voice, realizing the earring could be anywhere now.

Janelle and I searched the area as Drew asked the staff if they'd found anything, but it was no use. The earring was gone. I'd planned on returning them the next day before the charges could even go through on my card. Now, I was out money I didn't have to waste, and all I had to show for it was a stained outfit, Chris Stanson belittling me again, and Drew Williams awkwardly asking me questions with no good answers.

I officially wanted to go home. "We should head out."

Janelle sighed and looked around. "Yeah, this party is a bust, and I'm hungry."

"I'll make sure Chris orders more food next time," Drew assured us, like we'd be invited back to this house or anywhere near Chris Stanson ever again.

Still, my heart jumped a bit at the idea of seeing Drew Williams once more, some leftover remnant of a girl who used to swoon over dimple-faced boys in *Teen Bop* magazine until she hit puberty and replaced their photographs with deep-voiced androgynous rock stars like Kali. I'd dressed a few of the now-grown teenage stars from my childhood, and all of them were pompous pricks like Chris. Drew was the first I'd met who seemed legitimately kind. I suddenly felt bad that I'd been mean to the only friendly person in Hollywood. "Sorry I was a hangry bitch earlier."

"I blame Chris." Drew smiled.

"Good life plan." I chuckled.

"It was nice meeting you, Mr. Andy." Janelle shook his hand.

"Nice meeting both of you," Drew said, letting go of Janelle's hand and reaching for mine. I took it and met his gaze, those bright eyes so familiar from the movies staring back at me, even kinder in person. "Surreal, but nice."

I laughed at his reference while Janelle shook her head. Dropping hands after an awkwardly long embrace, we said our last goodbye, then headed down the steep driveway, trying to enjoy Chris's spectacular view one final time while we waited for our ride.

"We gonna talk about that little Andy moment back there?" Janelle asked when the car arrived.

"Oh yeah, all night long." I giggled, opening the door and getting in. "But first, fries."

"Fries before guys, always," she agreed, climbing in next to me.

Chapter Four

The sun was starting to rise when I got back to my sister's house in Arcadia, a suburb nestled on the edge of the L.A. basin, far from Hollywood. By the time I'd taken off my makeup and slid into bed, my niblings were up and playing not-so-silently in the room next to mine.

"Sshh, you're going to wake Aunt Didi," Reggie whispered loudly to her sibling.

I pulled out a pair of earplugs and a sleeping mask, hoping to push through the noise and get some rest, but my mind was racing, thinking about my interactions with Drew Williams. I replayed the whole evening, wondering what could have happened if I'd actually been nice to him instead of acting like a jerk. Questioning if Janelle had been right and he really was flirting with me.

I knew I wasn't the only person in the world lying in bed thinking about the famous movie star, but I told myself that mine was a different kind of longing. Sure, he was handsome and kind, but he was also a cishet man, and I hadn't been interested in one of those since high school. No, this weirdly twitterpated heart of mine couldn't be for Drew himself but what he represented: an opportunity to fast-track my dreams—one I'd stupidly given up by being hangry.

My stomach growled on cue, registering the scents wafting from the kitchen where Cecily was preparing our Sunday ritual of pancakes and painting.

"Wake up, lazy butt!" My sister opened my door, turned on the lights and fan, and threw her kids on top of me.

"Sleeping!" I yelled, clinging to the covers as my niblings tried to pull them off me, laughing hysterically. My mother used to do this to us. I hated it then, and I hated that my sister was perpetuating it now. Still, I was powerless to fight it, so I rolled out of bed, threw on some clothes, and met my sister in the kitchen. "You're the fucking worst."

"And a good morning to you, too," Cecily said as I grabbed a piece of bacon off the griddle and shoved it in my mouth before she could stop me, burning my tongue in the process. Cecily laughed at me for making the same mistake I made every Sunday morning.

"How'd you sleep?" she asked, flipping the pancakes.

"Dreamed of winning an Oscar," I replied.

"How's the script coming?"

"It's coming." I reached to steal a pancake off the griddle, but Cecily swatted my hand away before I could get one.

"So," she said, turning excitedly toward me, "tell me, tell me! I want to know everything about last night. Don't leave any detail out, especially one regarding a certain handsome host."

"Chris Stanson is a dick," I said, trying to grab at another pancake. "I've told you this before."

"Ugh, that party was wasted on you." Cecily swatted my hand again. "I should have been there. Why did I have kids?"

"I ask you that same question every day."

"Little brats ruin everything."

"They're kind of cute, though."

"Yeah, they are. I guess I'll keep 'em." Cecily poured new batter onto the griddle. "So, tell me, who did you see? Was it full of famous stars? Wait, no, don't tell me. I don't want to know who I missed out on falling in love with."

"How have you lived in L.A. for over a decade and are still this star crazy?"

"We live in Arcadia. Celebrities wouldn't be caught dead here."

"I keep telling you we should move to La Brea or Fairfax, maybe even Beverly Hills," I said, sweeping around her other side, grabbing for the plate of pancakes.

"And I keep telling you to win the lottery." Cecily slapped my hand hard with the spatula this time.

"If you're going to wake me up early, the least you can do is let me have a pancake."

"It's not my fault you stayed up past your bedtime."

"I have no bedtime. I'm a grown-ass adult who can do whatever she wants."

"You're basically my oldest child."

"Whatever," I brushed her off. I didn't want to get into the same argument we'd had a million times since we were kids.

Knowing it was best to walk away, I headed outside to help the kids set the table, watching Ellis haphazardly throw down the placemats while their older sister, Reggie, followed behind, straightening them and carefully placing a folded cloth napkin with perfectly aligned forks and knives on top, ever the perfectionist, just like her mother.

Once the table was set, Ellis and I lay out together in the grass, waiting for their mom to let us back in the kitchen to get some food. Their little body curled up into the crook of my arm, and we both sighed, soaking up that famous Southern California sun. It was a gorgeous day, even by L.A. standards. The sky was clear, but there were still wisps of clouds here and there for aesthetic effects. It felt like the studios set the perfect backdrop for a Sunday outdoor brunch.

It was images of days like this that had convinced me to move to L.A. in the first place a decade ago, when I was a starry-eyed eighteen-year-old leaving my small farming town on the Mexican border to enter film school in the shiny big city. While my friends had dreamed of marrying the latest TV heartthrob, I dreamed of working with Nora Ephron and directing Meryl Streep. I longed to be someone who inspired others, like I'd been inspired by Holland Taylor, Gabourey Sidibe, America Ferrera, Kate McKinnon, Lena Waithe, Janet Mock, Jane Lynch, Michaela Jaé Rodriguez, and Melissa McCarthy, to name just a few. Women and nonbinary folks who taught me that Hollywood wasn't just for straight, thin, white men.

I'd gotten close, too. A year out of film school, my senior thesis short film, *Lalo's Lament*, won a handful of awards, getting me an agent and helping me sell a full-length script—all by the age of twenty-three. As a congratulations gift, Janelle had somehow scored bleacher seats outside the Oscars, and we clenched each other's hands with excitement, knowing someday soon that would be us walking the red carpet, reporters asking who we were wearing, to which we'd indignantly reply, "Ask me about more than my clothes. Ask me about my work, my ambitions, my causes, like you do the men!"

That was years ago, back before I knew that studio execs would buy scripts with no real intention of making them, just to keep them off the market if they were about to release something similar. I wrote more scripts and put together a crew for another short. I pushed and hustled, putting in the work and refusing to accept rejection.

Then my brother was diagnosed with cancer, and everything stopped. Grief shattered me into a million pieces, and it took half a decade to gather back the bits that had been lost. Some, like my directing career, I worried I'd never see again. When Cecily got divorced, I gave up my apartment in Silver Lake, moved in with her in the suburbs, and spent the hours I used to attend industry events helping with the kids, my career as a writer and director a distant memory. I could barely watch movies these days. I hated wondering what my life would be like if cancer hadn't come in and chopped off a limb of my family tree.

"Breakfast!" Cecily yelled, coming outside with platters full of bacon and pancakes. Ellis and I stretched slowly and got up, meandering to the table where Reggie was already digging in.

"Slow down. You're gonna choke," Cecily said, and Reggie spat a giant wad of pancake out of her mouth.

"Lovely," her mother said.

"We raise ladies 'round these parts," I said, making a farting noise with my mouth. The kids joined in, fake farting and laughing so hard Ellis started choking.

"Either make farting noises or eat," Cecily said. "I don't want you dying of a fart attack."

Ellis chose to eat and shoved a piece of bacon in their

mouth. I got up and went into the house, returning with the butter dish.

"I already buttered the pancakes," Cecily pointed out.

"You call this buttered?" I plopped a pat on my plate. "Don't worry, I'll fix your mistake."

"If you don't like how I make pancakes, maybe get up early and do it yourself next time," Cecily replied.

"Thank you for making us breakfast," I said, genuinely grateful she cooked but still pissed off that she'd woken me up early.

"Can I have that?" Ellis pointed to the last piece of bacon.

"How can you possibly eat any more?" Cecily asked.

"I'm like a squirrel," Ellis said, grabbing the bacon. "Except I don't save anything for winter. I eat it all right now."

"Sounds very practical," I nodded, suppressing a laugh.

After breakfast, Reggie and I cleared the dishes while Cecily and Ellis gathered art supplies from the garage-turned-studio. It was the largest room in our house and full of canvases and materials we'd inherited from our grandfather, a farmer turned amateur artist. Her artistic background and bossy inclinations meant Cecily always took charge of our family art projects, and that morning she came out with a plan. We were all going to use the same color construction paper to cut up different patterns, then put them together to make one large piece of art.

After two hours of scissors, glue, and strips of construction paper flying all over the place, we had four highly individualized pieces of art that came together to form one cohesive unit. It was a bit rough around the edges, far from perfect, but that made it an even better representation of our little family.

"I bet they didn't have art this fancy at your bougie LACMA

fundraiser last night," Cecily said, placing our masterpiece on the wall.

"Chris Stanson ain't got nothing on us," I replied. "Who needs a Calder mobile in your entryway anyways?"

"That party was wasted on you." Cecily shook her head.

"More than you know." I sighed, thinking back on how I'd ruined my chance to network with Hollywood elites because I'd been hangry.

Even still, I refused to believe that meant my dreams were over. I didn't need Chris Stanson, Drew Williams, or any of their rich and famous friends. Janelle and I had made *Lalo's Lament* with a tiny crew and minuscule budget. We could do it again.

After pancakes and painting, I desperately wanted to go back to sleep or at least spend the day reading on the sofa, but instead I took my laptop to a local café and got to work. Nothing propelled me forward quite like black tea and spite, and I thought of rubbing my Oscar into Chris Stanson's smug face each time my eyes drooped. I would finish this script, send it to my agent, and make this film. And I would never again lose a night of sleep over Drew Williams.

Chapter Five

The doldrums of heading back to work after such an eventful weekend was dulled a bit, knowing my favorite client was coming into the store. Shamaya, a boisterous lifestyle blogger, lived a life of fortune and glamour. Her father was born in Jodhpur and moved to Mumbai to become a successful Indian film producer, and her mother had been a farmer's daughter from Guanajuato turned famous Mexican telenovela star, which meant Shamaya spent part of her childhood in India, part in Mexico, and part in the U.S.A. giving her one of those impossible-to-pin-down accents.

She was very popular online, with around a million followers on most social media apps and the kind of hits on her blog that would make major news sites jealous. She was known for two contrasting things: her signature comical vulgarity as she displayed the ridiculously over-the-top wealth and access that came from being a nepo baby, and her lovingly tender posts about body positivity and the way society treats fat women of color.

One day she'd post about her latest Neiman Marcus haul, and the next she'd show herself half-naked in the dressing room, all her insecurities laid bare. Shamaya appealed to a broad audience precisely because she never apologized for who she was, embracing every inch of the largesse that was her body and life. She was one of my biggest inspirations—and my biggest commissions.

Shamaya sashayed into the dressing room looking fabulous in a black-and-white striped jumpsuit with a peek-a-boo cutout on her belly, carrying overflowing bags from Tres, an upscale Mexican restaurant nearby.

"I'm starving," she declared, piling containers onto the small dressing room table. "Food first, fashion later."

"I like your priorities," Janelle chimed in, helping Shamaya with the spread.

With most of my clients, Janelle simply came up to consult on shoes, then quickly returned to her own department, but Shamaya had a particularly voracious appetite for fancy footwear, so Janelle's manager let her spend the whole afternoon with us when she was in town. Shamaya always insisted on taking her time to indulge in the pleasures of life, which for her included eating, shopping, and gossiping. Over the years of afternoons together, the three of us had become great friends, and we all looked forward to our "working lunches."

"Is that Premme?" I asked, pointing to Shamaya's outfit.

"This old thing?" She twirled around, showing off the jumpsuit. "It's my favorite to wear on days I want to be fashionable yet comfortable."

"I like that you consider those pointy Louboutins you

paired it with comfortable," Janelle said.

"A girl can't leave the house looking sloppy, my love," Shamaya answered, sitting down on the sofa next to me. "So what's the latest gossip?"

"Diana got hit on by Drew Williams," Janelle blurted out.

"I did not!" I insisted.

"Why else was he following us around?" Janelle asked.

"Maybe he was hitting on *you*?" I shot back.

"Yeah, like Drew Williams is into studs," Janelle said.

"Like Drew Williams is into fat femmes," I countered.

"Wait, stop, go back," Shamaya demanded. "This is too juicy. Start from the beginning, and don't leave a single detail out."

As we dug into the food, we regaled Shamaya with the events of the LACMA party. Janelle stood by her claim that Drew Williams had been hitting on me, but I insisted he'd taken pity on the two awkward plebs in the corner, especially after Chris had been such a jerk.

"What's he like?" Shamaya asked.

"Chris Stanson? I don't know," I answered. "Full of himself?"

"No, no, obviously he's going to be a narcissist, right? Any man that pretty is. I meant Drew Williams. What's he like? You can't tell from the gossip mags, now, can you? He's one of those guys who could go either way. I mean, he was fat—"

"He wasn't fat," I interrupted.

"Wasn't he?" Shamaya asked.

"Fat is when you can't shop in the regular sections at department stores," I said, then took a bite of my taco.

"Is that the official definition now? I should update my blog." Shamaya laughed, scraping the last of the ceviche onto a chip. We didn't waste food around these parts. "Wasn't he the fat kid in that TV show? And he always played the fat sidekick in those comedies. He was fat."

"He was chubby, not fat. There's a difference," I pointed out. "And he still dated that model… What's her name?"

"Gwen," Janelle said. She had an amazing knack for remembering celebrity names, which sat in contrast with how little she actually cared about celebrities unless she was filming them.

"Yes, Gwen." Shamaya spoke the name like she had beans stuck to the roof of her mouth. "One name. Gwen. Fat women can't catch a dick in this town to save their lives, and yet fat men get to date one-name supermodels. It's so unfair."

"I keep telling you to join the sapphic side," Janelle said.

"Not like it's much better," I added. "Remember my ex Sam? She loved the attention I was getting around *Lalo's Lament*, liked to show off my success online, and bragged that she was dating a filmmaker, but then privately she would nitpick everything I ate, say things about my body that she claimed were encouraging but were totally offensive, and even 'confided' in me that her friends didn't know why she was dating someone as fat as me."

"I still don't get why you stayed with her for so long." Janelle had always been protective of me when it came to Sam.

"Because I'm fatphobic, too," I admitted. "We all are. It's so ingrained in us that fat is the worst thing we can be, so when people say shit things about our bodies, deep down we wonder if they're right. I was put on my first diet at age seven, and my dad weighed my food before I ate it all the way into high school. Sam treated me better than my parents had. Better than most of society does. I thought that relationship was the best I could get."

"This is why I write my blog," Shamaya chimed in. "I know it looks all fluff on the outside, but at the core of it, I want fat girls to see a fat woman living her best life."

"I wish I'd had you as a kid to look up to." I often wondered what it would have been like to grow up with fat role models like her.

"You can look up to me now." Shamaya stood and twirled. "I'm quite inspiring."

"Especially in those shoes." Janelle pointed to Shamaya's heels.

"I know fatphobia is a big issue for gay men, trans people, and nonbinary folk, too," I continued. "And straight men don't have a pass from it, but life will always be easier for white, straight, cis men like Drew, even when they're fat."

"I thought you said he wasn't fat." Janelle smirked at me.

"Fuck off, Twiggy." I flung a bit of corn tortilla at her.

"Heyo!" Shamaya screamed loudly, pointing to an outfit in the corner. "Not near the Pucci!"

Shamaya walked to the dressing room, taking the gorgeous Pucci caftan with her. It was peach with umbrella-like circles radiating out of the sides in turquoise, black, and white, a pattern that screamed Shamaya. Luckily, Pucci was into the oversize look right now, so it fit her plus-size body perfectly.

Some designers had gotten better about carrying larger sizes, but it was still practically impossible to find high-end pieces above a ten. Shamaya was a size fourteen to eighteen, depending on the day or brand, so we sometimes lucked out and found stuff for her that fit. It was harder finding clothes for the larger bodies that came in, but I always tried to make them feel like they had the same amount of quality options thin people did, even if I had to special order items for them.

Janelle handed Shamaya turquoise Gucci heels to go with the caftan—leading to a long debate over whether you could pair Pucci and Gucci together—and I grabbed some big, chunky Kendra Scott earrings to complete the ensemble. The look was fabulous and would be a big hit on her blog. Already, her dressing room photos were blowing up social media, and her phone kept dinging with notifications.

"How can you stand all that noise?" Janelle asked when Shamaya's phone buzzed for what seemed like the thousandth time. Janelle was one of those very rare creatures without any social media presence.

"Eh, I don't notice it anymore," Shamaya said as she shut the ringer off on her phone. "And you never answered my question: what was Drew Williams like?"

Dreamy, a voice in my head said.

Dreamy, really? Dreamy? I hadn't called a boy dreamy since my crush on all of the Jonas Brothers in the fourth grade. And Drew Williams hadn't been dreamy. Mae Martin was dreamy. Kristen Stewart was dreamy. Dreamy was when you wanted to stare and swoon. Drew Williams was not dreamy. He was too awkward to be dreamy. So then what was he?

"A little weird," Janelle replied.

"Obviously, right? He's so awkwardly funny on screen—that kind of comedic timing can't be faked. But, like, what else?"

"Ask Diana. She was the one flirting with him." Janelle sipped on the iced tea Shamaya had brought us.

"Ooh!" Shamaya energetically elbowed me in the side. "You going straight for him now?"

In her excitement, Shamaya tipped over the small tray holding the food, sending leftover salsa flying. Luckily, it landed on the carpet, not the clothes. I went to the employee room to grab some napkins and checked my phone while I was there. I had a missed call from a random local number. It was probably spam, but I listened to the voicemail anyway.

"Hi, Diana Smith," a shockingly sensual voice said. "This is Susan Barry from LACMA, calling regarding your prize. Please call me back at 310-555-6649."

Stunned I'd won something, I wrote the number down on a pad of paper and tucked my phone into the lockbox, hurrying back to the dressing room, napkins be damned.

"Did you do this?" I asked Janelle, half excited, half accusatory.

"No, the bids were too high!" she said, then proceeded to explain to Shamaya how she'd put my name down for tea with Meryl Streep. "Did you do it in a hangry craze?"

"Of course not! The bids were up to $9,800."

"Then who did?" Janelle asked.

"Only one way to find out," Shamaya sang as she dialed the number and handed me her bright pink phone.

Susan Barry's voice was deep and sultry, like a phone sex operator from a bygone era. I wanted to ask her what she was wearing but instead opted to explain who I was and why I was calling. "I'm so sorry to do this, but I can't afford it. It was a joke between a friend and me. Besides, we thought I'd been outbid."

"My records show you already paid."

I heard her clicking a mouse as she verified that yes, indeed, this auction item was fully paid for. She could not tell me how, when, or by whom.

"I can double-check with accounting—that's not my area of expertise—but this is all paid up. I don't even get your information unless the account has been settled and money has been transferred. My job is to connect the prize winner with the person who donated the prize. Is this a good number at which Mr. Williams can call to arrange your tee time?"

"Wait, Mr. Williams? You mean Ms. Streep, right? I won tea with Academy Award winner Meryl Streep."

"No..." Susan Barry said, clicking and typing some more. "My records show you won a round of golf with Drew Williams."

This had to be someone's idea of a joke. I didn't even play golf. I tried to explain this to Susan, who gently reminded me that she had lots of other winners to call and if I didn't want my already-paid-for prize with a famous movie star, I could take it up with Mr. Williams himself. Apparently, he'd be calling me later today if I would kindly verify my phone number with Susan, which I did.

"You can borrow my clubs!" Shamaya squealed as I handed her cell phone back. "They're bright pink and have Louis Vuitton covers on the drivers."

"Of course." Janelle laughed.

"Picture it, you and Drew Williams golfing together, tabloids snatching photos, wondering who is this mystery girl." Shamaya took the Basille Georgette embroidered tunic dress I handed her.

"That image is hilarious." Janelle offered Shamaya her choice of multiple Tory Burch flats to go with the dress.

"Ridiculous is more like it," I said as Shamaya grabbed the green suede flats approvingly.

"But you're going, right?" Shamaya asked, shimmying into the outfit, not bothering to close the dressing room door.

"Of course I'm not going," I insisted.

"Do you know how many deals my father has brokered over

golf? This could be your chance to get him to read your script, maybe even take a role in your movie! You have to go, Diana."

"What do you think?" I asked Janelle as Shamaya came out of the dressing room and twirled around in the mirror, admiring her look.

"I think that outfit looks great on you, Shamaya." Janelle ignored my question.

"Fabulous, right?" Shamaya began snapping photos of herself.

"What about *me*?" I asked.

"You look fabulous, too." Janelle smirked. "As for the golf thing, I think that you asked for this from the universe, so you should take it."

"How did I ask for golf with Drew Williams?"

"You bid on yourself. You put your name down for your dreams, and the universe answered in its own way."

"You bet on Serena Williams, but I don't see you borrowing Shamaya's tennis racket."

"I'm still waiting for my call." Janelle smiled. "It's coming."

"Who even paid for this?" I wondered.

"Does it matter?" Janelle replied. "You get to network with one of Hollywood's biggest stars for free. Don't turn this down."

"Janelle is right," Shamaya agreed as I rang up her purchases. "I love visiting you here, you know I do, but this isn't where you belong. Either of you. Playing golf with Drew Williams is an opportunity to make the kind of connection that could propel your career exponentially forward. This is a gift from God or fate or chance, or whatever you want to call it. Don't return it."

"I don't know," I said, hesitant to accept this prize. It had been nice meeting Drew. He'd been friendly and funny. But small talk over appetizers at a crowded party was drastically different than sitting in a golf cart talking for however long a round of golf took.

"Don't overthink it," Shamaya scolded as I returned her AmEx Black card.

"That's what she does best," Janelle teased.

Shamaya kissed us both goodbye and strutted out of the store followed by three assistant clerks carrying armloads of designer goods and another filming the whole parade for her followers.

Reluctantly, Janelle returned to the shoe department, and I returned to the dressing room to clean up. I picked up some napkins from the employee room and grabbed my phone out of the lockbox, tucking it into the planter in the dressing room where no one else would see it. As I scrubbed salsa off the floor, I wondered if Drew Williams would actually call me and what I would say when he did.

Two hours later, I'd convinced myself this was all some elaborate prank when my phone buzzed, showing a call from an unlisted number.

"Diana Smith?" the familiar voice said when I answered. "Hi, this is Drew Williams. We met at the LACMA party."

"Hmm, I met a lot of people that night. Remind me again what you look like?" I wasn't trying to play it cool. There was just something about him that made me want to be a smart-ass.

"Somewhat tall, white man, with dark hair and dashing good looks."

"I met someone that matches that description," I said, "but he told me his name was Andy."

He laughed, and it was that same bottom-of-the-belly laugh that audiences loved, the nice-guy-next-door bit he was famous for. On camera, Drew made you believe you'd be best friends someday, if only you got the chance to meet in person.

"Ma'am, I hate to break this to you, but we're one and the same."

"Damn, and here I thought someone famous was calling me."

"I can try to get Chris Stanson on the line."

"Nah, that guy's a prick," I said, only half joking. "His friends are even worse."

"Too true," Drew replied. "But I hope that won't keep you from coming golfing with me."

"Yeah, about that," I began, not quite sure how to explain the situation but deciding honesty would be the best, "I don't know how this happened. I think they have me mixed up with someone else. I never bid on going golfing with you, and I definitely didn't pay for it."

"I bought it for you!" he sang enthusiastically, like someone jumping out at a surprise party.

"Why would you go and do a thing like that?" I asked.

"Some handsy older lady I really didn't want to spend time with signed up. I couldn't stand the thought of hours in a golf cart with her. So I put down the name of the first person I thought of who would be fun to go golfing with: Diana Smith."

"Shouldn't you give it to someone else? Who bid on it before her?"

"It doesn't matter. What does is you won! And now we get to go golfing together."

"First off, I didn't win. You did, since you put my name down and paid for it," I replied. "Second, and I don't mean to sound full of myself or misread the situation when I say this, but if this is some weird way to hit on me, I'm flattered, but I don't date cis men."

"You're a beautiful and talented woman," Drew replied.

"But that's not why I put your name down."

"Then why did you?" I asked.

"Like I said, you were the first person I thought of that wouldn't annoy me if I had to spend four hours with them. Plus, I thought it would be nice to hear what you've been working on since *Lalo's Lament*."

My heart sank. That would be four hours of nothing to talk about, then. *Not nothing*, I reminded myself, thinking about the script my agent was about to try to shop. Still, I didn't need to spend four torturous hours failing at golf in front of Drew Williams to get this screenplay sold.

"I'm flattered, but I don't golf."

"I can teach you," he said.

"I appreciate the offer, but the tee fees would be wasted on me."

"They're already paid for. The club donated them. So you've gotta go with me, or I'll be out there all by myself lookin' like a loser."

"Take Chris."

"Then I'd look like even more of a loser," Drew replied.

I chuckled. I liked the way Drew was willing to laugh at himself and his friends. Not mocking or cruel, but fun, jovial. It reminded me of my friends, my people—real people.

"Let's pretend for a second that I agreed," I said, questioning if this actually could be fun. "What would this golf outing entail?"

"I could pick you up, or we could meet there—it's a course called Brentwood that donated a few rounds of golf with various celebrities for the fundraiser. We'd tee off, play the first nine, have lunch at the clubhouse, play the back nine, then be done."

Even with Drew's humor to liven it up, that sounded

absolutely miserable to me. I couldn't imagine playing eighteen holes of golf at a stuffy country club, everyone staring at me, wondering what that fat, queer woman was doing with Drew Williams. It was one of my definitions of hell.

"I really appreciate that you're following through with this whole thing," I said, "but you put my name down. You can pretend someone else won it, someone who actually enjoys golf and snotty clubs and sandwiches cut into diamonds with little frilly toothpicks through them. That someone is not me."

"Okay, then what do you like? I owe you something if you don't want to go golfing."

"You signed my name, and you paid for it. You don't owe me anything."

"But I ruined your shirt," he replied.

"Is that what this is all about?" I asked. Of course Drew Williams was trying to assuage his guilt; he didn't actually care to get to know my work. Or me.

"It's all the other things, too. I just feel bad about that still."

"Don't worry, Andy. I got the stain out." It was a lie. The shirt had been ruined, but he didn't need to know that. "You don't owe me anything."

"You sure?"

"I'm sure."

"So we're good, then?" he asked.

I reassured Drew Williams that we were indeed good, and he promised he'd call on me the next time he needed a new suit. When we hung up, I sat staring at my phone for a while, wondering if I had done the right thing. Some girls would die to spend the day with Drew Williams. Most people would instantly regret giving up the chance to play golf with him. But I refused to be one of them.

Chapter Six

The next few days were a blur of monotonous routine, going back and forth from Arcadia to Rodeo Drive, trying to forget about Drew Williams, Chris Stanson, and every other celebrity in this city. When I first moved to Los Angeles, I was completely starstruck. Growing up in a small town, celebrities were otherworldly, and if I saw one, I would text everyone I knew. I'd been under this delusion that if I could get near famous people, I would somehow become famous myself, so I'd scour the tabloids for where stars hung out and tried to casually run into one, hoping they would want to collaborate on a project, just knowing they would love me if they met me. It wasn't long before I found out that famously gorgeous people only love other famously gorgeous people.

And I was far from famously gorgeous.

I could be pretty when I tried, and I was fashionable when my job required it, but thin, glamorous, and casually cool?

Nope, nope, and definitely not.

It was lonely trying to find my place in this city. I almost moved to Portland, Oakland, or Brooklyn, places known for celebrating queers and fatties like me, but I was invested in Tinseltown, even if it wouldn't invest in me. The few friends I knew from film school that still worked in the industry were struggling, giving it their heart and soul day after day, barely surviving the bloodied waters. A few years ago, our friend Lauren quit movies and went to law school, saying lawyers looked like saints compared to studio execs. All of this was to say that making it in Hollywood was hard. Really fucking hard.

But I wasn't going to let that stop me. I could do hard things. Sure, I'd taken a break from filmmaking, but I was back now, working on a new script based on Cecily and me—our grief, our sisterhood, and our multi-generational roots that went deep in the small, farming town on the Mexican border where we grew up. It was a movie about how women and queers build bridges, and hold each other up, and it showed the power of marginalized communities coming together to help each other survive.

It was good, better than anything I'd done before, so I was dedicated to making this movie on my own terms, not letting the gatekeepers of Hollywood suck out its soul. My most grandiose dream was to shoot the film with my own diverse crew of women. Men could produce it, I'd still take their money, but I wanted us making the art, bringing to life the characters, telling our stories with our own voices.

To do that, I needed even more money, so I'd started taking on extra clients at Roussard's. That morning, I had someone new named Mrs. Bertolli, coming in with her daughter "who refuses to dress like anything but a slob," and I was hoping it would be a big commission makeover.

One look at the kid when she arrived in her baggy pants and loose button-up shirt told me she wasn't a "slob." She was butch. Or genderqueer, trans, questioning, whatever they identified with, but the kid definitely wasn't a little girl who would willingly wear the form-fitting frilly dresses their mom wanted to force them into. As Mrs. Bertolli nitpicked her child in front of me, lecturing the kid to stand up straight, tuck in their shirt, and act like a lady, I knew I had a rough day ahead of me.

Keeping my job required placating the parents, the ones who paid the bill on their platinum Roussard's credit cards. But keeping my soul required me to stick up for the kids who came in here, awkward teens who reminded me all too much of my own childhood struggles to find comfort in a world that was constantly telling me how wrong and bad I was.

"So," I said, sitting across from them on the Personal Shopper sofas, "tell me about your event."

It was a wedding, a big one from the sound of it, full of important people whose names the mother expected me to know, but I didn't. Mrs. Bertolli explained that she wanted her daughter in something long, flowy, and maybe strapless, preferably with purple accents to match the wedding colors. "Everyone will be there." She pointed to her child. "And I can't have her looking like that."

"We'll find the perfect outfit for you." I tried to make eye contact with the kid, to let them know I understood their struggle, but they were staring at the carpet.

"Yes, you will," Mrs. Bertolli affirmed, matter-of-factly, like disobeying her was not an option.

"Now that I have the event details, why don't you go get a

coffee or snack while your child and I try some options?" I said, trying to be kind but forceful, letting Mrs. Bertolli know this was my domain, not hers.

"I'm not going anywhere." She crossed her arms defiantly.

"I appreciate your desire to stay here. I really do. Most mothers don't want to leave their kid alone, but I find that it helps the process immensely if it's just me and the person wearing the outfit. Plus, it adds an element of surprise to come back and see the end result."

"I don't like surprises." Mrs. Bertolli huffed. "I would prefer to stay here."

"You're welcome to go shopping, or get your nails done in the salon next door. My friends down in makeup could show you some new looks, or you can take this *Vogue* outside"—I handed her a magazine—"and enjoy a relaxing cup of coffee. We'll take about ninety minutes, and I'll have your child text you as soon as we're done."

The mother stood huffing for a moment, then declared she was going to get a manicure instead of wasting time waiting here, like it had been her decision all along. As soon as she was out the door, the kid visibly relaxed.

"So," I said, sitting back down on the sofa across from my client, "what name would you like for me to use with you?"

"My friends call me Alex," the kid replied. "But my mom says I have to use Alessandra."

"What name would you like me to call you today?" I asked.

"Um," the kid said, smiling shyly. "Alex is cool."

"Hi, Alex, nice to meet you." I extended my hand. They shook it, looking me in the eye for the first time. "Now, what pronouns would you like me to use with you?"

I guessed Alex was in middle school, and I wasn't sure what

they knew yet about queer culture, but I'd realized I was gay and gender nonconforming at twelve, and we didn't have the internet back then, so I assumed Alex knew something, if only just a hint within themselves of the desire to live differently. Still, I clarified, in case they didn't know they had options in how they wanted to live their life. "Do you like to be called she, he, or something neutral like xe or they?"

"I use they/them with my friends."

"Would you like me to use the name Alex and they/them pronouns here?" Alex nodded before I clarified, "Even in front of your mom?"

Alex sat quietly, thinking for a while before meekly saying, "Yes please."

"They/them it is." I smiled. "Okay then, Alex, what do you imagine yourself wearing to this wedding?"

"My mom said I have to wear a dress."

"Ah, yes, but again, she's not here. So tell me, what do you want? If you could wear anything at all to this event, what would it be? Dream big. No limits."

Slowly, Alex started opening up, telling me about how they hated dresses and the color pink but liked purple, that they'd seen this gray suit in a magazine and had dreamed of wearing it, but their mom would flip. I told Alex I'd deal with their mom and started taking measurements, their face lighting up at the excitement over getting to try on a suit.

As I headed out onto the floor to grab some options, I handed Alex the menu from the restaurant upstairs and told them to order whatever they wanted using the phone in the room. In a timid, sweet voice, they asked if I wanted anything. "I'd love an iced tea, please," I said, smiling as I left.

Alex was too small for men's clothes and too big for the

boys' section, but I pulled the options I could find, grabbing purple accent pieces, hoping to placate Mrs. Bertolli on the color scheme at least. I was starting to get nervous about Alex's mother's reaction as I walked back with the suits, but the giant smile on Alex's face made all of my apprehension go away. We'd find a way to get Mrs. Bertolli to capitulate. I just knew we could.

As they put on the suit, Alex transformed from slouched over and insecure to proudly admiring how handsome they looked in the mirror. They had chosen a silvery gray slim-fit suit, with a light purple plaid shirt, dark purple tie, and matching dark purple pocket square. It looked fabulous. Alex beamed. My heart swelled with pride. These were the moments I loved my job.

They stood on the pedestal fidgeting, worry all over their face, but when Mrs. Bertolli entered, Alex couldn't help but beam, throwing their arms out and twirling around. "What do you think?"

"This is a joke, right?" Mrs. Bertolli said.

Alex immediately deflated. The joy left their eyes. The slouch came back.

Mrs. Bertolli turned on me, glaring daggers. "Did I not specify that I wanted a long, flowing dress, maybe sleeveless, with purple accents? Did you not understand that?"

"Yes, Mrs. Bertolli, you said that, but that's not what Alex wanted."

"*Alessandra*"—Mrs. Bertolli emphasized her child's legal name—"would walk around in sweats and a baseball cap all day if we gave her what she wanted. But this is a civilized event, and she needs to look civilized, not like some cross-dressing lesbian."

"If you look at the magazines," I said, trying to ignore the way she spat those last three words, "you'll see that all the designers are putting their models in suits right now."

"I don't care about what's popular in fashion magazines; I care about my daughter looking like a lady. I care about you completely disregarding my wishes and putting her in this man's outfit, polluting her mind to think that this kind of behavior is okay."

"Ma'am, I think—"

"Oh, I know what people like *you* think. I should have seen it in you when we walked in. Alessandra, I will be waiting outside in the car. Take off that disgusting outfit immediately and meet me there. You"—she turned to me—"I'll be speaking with Mr. Roussard about this. He's a dear friend." With that, she stormed off.

I turned to Alex, who had tears in their eyes. "I'm so sorry."

"I should go," Alex said, taking one last glance in the mirror before changing back into their jeans and baggy shirt.

"It gets better," I apologized, hating myself for not having the right words to say, something actually useful, something actually true. I knew it might not get better, and chances were it would get a hell of a lot worse for Alex as they grew into themself, into who they truly were. I knew even if Mrs. Bertolli didn't make Alex's life hell, the rest of the world would. With trans healthcare bans in many states, conversion therapy on the rise, and the looming fear of gay marriage being overturned, I knew it never really got better for people like us, not fully, not like it is for straight and cis people.

As soon as Alex left the room, I sat down and cried: for them, for me, for my community, for the generation of elders we lost to the AIDS crisis while politicians mocked our deaths, for the queer and trans kids abandoned by their families, forced to grow up too soon in a world that shunned them. I cried for my gay friends lost to drugs and suicide. I cried for my younger queer self who turned to razor blades against her wrist to cope with the bullies in school and at home. I cried for my niblings, who I feared would do the same.

I cried and I cried and I cried.

Until Emmy walked in, reminding me where I was.

"I'm sorry," she said, her voice the same leveled professionalism it always was. "But there is a client here to see you."

"Tell them I'm busy." I pointed to Alex's suit discarded on the floor. "I need to clean this up."

"I will put this away." Emmy began gently placing the clothes back on the hangers. I couldn't tell if she was being nice to me or just doing her job, but either way, I appreciated her stoic nature even more in that moment. No questions, just practical support.

As Emmy cleared the dressing room for me, I sat on the couch, taking deep, calming breaths, clearing my head and steadying my heart rate. When I'd finally gotten my emotions tucked back down, I stood, looked in the mirror, fixed the mascara that had smeared down my cheek, and reapplied my lipstick. Patting the last tears away, I put on a fake smile and walked out onto the floor to meet with my awaiting client.

Chapter Seven

I didn't know what I was expecting to see when I came out of the dressing room, but it definitely wasn't the large smiling face of Drew Williams.

"Diana!" He pulled me into a hug. "Good to see you again."

"H-hello," I stuttered, confused at the familiarity with which he greeted me.

"I've got a party and need a suit," he explained.

"Okay." I nodded, trying to pull myself together. My heart was aching for Alex, for younger me, for all of the queer kids whose parents treated them like a curse on their house, on our society, a nasty problem to be solved. I had no desire or energy left to dress someone today, but I was in no place to turn down the commission a client like Drew Williams would bring me, especially after losing the Bertolli sale.

"You don't seem that happy to see me." Drew's expression fell.

"No, it's not you, it's me," I said, shaking my head and standing up straighter.

"It's not you, it's me?" He laughed. "What, are we breaking up?"

I knew Drew was trying to make a joke, but I had no humor left in me. There was no way I could dress him today. Commission be damned, I needed to go home. Now. "I'm sorry, sir, I was about to head out. My shift is over. Emmy is available, though, and she does great work."

"Don't tell anyone"—he leaned in to whisper conspiratorially—"but Emmy is very intimidating. Plus, I came here to see you."

"I'm sorry, sir, but I'm on my way out," I repeated, more forcefully this time.

"What's with all this 'sir' stuff? Call me Andy."

"I'm sorry, Andy," I said, frustrated that I wasn't in my car already, feeling the sting in my eyes as they were beginning to fill again. "But I can make you an appointment for another day."

"Are you crying?"

"It's been a rough day." I searched for a tissue in my purse to stop the tears leaking out of my eyes.

"Do you want to talk about it? I'm a great listener." Drew reached into his back pocket and handed me a white embroidered handkerchief with *D.W.* stitched on it. I'd never actually seen a man pull a hankie out and hand it to a woman before, much less one that was embroidered with his initials. It felt like something from a romantic comedy set in a bygone era. I didn't know what to do with it, so I just held it in my hands.

"Are you straight?" I asked.

"Mostly."

"Then no, I don't want to talk about it with you."

"Lady problems?"

"Bigotry problems." I handed him back his hankie. "Would you like me to schedule you an appointment before I go?"

"Want to play putt-putt?" he blurted out, his face lighting up like a six-foot-four ten-year-old.

I stared at him blankly in response, having no clue what that meant. "Putt-putt?"

"You know, putt-putt, miniature golf. Or we could race go-karts. Or play video games. Ooh, or bumper boats!"

"Thank you, but no," I declined, pulling up my calendar on the work computer. "I can get you in tomorrow afternoon, if you're free. What kind of outfit are you looking for?"

"It always makes me feel better."

"Buying a new suit?" I asked.

"Playing putt-putt. Plus, I owe you a round of golf."

"A round of golf you bid on and paid for, may I remind you."

"Tiny, insignificant detail." He pointed his finger in a circle toward me.

"*Love, Actually.*" I smiled as I recognized the quote.

"Yes!" He beamed. "See, you're feeling better already. Come on, I'll drive. It's thirty minutes away, tops. If you hate it, I'll bring you right back."

"I'm not really dressed for putt-putt," I offered as an excuse, not mentioning the change of clothes I kept in my car for after work. "Plus, I kind of just need to drive with the windows down and Indigo Girls blasting right now, but thank you for the invite."

"I've got a convertible. And *1200 Curfews* on my iPod."

"You like the Indigo Girls?"

"Mom's a lesbian," he explained.

"And you still use an iPod?"

"I'm old school," he said.

My head cocked to the side as I stood there taking him in. Drew Williams, action star, one of *People*'s Sexiest Men Alive (he lost the top spot to Chris), was offering to drive me to putt-putt in his convertible while the Indigo Girls played on an old-school iPod. I had no idea what to do with this information, so I just said, "Tomorrow at one in the afternoon work for you?"

"For putt-putt?"

"For your suit," I said, trying to keep it professional.

He looked at his phone. "Yeah, that should work."

"Okay, I have you down for one in the afternoon tomorrow."

"So no putt-putt?"

I didn't answer. I didn't know what to say. It sounded fun, but this guy could be a total asshole, like his buddy, and I really couldn't handle chauvinism right now. Plus, he was a famous client of ours; there were rules about this sort of thing at Roussard's.

"I don't know what happened to make you cry," Drew continued. "But I do know that driving with the top down blaring Indigo Girls on our way to play putt-putt and eat cheese fries will make it better."

"You didn't say anything about fries with cheese." I perked up. "That's a horse of a different color."

"So you're in?" His face lit up.

"I'm in," I said, wondering what the hell I was getting myself into. "Just let me get a change of clothes out of my car."

"Stupendous!" Drew threw his hands up in the air. "I haven't been to putt-putt in so long."

Drew stood there grinning while I gathered my things, told Emmy I was leaving, and clocked out. We headed to the parking garage together, passing a group of gawkers on the way out.

"Which one's yours?" he asked, completely ignoring the girls who were now openly taking photos of him.

I pointed ahead and led us to my white Subaru Forester parked at the end of the employee level.

"My mom has this same car," Drew said.

"She really is a lesbian," I joked, grabbing my clothes from the front seat. "I'll just run back in and change."

"You can change in the car. I promise not to look."

"And what about the other people we pass with the top down?"

"They promise not to look, too." He smirked.

I chuckled and ran inside for a quick change, glad to be free of my pointy shoes and tight clothes. When I came back out, Drew was taking a selfie with a young kid who looked about Ellis's age. A woman, I assumed it was her mom, stood next to them holding Roussard's bags and smiling.

"Thank Mr. Williams," she said to her daughter when Drew handed the phone back to her.

"Thank you, Mr. Williams," the little girl repeated shyly.

"Please," Drew replied, shaking the kid's hand, "call me Drew."

"I thought your name was Andy?" I said when the mother and daughter were gone.

"Shh." He put a finger to his lips and stared around furtively. "Don't give away my secret identity!"

Still acting like a stealth agent, Drew led me to where his car was parked, two levels up. I expected famous action star Drew Williams to have some flashy, new, souped-up Ferrari, with bucket seats and a vanity plate, but I was pleasantly surprised when he unlocked the door to a gorgeous orange-red antique convertible.

"Nice ride." I slipped into the passenger seat and ran my hands against the leather interior.

"1954 Chevrolet C1. You like it?"

"I love it!"

"It's yours, then," he said, throwing me the keys.

"Wait, for reals?!" My mouth gaped in complete shock.

"Just kidding." He laughed. "I love this car. I'd never give her away. But the look on your face was classic."

"Ass," I said, throwing the keys back at him.

"You can drive, though, if you want," he offered. "If that'll make you feel better."

"I'll take you up on that another day," I said as he rolled back the roof and got in. "Today, I want a chauffeur."

"At your service, ma'am." He bowed before pulling out an iPod and plugging it into an aux cable. The original radio had been replaced with a modern deck. Indigo Girls began to play. "Ready?"

"Ready." I raised my hands in the air as he spun out of the parking garage, Amy Ray and Emily's harmonized voices blaring through the speakers as we sang along with them to "I Don't Wanna Know."

"I can see why you chose Hollywood over Broadway," I poked fun as Drew belted the lyrics. He actually had a pretty decent voice, which wasn't surprising considering he got his start on a kid's musical show, but I wasn't going to tell him that. He looked over at me, feigning offense, and I caught him glancing down at my chest. My after-work clothes aimed for comfort over modesty, and Drew had apparently noticed how low-cut my old worn-out tank top was. "Hey there, buddy, eyes on the road!"

"Sorry," he said, immediately facing forward. "Bad habit."

He was blushing, and that made me blush in return. I didn't want Drew Williams in any sexual or romantic way, but it was still nice to know he appreciated what I considered to be my best physical asset.

"My brother, Henry, loved this song!" I screamed as "Galileo" came on. "His frat brothers made fun of him for it, but he didn't care."

"Sounds like a nice guy."

"Nah, he was a dick. But he did have great taste in music." Drew looked over at me questioningly. "Cancer. Five years ago."

"One more time, then"—Drew started "Galileo" over again—"for Henry."

We sang even louder this time, and I turned my head so Drew couldn't see the tears filling my eyes. It felt weird, crying in front of a total stranger, a famous movie star and potential client at that, but I couldn't stop the tears, not after today, so I let them run down my face and disappear in the wind. Drew said nothing, just handed me another embroidered hankie and kept singing until we pulled into the parking lot thirty minutes later and parked next to a ten-foot-tall tower with Rapunzel's hair running down it.

He got out and ran around the car, opening the passenger door for me and extending his hand. "Ready?"

"As I'll ever be," I replied, wondering what the hell I was getting myself into.

Chapter Eight

The whole fun center had a fairy tale theme with three giant blind mice greeting us at the entrance. Drew bought wristbands for unlimited play, and we raced go-karts and bumped boats while we waited for our tee time. It was weird, watching people interact with Drew in different ways—some staring, some being overly polite, some shooting photos from afar. If it fazed Drew, he didn't show it. Instead, he continually made jokes to cheer me up and checked in a bit too much to make sure I was enjoying myself, which I surprisingly was. He'd been right. This was exactly what I needed.

Soon it was our tee time, and while I picked out my putter, Drew ran off to the main building, returning a few minutes later with a giant popcorn tub full of fries with cheese.

"You're my new favorite person in the whole wide world!" I exclaimed, enthusiastically grabbing the tub from his arms.

"You only like me for my fries."

"It's true," I said, shoving a handful of warm, gooey, crunchy, salty goodness into my mouth. "Seriously, though, you're pretty chill for a movie star."

"And you're pretty."

"Pretty...what?" I asked.

"Just pretty." He smiled at me as we walked to our starting spots.

"Are you hitting on me?"

"Maybe?" He placed his ball on the dot, lining up his shot and hitting it perfectly along Hansel and Gretel's trail of crumbs.

"I thought we established that I'm more of the Indigo Girls type." I handed him the tub of fries before I stepped up to the tee-off line.

"I like the Indigo Girls."

"And I like girls," I emphasized as my ball ricocheted off the edge and came right back to me.

"Gender is a construct."

"Your lesbian mom teach you that one?" I asked as I hit my ball again, this time making it around the curve and almost to the Witch's Candy Cottage.

"Nice shot."

"I'm a natural," I boasted, taking the fries from him.

"Yes, my mother taught me that gender is more social than physical and that people are attracted to who they're attracted to." He paused to line up his shot. "But I wasn't hitting on you, just stating the fact that you are indeed pretty."

My heart skipped a few beats in spite of myself as he hit his ball perfectly into the hole. I tried to remind the butterflies in my stomach that I was not into cishet men, but still, it was nice to get compliments from someone—regardless of their gender or fame. Especially someone as sincere and thoughtful as Drew seemed to be.

"Nice shot." I smiled.

"I'm a natural," he echoed, reaching for the fries.

We headed to Hole Two, and I handed him the tub before bending over and lining my ball up on the little dot. I wasn't the competitive type when it came to sports, but I still didn't want to make an ass out of myself in front of Drew Williams. I swung lightly, following through with my stroke like I remembered my dad saying years ago when he tried to teach me. Yet still, my ball went flying, ricocheting off the wall and ending up behind us. "Now you see why I didn't want to go to the fancy golf course with you?"

"I just figured it was the lack of cheese fries." Drew held the tub steady as I dug my hand in for more.

"That, too," I said, mouth full. "And it's fries with cheese. Not cheese fries."

"Good to know. I'll remember that for next time." Drew placed his ball down, focusing on it as he lined up his shot. "So why were you crying at Roussard's today?"

I went and picked up my ball, stalling for time until I could figure out how much I wanted to share.

"You don't have to talk about it if you don't want to," Drew amended while tapping his ball easily into the Big Bad Wolf's mouth.

"No, it's fine. I probably should talk about it, and you deserve to know why you're cheering me up." I lined my shot up, tapped it gently, and completely failed to shoot my ball through the Big Bad Wolf's mouth.

"There was this kid." My heart began aching all over again thinking about Alex. "They were genderqueer, and the mom was horrible about it. A total bitch to me and the kid. It brought up a lot from my own childhood, people not accepting me being queer, and it made me feel terrible for this kid to have such an abusive, unaccepting mother."

"That sounds terrible," Drew said as I tried, and failed, another time to make it into the Big Bad Wolf's mouth. "Anything I can do to help?"

"This is actually helping a lot." I picked up my golf ball and shoved it into the wolf's mouth, only to have it immediately roll back out, making us both start laughing. "Who knew putt-putt with a friend was so therapeutic?"

"So we're friends, then?" Drew picked my ball up and handed it to me, writing a two down for strokes on my scorecard, a total lie that didn't matter, because he was a good ten points ahead of me only halfway through the course.

"We sang to the Indigo Girls and ate fries with cheese." I rummaged through the bottom of the tub he was holding, grabbing the last crunchy, salty, gooey bits. "That makes us friends in my book."

"And if I wanted more?"

"I'm sure we can go inside and buy some more."

"I wasn't talking about the fries." He tossed the container in the trash while I started on the next hole.

"I want an Oscar, but sometimes you have to settle for what life hands you." Trying to ignore the fact that Drew Williams was possibly hitting on me, and I was possibly liking it, I wiped my hands on my pants, lined up my shot, and sent my ball soaring over Cinderella's slipper and right into Little Red Riding Hood's basket two holes ahead of us.

"Keep making movies like *Lalo's Lament*, and you could win an Oscar." He retrieved my ball while the people playing that hole gawked at him.

"Thanks." I took the ball from Drew and hit it softer this time. "But the chances of me winning an Oscar are as likely as me winning the U.S. Open. I've just accepted it's not happening."

"Why not?"

"Because fat girl."

"You're not—"

"Please don't say I'm not fat," I cut him off. "That's like you pretending you're not famous. We both know the truth, so why lie about it?"

"Okay, but you're talented. I don't see why being fat would keep you from winning an Oscar."

I watched as his ball seamlessly soared up, around, and into Cinderella's pumpkin carriage.

"Have you ever seen a fat woman win an Oscar?" I leaned against my putter, waiting for the people in front of us to make it through the Three Blind Mice. "Hell, have you ever seen a fat woman in an Oscar-nominated film?"

Drew was quiet, as if thinking about it for a moment. "*What's Eating Gilbert Grape.*"

"She was the brunt of cruel jokes and torture in that movie. Plus, Leonardo DiCaprio is the only one who got accolades for that, and he was rail thin."

"*Precious.*"

"Again, a movie that allowed viewers to pity a fat girl and gawk at her life. Gabby Sidibe did an amazing job, such a brilliant performance, yet she's still not getting the roles thin actresses with half her talent are. And don't even get me started on the problematic bullshit that was *The Whale*. Hollywood barely gives fat people a chance, and only if we're making fun of ourselves or seen as the sad sack."

"I get it. I was the fat sidekick for a long time. It takes a full team of professional chefs, trainers, and nutritionists to get me to look like this so I can get decent roles." Drew walked us toward a giant Woodsman chopping an ax in front of the entrance to Grandmother's House.

"And yet you still starred in blockbuster movies and, if I remember the tabloids correctly, you dated a fashion model. Fat men have it rough, but fat women are pariahs in this town. No one in Hollywood would be caught dead hiring or dating a fat girl."

"My first girlfriend was plus-sized; she shopped at Lane Bryant."

"And how soon did you break up with her when you got famous?"

"She left me. Broke my heart, actually." He tapped his ball up and into Grandmother's House, completely avoiding the ax. "Married a mutual friend of ours who is a sound engineer at Universal. I still see them all the time. Went to their house last month for their kid's birthday."

"That's not awkward?" I tried to repeat his action, but my ball hit the side of the Woodsman and ricocheted back at us.

"I have a lesbian mom. I was raised to believe you stay friends with your exes."

I laughed at the all-too-true cliché. "Where do they live?"

"Pasadena."

"I live near there," I said, trying to make it through the chopping ax again. "I'm in Arcadia with my sister and her two kids. They're six and eight."

"Sounds like a wild house."

"It is," I admitted. I picked up my ball, after another missed shot, and shoved it into the entrance to Grandmother's House.

"It's official. I suck at golf."

Drew laughed and handed our putters to the teenager running the booth.

"Come back soon!" the kid shouted enthusiastically after us, taking out his phone and snapping a photo.

"Don't you worry people will see a photo of us online together?" I asked as we left the fun center.

"It would only boost my cred to be seen with the director of *Lalo's Lament* and a future Academy Award winner." I tried to ignore the way my heart skipped at the combination of his compliment and the smile he was directing at me. "Why, are you afraid to be seen with me?"

"Of course," I said, only partially joking.

"Well, get used to it because I plan on making you play putt-putt with me all the time now."

"You would put yourself through that torture again?" I pointed back at the Woodsman.

"If it makes you smile and forget about bigoted jerks, then yes."

"Can we skip putt-putt and just go straight for the fries with cheese next time?" I asked.

"Here, hand me your phone." Drew put out his hand, and I reluctantly handed it over. He typed something in, then handed it back to me. "Anytime you need me, just call."

Logically, I knew he'd simply felt pity for the crying shopgirl and invited me out to cheer me up. My mind knew that all his compliments were a part of that, and besides, I didn't like cishet men anyway. But still, I found myself holding my breath as I looked down at my phone and saw my new contact: "Fry Guy." I officially had the number of famous movie star Drew Williams—and I didn't know how I felt about it.

Chapter Nine

Drew unlocked the passenger door to his car and opened it for me to get in. "You know I can get my own door, right?" I asked sarcastically, sliding back into the Chevy C1's leather seats.

"No, you can't." Drew closed the door behind me, and I shot him a defiant look as he got into the driver's seat. "No, really, you literally can't open the door from the outside. That key sticks every time. I'm the only one who seems to be able to open the darn thing. But I'll let you try if you want. Maybe you'll have the magic touch."

I buckled my seat belt, still staring at him. I'd expected a pompous prick like his best friend, Chris, but instead I found a down-to-earth guy I was finding oddly endearing and magnetic. "Drew Williams, you have continually surprised me this evening."

"You can call me Andy, you know," he said as he maneuvered

out of the parking lot.

I didn't answer. Instead, I grabbed Drew's iPod and scrolled through his music options. The man had taste, I'd give him that. I landed on a mellow Bessie Smith album I used to listen to with my grandfather and settled back into my seat. "So, famous action star Drew Williams, tell me about this lesbian mother of yours."

"She's amazing," he gushed, pulling onto the freeway. "Wanted a kid, found a gay friend to donate some sperm, and raised me all by herself. She'd say not all by herself, since she had a group of gay men who took me to drag brunches and her best friends—Tammy and Joan—would babysit me for weekends she needed away. Really, though, when it came down to it, it was just her and me. She's the strongest, most accomplished, kindhearted, intelligent, and handsome woman I have ever met."

"You're a total momma's boy." My tone was joking, but I truly admired the way he lit up when he talked about his mom.

"Guilty," he gave in, a huge smile on his face. "What about your parents?"

"I don't see them much anymore, and when I do, we usually get into some kind of fight. They've never really been the same since Henry died."

"Of course not," Drew said. "How could they be after that?"

Bessie Smith crooned, *I got the world in a jug, the stopper in my hand*, and I stared out the window, thinking about the way my parents climbed into a bottle the day my brother died and never got out again. Things had always been tense between us, neither of them understanding the "alternative lifestyle" they thought I chose to live, but it was so much worse when they were drunk. I wondered what my life would be like if I'd had a lesbian mother like Drew's. Someone who not only accepted me but understood what it was like to face the vitriol of people like Mrs. Bertolli, knowing you were never completely safe as a queer person, even in liberal places like L.A.

"I'm sure you changed, too, after your brother died," Drew continued.

"So much," I admitted. "But I don't think it was for the better until about two years ago."

"What were you like before then?"

"Mean," I answered honestly.

"Mean?" Drew prodded.

"My grief made me mad, angry, bitter, and cruel at times."

"And you aren't that now?"

"Oh no, I still am." I chuckled. "But now it's more directed anger."

"At what?"

"Cancer. Grief. Death. The injustices in the world. I used to hate the whole world. Now I hate *my* world."

"Do you really hate your world?"

"No. That was too harsh," I said. "I actually love most of my life. I just hate the world of mourning. I've lived in it for so long. And now I'm coming out of it and trying to decide what to do next."

"You should write about that."

"That's actually what my latest script is about."

"Tell me more," Drew pressed.

An insecure panic began to ride up in me at the thought of sharing my story with him. His films grossed hundreds of millions at the box office. Mine had barely made the festival rounds. He was a star. I was some random shopgirl. But he looked at me with so much eagerness and excitement, I had to give him something. "Um, it's about two sisters going through some stuff."

There was a pregnant pause before Drew responded, "Well, that won't work."

His rejection hurt. "Why, because it's not some shoot-'em-up man thriller?"

"No. Because your elevator pitch sucks."

"I haven't worked on it, seeing as I'm still finishing the final draft," I snapped, pissed at him for rejecting my idea and mad at myself for not knowing better than to share it with him. What would a man like him understand about someone like me?

"That doesn't matter. You should have your elevator pitch from the start. You'll need it to sell the script—which, by the way, won't be the final draft. It'll change so much you won't recognize it by the time the film is out."

"What would you know?" I blurted, bitterness rising up in me at this unsolicited advice. "Don't you just show up and read the lines?"

"Actually, Chris and I are starting a production company," Drew said with pride in his voice.

"A production company? You two?" I laughed.

"What's so funny about that?" He sounded hurt.

"It's just, I don't know, you seem more of the smile-and-wave type."

Drew said nothing in response, but I could see by his face that I'd struck a chord. The hurt there reminded me of my ex Sam, the way she looked each time I lashed out at her, my insecurities taking over. I'd been so unstable dating Sam, never quite sure if she actually found me attractive. I always felt like she'd rather be with someone else, almost ashamed that she'd unwittingly fallen in love with a fat femme. One weekend, I overheard her friend casually comment that I was not the usual body type she went for. Sam told her I had a good personality and was really talented at my job, so that made up for it. I went back to our table, smiled, and drank my Negroni, trying to pretend I wasn't breaking inside. Sam denied it all when we got back to my place. We'd fought so hard, she packed her stuff and left for good, calling me abusive on the way out.

She'd texted my sister as she left, saying she still wanted to be her friend. I hated Sam for that, for reminding me that Cecily was the thin, normal, sane one that people loved more than me. But if Sam hadn't done it, I wouldn't be here today. My sister knew me well enough to immediately hop in her car and come to my apartment. She'd gotten there just in time to stop me from permanent harm.

I didn't want to be that person anymore, the one whose insecurities made her attack the people around her, who made her lash out at herself. I knew that only led to lying alone on a cold bathroom floor with a razor in my hand. I'd been through a lot of therapy since then, and I thought I had this demon under control, but I apparently still had work to do.

We all have work to do, I reminded myself, taking a deep breath and readying my body to apologize.

"I'm sorry. That was uncalled for." I reached out and touched my hand to his arm in a gesture I hoped he took as sincere and soothing. "You've been nothing but kind to me since we met. That comment was about me, not you. I actually think you'd be a really good producer. I can tell you're passionate about movies, and I think that will make you great. I know you're more than a pretty face. I didn't mean it. I just get insecure sometimes, especially around people like you who are hot, famous, and talented."

"Thanks for saying that." Drew looked down at my hand on his arm, as if he was wondering why it was there. I awkwardly withdrew it, feeling even worse than before and hating myself for ruining a perfectly good evening with my anger. I was trying to come up with something else to say to make it better when Drew turned to me and smiled. "So you think I'm hot, huh?"

"Don't forget famous and talented, too," I added, making both of us laugh and break the tension in the car. "Tell me about this production company you and Chris want to start."

"We want to help get the stories made that would otherwise be passed over. Like my mom's story. Single lesbian raising a kid on her own. Or Chris's cousin's biracial family, whose kids are treated differently based on their skin tones. Or our friend Kali's story, where Hollywood forced her to take diet pills, then rejected her when she got addicted to them. Stories like the ones you were talking about earlier, ones with positive fat characters. We want to help tell stories that are different from the normal narrative seen in Hollywood. We see groups of people struggling to get their stories told, and we want to help."

"So it's like a white male savior thing?" I asked, skeptical.

"My mom said the same thing when I told her our plan," Drew confessed.

"I like the sound of her."

"She's an amazing woman," Drew said, pulling into the Roussard's parking lot. "I get that Chris and I are privileged, and we are going to mess up at times, but still, we've gotta try. Action films are fun, but what I really want to do is make movies that have a positive impact on the world. This production company is my way of trying to do that. To use my fame to get the stories that aren't being told out there."

"And what is Chris's motivation?" I asked.

"Chris wants to win an Oscar and prove he's more than just a pretty face."

"Sounds like Chris." I scoffed. "Even his good deeds are full of ego."

"He's a better guy than he lets on," Drew vouched for his friend.

"I'm still waiting for him to prove it."

Drew parked next to my car and shut off the engine.

"You want to know the key to making this idea of yours work?"

"Absolutely." Drew turned to give me his full attention.

"Seek out people of color, queers, indigenous folks, women, trans people, people with disabilities, and other historically silenced and underrepresented folks. Hire ones with strong artistic visions and a solid sense of self. Give them a platform and then back away and let them do their thing."

"Hire people like you," Drew said.

"People like me but better."

"You don't think you're good?"

"I'm good, but I think a lot of what makes my films great is Janelle. She's amazing, one of the best cinematographers in Hollywood."

"Why haven't I heard of her?" Drew asked.

"When was the last time you were on a set with a Black DP?" I retorted.

Drew paused to think about it. "Never."

"And that's why she's still working at Roussard's," I said, pointing to the now-dark department store. I gathered my things from behind me and turned back to him. "I had a surprisingly fun time tonight, Mr. Drew Williams. Thank you."

"You don't have to act so shocked. I'm a fun guy." Drew smiled shyly, our faces startlingly close in this tiny car, his eyes staring right into mine.

"You are." I shook my head. It had officially been too long since I got laid if I was thinking about leaning in and kissing Drew Williams right now. Even if I wasn't super gay, I wouldn't be into beefed-out guys like him. Still, it had been nice to spend time with Drew. "Thanks again for turning my shitty workday into a delightful evening."

"You know, you should have your agent send me your script," Drew said as I opened the door to his car. "We're looking for movies to produce."

"It's not ready yet." I was suddenly back to being shy again.

"Send it anyways," he insisted. "You can't get anywhere in this town without someone greasing the wheels. And it just so happens I'm about to get into the grease business."

"That's a horrible line. You should never use it again."

"I regretted it even as it was coming out of my mouth." Drew laughed. "But I hope you won't let that stop you from going out with me again."

"As long as you're buying the fries with cheese, I'm there." I got out of the car and shut the door behind me.

Drew reached over and rolled down the passenger-side window. "I'll see you tomorrow at one, right?"

"Tomorrow?" I asked, confused.

"My suit fitting," he reminded me.

"Ah. Yes. Tomorrow it is, then," I answered, unlocking my car. "Thanks again, Andy."

"Anytime, Diana. I hope we can go out again soon."

As he pulled away, I sat there for a moment, letting his

words sink in.

I hope you won't let that stop you from going out with me again.

I hope we can go out again soon.

My brain spun. Had I just unknowingly gone on a date with Drew Williams?

Chapter Ten

Drew turned around on the pedestal in the private dressing room, examining his new suit. "Damn, I'm good-looking."

"And modest, too," I said, tugging on his jacket sleeve to check the fit. Drew had arrived the next day exactly on time, full of excited energy and greeting me like we were besties.

"Who would have known light gray was my color?" He admired himself in the mirror, tugging on his cuffs like he was James Bond.

"I would have." I smiled smugly.

"Now who's the modest one?" Drew smirked. "Well deserved, though. You're really good at your job."

"I look forward to the day people say that about my movies, not my ability to pick out clothes."

"I might be able to say that about your movie if you'd send me the script like I asked you to," Drew replied.

"It's not ready," I lied, hanging up a shirt Drew had passed on. It took until three in the morning, but I'd polished my draft up enough that I felt comfortable sharing it with him. A freshly printed copy was tucked away in my bag; all I had to do was reach over and pull it out. Instead, I picked up the phone and called down to alterations, and then to Janelle, asking her to bring up some shoe choices.

"I don't need alterations," Drew said when I got off the phone. "And I've got plenty of shoes."

"Yes, you do, and no, you don't." I changed his pocket square out for a more colorful one. "Where are you taking this suit for its debut?"

"I've got a hot date next weekend," he shared, a joyous smile crossing his face.

"That's fun." I wondered which actress or model he was dating these days, but years working at Roussard's had taught me not to pry. Besides, why should I care who Drew Williams dated? Instead, I handed him a purple tie to try.

"I'm really excited about it." He hooked the silk around his neck. "It's with the most amazing woman in all of L.A. She's smart, funny, accomplished, and gorgeous."

"Sounds like a wonderful woman."

Drew was glowing with excitement, and a part of me longed for someone, anyone, to talk about me the way Drew was talking about his date.

"She is. Although I'm partial." He caught my eye and winked. "Since she's my mom."

"You're buying a special suit to take your mom out on a date?" The shock in my voice must have shown on my face because Drew started laughing.

"I take her out about once a month." He chuckled. "It's her birthday, so I thought I'd surprise her this time with a fancy restaurant and new suit."

"That's adorable," I gushed as I undid the purple tie, which didn't work after all with his gray suit. "Tell me, do women fall for the mama's boy thing?"

"Only my mom's friends." He ducked so I could loop a black tie around his neck. "And they're all settled-down lesbians, so it doesn't do me any good."

"So you have a thing for lesbians, then," I teased, tying a Windsor knot on him.

"I have a thing for feisty, independent, intelligent women," Drew responded.

"Like I said, you have a thing for lesbians." I backed up to admire my work.

"Ha, well, maybe you're right." Drew fidgeted with the knot. "I never could figure out how to do a Windsor. How'd you learn?"

"Fucked the debate team in high school," I responded.

"I bet you had a nice grandpa. Liked ties on Sunday."

"I'm going to have to start quoting more obscure films around you." I held up two pairs of cufflinks for him to choose from.

"Come on, you can do better than that." Drew chose the ones in my right hand. "*Pretty Woman* is too easy. I know all the rom-coms. Try me."

"'I brought you *flours*.'" I emphasized the last word.

"*Stranger Than Fiction*," he said, catching the reference.

"'Well, nobody's perfect,'" I tried.

"*Some Like it Hot*," he guessed, correctly.

"'Today, I consider myself the luckiest man on the face of the earth.'" I made my voice sound like it was echoing through a stadium.

"*Sleepless in Seattle*, but quoting *Pride of the Yankees*." Drew smiled.

"Damn, you're good," I said, impressed.

"Mom's a romance writer." He shrugged. "Takes her job of educating me seriously."

"I'd like to meet her someday. She sounds like a great woman."

Drew turned to me, suddenly animated. "You should come next weekend!"

"To your mother's birthday party?" I asked.

"Yes! She'd love to have you there."

"Your mother doesn't even know me," I pointed out.

"Yet," Drew added, "but I told her all about meeting you."

"You told your mother about meeting me?" I asked, skepticism rising in me. "Why?"

"We saw *Lalo's Lament* together," he explained. "She loved it, too."

I had no idea what to say to that. On one hand, it could be really fun to hang out more with Drew and meet this lesbian romance writer mother he loved so much. On the other hand, it could be really awkward crashing a stranger's birthday party.

Luckily, Janelle arrived just in time to stop me from having to answer. Drew greeted her like an old friend, and she looked at him skeptically as she laid out his shoe options: black Bruno Magli leather cap-toe oxfords, dark gray Hugo Boss Kensington leather wingtip oxfords, and black Gucci leather fox head loafers with a gray stripe.

"The Guccis," Janelle and I said in unison.

"Don't I get a say in this?" Drew asked.

"No," Janelle answered, handing him the loafers.

Drew put them on as the tailor came in and got to work, pinning and tucking his suit until it fit him perfectly. Drew talked the whole time, asking Janelle about her recent projects and me about Cecily and the kids.

"He sure is acting friendly," Janelle whispered to me when Drew went into the dressing room to change out of his suit.

"We actually hung out last night," I admitted.

"And you're just now telling me this?" Janelle grumbled, smacking me playfully on the shoulder.

"It was nothing," I promised. "He came by to get a suit, but I was upset about a genderqueer kid's mom being a total bitch to her child and me, so he invited me to putt-putt to cheer me up."

"Putt-putt? Is that some slang I don't know?" Janelle asked.

"Miniature golf," I explained.

"You played miniature golf with Drew Williams?"

"We also rode the bumper boats," Drew shouted from the dressing room, his voice muffled through the clothes he was trying on. "And ate fries with cheese."

Janelle looked at me sideways and opened her mouth to say something, but Drew came out, back in the gray sweatpants he'd worn in.

"I'll have alterations rush this." I took his suit out of the dressing room and handed it to the tailor, who was patiently waiting by the door. "The event is next Saturday, correct?"

"Yes," Drew replied.

"We'll have it ready by Monday morning, sir." The tailor handed Drew a receipt and headed out.

"You both should come," Drew said as I packed up his accessories.

"Two invites in the last month," Janelle chimed in. "Who

knew Roussard's was the place for hanging out with the rich and famous?"

"Emmy knew," I said, handing Drew a pair of jeans and a shirt I'd pulled while the tailor was pinning his suit. "Go, try these on. I can't have you leaving in those crusty old sweats."

Drew protested that his sweats weren't crusty but went and changed anyway.

"Since when do you care about his pants?" Janelle asked.

I shrugged. "I could use the commission, and he could use a few paparazzi shots of him that don't include stained shirts."

"I can hear you," Drew said from the dressing room.

"That's the point," I shouted.

Janelle rolled her eyes as Drew emerged wearing a pair of dark wash jeans and a light blue cotton tee that clung tight across his chest.

"Much better." Janelle nodded in agreement.

"It's still weird," Drew said, staring at himself in the mirror.

"What?" I asked.

"Tight-fitting clothes," Drew responded. "I wore baggy sweats for so long, I don't know how to wear anything else."

"And that's why there are professionals like us to help you." I handed him a few more casual outfit options to try on, reminding myself that while men might have it easier in this town, it's still hard to be fat in Hollywood, regardless of gender. I could only imagine the tabloid images Drew had to deal with as a teen.

Janelle looked at her watch. "I should get back downstairs."

"Wait, before you go"—Drew poked his head out—"where should I pick you up for dinner next Saturday?"

"I'm not sure I agreed to go." Janelle cocked her head.

"You're gay, right?" Drew asked.

"Sure am," Janelle proudly replied.

"So are my mom and her friends. They're great—strong, independent, queers, and women of color. They'd love some fresh blood. You've gotta be there."

"We'll think about it," I cut in.

"Did I mention it's at Dos?" Drew added. "And it's my treat."

"Holy shit," I said. Dos was the hottest restaurant in town, impossible to get into, running about $250 a person. "I'm there."

"I should just start off with the food options if I want you to come somewhere." Drew laughed.

"It's the only thing that gets her out of the house," Janelle agreed.

"Send me that script of yours tonight," Drew encouraged me. "I want to read it before dinner."

"Why do you want her script?" Janelle asked, giving me the side-eye as she said it.

"To see if it would be a good fit for my new production company," Drew responded casually, like he wasn't offering some huge opportunity to me, one I wasn't sure I deserved but desperately wanted.

Janelle turned rapidly toward me, annoyance on her face. "How did you not tell me any of this? And why haven't you sent it to him?"

"It's not ready," I lied again.

"Bullshit," Janelle spat, looking around the room. "Where is it?"

"What do you mean?" I avoided her eyes while my brain rapidly tried to decide whether it could handle handing my script over for Drew Williams to read.

"You act like we haven't been best friends for a decade." Janelle began rifling through the room, lifting sofa cushions. "I know you brought a copy with you. So where is it?"

Unconsciously, I glanced over at my purse, hidden behind the dressing room loveseat. Catching my gaze, Janelle walked over, opened my bag, and pulled out the printed copy of my script with a satisfied look on her face.

"Here you go, Mr. Williams." She handed it over to Drew. "Your next big hit."

"Don't I get a say in this?" I asked.

"Nope." Janelle smiled smugly at me.

"Are you okay with this?" Drew asked me.

"Yes, she is," Janelle answered for me and crossed her arms, daring me to object.

"I guess I am." Nervous bile rose in my throat as I watched Drew flip through the pages.

"I'll read through it and let you know what I think on Saturday when I pick you up," Drew said. "Does five work for you?"

"Will you pick us up in a ridiculously long stretch limo, like prom?" Janelle asked.

"I'll even get a white one to make it that much more ridiculous if you'd like," Drew acquiesced.

"Sounds perfect." Janelle took a pen out of my purse and wrote her address and our phone numbers on the back of the script. "You can pick us up at five here."

"Great!" Drew exclaimed as he gathered his clothes. "I'm excited for you to meet my mom."

He changed, paid, and enthusiastically said he'd see us next weekend as he waved goodbye.

"Why did I let you give him my script?" I asked as Janelle

and I watched Drew maneuver gawking shoppers to get to the parking lot.

"Bitch, stop complaining. I just got you back into show business." Janelle wrapped her arm around me. "You can thank me in your Oscars acceptance speech."

Chapter Eleven

I tried to work, but all I could think about was the fact that Drew Williams was reading my script, and possibly Chris Stanson, too. I told myself that if they didn't like it, I'd be fine. My agent, Elise, could still shop it around like we'd originally planned. But if they did like it... My brain could barely fathom what that would mean.

Instead of fixating on the possibility of rejection—or even scarier, success—I focused all my energy on what I already knew I did well: fashion. I dug through my closet and found a form-fitting silver sequined ELOQUII cocktail dress that I'd bought years ago for a wedding and hadn't worn since. I had too many clothes like that, beautiful outfits I rarely took out, opting instead for my comfortable, favorite go-to pieces. Grief had left me living in sweatpants for so long that I'd forgotten how much I loved making a statement as I walked into a room. The LACMA party reminded me that I liked dressing myself as much as other people, but I was still recovering from the destroyed shirt and lost earring, wondering if I really could handle dressing up and going out with a celebrity, where paparazzi might catch us at any minute. The designer dress was stunning, but still, I felt like throwing it off, putting on some yoga pants, and feigning illness. At least that way I wouldn't have to face Drew as he rejected my script.

"He's here," Janelle said as her door buzzer rang. She wore an emerald crushed velvet suit with matching loafers and a perfectly folded goldenrod pocket square. She looked fabulously fashionable, and for a split second, I hated Janelle for how easily confidence came to her, before I remembered that she was a Black, queer, masculine-of-center woman in Hollywood—her swagger was hard-earned.

"Ready?" She looked over at me with excitement.

"No!" I said, my whole body tingling with nerves. "I think I'm going to puke. I don't think I can do this."

"Okay, I get it. That's fine." Janelle picked up her phone. "I'll call down and tell him we're not going."

"Really?" I was half hopeful, half heartbroken at the idea of staying home tonight.

"No, not really!" Janelle picked up my clutch and threw it at me. "This is a huge chance for both of us—you're not going to chicken out. You're going to suck it up, get your ass out that door, and have a damn good time tonight. You know why?"

"Why?"

"Because we're fine as hell." Janelle grabbed her suit lapel and posed in the mirror. When I didn't respond, she looked over at me expectantly. "I said, we're fine as hell."

"And sexy AF," I finished without enthusiasm.

"Excuse me, what? I didn't hear you." Janelle put her hand

up to her ear.

"And sexy as fuck," I said, louder.

"People are lucky to share space with us," Janelle encouraged, twirling around and sticking her ass out toward me.

I smiled. "They should pay us to be in their presence."

"Damn right." She smiled, opening the door for me.

I stood there, frozen. "What if he doesn't like it?"

"Then he's more of an idiot than I thought, and we'll find someone else to produce it." Janelle threw her arm around me. "Either way, you get a limo ride and a free dinner at Dos."

"I do love free food."

"See, the night is already a win!" Janelle hugged me tightly against her body, then pushed me away. "Now get your ass out that door."

I grabbed my clutch and Janelle's hand as we made our way downstairs where, true to his word, Drew had a ridiculously long white stretch limo waiting for us. He stood outside it with a goofy grin on his face and two corsages in his hands.

"You don't have to wear them all night," he said, slipping the flowers onto our wrists, "but I thought you might like them for the car ride."

We laughed and thanked him, climbing inside, where we were greeted by an older white woman wearing a black suit with satin trim, a thick black-and-white plaid tie, and a large, welcoming smile on her face. She waved at us, her corsage flopping around her wrist.

"He never went to prom," she explained, adjusting the band of flowers.

"Really?" I gasped as I scooted next to her.

"He was rather goofy in high school," she confided in me.

"He's rather goofy still," I joked as Drew got in.

She laughed, a deep belly laugh that at once put me at ease. "You must be Diana," she said, extending her hand to me. "I'm Jaqueline Williams."

"Why do I know that name?" Janelle asked, settling into her seat across from us.

"Because she's a super-famous writer, the first out lesbian to win a Pulitzer, among other prestigious awards," Drew said, beaming.

"Modesty was never his strong point"—Jaqueline offered her hand to Janelle—"but that is me. And you must be Janelle. And now that we are all acquainted, I think it is time to seal our new friendship with a toast."

Drew popped a bottle of champagne and handed us all glasses. "To Jaqueline!"

"To Jaqueline!" we cheered, clinking our flutes together.

"I could get used to this." Janelle lounged against the sofa-size seat she had to herself and sipped her champagne.

"I thought you didn't like big, fancy events," I teased.

"I don't," she insisted, letting her legs stretch out. "But I do like big, fancy cars."

I laughed and noticed Drew fussing with his tie in the window's reflection.

"This won't do." I squatted and made my way past Janelle to the far end of the limo where he was sitting. "As your stylist, I can't let you out in public like this."

"Windsor knots are impossible." Drew yanked and pulled his crooked tie tighter.

"You're impossible." I tugged on his neck, trying to loosen the wonky knot.

"I read your script," he said.

I stopped breathing, my hands pausing against his neck.

"And?" I responded, focusing intently on the tie so he couldn't see the nervousness in my face.

"It's amazing," he replied, trying to catch my eye.

"It's good," I corrected, still not looking at him. "I wouldn't call it amazing."

"Diana." Drew leaned over and forced me to look into his eyes. "This script is really, really good. With the right cast and crew, I think it could win awards. Big ones."

"You think so?" I asked, my fingers shaking against his chest, a blush starting to take over my face.

"I do." The beam on his face told me he meant it. "And so does Chris. We want to produce it."

I froze, dropping his tie, the knot falling loose. "You want to what?"

"Produce it." Drew grabbed the pieces of silk and tried to tie them together himself. "With you as the director."

"Janelle..." I looked over my shoulder at my best friend talking with Jaqueline farther down the limo. "Janelle, I need you to hear this."

"We're almost there," Jaqueline announced. "Andy, fix your tie."

"I'm trying." He flipped the silk over and under itself. "Windsor knots are impossible."

"Drew," I squealed, "repeat what you told me, loud enough for Janelle to hear."

"Windsor knots are impossible," he yelled, smiling coyly at me.

"You know what I mean." I pushed his fingers away and yanked out the tangled knot he'd created.

"Chris and I want to produce Diana's film," Drew said, loud

enough for everyone to hear. "With her as the director."

Janelle shot up, looking from me to Jaqueline. "Is he for real?"

"Andy talked about your script the whole way here," Jaqueline confessed, "which is a good sign for him and a project."

"So, then, what do we do now?" I asked.

"I think you should start with fixing his tie," Jaqueline replied.

I laughed and flipped the material around, my hands practiced from working at Roussard's. Seconds later, Drew had a perfectly tied Windsor knot around his throat.

He thanked me as he glanced at his reflection in the window. "Looks good."

"Now, tell us what's next for this film," Janelle said.

"We don't need to talk details right now," Drew reassured us as the limo pulled over in front of Dos. "But if you're interested, I'll have my people call your people."

"So they really do say that in Hollywood." Janelle shook her head.

Drew smiled as he looked me up and down. "You look like a disco ball."

"Thanks?" I didn't know how to take that. On one hand, my silvery sequined dress did look like a disco ball. On the other hand, I didn't know Drew well enough yet to tell if that was a fat joke.

"In a good way," he added quickly. "A *really* good way. You both look stunning as well," Drew said to Janelle and Jaqueline. "I'm the luckiest guy in L.A."

"I'd say you're lucky, showing up with a limo full of hot queer women," Janelle said as the driver opened our door.

Drew stepped out of the car first, and a sound like distant gunfire went off around us.

Jaqueline grabbed my arm. "Wait a few minutes. Let the cameras die down. Avoids a crotch shot in the news tomorrow."

I thanked her for the advice and looked through the windows as Drew waved to the paparazzi. I smiled, excited that it might be me soon, standing on a red carpet posing for photos at the opening of my film. A film Drew Williams and Chris Stanson wanted to produce! With their names attached, this script had a great chance of being made. I pinched myself as Drew raised his hand, indicating he was done, then ducked back into the car. "It's safe to come out now."

Jaqueline grabbed a silver-tipped cane from the floor and scooted toward the door. Drew helped us each out of the car, and together we made our way to the front of the restaurant as paparazzi snapped shots and shouted questions.

"What brings you here tonight, Drew?" a woman with a notebook yelled.

"Tacos." Drew smirked. The woman laughed.

"Who are you here with tonight, Drew?" a man with a camera shouted from the group.

"My brilliant mother, the award-winning writer Jaqueline Williams, and two talented filmmakers, Diana Smith and Janelle…" He paused, looking at Janelle.

"Zenon," Janelle added.

"Janelle Zenon," he said loudly. The man wrote something down on his notepad as we walked inside.

"That was intense," Janelle said as we approached the host stand. "Does that happen to you everywhere you go?"

"Not everywhere," Drew admitted.

"This row of restaurants is popular with famous people, so

the tabloids keep a crew outside on the weekends," Jaqueline explained.

"Right this way, Mr. Williams." The hostess escorted us away from the entrance and to a door in the back of the restaurant. When she opened it, I expected a small, secluded space just for our party but instead found a whole other dining room, this one completely full of celebrities.

"Do all restaurants have a secret famous person room?" I asked as we passed Hugh Jackman sipping scotch with Ryan Reynolds.

"Just the most pretentious ones," Jaqueline said as we reached our table where two handsome women in tuxes sat. "Tammy and Joan, this is Janelle and Diana."

"Nice to meet you," Tammy said in a Southern drawl.

"You, too," I replied, "and might I add that you both look very handsome in those tuxes."

Tammy laughed and winked at me. "If only I were twenty years younger."

"Maybe I like my women refined with age," I said, winking back.

"Then you can sit right here." Joan patted the seat next to her.

I accepted the offer and sat down as Drew pulled the seat out for his mother on the other side of Tammy and hooked her cane on the back of her chair. Janelle sat next to me, with Drew next to her, and two empty chairs between him and his mom.

Dos was a lavish homage to 1950s Mexico City, with royal purples and rich maroon walls contrasting with bright gold and brass fixtures, all of it accented with bouquets of fresh flowers and lush green vines. Our table itself was a work of art, a copper-and-glass frame lit by a jumbled string of tiny, white lights embedded inside. Janelle ran her hand over it admiringly as I pointed out the chandelier, its waterfall of shining crystals a crown encircling us all. Across the room, a similar chandelier dangled above the well-stocked brass bar, creating a halo around the bartender's head, like a Byzantine saint serving up redemption.

It was by far the nicest restaurant I'd ever been in.

"Look who made it." Jaqueline nodded toward the entrance, a warm smile crossing her face. I held back a groan as I looked up and saw the hostess escorting Chris Stanson to our table.

"Ah, Jaqueline, beautiful." Chris kissed her on both cheeks in greeting. "It's been too long."

"And whose fault is that?" She smacked him with her hand.

Chris faked being hurt and then pulled her into a long hug.

"I miss you, son." She returned his embrace. "Where's Kali?"

"Couldn't make it," Chris said, giving a glance over at Drew.

"Chris, you remember Tammy, Joan, Janelle, and Diana." Drew pointed to each of us.

"Yes, lovely to see you all again." Chris sat down next to Drew and let the waiter know there'd be one fewer person.

As the staff took away the extra place setting, I internally freaked out a bit as it dawned on me that they were talking about *the* Kali, as in the lesbian rock star I'd grown up idolizing. Chris, Drew, and Kali had all been in a show together as teens, and the tabloids said they were still best friends, but I hadn't even contemplated that she might also be here tonight. Part of me was devastated at the missed chance to meet her, but my nerves were glad to not have another celebrity to impress tonight.

"So, Coffee Girl." Chris turned to me. "I loved your script."

Before I could remind him that my name was Diana, not Coffee Girl, Janelle grabbed my arm and squealed. "Oh my god, it's Lena Waithe!"

Janelle had the hugest crush on the screenwriter and actor, and I couldn't blame her. Lena Waithe was the complete package: smart, funny, and exceptionally well-dressed. "She is so hot." Janelle beamed, and all the queers at the table enthusiastically agreed. "Or wait, do they use they/them pronouns or she/her?"

"I know they're enby, but not sure about pronouns?" I replied. "Either way, so hot."

"Are you both lesbians?" Joan asked.

"I prefer queer, but yes, definitely super gay," I answered.

"Why do the young kids love the word 'queer' so much?" Tammy asked. "Back in my day, that was the term used to beat us up. Not one I relish."

"I get that," I said. "I think that's why our generation decided to reclaim the term."

"We call ourselves queer to embrace our differences," Janelle explained. "To me, being queer means my sexuality, my gender, my kinks, my lifestyle, my politics are all different than the heteronormative, patriarchal, white supremacist society."

"Exactly," I agreed as people appeared with dishes for the table. "Plus, many of the people I date don't identify as women, and I'm genderqueer myself, so 'lesbian' isn't really accurate for me. Queer is more encompassing of the full rainbow of my life."

"We'll start with a little palate teaser of oysters," our server interrupted, placing a small plate in front of me, "fresh up today from Ensenada and topped with a house-made jalapeño granita. "The whole meal is gluten, dairy, and soy-free, as requested. Enjoy."

"Oh my god, that was so good," Janelle gushed, finishing

hers in one bite and slurping the last bits of granita out of her oyster shell.

Good was an understatement. It was crispy and cool, salty and acidic, fatty and fresh all at once. My tongue had reached nirvana. This one bite held more complexity than whole meals at other restaurants, and I knew we were about to embark on one hell of a culinary adventure.

"Oh, just you wait," Jaqueline promised.

"We came here for our anniversary earlier this year, and I still dream about that meal." Joan pulled Tammy into a hug.

"How long have you two been together?" I asked.

"Twenty-two long, tedious, painful years," Joan bemoaned, and Tammy pushed her away. Joan pulled Tammy back toward her with a smile. "And I've loved every second of it."

"I officiated their wedding," Jaqueline chimed in. "Drew was a flower girl."

"Flower girl, eh?" Janelle asked.

Drew shrugged. "We're not big on gender norms around here."

"I'm going to need photos," Janelle teased.

"How have you made it last?" I asked the couple.

"Communication, collaboration, and vibrators," Tammy confessed, making the table laugh.

"And non-monogamy," Joan added.

"So you have sex with other people?" Chris asked.

"Why, honey, you interested?" Joan quipped.

"We realized early on that we couldn't always meet each other's every need," Tammy elaborated while squeezing Joan's hand, "so we opened our lives up to people who could."

"Doesn't that cause drama?" Chris asked.

"Says the boy with a different tabloid headline breakup

each month." Jaqueline sneered.

"Have you ever?" Chris looked back and forth from Jaqueline to Joan.

"How do you think we met?" Jaqueline lifted her glass to Joan's. They clinked and drank, smirking the whole time.

"Lesbians are so complicated," Chris said.

"Look who's talking," Jaqueline said. "Your sex life is like a box of puzzles all thrown together with a few pieces missing."

"Just how I like it." Chris raised his glass to her, and she pulled him into her side, their affection for each other apparent. There was something about Jaqueline loving Chris that warmed the coldness I had toward him, and something about Chris showing up for Jaqueline like this that made me think he might deserve a second chance. *Might* being the key word.

After the delightful oysters came urchin tostadas with sea snail ceviche, followed by the most exquisite guacamole with house-made chips and chapulines—seasoned spicy grasshoppers—to sprinkle on top. I thought about how Reggie and Ellis would laugh at me for eating snails and grasshoppers, but I loved every crispy bite. A cactus flower sorbet cleansed our palates before an entree of wild boar tamales with a peanut mole, followed by quail with adobo sauce over cilantro rice.

The meal went by in a blur of laughter and mezcal, with Janelle pretending to pee every five minutes so she could get another glimpse of Lena Waithe. For dessert, the restaurant sent over a simple yet elegant deep-fried churro—shockingly gluten-free—presented on a wooden board with a miniature chocolate piñata Jaqueline had to break open to get at the creamy coconut cajeta center. As we sang her happy birthday, I swore I heard Hugh Jackman join in. When the check came, Drew insisted on paying it in full, and I didn't protest, knowing the meal probably cost my whole paycheck.

"Happy birthday, young thang." Joan yawned as she and Tammy kissed Jaqueline good night. "It was a pleasure meeting you, Diana and Janelle."

"The pleasure was all mine," I said, getting up and hugging both of them.

"I should get home, too," Chris declared. "Early morning photo shoot."

"Please tell me you ladies aren't party poopers as well." Jaqueline grabbed her cane and stood. "The evening has just begun."

"What did you have in mind?" Janelle raised an eyebrow.

"Let's go to Drew's house and watch a movie. He has a very big screen."

"Overcompensating?" Janelle joked.

"If he's anything like his sire was, he has nothing to compensate for." Jaqueline looped her arm through Janelle's.

"You two?" I said, making a lewd hand gesture.

"Cheaper than a sperm bank." She shrugged, pulling me to her other side as we left the table. "Chris, my darling, can I convince you to join us?"

Chris looked at the three of us, arms linked, smiling conspiratorially, and shook his head, a definitive no.

"Suit yourself." Jaqueline headed into the restroom. Janelle joined her, and Drew went into the men's, leaving Chris and I standing alone together. He leaned back into the corner of the room and stared at his phone.

"What's your photo shoot tomorrow for?" I asked, trying to fill the awkward silence settling between us.

"What?" Chris looked up at me from his phone.

"What is your photo shoot tomorrow for?" I repeated,

leaning into him and shouting over the ambient noise surrounding us. As I did, a flash popped off, and I turned to see a man carrying a camera running out of the restaurant, a large security guard following him.

"I'm starting to hate those guys," I complained as my eyes adjusted.

"You never really get used to them."

The manager came over, apologized, and offered to show us out the back of the building.

"Lead the way," Chris said once everyone was out of the restroom.

We wound through the kitchen and out a delivery door, where our limo was waiting.

"Your car will be around shortly," the manager said to Chris, who looked put out at having to wait.

"You mean the world to me, son." Jaqueline pulled him into a tight embrace and kissed the top of his head. "Drive safely."

Chris lingered in Jaqueline's arms, and for a moment I saw the little kid he must have been. Saying a brief goodbye to Chris, I climbed into the limo, followed by the rest of our party. With one last wave at Chris standing alone on the curb, our limo took off, Aretha Franklin blaring, Jaqueline already singing along.

Chapter Twelve

We pulled up to a simple white house with a beautifully lit, cactus-lined driveway. It was a lot smaller than I expected of action star Drew Williams, and it stood in contrast to Chris Stanson's massive mansion. Drew entered a code on the keypad, and a modern white security gate opened to reveal a large entranceway where Drew's vintage red convertible and a black Tesla SUV sat parked next to each other. Floor-to-ceiling windows lined the house, revealing a much grander estate than I had guessed from the outside.

The limo pulled up diagonally at the front door, and we filed out, Janelle and I the last to leave. We raised our eyebrows at each other, a nod to how chic this place was, then exited the car. Jaqueline unlocked the door, and we followed her inside while Drew tipped the driver.

The spectacular view hit me as soon as I entered his home. Giant windows exposed a stunning panorama of Century City skyscrapers in the forefront and the whole Los Angeles basin beyond them. With the exception of a few obligatory Southern California palm trees, Drew had a completely uninterrupted and breathtaking view of the valley below.

The house was modern without being cold, masculine without being brutish, and done up in shades of gray with the occasional pop of color, mostly coming from an impressive modern art collection that included a large Catherine Opie print in the front entranceway.

"How much of this was you and how much of this was him?" I asked Jaqueline as she showed us around.

"You don't spend your whole life around lesbians and gay men and not absorb some of our fabulousness." She led us into a meticulously organized black-and-gray kitchen. "Shall we have a charcuterie plate with our movie? Popcorn for dessert?"

"Sorry, Janelle, Jaqueline is my new best friend," I declared as Drew's mom opened a long, black cabinet door to reveal an almost-empty refrigerator.

"Andy never has food in his house anymore." Jaqueline sighed. "I miss the days when he was the chubby sidekick."

"Check the catering kitchen." Drew pointed to a hidden door off the side of the room. "That fridge should be full."

"It's cool, I have a catering kitchen with a second fridge, too," I said as Jaqueline walked into the other room, this one all white. "We just call it our garage."

"And I have a wine rack just like that." Janelle pointed to the glass-enclosed cellar that took up a whole wall. "But, you know, under my sink."

"You're making fun of me, aren't you?" Drew said, grabbing four wine glasses from the cabinet.

"Somebody has to," I replied, noticing a sculpture of a curvy, naked woman reaching up into the glass from outside.

"Is it too much?" Drew asked.

"Oh no." Janelle walked to the wine cabinet and opened one of its four glass doors. "It's just right."

Jaqueline reentered with an assortment of cheeses and cured meats loaded in her arms. "I'm glad Serena keeps food for your guests to eat, or we'd be starving."

"You just ate a five-course meal," Drew pointed out.

"Who's Serena?" I asked, helping Jaqueline lay out an array of food.

"His personal chef," Jaqueline explained.

"Fancy," I replied.

"Luckily she still keeps salami and popcorn in the house." Jaqueline handed me a link of cured meat, and I began unwrapping it.

"What wine goes with salami and popcorn?" Janelle slowly walked down the rack, examining every bottle.

"Actually"—Jaqueline reached into her purse and took out a paper bag with a green cannabis cross on it—"I was thinking maybe some of this instead."

"Yes!" Janelle and I squealed in unison.

Drew shook his head. "What have I gotten myself into?"

I wondered the same thing as his eyes met mine and my heart fluttered a bit. Drew Williams was a handsome, funny, charming, rich movie star. He was the definition of irresistible, and apparently, I was feeling the allure since my stomach filled with butterflies each time he looked at me. Who wouldn't long to be sucked into his world of personal chefs and celebrity-packed secret dining rooms?

I had to remind myself that I was enamored with the dream,

not Drew, as Jaqueline handed me a package of aged ibérico to open.

"You two go pick out a movie," Jaqueline ordered Drew and Janelle. "Diana and I have this."

"This place is unreal." I gawked at Drew's kitchen—one of two, I reminded myself—which now felt even larger with just us in it. "This whole night has been unreal. I'm not used to hanging out with famous movie stars."

"Try being the mother of one," Jaqueline replied.

"Tell me the truth," I said, struggling to open the package of ibérico. "Does Drew really like my film, or is he desperate to produce something and I'm cheap?"

"It must be good if Andy likes it," Jaqueline reaffirmed, handing me a pair of scissors. "He has a keen eye for great scripts."

Then why has he been in such shitty movies lately? I thought, slicing cucumbers to eat with the cheese instead of crackers, which Drew didn't have.

"I can feel you rolling your eyes." Jaqueline handed me another cucumber to cut. "But those *Total Destruction* movies paid for this house, and they will pay for your film. Drew was looking for a cash cow franchise, and he spotted it among the hundreds of scripts that flopped before they even began. He knows what makes a good story, he knows this business, and most importantly, he knows what moviegoers want to see." Jaqueline paused, grabbing a large wooden serving board from the cupboard. "I worked hard to raise a sensitive, kind, intuitive boy," she continued, placing the board down in front of me. "He has turned into a handsome, rich, famous man, so too often people forget that he's still that tender boy under it all."

"I can see that." I nodded.

"He took you to putt-putt," she explained.

"Is that supposed to mean something?" I asked.

"And he invited you here," she continued.

"He invited Janelle here, too," I pointed out.

"He didn't take Janelle to putt-putt," she countered, like that explained it all.

"I didn't realize miniature golf was such serious business," I joked, trying to lighten the tension.

"He likes you," Jaqueline said. "That's a good sign. For your movie and your ability to work together."

I didn't know how to respond, so I decided to change the subject. "Does he have any honey?"

"I think in there." Jaqueline pointed to a cabinet on the other side of the stove that matched the fridge. "Don't let the tabloids fool you into thinking my Andy is anything like the man he plays on screen."

"Don't worry," I said, "I don't expect him to save the world from an impending nuclear disaster."

"God help us all if he were our only hope." Jaqueline laughed, turning away to place chopped walnuts in piles between the chunks of cheese. "What I'm trying to say is he's picky. If he's taking you to putt-putt, bringing you to my birthday, and inviting you here, then you're special. And that means your script is also special. Just don't take advantage of him, or you'll have to deal with me." Jaqueline pointed a knife at me, only half joking.

"I won't pretend like the perks of hanging out with him aren't nice"—I gestured around the house—"but I'm not some gold digger trying to manipulate your son. If this movie gets made, I want it to be because of the quality of my script, not because he took pity on me one day."

"Good for you." Jaqueline lifted the charcuterie board in one hand and her cane in the other. "Make sure you keep it that way," she said on her way out.

I stood there in the kitchen, shocked. Was Drew Williams's mother really worried I'd hurt her rich and famous son? I assured myself that she was simply being an overly protective mother—rightfully so, considering how sweet, trusting, and instantly open with people Drew was. Someone could easily take advantage of him. But I wasn't one of those people.

Shaking off our conversation, I grabbed the rest of the food and found my way to the living room, which had been converted into a luxurious screening area complete with plush reclining chairs and a vintage movie theater popcorn maker. Drew beamed at me when I entered. He looked so happy and proud right then, a little kid excited to show off his toys to new friends.

"Before we begin, shall we?" Jaqueline reached into her little bag with the green cross on it and pulled out a joint. We all jumped up excitedly and followed her to the edge of the backyard, Los Angeles laid out below us, rare rain clouds brewing above. As Jaqueline lit the joint, Drew pointed to his indoor/outdoor pool and told us it was heated if we wanted to go swimming later.

"This place is a real shithole," Janelle declared.

"Complete dump," I agreed, taking the joint Jaqueline offered me. I took a puff and then handed it to Drew, a spark of electricity zapping us as we touched.

"Looks like a storm is coming," Jaqueline noted, her head lifted, her voice deep and husky. "Let it rain."

Her words sparked a memory in me, and I started singing "The Late September Dogs," my favorite Melissa Etheridge song, all about the rain setting love free. As if we'd cast a spell, the sky opened, and water started pouring down on us. We continued singing, grabbing each other's arms and twirling as Janelle and Drew ran for cover.

"This song was playing when I kissed my first girl!" I confided in Jaqueline.

"I once had sex in a rainstorm to this song!" she countered, and we both laughed at the absurdity of it all, dancing in circles and continuing to sing as our clothes and bodies got drenched. Drew and Janelle yelled at us to come inside, but we ignored them, giddy with the kind of feral joy that came from magical moments of connection.

"Come join us!" I yelled at my best friend.

"We're both wearing Gucci shoes!" she yelled back.

"Take them off!" I cried, throwing my own now-ruined footwear under the awning where they were standing and grabbing each one by the hand. "Come on!"

Janelle released my grip as she carefully discarded her designer items, but Drew held on tight as we ran out into the rain, clasping on to each other. I looked over at him, and his eyes locked onto mine as we twirled in the tempest, Jaqueline continuing to croon.

At once, I was two places in time. I was a teenage girl sitting on the hood of a purple Geo Prism parked on a country dirt road, a Melissa Etheridge CD blasting from the cracked speakers, surprised to find my lips pressed against another girl's for the first time. And I was also a grown woman, standing in the lawn of a mansion overlooking Hollywood, shocked to find myself longing to press my lips against a man's for the first time in years. Time stopped. My heart stopped. Drew moved closer, and my whole world felt topsy-turvy, my axis tilting. I worried I would slip and fall, but Drew was there, his arms strong, holding me up as we spun faster and faster.

Janelle squealed loudly as she entered the storm, breaking my trance and reminding me where I was—and who I was. Not the kind of girl who dreamed of kissing men in the rain, that's for sure. I dropped Drew's hand and took hers, gaining some distance before I did something I couldn't take back. Unlike me, Drew seemed unfazed by the whole situation, grabbing his mother with one arm and Janelle with the other, creating an adult version of "Ring Around the Rosie," everyone belting out Melissa Etheridge at the top of our lungs as we swung around. We'd probably all have pneumonia in the morning, but it would be worth it. This was a moment I'd never forget.

When we'd had our fill, we giddily ran back inside, Janelle and I shivering as Jaqueline grabbed us all towels and Drew ran to find a change of clothes. He returned with two old shirts and some sweatpants for us to lounge in. I took the larger black pants and Guns N' Roses shirt, and Janelle took a cozy-looking white shirt with gray sweatpants, then both of us ran off to change in the guest bathroom off the kitchen.

"This evening just keeps getting better." Janelle smiled as the smell of popcorn started wafting through Drew's house.

"Get comfortable," Jaqueline insisted as she walked over to the vintage popcorn maker and filled up bowls for all of us, placing them next to the charcuterie board I'd almost forgotten we'd made earlier.

Drew pressed play on the movie, and the sights and sounds of Italy filled the room as the opening credits rolled for *Roman Holiday*.

"Good pick." Jaqueline smiled as she reached for some popcorn.

"One of my favorites," I admitted, grabbing a bit of salami.

"Janelle gets all the credit," Drew said as Audrey Hepburn's face lit up his giant screen.

It felt wonderfully cozy there in our reclining seats, faux-fur blankets tucked around us. Drew's equipment was state of the art, and I wondered if this was what it was like seeing *Roman Holiday* when it first came out in theaters. Audrey Hepburn's Princess Anne sounded even more poised in surround sound, and Gregory Peck looked exceptionally handsome in high definition.

When the movie was over, the popcorn was gone, and the charcuterie plate was wiped clean, Jaqueline invited us outside to finish the joint with her. Drew and I both abstained—I'd had enough for the night—but we still went to keep Janelle and Jaqueline company under the now-clear sky.

"William Wyler sure did know how to tell a good story," I gushed.

"I met him once at a friend's wedding. She was a close childhood friend of his daughter Catherine," Jaqueline claimed.

"What was he like?" I asked.

"Old." Jaqueline coughed through her laughter. "I think he died about a year later."

"He has three Oscars for directing," I noted. "Second only to John Ford."

"Okay, Professor McBride." Janelle laughed.

"We went to film school together," I explained, answering Jaqueline's questioning look.

"Ah." She took one last hit of her now-tiny roach.

"This has been so great." I let out a yawn. "But I really should head home."

"You're not going anywhere," Jaqueline declared. "It is too late, and this night has been too magnificent for it to end. You will stay here—Andy has plenty of room and amenities."

We tried protesting, but Jaqueline wouldn't hear it. Instead, she led Janelle and me down a hallway and into two guest rooms with an adjoining bathroom between them.

"Help yourself to anything in here." Jaqueline opened the drawers to reveal top-of-the-line toiletries, including Nopalera soap and a full lineup of JVN hair products. She walked to the hallway and returned with a washcloth, hand towel, and bath sheet (apparently that's what you call a very large towel) for each of us.

"I stocked this place myself for visitors," she beamed proudly.

"You did a great job," Janelle complimented, admiring a brand new beautifully sleek electric toothbrush.

"I took all kinds of needs into consideration"—Jaqueline reached her hand into a drawer and came out with a silk bonnet for Janelle's hair—"but obviously I have blind spots, so let me know if either of you find the supplies lacking, and I will remedy that."

"Thank you again for everything tonight." I felt overwhelmed with gratitude for how welcome they'd made me feel in their lives.

"Our pleasure." Jaqueline hugged us both good night. Drew followed suit, and soon Janelle and I were alone standing in the bathroom surrounded by expensive toiletries and designer towels. We looked at each other and started giggling, the high of the evening hitting us. I ran and jumped on Janelle's bed, prompting her to run and jump on mine.

"Switch?" I yelled, hopping up and heading back to the room I'd started in. Janelle didn't move, so I flopped down next to her.

"I think I like your room better," I said, laughing at my own joke. Both rooms were identical, down to the last pillow sham. We giggled some more, letting the effects of the evening settle in. "I can't believe this night."

"Same." Janelle opened a drawer next to the bed to find earplugs, eye masks, tissues, lube, condoms, and even dental dams, all neatly arranged together. "How did we get here?"

"'I led you here.'" I grabbed an eye mask and placed it over my face like sunglasses. "'For I am Spartacus.'"

She smiled, hugged me, and headed into the other room. We both washed our faces with expensive soaps, applied lavish lotions, brushed our teeth with fancy electric toothbrushes, and said good night, heading to our respective plush beds.

Tugging off Drew's sweats, I climbed in, the giant, white comforter engulfing me like snow. I giggled with delight as I made angels in the high-thread-count Egyptian cotton sheets, kicking my feet up and down under the covers. Adult me had kept her cool all night, but the teenage girl inside was jumping with excitement at the evening's events. It was all too much, and yet every molecule of my being wanted more.

This was the life I wanted.

This was what I'd been waiting for.

I shot up in bed, too excited to sleep. Instead, I got up and padded out into the house, heading for the kitchen. *Kitchens*, I reminded myself, laughing at the ridiculousness of being in a house with two separate kitchens, each at least twice the size of ours at home. I searched cupboards and ransacked the fridge, but everything I found was empty.

"Looking for something?" Drew said from the other side of the refrigerator door.

I jumped, startled, and yelled a bit too loudly at him. "Snacks!"

"This way." He chuckled, taking my hand. I didn't let go as he led me through a set of doors and into his all-white second kitchen. "Sorry, but I don't have any cheese fries."

"It's fries with cheese," I corrected him as he let go of my hand and opened his fridge. Food packaged in labeled glass containers filled the shelves, with some liquids and condiments on the door.

"I don't have any fries with cheese, either, but I do have this." He handed me a large container marked "munchies."

"Wait, your private chef makes you food to eat when you're high?"

"Not only for when I'm high." Drew closed the fridge. "I don't smoke that often, but I've got a sweet tooth, and she makes sure it's satisfied in a way my trainer approves of."

I opened the container to find small dark truffles, mounds of coconut dipped in chocolate, and what looked like peanut butter cups.

"Here"—Drew picked up a truffle and handed it to me—"try this."

The rich ball of chocolate melted seductively on my tongue. "Holy Goddess! Is that cayenne and cinnamon?"

"She says they're good for you." Drew popped a chocolate ball in his mouth.

"My taste buds agree." I reached for a coconut cluster, which was equally delicious.

"Nice outfit." Drew gestured at my baggy T-shirt, smiling at my bare legs. In my euphoria and excitement, I hadn't bothered to put on the pants he'd given me, and my lacy see-through underwear poked out from under his Guns N' Roses shirt.

"I'm Porky Piggin' it, as my sister would say," I replied, trying to tuck my shirt down a bit more. "I kind of wish I'd worn less revealing lingerie this evening."

"It's sexy." Drew looked me in the eyes.

"It's the Guns N' Roses shirt," I deflected, trying to ignore the shiver in my body as he gazed at me. "You get some of Axl Rose's allure by proxy."

"It's you," he insisted, and I found my hand brushing against his.

"You're high." I felt my body gravitating toward his.

"I'm sober now," he said as I intertwined my fingers with his. "Are you?"

I nodded, not trusting myself to talk.

Drew used his free hand to pick up another truffle and offered it to me. I parted my lips, and he placed the chocolatey goodness in my mouth, fingers lingering as he brushed his thumb against my face. I sighed as the dual sensations of decadence and desire flooded my body.

Drew smirked and moved closer to me, bending over, stopping inches away from my lips, close enough for me to feel his breath against my neck but far enough apart that I was given the option of what to do next: lean in or pull away.

Lean in?

Or pull away?

Lean in or...

"Diana," a voice whispered rather loudly from the other room, and I quickly untangled myself from Drew's body. "Diana!"

"In here." I opened the door to let Janelle into the white kitchen. "You okay?"

"Mad munchies!" Janelle declared.

"Here." Drew handed her the box of sweets.

"Your chef makes you munchies?" she asked, reading the

label. “I can’t wait to be rich.”

Janelle dug into a peanut butter cup, moaning loudly. Behind her, Drew grabbed my hand and gave it a quick squeeze before letting it go again.

What the hell just happened? a voice asked in my head.

I had no idea how to answer it.

Chapter Thirteen

An hour of laughter and delicious snacks later, I was back in the guest bed, eyes wide open, wondering what my life had become. I pinched myself, just to make sure this wasn't a dream. Sleep was impossible, I didn't even try, so I lay there wondering what I would have done if Janelle hadn't walked in.

Leaned in?

Or pulled away?

My head said pull away. But my body shivered with the idea of leaning into his, bringing up feelings in me I'd long thought dormant.

Drew seemed so accessible there in his kitchen, like a guy I'd have approached in high school or college, when I was still figuring out who and what I wanted in my life. I tried to remember if there was an exact moment when I ruled out men or if it was a gradual thing, brought on by a collection of appalling encounters that all too often ended in a form of assault, coercion, or at the very least emotional negligence. If boys hadn't been so horrible to me, would I have ruled out dating men completely?

Growing up in a conservative town, I often argued that sexuality wasn't a choice. If I was born this way, then the Bible-thumping Jesus-lovers would have to accept me for being gay, just the way God made me. However, I was starting to wonder if maybe I had chosen to limit myself somewhere along the line. Not that I didn't like dating women, I very much *loved* dating women. But I'd dated all along the gender spectrum, and I wasn't quite sure when I'd decided that array wouldn't include cis men anymore.

Yes, actually, I could remember the exact moment. Sophomore year in college, visiting a girl I liked in San Francisco, watching *The L Word* at the Lexington—my favorite lesbian dive bar until gentrification pushed it out. The character Dana had been giving her best friend Alice shit for liking men and women, insisting she needed to choose one. My date turned to me and said I needed to do the same.

"Don't be one of those women who breaks everyone's heart by going back to men," she'd said over drinks when the episode finished. "Just admit you're a dyke now and save everyone the trouble."

I'd sat there at the bar holding my vodka tonic, thinking about *Chasing Amy*, one of the most influential movies for me as a young queer. In high school, I'd watched Joey Lauren Adams jump off the stage and into the arms of a hot blonde over and over again, their kissing and groping the closest thing to lesbian porn I got as a teen.

I'd craved moments like that, sitting in places full of women kissing, and finally getting it at the Lex filled my soul with joy.

That night at the bar with my friend, I thought back to a later scene in *Chasing Amy*, where Joey Lauren Adams's circle of lesbian friends find out she's been dating a guy.

"Another one bites the dust," one woman mourned, all of them shaking their heads, the whole group disappointed in her choice to sleep with a man.

In the end, Ben Affleck turned out to be a total dick, breaking Joey Lauren Adams's heart and solidifying in me this idea that falling for a guy would only end in both emotional pain and a loss of lesbian identity and community, something I'd desperately needed to survive as a young baby dyke.

Lying there in Drew's bed a decade later, I could recognize intellectually that these thoughts—and the vile words and antiquated beliefs that put them in my head—were moments of blatant biphobia, horrible biases about a large group of people with a totally valid and real sexual orientation. I felt forced to choose between straight and gay, man and woman, like those were the only identities allowed. Straight had never been an option for me, so I chose gay. It was years before I realized that gender and sexuality were more fluid than that, and I started dating all along the beautiful spectrum. Had I closed off a part of my sexuality by not including cis men? Maybe. But even if I did decide to open that door again, I sure as hell wasn't doing it with someone like Drew, where the whole thing would play out in the public eye and my moviemaking dreams could be at stake.

Eventually, I gave up on the idea of sleep, threw on the sweats Drew had given me, and meandered around the house, searching for something to distract me from my own spiraling thoughts. I went outside and was pleasantly surprised to find Jaqueline on the still-damp back patio with a spread of food around her, engrossed in the *L.A. Times*. We said our good mornings and she invited me to sit down next to her and help myself to a pile of sections she'd already read.

"I didn't know people still got the physical paper." I grabbed the comics section, the only part I could read without my glasses, and began perusing.

A short, curvy, Latina woman came out and greeted me, asking if I'd like some fresh-pressed juice or coffee. "Serena, this is Diana—Diana, Serena," Jaqueline introduced us.

"I'm a big fan of your work!" I exclaimed.

She laughed. "I did notice the munchies container was empty this morning. Would you like a smoothie or an egg-white omelet?"

"I'd love some tea and maybe an avocado if you have one," I said.

"Would you like the avocado on toast?" she asked, a bit of a Spanish accent coming through.

"No, thanks, I can't eat gluten."

"Oh, honey, this house hasn't had gluten in it for years," Jaqueline said from behind her paper.

"I swear I'm not one of those L.A. types who watched an episode of *Dr. Oz* and jumped on the anti-gluten bandwagon but like, secretly eats a loaf of bread each night alone in their room," I explained, making Jaqueline chuckle. "It actually makes me really sick."

"You never have to explain yourself to me, darling," Jaqueline soothed, patting my hand.

"I just made a fresh chestnut baguette," Serena offered.

"That sounds great, thank you." I smiled as Serena floated off toward the kitchen, leaving Jaqueline and me alone with our paper. "She's perky for early on a Sunday morning."

"It is almost noon," Jaqueline said.

"Noon!" I exclaimed, standing up. I must have gotten more sleep than I realized. "I gotta go."

"What's the rush?" Drew stepped outside in nothing but tiny gym shorts and bright blue Nikes. He'd obviously been working out, and I tried to remind myself I wasn't the kind of woman who stared at sweaty pecs glistening in the sun.

"I promised my sister and her kids that I would be home for pancakes and painting," I explained. "I missed pancakes already, but I don't want to miss painting."

"You should grab some breakfast, then," Drew suggested. "Since you missed pancakes."

"Mmm, breakfast." Janelle yawned as she walked outside into the light.

"Serena is here." I turned toward Janelle. "She's making breakfast."

"That's it, I'm never leaving." Janelle sat down next to Jaqueline.

"Stay?" I tried to ignore the hint of longing I thought I heard in Drew's voice. There was a lot about him I was trying to ignore at that moment. He had that distinct smell masculine people had after working out, like testosterone and dirty gym socks. It was a smell I associated with my athletic ex, gay men dancing at clubs, and one sixteen-year-old boy who, years ago, had pumped away on top of me with no clue what he was doing. It was a primal smell, full of pheromones, and as I breathed in Drew's scent, I wondered if that's why I found myself so drawn to him. Even though I didn't want kids or cis men, there was still some instinctual desire to procreate with the most physically fit person in the tribe.

Pull back! a voice in my head warned. *Pull back now!*

"I really must go," I insisted. Janelle sighed and reluctantly joined me inside.

"Why are we hurrying out of here?" she asked as she dressed.

"I promised Cecily and the kids I'd be home by now." I grunted as I wrestled my body back into my outfit from the night before, yanking up my tights and adjusting my bra. Fancy outfits were never as fun or glamorous the next day. They always had a snagged bit here or a torn piece there, adding to the walk-of-shame feel they gave, like I was announcing to everyone what I did last night, the assumption being I'd scandalously had sex out of wedlock the night before. Men have it easier. Their outfits aren't as delicate—and neither is their virtue. Both can survive a romp in a way a woman's can't.

"You sure you're not running away from a certain movie star I saw with his arms around you in the kitchen last night?" Janelle smirked as she handed me a container of baby wipes she'd found in the bathroom drawers.

"He was just sharing his munchies with me." I wiped my pits, trying to get the smell of nervous sweating off me.

"Is that what they're calling it these days?" Janelle lifted her eyebrow at me. I ignored her and brushed my teeth with Drew's fancy paste, wiped some Megababe I'd brought onto my inner thighs to avoid chafing, grabbed my stuff, and headed out.

Drew was waiting for us by the front door. "I called my driver; he should be here soon to take you home."

"We can take a cab," I declined, regretting the coldness in my voice. I didn't know how to take the distance I needed without pushing away.

"Let him be nice to you," Jaqueline voiced, making her way in from outside, looking at me poignantly.

"Okay," I reluctantly agreed, my chill warming. "That would be lovely. Thank you for the ride."

"Don't be strangers." Jaqueline gave Janelle and me each a big hug and handed us her card. "My house isn't as fancy as this one, but you're welcome over any time."

Jaqueline Williams, author, it read with her email and phone number on it. It was somehow both old-school and chic, just like Jaqueline. "I'm excited to read your books," I said, giving her another hug.

"And I'm excited to see your movies," she replied, squeezing me back.

Serena emerged from the kitchen, handing Janelle and me each two containers, one marked *breakfast*, the other marked *munchies*. "A little something for the road," she explained.

"I'm in love." Janelle swooned as she watched Serena head back to the kitchen.

"You'll have to come back for dinner sometime," Drew said as he opened the door. A man in a suit stood in the driveway with a black Lincoln Navigator parked behind him. "She makes a delicious eggplant parmesan. Vegan and gluten-free, of course."

"Of course it is." Janelle laughed as she headed out to the car, turning around before climbing in. "Thanks again for a great night!"

"We'll do it again soon," Jaqueline promised.

Drew turned to me. "See you soon?"

"Yes, we have to talk about the movie." I awkwardly reached my hand out to shake his. "Thank you again for your hospitality."

"Anytime." Drew took my hand and shook it before escorting me to the car.

“I can’t believe we just spent the night getting high with Drew Williams and his mom,” Janelle said as the driver pulled away. “And I really can’t believe that you were flirting with him!”

“Was not!” I pushed her away.

“We’ve got twenty minutes.” Janelle leaned back in her seat and opened both of the containers marked “munchies.” “Tell me everything that happened in that kitchen before I got there. Leave no detail out.”

Chapter Fourteen

Janelle and I analyzed every bit of my interaction with Drew in the kitchen until the car dropped us off at her house. We thanked the driver and got out, saying a quick goodbye before I hopped in my Subaru and hurried home, blasting Alabama Shakes and singing along with Brittany Howard to keep myself awake and distracted.

"You missed pancakes," Ellis yelled from the garage when I got home.

"I hope you saved me bacon!" I yelled back, searching the kitchen but coming up short. I walked into the studio to ask Cecily where the bacon was but only found Ellis and Reggie there. "Where's your mom?"

"Crying in her room," Reggie said in her matter-of-fact tone.

Ellis pointed to the clock. "She said we couldn't come get her until the big hand is on the twelve and the little hand is on the one."

I left the kids to paint and headed down the hall, knocking gently on my sister's door. "Hey, it's me."

"Come in," her weary voice replied.

"What happened?" I demanded, my heart stopping. Since Henry got sick, I panicked easily, expecting all news to be bad. Back then, every phone call was a new disappointment, another bit of hope lost as the cancer spread to other parts of his body and he ran out of options to stop it. Then the ultimate bad phone call. I was there when he died. Cecily was hundreds of miles away, and we couldn't get ahold of her. I'd called and called and called and worried someone else would get to her before I could. When she finally answered, she said, "Please let it be Poppo..." and we cried, because it hadn't been our ailing ninety-two-year-old grandfather who had died that morning but our vibrant younger brother.

We buried Poppo four months after Henry. Another shitty set of phone calls I'd had to make.

"Fucking Greg." Cecily broke down into sobs. Selfishly, I sighed with relief. Ex-husband issues I could handle.

I sat down next to her. "What did he do this time?"

"He gets all the fucking credit while I do all the work. Did you know he showed up for the volunteer breakfast at school on Friday? He didn't volunteer once this year, but he shows up and goes to the front of the line, all important-like, saying he's got some big meeting to go to, so he has to eat first. Those bagels are for volunteers only, you prick! I should know because I woke up early to buy them. Because I actually help out around the school."

"God, I hate male entitlement."

"And this morning I got an email saying he wants to pay

me less alimony." Cecily sobbed. "Says I should get a real job, that he needs to save up for the giant wedding his new fiancée is planning. The poor girl—I wouldn't wish him on anyone, even a blonde. He had the audacity to suggest he start taking the kids half-time, which is only a fucking ploy to pay less child support. The nights he has them he just puts the kids in front of their iPads while he watches football. The cheap bastard doesn't want them more. He just doesn't want to pay me more. I gave up my career to follow him around the country going from job to job; that motherfucker can pay for my lost wages."

"Prick," I spat, glaring at the hole in the family portrait by Cecily's bed that used to be his face. I'd cut it out a few weeks after moving in. No point wasting a perfectly good photo simply because he was in it. "Did you know I have him in my phone as Fuckwad Shitface Turdbrain?"

"You do not," Cecily sobbed.

"I do! I'll show you." I pulled up her ex-husband's contact in my phone and Cecily laughed so loudly that Ellis came rushing into the room.

"What are you laughing about?" they asked.

"Your face!" I pulled them into me.

"Your butt!" Ellis squealed as I tickled them.

"Your mom's butt!" I shot back.

"Your mom's butt's face!" they yelled.

Reggie ran into the room to see what she was missing, and Cecily grabbed and threw her on the bed with us, making a pile of giggling tickle bugs squirming around. The kids wiggled away from us and ran back into the studio, shouting about finishing their painting of poop emojis.

"I'm sorry Greg is such a dick," I began, lying next to Cecily in her bed, "But unless he wants to take you to court, he can't make you give him more custody. And he's too cheap to pay for a lawyer. I'm sure this will pass and you'll be okay. Whatever happens, we have each other."

"Unless you leave me for your new boyfriend," Cecily threw in.

"What are you talking about?" My heart stopped, wondering how Cecily knew about my confusing feelings for Drew.

She pulled Star Watch, her favorite guilty pleasure gossip website, up on her phone and handed it to me. Right there on the homepage was a photo of Chris Stanson leaning forward to kiss an anonymous plus-size woman in a silver, sparkly dress.

"Oh god, I totally forgot about that," I said, mortified.

"How do you forget about kissing Chris Stanson?!" Cecily sounded incredulous as she grabbed her phone back.

"We aren't kissing!" I snatched her phone again to look at the image. "I was leaning in so he could hear me."

"It looks like you're fully making the moves on him." Cecily zoomed in on the photo.

I had to admit, it was a good shot, taken at just the right angle, at just the right moment. It looked like I was cornering him and forcing him to kiss me.

"Ugh." I sighed, seeing a comment that read, "Shamu tries to eat off Chris Stanson's face." I handed Cecily her phone, not wanting to see any more. The responses to this photo would be horrible. I knew it like I knew Reggie would throw a fit every time I asked her to eat a vegetable. The internet is full of babies who protest against anything different or new, and trolls had a special hatred in their hearts for fat people.

I really didn't want to be known as the woman who attacked Chris Stanson at a restaurant, which was how the gossip websites seemed to be framing it. Fat women were always portrayed as desperate and insatiable, molesting everyone and everything around them. Even rides like Pirates of the Caribbean at Disneyland played into this horribly biased trope. First, no one was bidding on the fat woman, even though everyone else was crying and she was standing there with her hands together, smiling like a good subservient wife. Then you floated into an area where all the thin women were being chased by men wanting to assault them, and the fat woman was chasing a man wanting to assault him. Or at least you did until they changed it all to be slightly less offensive. But still, the impression it left on me as a kid remained: thin women had to run away from the danger of men who wanted to violate them, fat women had to chase men who would never consensually want them. As if men were any less of a threat to us. As if they didn't speak of our assaults like a goddamn favor.

I didn't want to be seen as either. I wanted out of that narrative completely. I wanted to create a new narrative where women weren't chasing or being chased by men, but instead chasing their own dreams and careers. The women in my stories rescued themselves and each other, just like Cecily and I had done.

"Oh god, please tell me Chris Stanson's bed is not where you were all night." Cecily's question brought me back to the present. She dramatically threw herself back on her bed before prodding further. "I don't think I could handle my jealousy if you slept with him."

"Don't worry, we ditched him at the restaurant." I lay down next to her.

"Why were you with him again in the first place?" she asked. "And more importantly, why didn't you invite me along?"

"It was Andy's mother's birthday party. They know Chris."

"And who is Andy?"

"Someone I met at the LACMA party." I knew one day she'd find out Andy was Drew Williams, and there was no point in building a bubble around him since it would someday have to burst. I just wasn't ready to talk about him to my celebrity-obsessed sister. Drew Williams the star felt otherworldly, as unrealistic as the action hero characters he played. The Andy I've been getting to know still felt real, like someone tangible that I could touch, had touched, and maybe wanted to touch again. I didn't know where this thing with Drew would go, but I knew it was too early to let Cecily near it.

"You're living the glamorous Hollywood life." My sister sighed. "Going to fancy galas, attending birthday parties with famous stars. And I'm over here doing laundry and cleaning spilled mac 'n' cheese off the floor."

"Yes, because living in my niece's bedroom in the suburbs is living the dream," I countered.

"I don't know, this looks pretty dreamy." Cecily pulled back up the photo of Chris Stanson and me. "I think I'm going to print this out."

"Oh god, please don't." I got up and headed back out to the kitchen to eat Serena's "breakfast" container. She hadn't lied; this bread was delicious, the best gluten-free loaf I'd had in a while. I took another bite, wondering how expensive it would be to get Serena to make it for me every day.

...

Two days later, I was cleaning up breakfast with Cecily when my phone rang.

"Fry Guy? Who's that?" she said, picking it up.

"A friend." I reached for my phone.

“Is it Andy?” She held it out away from me. “It is, isn’t it? You’re so into them! I remember you having this look on your face when you first met Sam.”

“I do not have a look,” I lied.

“Don’t go falling for them hard like you did Sam, okay?”

“They are not Sam,” I replied, grateful Cecily was used to me using gender-neutral pronouns for people in my life.

“I’m not saying they are,” she said. “I just know that look and don’t want you ending up back where Sam left you.”

“I’m not the same person I was back then,” I reminded her.

“I’m not saying you are.”

“Then what are you saying?” I asked.

“I guess I’m telling you to be careful.” She handed me back my phone. “We both know you go off the deep end when you fall for someone.”

“I didn’t realize my heartbreaks were such an inconvenience for you. How unthoughtful of me since your relationships have never impacted my life, ever.” I threw my arms around at the house.

“You don’t have to be an asshole. I’m just asking you to be cautious. For both of our sakes.”

“Well, you don’t have to worry, because Andy is just a friend.”

“Sure, just a friend.” Cecily rolled her eyes pointedly down at my phone, where I had two new texts from “Fry Guy.”

I stared at the screen, confused. “I wonder what’s up.”

“I don’t know, maybe you should call them back and find out.” Cecily’s tone told me she was as annoyed with me as I was with her.

I sighed. I did not want to spend my day off fighting with my sister. Maybe she was right. Maybe I was being an asshole.

But so was she. We were both assholes, in the way only siblings got to be. We were raised by alcoholics who settled everything with verbal fights, the winner being the one with the sharpest barb. We hadn't learned to apologize. No one taught us how to make amends. We would all just retreat to our corners to lick our wounds until Henry inevitably made a joke to cut the tension. But Henry wasn't there anymore, and he never would be again. Without him, I didn't know how to end an argument. So I stayed silent and opened my texts.

Call me back when you can.

It's about the film.

I bolted up. Drew wasn't checking in about our moment at his house, like I'd awkwardly assumed. He was calling about the movie. *My* movie. Was it good news? God, I hoped it was good news. I needed some good news. Nervously, I dialed him back.

"Hi, Diana," Drew answered, sounding both anxious and excited.

"What's up?" I tried to sound casual, but my voice cracked with nerves.

"Chris showed your script to Silvia Cortez at Focus," Drew began. "She wants to meet with us on April first."

"Holy shit." I gasped.

"Nothing is set in stone yet, but we have a meeting, and that's a huge first step."

"But who's involved?" My mind flooded with questions, unable to process it all. "What are the terms?"

"That's what we'll talk about in the meeting."

I pulled up my calendar. "I have to work at Roussard's that day."

"Not anymore you don't," Drew said.

"This is really happening?" I asked.

"Looks like it," Drew replied.

I stood there for a moment, the phone still up to my ear, unsure of what else I was supposed to say to this man who had swept into my life and started making my dreams come true. "Thank you," I croaked out feebly.

"All I did was make a few calls," Drew answered humbly. "The rest was you."

"I wouldn't be in that meeting without you," I insisted.

"Yes, you would have someday." Drew sounded full of confidence. "I only helped make it go faster."

"Thanks for getting me in the door before I'm too old to appreciate it."

"I believe in you, Diana, and I believe in this script." Drew paused briefly. "Speaking of which, I'm sending over some edits Chris and I had. They're minor, but we're moving some bits to the top that we think would grab Silvia's attention."

I was nervous at the idea of Chris and Drew messing with my story, but I promised to keep an open mind. We solidified a few more details before Drew hung up, and I stood there staring at my screen in disbelief.

In a daze, I made my way to the garage where Cecily had started setting up her painting supplies. "Oh no, bad news?" She saw my face and came rushing to my side, concern making her forget our disagreement.

"I have a meeting on April first." I dazedly looked up from my phone to her. "With an executive at Focus Films."

"What?!" Cecily squealed. "With that look on your face, I thought someone had died. Why aren't you more excited?!"

"It feels too good to be true," I admitted. "I keep waiting for the catch."

"Maybe the catch is that this family has suffered enough and we finally deserve a win!" she said, jumping up and down.

"Oh my god." A smile crept up onto my face. "Oooohhhh. Mmmmyyyy. Gggoooooodddd!" I screamed. As I stood there letting the situation sink in, Cecily ran over to her computer and started playing our favorite celebration song.

Salt-N-Pepa's "None of Your Business" came on, and we sang loudly, laughing and dancing around the house until we fell into a pile of exhausted excitement on the sofa.

"What if I did wanna take a guy home with me tonight?" I asked, thinking about Drew and our almost-kiss.

"That would be so weird." Cecily snorted.

"The correct answer is, it's none of your business," I said.

"I'm your big sister. Everything you do is my business," Cecily asserted, throwing her arm around me. "I figured you knew that by now."

"I thought that just applied to me breaking the rules in school or not doing the dishes."

"Oh no, big sisters rule over everything. Just ask Reggie."

I chuckled as my eyes made their way to the carefully crafted chore board Cecily and Reggie had made for our house, their chores all marked complete while Ellis and my chores were only about a quarter done. My eyes caught on a photo next to it, and I stood, walking quickly over to the corkboard.

There, next to our chores, was a printed copy of the tabloid photo of Chris Stanson and me kissing, except Cecily had photoshopped her face in place of mine. "What is this?"

"I was wondering when you'd notice that." Cecily laughed.

"You are ridiculous!" I yanked the photo down and threw it at her.

"You're hanging out with celebrities now, making movies

with them, being all fancy and famous. Let me at least have my Chris Stanson crush, okay?" She got up and pinned the photo back on the board.

"What if I was actually kissing Chris Stanson?" I asked.

Cecily scoffed. "Please."

"What? It could happen!" I was offended at how easily she dismissed the idea.

"If it was Tessa Thompson or Kate McKinnon, maybe I'd believe it, but you're too queer for me to take the idea of you and Chris Stanson seriously. Can you even imagine you and some straight dude like him? He's basically everything you hate."

"And yet here I am, hanging with him while all you have is a photoshopped picture of you two kissing," I threw at her.

"Oh, honey, I didn't mean to offend you." Cecily pulled me into a hug and kissed my forehead. For a moment I felt more like her daughter than her sister. "I'm so, so, so proud of you. Your movie is getting made! That's amazing! You obviously can do anything you want. Including dating Chris Stanson. I think it's funny because you're so gay and he's so straight, that's all."

"It would be funny." I pulled away from her. "Dating a man."

"Hey, if you wanna take a guy home with you tonight, it's none of my business." She smirked at me. "And guess what?"

"What?"

Cecily pulled me up from the sofa, grabbing my arms and jumping up and down. "Your movie is maybe getting made!"

"My movie is maybe getting made!" I screamed, jumping with her, the excitement contagious.

"I'm so damn proud of you!" Cecily hugged me so hard I thought my eyes would pop out of their sockets. We weren't perfect, and we disagreed all the time, but Cecily was my person, and it felt great to celebrate this with her.

"Now, the important question," she said, a giant smile on her face. "What are we going to wear to the Oscars when this wins?"

Chapter Fifteen

A combination of intense nerves and giddy excitement washed over me as I drove up to the Lankershim gate at the Universal backlot and handed my ID to the guard.

"You're not supposed to be here." He handed my driver's license back to me and turned around.

Panic sank in as I realized today was the first of April, and I wondered if this was all some kind of twisted April Fool's joke Chris and Drew liked to play on naive screenwriters. How stupid I had been to think two major movie stars would want to produce my film. How idiotic to think I could get a meeting with an executive so quickly. Shame filled me as I put my car in reverse, hoping to flee the scene before someone could come out with a camera and tell me I'd been punked. Just as I was starting to pull away, the guard handed me a paper map with two *X*s marked on it.

"Your meeting has been moved from the Carl Laemmle

building to this backlot bungalow." He pointed to one *X*, and then the other. "You need to enter at this gate here, then you can park here. I'll let them know you're coming."

With a giant sigh of relief, I thanked the guard and made my way to the other security checkpoint. *I belong here,* I reminded myself as I handed my ID to the other guard, who waved me through quickly and wished me a good day.

I found the parking area easily enough, but the bungalow was a bit more difficult to pinpoint, and I wandered around trying to look like I knew where I was going, the heels I'd stupidly let Cecily talk me into wearing painfully digging into my feet. Finally, I found the bungalow marked on my map, took a deep breath, and headed inside.

"Hi," I said to a busy-looking receptionist typing away on her computer. "I'm here to see Silvia..." Shit, I'd forgotten her last name.

The receptionist looked up from her screen and appraised me. "Are you an agent?"

"No, I'm a writer and director." She gave me a *Who isn't these days?* look. "I'm Diana Smith. She's expecting me."

"Why are you wearing a suit?" She tilted her head to the side, like I was something interesting to analyze.

"Why, what?" I looked down at my outfit, confused, wondering if I'd spilled something on it.

"Only agents wear suits. Lose the jacket, and wait over there." She nodded toward a group of chairs tucked into the corner of the room.

"Thanks?" I didn't know whether that tip was helpful or insulting, but I took off my jacket anyway before sitting down, suddenly very self-conscious. Minutes before, I'd felt powerful in this outfit. Now it felt like a flashing sign that I was basically a kid playing dress-up with no idea what I was doing.

The office was small, about the size of a studio apartment, and I was nervous sitting there under the receptionist's watchful eye. My stomach gurgled loudly, reminding me that I'd never eaten the protein bar Cecily had thrust in my hand when I left the house. I wondered if I had time to go back and get it, but decided my car was parked too far away and my feet were hurting enough as it was in these shoes. I kept fidgeting with my papers, my skirt, the chair, anything to keep my mind busy, annoying the receptionist enough for her to look over and ask if I needed anything.

"I think I'll wait outside." I stood and got out of there as fast as I could in heels, trying to find a bench to sit on and wait.

A black Tesla pulled into one of the reserved parking spots across from the office, and Drew got out. My stomach did flips seeing him there. Somehow his presence made this all feel more real. Drew stopped and greeted someone—I assumed a sound guy from the equipment he carried—and they embraced like old friends. I stood there awkwardly watching their interactions, waiting for Drew to look up and see me, wanting desperately to appear poised and professional when he did.

The backlot was a big attraction for the Universal Studios amusement park, and a tram full of tourists drove by, stopping to point out Drew, who smiled, waved, and posed for photos. He looked completely at home there. Meanwhile, I was nervously sweating and spinning my thumbs in circles around each other, unable to tell if I needed to run, vomit, cry, or laugh.

At some point, Drew would make his way over here, and then what? A couple months ago he was some actor on the screen that I never dreamed of meeting, and now he was…what? My boss? My colleague? My friend? Some guy I maybe almost kissed? Since meeting him, he'd taken me to a kitschy putt-putt golf course, a fancy restaurant for his mother's birthday, and his gorgeous home in the Hollywood Hills. In a matter of weeks, Drew had been able to arrange the kind of meeting I'd been waiting five years to get. How was I supposed to act around someone with that much power?

Drew looked up and saw me staring at him. He smiled and offered a friendly wave before a sporty, dark green Porsche revved into the spot next to him. Chris Stanson got out and immediately embraced the sound guy, then Drew, patting them both on the back and laughing about something I couldn't hear. I stood there waiting awkwardly as they chatted, hyperaware of my toes being squashed into the ends of my heels. *Never again*, I vowed as Chris and Drew said goodbye to the sound man and headed my way.

"Coffee Girl," Chris greeted me. "You ready for this?"

"Born ready," Drew and I said in unison.

"Look at that. Already in sync." Chris smiled cockily. "That's good. You'll be spending a lot of time together these next few months. You'll need that synergy."

"And you?" I asked, trying not to think about what spending months intimately working with Drew would feel like. "What's your role in all of this?"

"I'm going to get us the money," Chris said, then raised his arms open toward the woman walking our way in impressively high heels and a dangerously tight skirt. Drew straightened up, and from the wide grins both men plastered on their faces, I assumed this was the studio executive walking toward us.

"Silvia!" Chris pulled her into an embrace and kissed both her cheeks. "Looking gorgeous as always."

"Flattery will get you everywhere, Chris," Silvia replied.

"You know Drew, I assume." Chris pointed to his friend.

"Only by reputation." Silvia extended her hand to Drew. "It's nice to finally meet you in person."

"The honor is mine," Drew said.

"And this must be your writer," Silvia questioned, turning to me.

"Diana Smith. Meet Silvia Cortez."

Cortez! That's her last name, I thought as Silvia gave me a firm handshake.

"Now," she said, letting go of her vise grip on my hand. "Let's go inside and talk about this little film you've brought me."

Chapter Sixteen

I couldn't stop smiling as I turned into Chris Stanson's driveway. The last time I was here, I was invited to his home out of pity and solely because Emmy didn't want the invitation. Today, I was arriving as a colleague, here to collaborate with two of Hollywood's most famous stars mere days after our meeting with a movie executive about the film we are making together.

What is my life?! I thought, my heart beating rapidly with anticipation as I parked and grabbed my things. Stepping out of my car, I couldn't believe I'd made it this far, and I wasn't sure I could go any further. Suddenly my feet were lead, dragging me down as I trudged up the steep entranceway and knocked on his giant black door.

"Welcome." Chris opened it wearing nothing but low-cut jeans. He immediately turned around and walked away, his naked back retreating into his home.

Confused, I stood there in his doorway, wondering why he

wasn't dressed. Did I have the time wrong for the meeting? Was I supposed to follow him? Not knowing what to do, I stayed where I was, awkwardly glancing around at his perfectly kept home, able to experience it fully now that it was empty of people. The building itself was a work of art, the architecture crisp and modern with geometric lines and an open, airy floor plan allowing seamless movement from one room to the next.

"You coming, Coffee Girl?" he called from the other room.

I rolled my eyes, walked inside, and closed the door, which was surprisingly light considering it was a two-story-tall piece of solid wood. *There's so much ease when you're rich*, I thought, trying to figure out the mechanism that made this massively heavy piece of lumber move so effortlessly.

"What are you doing?" Chris asked.

I spun around to see him standing in a doorway, staring at me. "This is so fascinating." I was aware that I probably looked like a crazy woman repeatedly opening and closing his front door, but I didn't care. I was so fascinated by how it worked.

"My door?" he asked.

"Yes, your door," I said.

"You're a strange one, Coffee Girl." Chris headed back into the house.

"And you take for granted the things around you!" I yelled after him before walking into the living room, where he was standing topless. "And please stop calling me Coffee Girl."

"I thought you liked my little nickname for you," Chris replied. He grabbed a small mug off the side table where it sat next to a pile of scripts and took a sip.

"You thought wrong."

"You're a feisty one, aren't you?" Chris gathered up the

scripts and placed them into an expensive-looking black leather briefcase. "You should get laid. Silvia's assistant told me she thought you were cute."

"Why?" I asked as Chris walked over to the marble bar in the corner of the room and turned on a small black espresso machine.

"I have no idea." Chris dumped out old grounds and poured fresh beans from a matte pink Flamingo Estates bag into a grinder. "But apparently people are attracted to you."

"Thanks for the heartfelt compliment," I yelled, trying to be heard over the noise of the machine. It turned out that Chris Stanson did get his own coffee once in a while. "I meant why did she talk to you about me?"

"We're friends," he said as liquid dripped its way through the machine.

"That's weird."

"That I'm friends with her?"

"That anyone would be your friend," I said, immediately regretting the words. Jerk or not, Chris was now my boss, and I needed to be professional if not friendly. "Sorry. That was mean."

Seemingly unfazed, Chris handed me the espresso he made. "You need coffee."

I handed the tiny mug back to him. "I don't drink coffee."

"That explains so much." He picked up the cup for himself.

"Do you have any tea?" I asked.

"That disgusting pond water?" Chris shook his head in disgust. "No, thank you."

"I love tea," I protested.

"Must be a lesbian thing." He led me outside. "Jaqueline loves it, too."

"I identify as queer, not lesbian," I corrected, following him to the patio where I'd seen Kali, Beanie Feldstein, and Brad Pitt talking at the LACMA party, still unsure how I'd gotten here so quickly. Chris's backyard—one of a few he had—was perfectly manicured and decorated. It was a typical smoggy L.A. day, but Chris's house sat above it all, looking over the haze to the ocean beyond. The view was beautiful, but I was eager to get started. "Where's Drew?"

"You're early." Chris stepped into a sunken area full of plush furniture surrounding a fire pit.

"I was told ten," I said, sitting down on one of the sofas.

"Ten means eleven around here," Chris explained as he pushed a button on the side of the building and a shade started uncoiling in our direction. Tucked in corners were switches that controlled not just the lighting, like in normal homes, but the walls, ceilings, furniture, appliances, and technology as well, all of them perfectly labeled for ease of use.

"Then why don't you just say eleven?" I was grateful for the shade but still very annoyed at Chris.

"Because everyone knows ten means eleven."

"I didn't know that."

"Everyone who's anyone does."

I stood. Fancy shaded backyard or not, I wasn't going to sit here and be insulted. "I'm going to go wait in my car."

"No, stay." Chris sat down across from me. "I want to chat with you."

"Don't you have someone you can pay to listen to you talk?" I shot back, worried I'd ruin this project if I was left alone with Chris any longer.

"Why do you hate me so much?" Chris asked.

"I don't hate you." I sighed and sat back down, resigning

myself to this situation. "I'm just annoyed by how little you see of the things around you."

"You hate me because I don't see you?"

"Not me," I corrected, although that wasn't entirely true. It irked me that Chris barely looked my way until he thought my script could bring him money and acclaim, but I didn't want to open that can of worms right now.

"If not you, then what?" He leaned back into his seat and gestured to the world around him. "Tell me, Diana, what am I missing?"

I looked around his backyard. The outdoor furniture was in better condition than the indoor pieces at our house, and there wasn't a single weed in sight. I wondered how many people it took to keep this place so pristine and where those people hid when he had guests. "It's like your door. I bet you don't even notice it."

"You hate me because I don't see my door?" Chris looked confused.

"Your door is a giant piece of wood, and yet you don't have to exert any energy to open it. It just opens for you. And you assume you deserve that ease because you worked hard to have the kind of life where doors just open for you. But, really, you simply won the lottery of looks. And those same doors that open with ease for you are shoved closed in my face and the faces of my friends. Your ease is our obstacle. Your privileges our burdens."

"I work hard," Chris retorted. "I went to Yale."

"Dropping Yale into a conversation about privilege just makes you sound more pretentious."

"Fair enough." Chris chuckled. At least he could laugh at himself.

"I'm sorry, I'm being rude. I'm just..." I stopped, not sure what I was.

"You're just passionate about this stuff," Chris continued for me.

"Yes." I leaned back into my chair. "I am."

"That's what makes your script good," Chris said as a bell chimed somewhere in the bushes. "But it's also going to be our biggest obstacle."

As Chris got up, I thought about what he'd just said. Chris and Drew liked me and my script because of my passion, but how many people had liked my fiery nature at first, only to get burned in the end? They might appreciate it now, but I knew I had to reel myself in more if I wanted to make this movie work. There was only so much room fat, feminist, queer women got to take up in this town before they were shut up and shut out.

Drew squinted as he emerged from the house, looking around in the bright sun. "Chris went to go find a shirt," he said as he sat down on the cushioned bench next to mine.

"About time," I said.

"Not a fan of staring at Chris's pecs?" Drew raised an eyebrow.

"I prefer my business meetings to be conducted with clothes on," I clarified. "And on time."

"I'm sorry," Drew said. "I figured you knew ten meant eleven for Chris."

"Why would I?"

Chris joined us again, this time with a shirt on and carrying a designer tablet Roussard's sold to rich people who were too good for Samsung or Apple.

"In the future, let's please have meetings at the time we say we're going to have them," I insisted.

"Anything for you, Coffee Girl. Sorry," Chris quickly added as I shot him an angry look. "Old habit and all. From now on, I will call you Diana and meetings will be at the time we say they are. Happy?"

"Thank you," I said. "So what's on today's agenda?"

"As you heard Silvia say, we need to lock in some of our cast and crew before we can move on to get her approval and funding," Chris explained, swiping open his tablet and sitting up straight, suddenly very serious. "Today, I'd like us to come up with two to three options, ranked of course, for each of the main positions. I made a list of the order in which we need them, starting with the casting director, production manager, line producer, location manager, director of photography, gaffer, grip, production designer, costume designer, editor, and sound designer."

I turned to Drew. "When did he get so organized and serious?"

"He's always this serious. He just plays dumb on TV," Drew responded, making me laugh and Chris throw us both a dirty look. On *Geek Patrol*, the show they'd starred in as kids with Kali, Chris Stanson played a sexy-yet-stupid heartthrob, and for much of his early career, Chris played the idiot sidekick. He'd broken out as a blockbuster action star about eight years ago, but he was often still the brunt of dumb blond jokes.

The look on Chris's face told me he didn't appreciate our laughter, and I began to better understand his over-the-top philanthropy, the touting of his degree from Yale, and his obsessive need to win an Oscar. Turned out, Chris Stanson also had social stigmas he was trying to shed.

"Silvia suggested Francine Beaumont as casting director."

Chris changed the subject back to the film. "She's free right now, and I think we should grab her while we can."

"Francine is great," Drew agreed.

"Tell me about her." I didn't want to accept their suggestions for my crew without vetting them myself as well.

"French woman who worked at the Cannes Film Festival for years, so she knows everyone," Chris said. "Now she lives here and does casting. I've auditioned for her a few times, and she's great at creating chemistry."

"You would know." Drew turned to me. "Chris is infamous for sleeping with his costars."

"I'm sure you have no room to talk," I rebutted.

"Oh no, not Drew." Chris patted him on the back. "This guy is way too sentimental to sleep around. A shame, really. All that working out and nothing to gain from it."

"Nothing except multimillion-dollar movie deals," I pointed out.

"Francine's mother is from Ghana, and her father is from Bordeaux." Drew brought us back to the matter at hand. "So she understands minority voices and aims to cast diversity."

"Can I meet her first?" I asked.

"Of course," Drew said.

"But make it soon," Chris added. "Francine sells out quickly."

"Sells out? She's not a show. She's a human."

"You know what I mean. Don't drag your feet on this."

"Will do, boss." I saluted Chris mockingly.

"Now on to money." Chris put down his tablet. "Focus offered us a preliminary five million dollars."

"Holy shit, five million dollars!" I yelled excitedly, but Chris and Drew did not seem to share my enthusiasm. "You two are acting like this is bad news?"

"Have you ever tried to make a film for five million dollars?" Chris asked.

"That is about $4,980,000 more than I've ever had to make a movie."

"We won't get the people we want." Chris ignored me and talked to Drew. "Jennifer's already at her lowest."

"Jennifer?" I asked. "Lawrence? Aniston? Lopez?"

"Conger," Chris answered. "The director of photography I wanted."

"Janelle is our DP." I sat up, not liking where this conversation was headed.

"I hadn't had a chance to talk with her about it yet," Drew explained when Chris gave him a look.

"Talk with me about what?" I sat up even straighter, trying to sound as confident as possible. "There's nothing to talk about. Janelle is our DP. End of discussion."

"Focus wants a more experienced crew," Drew explained. "Since you're a relatively inexperienced director."

"I've directed multiple short films," I corrected him. "One of which you loved so much you asked me to direct this movie for you."

"So what if you shot a little film that was better than the other little films submitted to some festival that is now shut down?" Chris said. "You've never done a feature. We don't know if you can hold an audience for that long. Silvia is right; we need an experienced crew to make this movie work."

"Janelle is a highly experienced cinematographer. Look at her IMDb profile; she's got loads of credits to impress Silvia."

"As an assistant," Chris added. "She's never run the show. And neither have you. We need fewer amateurs, more professionals. And we can't get them with only five million dollars."

"We can afford Janelle at that rate," I pointed out, but Chris wasn't listening to me.

"I can add two," Chris said to Drew, "maybe three."

"Two what?" I asked, trying to keep myself in the conversation.

"I've got one," Drew responded, "but I might be able to scrounge up another one when *Total Destruction 3* is done."

"So that's about four total." Chris typed on his tablet and ignored my glares. "I'd like at least one more."

"Four of what? I'm the director. Shouldn't I be involved in the finding of things? I've got connections, too," I lied, not wanting to feel left out. "Maybe I can get one, too, if you tell me what we're looking for."

"Sure, Coffee Girl." Chris smirked. "You go ahead and find one."

"Great." I smiled, glad to finally be involved in the conversation. "Now, what am I finding?"

"Millions of dollars," Chris said, broadening his grin.

"Millions of dollars?" I said, shocked. "You both are putting millions of your own dollars into this film?"

"We believe in its success." Drew smiled at me.

"But it's not going to happen with Janelle as DP," Chris said, his tone final.

Chapter Seventeen

All the way home from Chris's house and into the evening, my mind raced, trying to come up with ways to keep Janelle on this project. She wasn't just my best friend, she was also the best director of photography I knew and my right-hand person on set for so long I didn't know how to make a movie without her. I tossed and turned all night, composing long diatribes in my head that I wanted to yell at Chris and Drew and imagining convincing Silvia myself to let Janelle stay. By the time morning came, I was so exhausted that it took me twice as long to get ready, making me half an hour late to work.

Janelle was standing by the door when I arrived, and she grabbed and pulled me into designer dresses as soon as I got in. "Where the hell have you been?"

"Rough night," I said as Janelle fixed the collar of my jacket. "What's going on?"

"Mr. Roussard is here," she whispered. "With that mom."

"What mom?" I asked.

"The queer kid's mom."

"Fuck." Mrs. Bertolli had threatened that she knew the Roussard family, but everyone pretended to know someone in this town.

"Indeed." Janelle picked a piece of lint off of my shirt and tucked it further into my pants. "I didn't want you going into battle unprepared."

"Thanks for having my back."

"I always have your back." She turned me around to pull more lint off of my shirt. "That homophobic bitch is going to give you shit, but just remember: you're fine as hell."

"And sexy as fuck," I said, standing up straight and tall.

"People are lucky to share space with us," Janelle continued.

"They should pay us to be in their presence."

"Damn right," she finished off, patting down my hair. "Now, go show them who's the real boss around here." Janelle walked out of Couture Gowns and straight down the escalators, like nothing unusual was happening.

I tried to compose myself in the same confident manner as I made my way to Personal Shopper, but I stumbled when I saw the short, round, mustachioed man standing next to Mrs. Bertolli.

"That's her," Mrs. Bertolli yelled before I'd even fully arrived in the department. "The vulgar dyke."

"No need to be vulgar yourself, Olivia." The man walked up to me. "Ms. Smith, do you know who I am?"

"Yes, sir." Even if Janelle hadn't warned me, I'd know Mr. Roussard's face from the images of it plastered all over the store.

"And do you know why I'm here?" he asked.

"I assume it is because Mrs. Bertolli did not like the suits I picked out for her child, Alex."

"Alessandra." Mrs. Bertolli hissed the name. "Her name is Alessandra, not Alex."

"Your child asked me to call them Alex, so I will respect that and call them Alex."

"See, Richard," Mrs. Bertolli fumed, "even now she's pushing her lesbian agenda."

Mr. Roussard sighed, looking almost as frustrated with Mrs. Bertolli as I felt. "Ms. Smith, I would like for you to apologize to Mrs. Bertolli."

"With all due respect, sir," I began, "I believe Mrs. Bertolli owes me an apology. And one to her child as well."

"How dare you?" Mrs. Bertolli exploded. "I owe you nothing."

"That was not a request, Ms. Smith," Mr. Roussard said, looking even more fidgety than before. "Mrs. Bertolli is a very special customer, and we respect our customers' wishes here at Roussard's."

"Alex was my customer, too, sir, not just Mrs. Bertolli." I stood firm in my belief that everyone deserved to have their chosen name and pronouns respected, even children. "I am doing my job by respecting their wishes."

"*Alessandra* doesn't know what's good for *her*," Mrs. Bertolli spat, emphasizing her child's birth name and gender.

"I believe your child knows better about their wants and needs than you do." I knew I should pull myself back in front of Mr. Roussard, but I couldn't stand there and let her hatefully misgender Alex like that.

"Are you going to put up with this kind of insolent behavior, Richard?" Mrs. Bertolli demanded.

Mr. Roussard sighed and looked at me. "I've seen your work history. I would hate to lose you, but you leave me no choice if you refuse to apologize for upsetting a customer."

"Then I'll take the choice away from you." The years of painfully experiencing queer and trans erasure caught up with me, and anger overrode rationality in my mind. "I quit."

Panic set in the minute the words left my lips, but there was no going back now. I couldn't stay working here, not anymore, not after this.

"You can't quit, because I'm getting you fired!" Mrs. Bertolli shouted.

"You can't get me fired, because I quit!" I said, feeling childish yelling back at her but also more empowered than I'd felt in a very long time. I would never again apologize to a bigoted, transphobic, homophobic, entitled bitch like her, even if it cost me my job. I had savings and a movie deal in the works. I didn't need this bullshit. "I will pack up my things and be out of here in an hour."

"Now, no need to be hasty," Mr. Roussard cautioned. I could tell his mind was weighing my outstanding sales record with the fortune Mrs. Bertolli spent here annually. "Let's talk this through."

"There's nothing more to say." I was calm and confident now that my decision had been made. "You want me to apologize to a customer for standing up for myself against her homophobic and transphobic remarks, and I refuse to do so, personally and legally."

That got his attention. "We don't need to bring legal into this."

A group of customers and employees had gathered around us, far enough away to not be pulled into the tussle but close enough to hear it all. Mr. Roussard looked around, unsure of what to do next, especially with a crowd gathering. I saw Emmy standing there, arms crossed, scowling. I wondered if she was mad at me or Mr. Roussard. It didn't matter, I wasn't going to stop now.

"You're right. And the generous severance package you're going to offer me should guarantee that we don't have to bring our lawyers into this."

Before I could lose my nerve, I turned around and walked to the employee room where I kept my things. It took everything in me not to turn around and beg for my job back, but I could hear Mrs. Bertolli huffing about my unworthiness of any such benefits, and my relief at never having to work with someone like her again outweighed my fear of being jobless. I was high on self-righteous indignation. I felt strong, victorious, like Harvey Milk on his soapbox or Marsha P. Johnson throwing bricks at Stonewall—except obviously on a smaller scale. Still, I hoped that Alex heard about this encounter and felt empowered knowing that someone out there was willing to fight so they could wear whatever the hell made them feel like the fabulous human they were.

I grabbed my phone and texted Janelle a brief overview of what had just happened. She arrived minutes later, flushed from running up the stairs.

"That's it, then?" she said.

"That's it," I replied, putting the last of my things in a bag.

"No going back?"

"I burned that bridge."

"Good for you." She gave me a big hug. "On to bigger, better, gayer things."

My eyes started tearing as she squeezed me, and I pulled

back, not wanting to fall apart here. "You should get out before Mr. Roussard sees you."

"It's not going to be the same without you here," Janelle said. "Maybe I should walk away, too. Go out in a blaze of glory together."

"Please don't," I begged, panic rising in me at the thought of Janelle quitting her job only to find out she wasn't DP for this film after all.

"Don't worry." She laughed. "I'll let you have your big moment all to yourself. But, hey, at least we'll be on set together soon."

Not sure what to say, I hugged my best friend, feeling like a complete asshole. Janelle had my back, always and forever, and here I was about to let her be kicked off my movie. *Our* movie! I needed to fight for her. I needed to not back down.

"You're fabulous." She pulled me in extra tight. "Don't let anyone make you forget that, okay?"

With one last squeeze, Janelle let go and went back to work, leaving me alone. As I looked around the Personal Shopper room for probably the last time, the reality of the situation hit me.

Drew and Chris had bought the holding rights to my script, but they still had time to back out. No contract had been signed for me as director, and Focus refused to commit. This project could end up in the bin tomorrow, and where would I be?

It wasn't my ultimate dream, but Roussard's had been good to me. Sure, this place was full of superficial people severely out of touch with the way the average person lived in this world, but through Roussard's I'd met queer kids like Alex, fabulous people like Shamaya, and yes, even the occasional movie star or two. This job had allowed me flexibility when my brother died, good health insurance, and above-average pay. That was more than most people could say of their work. I always imagined I'd walk out of here with my head held high, a decision I'd made consciously, not in response to some horrible client.

My phone pinged, and I pulled up a text from Janelle with a photo of us together years ago on the bleachers in front of the Oscars.

On to bigger, better, and gayer things! she wrote.

I smiled, wiped my face, and stood.

It was time for me to move on.

I gathered my things and was almost out the door when Emmy stopped me. "Diana, a word before you go."

I nodded and followed her into the room where we'd dressed Chris Stanson together, not sure from her stoic face if I was going to get a lecture or a hug goodbye.

"I am very good at my job." She presented this as fact and did not wait for me to agree before she proceeded. "Dressing people is my profession and my life."

"Okay," I said, no clue where this was going.

"You are making a movie with Chris and Drew, correct?"

"Correct." I wondered how she'd found out but then remembered Emmy had her ways.

"Then take this." She reached into her pocket and handed me a card that read EMMY MILLER, COSTUME DESIGNER.

"Are you asking me for a job?" Realization dawned on me.

"I am presenting myself for a position," Emmy stated. "One I am extremely qualified for."

"I consider you a strong candidate," I agreed. Then, without thinking, I hugged her, catching both of us off guard. "It's been nice working with you these past few years."

"You as well," she said, extracting herself from me and

pressing down her skirt. “Thank you, by the way, for standing up for Alex.”

“Of course.”

“Very few people know this, and I prefer it to stay that way”—she looked me directly in the eyes—“but I am trans.”

“Oh,” I said, never sure what to say when people came out to me, even after decades of being out myself.

“I was Alex as a kid,” she continued. “I haven’t spoken to my mom, or anyone from my childhood, since I was fifteen.”

“Thank you for sharing your story with me.” I was genuinely touched.

“I trust you to keep this information between us,” Emmy said, turning around and walking out of the dressing room without looking back or saying goodbye.

And with that, my days of being a shopgirl were officially over.

Chapter Eighteen

When I got to my car, I sat there for a while, unsure of what came next. I was all dressed up with nowhere to go and a whole afternoon free. I thought about checking out the new exhibit at LACMA or going to Joan's on Third to eat my way through the cheese counter, but then my phone pinged with a picture of Janelle flipping off a photo of Mr. Roussard, and I knew what to do.

It was time to fight for my best friend.

Thirty minutes later, I pulled up to a little Mediterranean bungalow in Studio City and parked behind a white Subaru that looked just like mine. Gathering my courage, I walked up the steps and rang the bell. No one answered, so I double-checked the address and rang again. Still no answer. Frustrated, I started heading back to my car when I heard a familiar voice giving out orders in the backyard.

"No, no, no, that's all wrong!" Jaqueline shouted as I

unlocked the gate and made my way inside. “Have we tried to the right?”

“We tried there already, and you insisted the lighting was wrong,” Drew said as he put down a giant wicker chair.

“You could get a lamp,” Tammy suggested.

“Where would she plug it in?” Joan asked.

“I could get an extension cord,” Jaqueline offered.

“Or you could leave it where it is under the light,” Joan said.

“But the light attracts bugs,” Tammy pointed out.

“Am I interrupting?” I asked, making my way over to the group.

“Diana, darling, I’m so glad to see you!” Jaqueline opened her arms and engulfed me in a warm hug, one arm tight around me, the other holding on to a particularly dapper cane. “Help me convince my son that this chair must be moved.”

“She’s moved it five times already,” Drew cut in, wiping his hands on his jeans.

“Do you expect me to just sit there, being eaten alive by bugs while I write?” Jaqueline countered, still embracing me.

“Don’t you have an office inside for that?” Joan reasoned.

“I hate writing in there.” Jaqueline waved her off. “So stuffy. I like being a part of nature.”

“Honey, nature bites,” Tammy said in her thick Southern drawl.

“Tell me about it,” Jaqueline said, letting go of me to scratch her arm.

“You could get one of those blue lights that zap bugs,” I suggested. “Or a citronella candle.”

“Citronella makes you hallucinate,” Jaqueline said.

“Maybe it would make you write better,” Drew quipped.

“There, there, no need to get mean just because you’re not

strong enough to carry a little chair from left to right." Jaqueline used her cane to point out how short the distance was.

Drew threw his hands up in the air, turned around, and walked into the house.

"What's the point of all those muscles if you won't help your poor old mom?" Jaqueline yelled dramatically after him, a smirk on her face. "Don't worry, he'll be back." She winked at me. "Now, darling, you are here in the middle of the day all dressed up needing to talk to my son, which means something salacious happened. Tell us everything, and don't leave a single detail out."

Jaqueline, Tammy, Joan, and I sat down on wicker furniture under a big umbrella, and I told them everything, about Alex and their mother getting me fired, about the Focus meeting and Janelle being kicked off the film, I even told them about my fear of paying my bills and my absolute terror of being a horrible director. Drew brought out some iced tea for all of us but disappeared again when Jaqueline shooed him away. The women were so easy to talk to that it was almost an hour before I sat back with a sigh, completely spent.

"Oh, to be young and excitable again." Tammy sighed.

"I'll take old and wise," Joan rebutted. "Such drama these young kids have."

"Tell me about it." I smiled at Joan.

"And you're never dramatic now?" Tammy raised one eyebrow at Joan.

"I am not dramatic," Joan insisted. "I'm theatrical. There's a difference."

"You know what you need to do, darling?" Jaqueline said, handing me an embroidered hankie to blow my nose.

"No, I don't. God, please tell me what to do." I sat up

straight, dabbing my eyes with the hankie while waiting for her magical words of wisdom that would make everything okay.

"You need to get high." She reached into her pocket and pulled out a joint.

And because I had nothing better to do with my day, I did just that.

• • •

Hours passed in a haze of giggles, ice cream, and multiple Tegan and Sara albums. At some point I stripped out of the ELOQUII pantsuit I'd worn to work and ended up in Jaqueline's pool wearing nothing but my bra and underwear, competing with Drew for who could create the biggest cannonball splash. Jaqueline, Tammy, and Joan acted as judges, holding up crooked signs with our score scrawled on them. Sober, I might have felt self-conscious mostly naked in front of practical strangers, one of them a famous movie star known for his newly ripped physique, but stoned I simply enjoyed the feeling of my body floating in water. I spent a ridiculously long period of time admiring how perky my boobs looked in the pool and ate a whole bag of Pirate's Booty Jaqueline brought out for me. I didn't think about Roussard's once. I also didn't talk to Drew about Janelle, a fact that my sobering brain realized around sunset.

Tammy and Joan had left long ago to avoid traffic, and Drew was inside doing dishes, leaving Jaqueline and me alone. She'd made Drew move her furniture one more time, back to the spot it had originally been in, and we sat together swatting mosquitoes as they gathered around the light above us.

"What am I going to do about Janelle?" I sighed, leaning my head against Jaqueline's shoulder.

"The solution, my beautiful darling, is simple. A sacrifice was demanded, so a sacrifice must be made."

"I cannot sacrifice Janelle."

"Then you must find something else to die for her," she declared. "And until you find that sacrifice, you must be honest with her. She needs to know that her life is on the line."

"I wouldn't say life," I argued.

"Then her livelihood. But you should know that's the same thing to those of us outcast by society, my dear." She paused as Drew emerged from the house carrying two large glasses of water. "Now, I shall revel in the privilege growing old affords me and retire early for the evening with good wine and a great book. You two stay as long as you want and help yourself to anything in the icebox. Except for the last piece of cheesecake. That is mine."

Jaqueline kissed both of us on the forehead, then headed inside.

"Your mother is truly wonderful," I said to Drew.

"She's a pain in the ass," Drew taunted after her. "But I absolutely adore her."

"I've definitely overstayed my welcome." It had gotten dark, and there was a chill in the air. "I can head out—I'm sure you've got glamorous places to be this evening."

"There's nowhere I'd rather be right now than here with you." Drew smiled, handed me a glass, and sat down next to me.

"I find that very hard to believe"—I took a sip of water—"but I'm flattered."

"Do I get to know what happened today? Or is that information just for your queer elders?"

I folded my feet up under me and gave him an abridged

version of my day. He asked questions and told me a story of growing up the son of a single lesbian, being teased for wearing dresses to school, not understanding why he couldn't. I enjoyed the ease with which we conversed, just two people talking about our lives, not a famous actor and some random shopgirl. I guessed I wasn't a shopgirl anymore. Now, I was a director spending the afternoon with my producer and his mother. It was surreal and yet it felt right, like I'd always belonged right there on that sofa next to Drew.

I shivered as the Santa Ana winds picked up, and Drew went inside, emerging again with a big, fluffy blanket. "Can I ask you something?" he said, throwing the cover around me.

"Sure," I said, tucking my toes under the blanket to stay warm.

"I know it's been years, and you probably had lots of people vying for your attention at that time, but I just need to know. Why wouldn't you meet with me?"

"After LACMA?"

"No, after *Lalo's Lament*."

"I don't know what you're talking about."

"I've always wanted to do a rom-com," he explained, "something my mother would love, maybe even based on one of her books. I had an idea for a project, and I thought your style would be perfect for it. I made my agent call yours and ask for a meeting, but you turned me down. I know it's silly. It was years ago. It's just been bugging me since I met you at the LACMA party, so I had to ask."

I was speechless. I had no idea any of this had happened. "It wasn't personal."

Drew's shoulders shrank, and he chuckled a bit. "I thought you hated that line."

"I do!" I insisted. "But in this instance, it really wasn't personal. I didn't even know that you called."

"Your agent never told you?"

"She told anyone who called that I was too booked to talk."

"That's a baller move."

"I wasn't trying to be cocky. I just needed space."

"Hollywood can be overwhelming when you're in demand," Drew agreed.

"And lonely when you're not," I added.

"But you answered those calls eventually. Why not mine?"

I paused, not sure how much I was willing to share. Drew was friendly, maybe even a friend by now, but few people knew about those months after *Lalo's Lament* came out, and talking about it always sent me into a downward spiral. But if this movie was going to work, Drew needed to know the story behind it, and the person behind the story. So, taking a deep breath, I opened up.

"Henry, my brother, was diagnosed with cancer right after the movie came out." I shivered, my body reacting to the change in both weather and subject. Drew tucked the blanket around me, and his proximity and warmth encouraged me to keep going. "It's hard to deal with Hollywood when you're living in a hospital, watching someone you love die. He had his jaw removed the week I won Best Short. He died in my arms a month later. Offers came pouring in, and all I could do was move from my bed to the sofa to binge-watch old sitcoms. Some days I couldn't even do that. I ignored my agent, and she told everyone I was booked. That seemed better than saying I was in a deep hole of despair. I wasn't trying to be cool or seem in demand. I was just trying to stay alive. When I reemerged from my black void of mourning, my career had died along with my brother."

Drew paused, taking it all in. "I don't know what to say, except I'm so sorry, and fuck cancer."

"Fuck cancer indeed."

"This whole time I thought... It doesn't matter what I thought."

"It matters to me."

"I thought..." Drew spoke more to the blanket than to me. "I thought you didn't want to work with me, because I was the broke, fat, jovial sidekick. And now you will because I'm—"

"Ripped and famous," I finished for him.

"Don't forget rich," he added.

"Oh, I can't forget that." I gestured around his mother's gorgeous backyard. Drew chuckled. "I'm not going to pretend that you being rich and famous isn't a bonus. It got me a meeting I've waited years for and will help get this movie made. But that's not the reason I'm here right now. You don't see me getting high with Chris's mom."

"She's a teetotaler. Doesn't even drink the sacramental wine at church."

"That explains so much." I shook my head. "I'm not here right now because of your money and fame." He looked up at me, our eyes meeting, his face nervous, like the butterflies in my stomach had taken up residency in his as well. "I'm here because of your heart and soul."

Without thinking, I leaned forward and pressed my lips to his. I pulled back quickly, unsure of what I'd just done. We stared at each other again for a split second before both of us plunged forward, bonking our heads and laughing. Drew let go of my hand and wrapped his arms around me, pulling me toward him. Our lips met again, gently at first but gaining in voracity as I climbed on top of him, feeling his eagerness grow. He grabbed my back and pulled me closer while I lifted my hands to touch his face.

My body wasn't used to kissing people with five o'clock shadows. The scruffiness of it shocked me. I became acutely aware of Drew's muscles, his scent, his hardness beneath me. The way his tongue pushed into my mouth, eager for more.

But what would more look like? His hands on my fat rolls. Broken condoms and begging my period to come. The inevitable heartbreak when he never called me back. The lack of emotional awareness if he did. I'd been with men before. I knew the drill. I wanted no part of it.

"I can't do this," I said, pulling away.

"I'm sorry, did I do something wrong?" Drew asked as I climbed off him. "Are you okay?"

"It's not you, it's me."

"You're going with that line again?" Drew chuckled.

"Sorry, it's just that this is a very bad idea."

"I like you. I think you like me." He entwined his fingers with mine. "Maybe this is a very good idea."

"Good for you, sure. You'd get praised for being an open-minded feminist, accepting all bodies and sexualities. The newspapers would eat it up. But me, I'd be the fat dyke who doesn't deserve famous Drew Williams, and people would think my movie only got made because we were sleeping together."

"What happens when this movie is made and you're more famous than I am?" he asked.

I rolled my eyes. "First off, that won't happen. Second, I don't want to just be famous, I want to be respected. I want to have creative freedom. I want to make movies about girls like me. I don't want to be some old tabloid headline, the fat girl Drew Williams once fucked."

"I'm not going to just fuck and leave." He was suddenly serious. "I like you more than that."

"So what, we date?" I posited. "I don't even know how that works. Forget that you're rich and famous. You're also my boss. And a cis man."

"We'd find a way." He sounded so sure of himself that I wanted to believe he was right.

"Have you thought about what dating me would mean for your career?" I pondered, enjoying the feeling of his hands in mine but still not sure it was a good idea to keep touching him. "There are expectations people have of A-list actors. You're a contender for the next Bond, for fuck's sake. People expect Bond to have a Bond girl on his arm, not someone who looks like me."

"That's really unfair."

"You're right, it is unfair." I nodded. "But just because it's unfair doesn't mean it's not true. If people saw me with you, the backlash and hate would be too much. For both of us."

"You know I don't care about that stuff."

"You don't have to care. Your privilege allows you to rise above it. You're an action star—you can jump over hurdles. But me, I've got barricades ten stories high with sharpshooters trying to take me down while I climb to the top. It's not the same for us. Even if I want this, I can't have it. There's just too many walls between your world and mine."

"Then we take down the walls." Drew put his hands on my face and looked me in the eyes. "People will always talk. The paparazzi will always spin whatever story they think will sell. But there's something special here. You're something special."

I touched his hand on my face and realized it was wet. Somewhere in there, I'd started crying.

"I like to think of myself as a courageous person." I pulled both our hands away and placed them intertwined on my lap. "I like to think I don't make decisions based on what other people would say. But courage takes energy, and I don't have the energy for what pursuing this would take right now. I've got too much to do. I have to make this movie. I have to rebuild my career. I have an Oscar to win!" I sobbed, placing my head on Drew's shoulder.

He held me as I cried, wishing it weren't all so complicated, that sexuality and attraction and body size were all so much more fluid than society let them be, and wondering how I was going to focus on this film with my confusing feelings for Drew clouding every move. It felt like years had passed since I quit Roussard's, decades since I left Cecily's house that morning. So much had changed in less than twelve hours. I wanted to crawl into Drew's arms and stay there, comforted and protected. But I couldn't imagine a world where that ended well, couldn't dream of a way to make it work. So instead, I pulled myself together, wiped my eyes, and sat up.

Drew handed me a hankie from his back pocket. "When you win an Oscar for this movie, will you date me then?"

"*If* I win an Oscar for this movie, you can fuck me right there on the stage." I laughed at the absolute absurdity of the idea. "Just wait until after my acceptance speech."

Drew lifted up his little finger. "I, Drew Williams, pinkie swear to keep it purely professional between Diana Smith and me until this movie we're making together wins an Oscar."

Smiling, I lifted my little finger and wrapped it around his. "I, Diana Smith, promise to fuck Drew Williams on the stage if I win an Oscar for this movie. Right after my acceptance speech, that is."

"It's agreed, then." Drew twisted his pinkie around mine and pulled both our fingers down in a shake.

We sat there for a while, our hands held together, my body aching for his. I wanted to lean in, to give in, to kiss him and straddle him and let him fill me. Our bodies pulled toward each other. His forehead touched mine. My lips grazed his.

"I should go," he whispered, "before I forget my promise, scoop you up, and take you to bed."

"You couldn't lift me."

He leaned in farther, his lips brushing past mine as they made their way to my ear. "I can hold all of your greatness, Diana."

Drew's whisper sent erotic shivers down my spine. I pulled back from him and looked into his eyes. We were inches apart and my whole body was begging to kiss him. "I can't..."

"I know," he lamented, moving away from me.

I stood up, already missing his warmth. "I should head out."

"Are you good to drive?" Drew asked. "I can call you a cab."

"It's been a few hours since I smoked." I grabbed my bag and fished out my keys. "I'm good."

"Need directions out of here?"

"I've got this wonderful invention called a cell phone." I smirked. "Not only does it answer calls, it gives me directions, too."

"Just trying to help." He smiled back at me. "Drive safely, okay?"

"Will do," I promised. "Thanks for today. I needed it."

"Anytime," Drew said, and I knew he meant it. He was the

kind of guy who would hand you his whole world. But I wasn't the kind of gal who could take it.

"Goodbye, Andy." I turned around and forced myself to leave.

"Goodbye, Diana," I heard as the gate closed between us.

Chapter Nineteen

Janelle opened the door to her apartment wearing an emerald crushed velvet suit with no top underneath. Her hair was disheveled, and she had a flush to her face that told me she wasn't alone.

"Shit, am I interrupting?" I whispered, looking into her apartment.

"Who is it?" someone asked from the other room.

"A friend." Janelle pushed us both into the hallway and closed the door behind her. "I've got someone over."

"I see that." I wiggled my eyebrows at her.

Janelle's door opened, and a curvy woman with long dark locks wearing a stunning copper cinched satin dress stood there. "Did you double-book yourself?"

"I'm so sorry for interrupting." I hurried back toward the elevator, feeling like a total asshole for showing up on my best friend's doorstep without warning. This was Janelle, after all.

That woman always had a date.

"Diana, wait." Janelle ran after me. "What's up?"

"She looks mad." I nodded over at where the woman was gathering her purse and keys.

Janelle ran back to her apartment and took the woman's hands in hers. "Crystal, this is my best friend, Diana. I swear, I didn't know she was coming over."

"I'm really sorry!" I yelled back at the doorway as I stepped into the elevator. "I love your dress!"

The doors started closing, but Janelle's hand shot out between them, stopping me from leaving.

"Go back to your date. I'm fine," I insisted.

Janelle stood firm, staring at me. "What happened?"

"What, I can't just come surprise my best friend?"

"You are horrible at surprises," Janelle said, still blocking the elevator door.

"Am not!" I protested. Janelle raised her eyebrow at me. "Fine, I am."

"So what's up?" Janelle pulled me out of the elevator.

I looked over at her door, which had shut with Crystal inside. At least her date wouldn't be around to hear this. I took a deep breath, grabbed her hand in mine, and said the words I'd been dreading to tell her for weeks. "They want to hire someone else to be director of photography."

"Motherfuckers." Janelle dropped my hand and started pacing the hallway. "I'm sorry, I know you're all buddy-buddy with them now, but motherfuckers."

"They're not my buddies!" Chris barely gave me the time of day, and Drew was in a gray area between colleague and… something else. "They're my producers. You're my best friend."

"And what did you tell your producers when they said your

best friend was off this film?" Janelle glared at me.

"I fought for you."

"How hard? Did you flex your right as director? Did you demand they put me on the film? Did you offer to give up something else in return? Did you keep fighting until they had to give in? Or did you give up as soon as they said no?"

I couldn't answer her, because she was right. I hadn't done all I could. I'd spent the whole day with Drew and hadn't even brought her up with him. Sure, I complained to Jaqueline, but I hadn't advocated for Janelle, not really, not like my best friend deserved.

"Right," Janelle said, interpreting my silence. "So it's like that, then."

"I don't want it to be like that!" I cried. "Hollywood makes it like that. This business breeds betrayal and backstabbing."

"Every job does that!" Janelle threw her hands in the air. "This whole town is the same. This whole world is the same. Humans are selfish. Capitalists are greedy. The only thing that ever keeps us from being like the assholes we hate is the choices we make in our lives. And you chose them over me."

"I fought for you," I repeated meekly.

"Fought. Past tense." Janelle leaned against the wall. "So it's over, then."

"I'm going to keep fighting for you." I reached for her hands. "I'm going to get you on this film. I promise."

"Don't make promises you can't keep." Janelle pulled away from me and pointed to her place. "I should get back in there."

"Yeah, sure," I said, letting my hand drop from where it had been reaching out for my best friend. "I'm sorry again."

Janelle nodded and opened her front door, pausing halfway. "You know, this film was my dream, too. I sat at the Oscars with you, staring at that red carpet, envisioning the day we'd walk it together. All those late nights in film school and early mornings at Roussard's. I started this journey with you. It sucks that we don't get to finish it together."

"I'm sorry," I said, again, my voice cracking as she closed the door behind her without saying goodbye.

Fuck! I screamed internally, shaking my whole body out as I walked back to the elevator. That had gone all wrong, and there was no way to take it back. She was right; this movie wasn't just my dream. It was ours. What was the point of making it come true without her by my side?

Back in my car, I pulled out my phone to play some distracting music and noticed dozens of texts and missed calls from Cecily.

Shit! I thought as I read the ever-increasing agitation, then eventual disappointment in her texts. I'd missed the kids' school performance, something I'd promised them I would attend.

"They're already asleep," Cecily answered when I called her from the freeway.

"I'm so sorry!" It was a phrase I seemed to be using a lot lately. "I got caught up at work."

"Roussard's closed hours ago," she pointed out.

"Movie stuff," I replied, which was technically true. I didn't think Cecily would appreciate what I'd really spent my day doing.

"This performance has been on your calendar for months," she lectured in her mom voice, talking to me like a teenager who had broken curfew.

"Work stuff came up, and I had to deal with it." I tried to remind her with my tone that I was a grown adult who was allowed to stay out late if I wanted to.

"Work is always going to come up," Cecily said, "but you have to be there for your children when you say you're going to."

"Except they're not my kids. They're yours," I pointed out. "I chose making movies over having kids years ago. I'm going to keep making that choice."

"Fine, they're not your kids," Cecily accepted, "but they're still your niblings, and you made a promise to them. I know you've got your fancy movie deal now and you're too good for an elementary school play, but this was a big deal to them. You not showing up hurt. So while you were out with whatever latest movie star friend you've made, I was holding Ellis as they cried themself to sleep, wondering why Aunt Didi didn't show up when she'd promised she'd be there."

I could hear the tears in Cecily's voice and felt my own coming on. Little Ellis had been practicing their two lines over and over again, so excited to deliver them to the crowd. Just that morning, they'd recited them before school, beaming up at me and making me promise I'd get there early for a front-row seat.

With everything that had happened that day—quitting Roussard's, kissing Drew, fighting with Janelle—I'd completely forgotten that promise. Ellis was crushed, and Cecily had every right to be mad at me.

"I'll make it up to them," I promised.

"Stop making promises you can't keep." Cecily hung up the phone.

Her words joined Janelle's in my head, a loud, insistent echo, pointing out all the ways I'd disappointed the people I loved today. How much I'd disappointed myself. I'd quit my job without any guarantee of a paycheck from this movie. I'd kissed my straight, cis male producer, both complicating and compromising this film being made. I'd severely let down my best friend, broken a promise to my niblings, and fought with my sister. All in less than twenty-four hours.

Needing to scream and cry all at once, I opened my phone and turned on Brandi Carlisle. Tomorrow, I'd start fixing all of this. Until then, I'd let myself escape into the deep soulful music of the queer queen of Americana, who always made me feel better.

Chapter Twenty

The next few weeks flew by in a sleepless blur. It took a heartfelt apology and five days of making pancakes for breakfast every morning, but the kids eventually forgave me. Cecily wasn't so easily bought, and the house was thick with the tension of an uneasy truce.

Janelle had asked for space, and I was trying to respect that, checking in every couple of days and only getting curt responses in return. I'd brought up the director of photography positions a few times on the phone with Chris since then, but he was insistent on using Jennifer Conger, eventually telling me rather firmly to drop it. Drew might have been helpful, but I couldn't bring myself to call him, which just made me feel worse about the whole situation.

Nervous dinosaurs roamed my stomach as I made my way to Chris's house for our first in-person production meeting since my kiss with Drew. I parked my Subaru next to a custom matte-black Mercedes G-Wagon and sat there, frozen with worry that Chris's big black door would be slammed in my face. I knew in my logical brain that Drew and I had left things on good terms and we were both adults who could handle this situation, but my stomach still lurched as I got out of my car, walked up to Chris's house, and rang the doorbell.

A handsome man answered the door, but not the one I was expecting. Instead of Chris, standing in front of me was a guy wearing a Virgen de Guadalupe apron over his teal shirt and jeans. His eyes sparkled mischievously, and his dimples dug deep into his cheeks as he smiled at me and said, "Buenos dias, bonita."

"Hola, guapo," I replied, intrigued by this fabulous gay guy answering Chris's door. "Soy Diana."

"Diana, la diosa." He kissed my hand. "Soy Simón. ¿Tienes hambre?"

"¡Siempre!"

Never one to turn down food, I followed Simón into Chris's kitchen, which was a simple yet elegant space, fully loaded with everything you'd want for cooking. Simón made his way around, grabbing items from cupboards and drawers that opened and closed for themselves with a simple push.

"I would like to make you an omelet with nopales, queso fresco, tomato, and onion." Simón surveyed the goods he'd placed on the counter. "Maybe some chile rojo sprinkled in, if you can handle a little drama in your mouth?"

"Oh, I can handle it," I bragged.

"I'm sure you can, darling diosa." Simón winked at me and got to work, chopping up some cactus.

"I just can't handle gluten." I sighed.

"Don't worry, no wheat here," Simón promised, already at

work on my meal.

"Where is everyone else?" I'd been so distracted by Simón that I had forgotten about our meeting.

"No one matters but you and me right now," Simón said, "but if you are looking for Chris, he is downstairs getting a massage."

"And Drew?" I asked.

"Sólo Dios sabe," he said, chopping nopales.

I didn't know whether to be frustrated that I was sitting here, waiting for everyone again, or relieved to have a moment of respite—and food—between my drive and our meeting. My anxiety was still there, but the panic had gone since meeting Simón. He had a soothing energy about him, like all would be okay if I just let him feed me. Which, knowing how angry I got when I was hungry, was probably closer to the truth than I wanted to admit.

"So tell me about yourself," I said, figuring I might as well make the best of my waiting. "What do you do when you're not making food for Chris?"

"Oh no, Chris makes his own food," he answered as he whipped the eggs in a fast yet delicate motion that spoke of years of practice.

"Sorry, I assumed you were his chef."

"I am a chef, but I am not *his* chef," Simón emphasized, stirring onions in the pan. "I am owned by no one."

"I can respect that." I was in awe of the way Simón moved around the kitchen. "So then what do you do for Chris?"

"Who said I have to do anything for him?" Simón smirked. "Maybe he does things for me."

"I can't see Chris doing much for anyone but himself."

"He is actually a very good cook. Could be a chef, but alas, too beautiful."

"Huh, Chris Stanson cooks his own food." I gawked as Simón slowly poured the eggs into a pan. "Who would have guessed?"

It was beautiful watching Simón work. The mesmerizing way he slowly stirred the eggs, tapping the sides of the pan to make sure none stuck. Plopping bits of queso fresco into the batter and letting it melt just so before sprinkling in the chiles. Folding the whole thing over on itself, tapping the pan again to keep it from burning on the bottom.

Obviously, Simón loved food, I could tell from the way he treated it, but it was more than just love. It was talent beyond measure, like watching Mozart perform a piano solo he'd written himself.

Simón plated the omelet, placing a dollop of fresh crema and a sprinkle of cilantro on top. I expected a flourish as he handed it to me, but the loving care he took with the preparation was absent in his delivery. He simply handed me the plate and walked back to the sink to do dishes.

I wondered how someone could put all of that effort into creating a piece of art and not want to see the audience's reaction to its unveiling. I thought about how someday soon I would be sitting in a theater with people watching my film and how horribly nerve-wracking it would be. My self-worth as a filmmaker would be dependent on their every reaction. Simón had it right. If I could create art and then walk away without having to worry about other people's opinions, I would do that, too.

But making an omelet is nothing like making a movie, I thought. *I'm sure this is nothing to him.*

And then I tasted it.

"Simón"—I gasped, and he turned around expectantly—"this is fucking amazing."

"There's no need to cuss." He smiled. "It's just a simple omelet."

"Yes, and the *Mona Lisa* is just a simple painting." I scooped up another bite and savored the creaminess.

"And there's no need for hyperboles, either." He was playing humble, but even with his back turned, I could tell he appreciated the compliment.

"I'm not kidding here." I tried to make myself slow down so I could appreciate every bite. "This is absolute perfection. Salty, spicy, bitter, sweet, all in one bite. It's pure genius." I took another bite before continuing. "There's this restaurant by where I used to work, a couple blocks off of Rodeo Drive. It's called Tres, and it has the best omelet in the world. Or that's what I thought before I tried this one. It's this wonderful Cuban-Mexican fusion place known for its beyond amazing egg dishes, but you've got them beat. You should go and try it sometime, just so you can compare how much better yours is." I realized I was babbling, but I couldn't stop. Really good food (or really good sex) had that effect on me. "Do you know Tres?"

"I have been to Tres a few times, yes." Simón smirked.

"So good, right?" I was sadly halfway through my omelet, trying to make it last as long as possible. "Did their omelet inspire yours?"

"My omelet inspired theirs."

"Oh, do you know the head chef there?"

"I am the head chef there."

"Oh. My. God." My mouth hung open so far that a bit of nopales fell out. "You're Simón Barboza!"

"Soy él," Simón admitted, taking a dramatic bow.

"That means you also run Uno and Dos."

"Sí." He smiled proudly.

"I can't believe I've been sitting here chatting with Simón Barboza! And you made me breakfast!"

I felt like an ass. I just assumed Simón worked for Chris, like Serena did for Drew, since he was in his kitchen. I hadn't even thought to put his name together with the food in front of me. Of course he was Simón Barboza—who else made omelets like this? I just had a personal meal made by one of the top chefs in the world, a man famous for his complex and fresh takes on Cuban and Mexican food, merging the two sides of his family together. An activist known for advocating for Latin-American populations and immigrant rights. He was notoriously private, refusing to pose for any magazines or come to the front of house at the restaurant to greet famous guests. That's why I hadn't realized who he was. Unlike the rest of Hollywood, he preferred to stay unrecognizable.

"Tres is one of my favorite restaurants; I used to eat there at least once a week when I worked at Roussard's." I'd completely lost any semblance of cool, but I didn't care. "I went to Dos a month ago for Drew's mom's birthday, and it was the most fantastic meal I've ever had in my life. I still can't believe you're Simón Barboza! I just had an omelet made for me by Simón Barboza!"

I forced myself to stop talking, blushing with embarrassment over how I was acting. I'd worked around many famous people in my life, but it had been a while since I'd been this excited about meeting someone. "I'm sorry, I'm just not used to being fed by famous chefs."

"I'm sure you meet even more prestigious people all the time," he said, putting away the bits he hadn't used. "You are friends with Chris Stanson, after all."

"He's just a pretty face with good genes. But you! The things you do with food, it isn't genetics, it's genius. It's talent and hard work combined. It's art."

"Thank you"—Simón bowed—"but I wouldn't dismiss Chris so easily. It takes more than just looks to get to the level of success he has."

"Eh, Chris can't do this." I used my finger to scrape the last of the crema off my plate to emphasize my point.

"What can't I do?" Chris came into the kitchen with a towel wrapped around his otherwise naked body, his forehead still marked from the massage table's face cradle.

"Simón Barboza just made me breakfast!" I blurted out, too excited to care that he was showing up to yet another meeting half naked and late.

"Look at that," Chris remarked, "Coffee Girl does get starstruck."

"He's the hottest thing in town," I gushed, ignoring Chris's little nickname for me. "Every lesbian I know wants in his kitchen, and every gay guy I know wants in his bedroom."

"You'll have to send me some names." Simón winked.

"One name: Matt. He's a film director who will fuck your brains out and make you beg for more." I caught myself as I remembered his response to my cussing earlier. "Pardon my French."

"Even a prude like me can enjoy the sound of that," Simón said as we exchanged numbers. "I have to go, but it has been a pleasure meeting you, Diana. You must come by Dos again sometime. My treat."

"Oh my god, really?" I shook his hand a bit too vigorously. "I will! Thank you!"

"I'm curious," Chris said, after Simón was gone, "do you lose your shit over every chef or just Simón?"

"And I'm curious," I shot back, leaning toward him, "why Simón Barboza was at your home so early in the morning."

"I was hungry." Chris shrugged.

Of course, Chris Stanson was the kind of guy who would call up a famous chef to make him breakfast.

"So where is everyone else?" I looked around, wondering about our production meeting.

"Drew and Francine will be here in about an hour."

"Did you give me the wrong time again?" I fumed. Sure, I'd gotten to meet Simón Barboza and eat the most amazing omelet of my life, but still, I hated that Chris kept disrespecting my time.

"No, you're on time." Chris smiled. "I just arranged a special meeting beforehand for you downstairs."

"Who am I meeting with downstairs?" I asked.

"My massage therapist," Chris said, patting me on the back. "You're way too tense."

Chapter Twenty-One

An hour and a half later, I stumbled my way back up the stairs, only half conscious after the most heavenly massage of my life. I'd had a knot in my shoulder for god knew how long that was now gone, and my feet felt like I was walking on air, all the tension released from my body. I saw Francine in the sitting room off the kitchen, but I barely registered her presence, my body instead focusing solely on the sunlit sofa next to her.

"Are you stoned?" Francine asked as I staggered over and plopped down on the cushions.

"High on Melody," I explained.

"Melody, like music?" She looked at me like I was unstable.

"Chris's massage therapist." I closed my eyes, grateful I was wearing a stretchy Nooworks jumpsuit so I could cuddle up into the cushions.

When I opened them again, Francine was gone. Dazed, I glanced around looking for some sign of my production team but found no one. Wiping a bit of drool off of my chin, I stood and began to search the house. They weren't in the kitchen, living room, entryway, or dining room. They weren't outside on the upper or lower lawns, and they weren't in the gym, garage, pool house, lounge, or game room downstairs. Tentatively, I headed upstairs, past where Chris usually kept a security guard during parties to avoid people going into his private rooms. Having never been invited upstairs before, I was hesitant to start opening doors randomly, so I pressed my ear against them instead, searching for some sign of the production meeting I was supposed to be attending. Nothing.

Heading back downstairs, I wondered how long I'd been asleep. The house was big, but not so massive I wouldn't be able to hear people talking. They must have gone somewhere. Feeling horribly awkward, I grabbed my bag and keys and headed to leave when I saw a wall open, and Drew emerged from it.

My heart skipped in a way that made me long to be someone else, the kind of woman who could walk over right now and kiss Drew Williams and not have it wreck her life. I wished I was Cecily, unashamed in her obsession with men, unabashed in her need for them. But I'd seen the consequences of that kind of lust. I didn't want to end up losing my queer community, or worse, pregnant in Arcadia. The only little man I wanted Drew to help me get was an Oscar, and that wouldn't happen if I kept being pushed out of meetings.

"Where were you all?" I asked.

"In the screening room." He pointed to the invisible door behind him. "You were sleeping, so we started watching clips."

"You didn't think to wake me for the meeting?"

"You looked like you needed the rest."

"Thanks." I didn't know if that was kindness or commentary on the bags under my eyes. I did need the rest—he was right about that—and the combination of massage and nap had been lovely, but it meant my team had started without me, possibly even made decisions without me. I couldn't let it happen again. "In the future, please wake me up for all meetings."

"You didn't miss anything."

"Obviously, I missed something," I said, pulling my giant production notebook out of my bag, determined to catch up. "Tell me about each clip. Or better yet, let me watch them."

"I don't think you'll find them as funny as we did," Drew said, opening the door.

"We'll see." I pushed my way past him and into the room, where Chris and Francine were laughing at the screen. On it, Chris and Shelene Elliot were continually breaking character with bursts of giggles as they tried to kiss.

"What's this?" I asked, pointing at the scene.

"It's the *Tendered Secrets* gag reel." Drew chuckled as the director yelled at on-screen Chris and Shelene. "They made a special one for the cast and crew that won't be released to the public, because Chris looks like an idiot. He insisted on doing his own stunts for the first few days until he fractured his wrist."

At that moment, on-screen Chris slid past his mark, bumping into a wall, sending the crew on screen—and Drew and Francine off screen—into hysterics.

"Laugh all you want, but that hurt!" Chris exclaimed while his on-screen self moaned in pain as the medic rushed toward him.

"I thought you were watching screenings of actors for our movie," I said.

"We wouldn't start without you," Drew answered.

"Oh." I softened as I realized that the only thing I missed was Chris making a fool out of himself. My team had been kind and waited for me. "Thank you. I appreciate that."

Drew gave me a big, reassuring smile as I sat down next to Francine, who was chuckling as Shelene Elliot begged on-screen Chris to please let the stunt doubles do their jobs.

"Okay, enough laughing at me for one day." Chris turned off the projector. "Let's get this meeting started."

"I'm sorry for being late." I was suddenly aware we were two hours behind schedule thanks to my massage and nap.

"It's only a few minutes; we'll make it up," Francine said.

"Weren't we supposed to start at ten?" I asked, looking at my watch.

"Noon." Francine pressed play on the remote Chris handed her.

"You did it again." I glared at Chris.

"Always so regimented," Chris said, sitting down on the other side of Francine. "You should be thanking me for the massage."

I took a deep breath and sighed. "I am grateful. Thank you, the massage was a lovely gift, but please just tell me the truth next time."

"Chris likes his little games." Francine's tone made me wonder what kind of games Chris had played with her. I didn't get a chance to pry, though, as she passed out binders to each of us.

I liked Francine. Her organization and preparation rivaled mine. When we met over tea for the first time, she came with a full presentation of ideas and options for casting the script, all of which I loved. During our read-throughs with actors, she'd been professional and serious about her work, while also bringing levity and humor when it was needed to break the nerves of the actors. She wasn't flashy like most people in Hollywood but had the kind of minimalist sophistication of style that you only saw in Paris or New York. Best of all, she didn't fawn over Chris, Drew, or any of the other celebrities we encountered during our auditions. She'd been in the industry long enough that star power had lost its appeal. Instead, she was interested in casting based on talent and chemistry, which I loved for our movie.

"My team and I have put together a compilation of possibilities for casting," Francine explained as she plugged her computer into Chris's projector. "I'd like to start with our two leading ladies. Open to the tab marked 'Laura and Mikayla,' and we'll begin."

Francine had been busy. The perfectly labeled and organized binders she'd handed us were full of headshots, resumes, and in-depth charts with various options for casting.

"My top choice for Mikayla"—Francine pressed play on the projector—"is Miel Garcia."

The screen lit up with a light-skinned, dark-haired woman with doe eyes and a confident smile. She was wearing a simple cotton T-shirt, boyfriend-cut jeans with a little paint on them, and ballet flats. Her hair and makeup were done simply as well, but despite the girl-next-door wholesomeness of the look she'd chosen, Miel was still impossible to take your eyes off of, alluring and completely comfortable in the spotlight. There was no denying Miel Garcia was a star, one that would shine in this role.

Unfortunately, she was competing against other, more established stars for the part. Drew and Chris had called in favors, and we got some famous actors to come in and read for Mikayla, including Kristen Bell and Anna Kendrick, among many other lesser-known but equally talented women, all of whom we watched play out their version of my sister on the screen.

About an hour after starting, Francine turned off the screen. She then pulled over a big corkboard with the character names on it and grabbed a stack of headshots. “Thoughts on Mikayla?”

“Obviously we’re going with Anna Kendrick,” Chris said, closing his book.

“Not obviously,” I quickly added. “I love Anna, but she’s not the right fit. I think we should go with Miel. She felt the most natural for the part.”

“Miel was great, but she’s a no-name,” Chris rebutted. “We need a star.”

“Diana is correct—I think Anna is great, but not for this role.” Francine moved headshots around her board. “I like Miel if we go with Henry Murdoch as the father. Explains her height.”

“And if we go with Stan Brown?” Drew asked.

“Then we should go for Reese Witherspoon,” Chris said.

“Ooh, if we go with Reese, we should try for Fred Dalton.” I loved the idea of Reese and Fred as father and daughter in this movie. “He’s tall and has the regal Southern feel like the dad in the story.”

“He’ll be hard to get,” Drew said.

“Is he expensive?” I asked.

“No, he’s dead,” he explained.

“Oh, damn, that sucks,” I replied.

“I’ll tell his family you send your condolences.”

I couldn’t tell if he was joking or if he really knew the Dalton family. With Drew, it could be either.

"We can't get Reese. She's booked with her own projects." Francine pointed to Chris's binder. "Hence why she's not in here. Can we stick to people we know are available, please?"

"Miel is available," I noted.

"I don't understand why you'd settle for a no-name when you can get a real star," Chris complained. "Fine, Anna isn't right for the role, but Kristen Bell is available and hugely popular right now. People will come just to see her, and we need asses in those seats or all of us are screwed."

Chris was right. I hated to admit it, but he was right. People would come to see Kristen Bell. Still, Kristen didn't fit like Miel did.

"We go with you." I pointed to Chris.

"Thanks, but I don't think I'm right for the role of Mikayla."

"But you're perfect for her husband," I countered.

"Take on a minor role of an asshole, abusive husband? My agent would flip."

"You're investing in your own film," I said. "Showing your broad range as an actor. Your agent could spin it."

"The brother-in-law barely has any lines," Chris pointed out.

"We can fix that. I know the writer." Ideas were already flowing in my head. "And he has a hot sex scene where you could show off your famously rock-hard abs and tight ass. The ladies, and multiple men I know, would come just to see that."

"Sure you don't just want to see Chris naked?" Drew smirked at me.

"Please"—I scoffed—"half the time I'm begging him to put a shirt on around here. But you can't deny people would come to see that."

"You know I'm not just a piece of meat." Chris's tone was

playful, but there was an underlying note of insecurity.

"This would be different than anything you've ever done," Francine considered.

"You've wanted to show range as an actor," Drew added.

"If I did say yes, which I'm not saying, we still need more big-name supporting actors if we're going with Miel as Mikayla," Chris rebutted.

"Okay." I flipped through the notebook Francine gave me, a plan coming to mind. "Drew as the ex–football star neighbor."

"Assuming I'm done with *Total Destruction 3* in time," Drew said.

"You'll be done," I reassured myself as much as him. I needed Drew on set; I couldn't deal with Chris on my own. "We can push your scenes until the last weeks to make sure."

"Miel as Mikayla"—Francine moved headshots around on her corkboard—"Chris as the husband, and Drew as the neighbor. I like it."

"Me, too," I said.

"Me, too," Drew agreed.

"If we go with Miel, we need someone big for Laura," Chris insisted.

Francine pulled out her options, and my heart broke a little. I'd always imagined being a triple threat, starring in the films I wrote and directed. But one screen test told us all that I should leave the acting to the professionals.

Still, I was protective of this role. I'd fictionalized the plot, changed details, and amped up drama for the movie, but at her core, Laura was me. I was the fat queer kid who grew up in a small, conservative farming town. I was the teenager who ran off to the big city the minute she graduated to find gay people like her. And I was the adult who got dragged back to that same conservative town full of my complex and complicated family when my brother died.

Every time I felt like giving up, every time I thought I would end it all, I told myself, "This will make a great story someday." I imagined myself up on the screen, playing out the happily ever after that I'd desperately needed to believe would happen. I'd lived for that moment, and I wasn't going to give that part of myself away to just anyone.

"I think we go with Kali," Chris said.

"Absolutely not," Drew rejected.

"She's too thin for the role," I pointed out.

"She's gained some weight back," Chris said.

"What she's gained is a reckless and out-of-control drug habit, from what I hear around town," Francine countered.

"Not to be an asshole, but how much weight are we talking?" I asked. I hated that we were debating the size of a woman's body, but I refused to let my fat character be played by someone who didn't have to shop in the plus-size section of stores. Kali used to be a fat icon, and a few years ago she'd have been perfect for this role, but lately she'd been on some kind of crash diet—or drug binge, depending on which tabloid you read—and had gone from a size eighteen to a size six.

"She can gain enough for the role," Chris affirmed.

"It doesn't matter, because she's not doing it," Drew said.

"Drew, please," Chris said, and it was the *please* that made me pause. Chris was pleading, which meant this wasn't just business. It was personal.

Chris, Kali, and Drew had been inseparable as teens, constantly seen in all the tabloids together, a modern-day Brat Pack growing up with all of their awkward and rebellious years broadcast for the world to see. But lately, Kali had been missing from their trio, and the gossip sites were full of rumors that Kali and Drew were secretly lovers, and Chris had been jealous and broken up the gang.

Had famously gay Kali fallen for the kindhearted Andy like I had? Did Drew really have a thing for queer women? Or were Chris and Kali the ones secretly in love, leaving Drew scorned? Also, why hadn't Kali shown up to Jaqueline's birthday?

I shook my head, realizing I sounded like one of Cecily's gossip magazines. It didn't matter what had happened between the three of them in the past; what mattered was who would be playing Laura in the future.

"Is she any good?" I asked Francine. "I didn't see her in the auditions."

"That's because she didn't show up," Francine said.

Drew threw out his hands in an exasperated gesture.

"You know she needs this," Chris appealed.

"She can't even show up for the fucking audition!" Drew yelled, getting up and pacing the room. "I'm sorry, Chris, I really am, but I don't want Kali on this film."

"You don't give up on family." Chris stood up, facing Drew head-on.

The two men stared at each other, a standoff between friends, with Francine and me as bystanders. I'd never seen either of them this heated, and I didn't know whether to speak up or let them glare each other to death.

"I think we should stop for the day." Francine stood and walked between the men, breaking the tension. "We can return to Laura later."

"I leave for filming tomorrow." Drew ran a hand through his hair and sat down in a chair.

"And I meet with Focus next week," Chris pointed out.

"Silvia is going to expect our top picks."

"We've all agreed Miel, Drew, and Chris are in?" Francine said, and everyone nodded their approval. "Then I can package them up and send it over. That should buy us some time to agree on a Laura."

"Fine," Chris seethed, his jaw clenched as he picked up his phone and headed toward the door. "Now, if you don't mind letting yourselves out, I need to make a call."

"Wait." I ran after him, my heart racing. I wasn't going to let this conversation end without standing up for my best friend. "We need to talk about Janelle."

"What about Janelle?" he shot back.

"I won't do this film unless she is my DP," I declared.

"Then don't do the film," Chris replied coldly, his jaw set, eyes red. He turned and walked away, leaving his words to linger like a dagger in my heart.

I turned to Drew, desperate for an ally in this fight. "Can you please talk with him?"

"Let it go, Diana," he mumbled, his face in his hands.

"Drew," I pleaded.

"Not now, Diana." Drew stormed off after Chris.

"What the bloody hell was that about?" Francine stood, dumbstruck.

"I was hoping you would know." I shook my head.

Together, we packed up the binders, tidied up the screening room, and headed out, speculating the whole time about what might or might not be going on between Drew and Chris, our guesses getting ever wilder until we were giggling at ridiculous theories involving orgies and sacrificial pets. We hadn't solved our casting issues, but I left there feeling a little more hopeful and a lot closer to Francine.

"It will work itself out." She patted me on the back as we headed toward our cars.

"Promise?" I leaned into her.

"No." Francine laughed. "But you've gotta keep the dream alive."

With that, she got in her car and drove off, leaving me standing alone in Chris's driveway, wondering if today's turmoil was a normal part of the movie-making process or if we'd just irrevocably lost the jovial nature of our producers. Part of me wanted to go back inside and demand that Chris tell me what the hell was going on, and another part of me wanted to run after Drew and kiss away any tension. But the bigger part of me, the part that saw through all this Hollywood bullshit to the core of my longing, really just needed to be able to talk to my sister and best friend about all of this, but neither of them wanted much to do with me right now.

Chapter Twenty-Two

Things felt tense in the group texts and emails we had for the next ten days, but Francine kept promising me it would all blow over. Chris had insisted that he and I drive together for our meeting with Focus, saying it was important to show up as a unified front. I loathed the idea of spending any time trapped in a car with him right now, but I acquiesced, promising myself I would let my annoyance with Chris fuel my fight for Janelle once we arrived.

"You're late," he said as soon as he saw me.

You're lucky I came at all, I wanted to respond, but instead I silently seethed as I slid into the passenger seat of his pretentious green Porsche.

Chris wove his way through the Hollywood Hills, past the homes of some of the country's richest and most powerful people, the people who decided which stories defined our culture, who got a voice and who was left out of the conversation. I'd spent so much of my life dreaming of access to these homes and the powerhouses within them, but now I was sitting in the car with one of them, and all I wanted to do was escape.

"You're shockingly quiet," Chris said as he pulled onto the 101 freeway.

"I have nothing to say to you," I replied.

"I thought you'd spend the whole car ride fighting for Janelle as DP," Chris admitted.

"I'm tired of trying to get straight white men to see things my way," I explained. "I'm saving my energy for Silvia."

"You think she's going to be any better?" Chris laughed without any humor behind it. "Who do you think I'm taking orders from?"

"Don't act like you're the innocent victim here," I rebutted.

"We're all victims to the machine of Hollywood," Chris countered as he pulled up to the Lankershim gate. "And none of us are innocent."

Chris flashed the guard his million-dollar smile and was waved through without having to show his credentials. He drove directly to Silvia's production office and pulled into a spot that said, Reserved for Chris Stanson and Associate.

That's what I would always be to him. An associate. That shopgirl who helped out Emmy one day, the Coffee Girl he continually overlooked. But this was my movie, my dream, my day. Yes, Drew and Chris had opened the door for me, but that didn't mean I didn't belong in the room. As we got out of the car and walked toward Silvia's office, I stood tall and strong in my resolve to fight for Janelle, not because she was my best friend but because she was the best cinematographer for this project, and she deserved to be in these rooms, too.

I followed Chris into Silvia's office, stopping abruptly when

I saw her assistant at the reception desk, remembering Chris's comment that she thought I was cute. I waved at her awkwardly, then went and sat down next to Chris.

"Go talk to her." He nudged me. "Get laid for all of our sakes."

"Have you no semblance of decorum?" I retorted as Silvia's door opened and her assistant beckoned us inside.

Chris turned on his charm, I plastered on my most confident smile, and together we headed into the executive's office, the professional imitation of a united front.

"We have a problem," Silvia said as a greeting, turning her computer toward us and showing a graphic image of two people having sex.

"And you lecture me on decorum," Chris remarked.

Silvia pressed play, and the camera panned out to show the moaning face of a young woman.

"I'll be damned," Chris let out.

"Meet Honey DeLucca, a.k.a. Miel Garcia." Silvia paused the film on a shot of Miel's ecstatic face. "Obviously, she's out."

My heart sank at the idea of replacing Miel. Not only was she great for the role of Mikayla, but she was also a lovely human. Miel had been friendly and kind during casting calls, and a quick search of her online showed an out, queer Latina who was active in her community. She was exactly the kind of person I wanted on set. If anything, being a sex worker made me like Miel even more.

"Who cares if she's worked in porn?" I asked.

"Hollywood hates porn valley," Chris explained.

"But Miel is perfect in the role. If anything, this just proves she's a great actress." I pointed to her face on the screen. "Because, really, there's no way she's enjoying herself that much."

"I'm sure you want your little friend to keep her job," Silvia said, "but we can't have this kind of thing popping up when we promote the film."

"It's not personal. It's business," I said.

"Precisely," Silvia affirmed.

"No, I meant I don't want to keep Miel because I like her personally. I barely know her. I want to keep her because she's good for this movie."

"A promiscuous woman is never good for a movie," Silvia chastised.

"So it's okay if Chris practically has sex on screen in this film and is considered the playboy of Hollywood, screwing his way through every famous starlet, but Miel has to be a virgin?"

"I don't make the rules." Silvia shrugged.

"But you'll enforce them." I scoffed.

"Chris, talk some reason into her," Silvia said, exasperation in her voice.

"I'm actually with Diana," Chris said, shocking us both.

"You are?" I muttered.

"It's not personal. It's business. The reason porn stars don't usually cross over is because they can't act. Miel can. She's perfect for this role. Plus, she'll bring fans with her." Chris turned his tablet over. "Look at how popular she is on PornHub."

"We can't take the Bible Belt press on this one," Silvia said. "Replace her."

"We really love Miel for this role," I insisted.

"And you'll really love whoever I get to replace her," Silvia said. "Now, who do you have for Laura? You're not seriously considering Kali, are you? That was a joke, right? Because if you think I'm going to fund a movie with that irresponsible, drug-addled shit show as its lead, you're stupider than you look, Chris."

Wow, there was so much problematic bullshit in that, I don't even know where to begin, I thought, sitting there fuming as Chris explained that Kali was doing better now, how she'd gained some weight and would be perfect for this role.

"I said no." Silvia's voice was firm, leaving no room for argument. "Which means you're here at a casting meeting with no cast. So what are you doing here besides wasting my time? You haven't even signed Jennifer Conger yet like I told you to do."

My heart stopped. Chris hadn't signed Jennifer yet. That meant there was still a chance for Janelle to be director of photography. "That's because we're going with Janelle Zenon instead." I grabbed Silvia's laptop, ignoring the look Chris gave me, and pulled up Janelle's IMDb profile.

"She's done nothing of substance." Silvia waved it off. "A few assistant jobs here and there. Why would you go with her instead of an award winner like Jennifer?"

"Budget," Chris responded, and I shot him a furious glance. I did not want Silvia thinking we were going with Janelle because she was cheap. We were going with her because she was talented and they were going to pay her what she's worth.

"And I set your budget," Silvia replied. "I don't want a nobody. I want Jennifer."

"Janelle is one of the most talented cinematographers I've ever met." I opened another browser and tried to find Janelle's sizzle reel online. "If you'll just watch—"

"I want Jennifer," Silvia interrupted without looking at the screen.

"And I want Janelle," I insisted, trying to keep my voice

steady. "I'm the director. Shouldn't I get a say in who my right-hand cinematographer will be?"

Silvia stared at me, taking my measure before turning to Chris. "Solidify that contract with Jennifer this week."

"I would really like you to reconsider," I said.

"And I would really like you to stop making this all so personal," Silvia shot back. "This is a business, and we're in it to make money. Jennifer will make us money, so she's in. Miel, Kali, and Janelle will not, so they're out. If you can't comprehend that simple, basic concept, then maybe you need to be out, too."

"Got it." I sat back in my chair, utterly defeated. There was nothing more I could do or say without risking my own role as director on this film, one I'd desperately wanted since I was a kid, and one I needed now that I'd quit Roussard's. I couldn't keep fighting for Janelle and Miel if I lost the only power I had. My hands were tied. I had to sit back and wait for another chance for all of us, hoping it came.

• • •

The rest of the meeting was a barrage of details, the little boring things that you don't think of when you're fantasizing about making a movie: catering budgets, production assistants, and whose trailer needed to go where to make this all happen. The sketches of the sets were coming along, and it was surreal seeing a backlot transformed into my little hometown. We'd have to do a few shots in the field, but mostly we'd be filming on a soundstage at Universal. Any other time, these details would have sent me into ecstatic excitement, but my dream for this film had always included a diverse cast and crew, and that dream was dwindling with each meeting we had.

"Chris, a moment alone," Silvia said as we were packing up to leave.

Chris nodded me on, and I didn't have the energy left to protest that I should be included in their conversation if it involved this film. Instead, I waited outside, watching people come and go, some carrying equipment, others dressed like zombies or store clerks. I thought I saw America Ferrera, but she disappeared too quickly for me to be sure.

"Let's go." Chris emerged a few minutes later, not waiting for me as he strode toward the car. I followed him, my emotionally exhausted body flopping into the passenger seat.

"What did you and Silvia talk about?" I was afraid to know the answer but had to ask.

"Budget stuff," Chris replied dismissively.

"Anything I should worry about?" I asked.

He started the car. "I'll take care of it."

"You sure?" I prodded, unconvinced.

"I said I'll take care of it," he responded, his voice angry.

"Okay." I put my hands up. "I'll drop it."

"Put on some music, will you?" Chris said as we left the Universal lot. "I'm tired of hearing my own thoughts."

Not sure what had gotten into Chris or what kind of music he liked, I put on Lucy Dacus's cover of Springsteen's "Dancing in the Dark," a song I turned to when life felt overwhelming and I needed a reminder that I've got this.

I put on boygenius's self-titled album next, and we let the music wash over us, singing along when we knew the words, which Chris surprisingly did. His voice was beautiful and in perfect pitch, reminding me that he got his start in musicals. It gave me flashbacks to Cecily playing his songs over and over again as a teen. My voice was not great, but I didn't care. I sang along anyway, not wanting to let my brain wander back to Silvia's office and what she might have said to Chris.

We made it through most of the album before Chris pulled into his driveway and parked next to my Subaru. He turned off the car, ending the music as he did. The contrasting silence sat heavily between us. I could tell he was readying himself to say something, and I dreaded what it would be. He took a deep breath, and let it go in a sigh. "Silvia said you're out."

I should have expected this. I should have known that's why they'd met without me. Still, Chris's words hit like a sucker punch to the gut.

I couldn't breathe. Couldn't get enough oxygen to my brain to think about what this meant. For me. For my movie. For my dreams.

I started gasping for air. I needed out of this car. I needed away from Chris.

Panicking, I opened the passenger door, falling down as I tried to get out, running away from it all, running away from Chris, the man that I'd stupidly thought for a brief moment today was in this together with me, a united front.

Of course that's what Silvia had wanted.

Of course Chris had agreed.

Of course I was out.

I was never in to begin with.

Chapter Twenty-Three

Chris's mansion felt gargantuan as I pushed myself through the large front door, tearfully making my way to the screening room. I went to the desk we'd set up in the corner for production material and started packing up my paperwork, the last remnants of my input on this film. I wanted to leave them there as proof that I existed, that I'd been a part of this team once, but I was too sentimental to abandon mementos. I might no longer be on this crew, but it was still the closest I'd gotten to directing a feature film. I wanted to keep a bit of the dream come true. I needed to remember I'd gotten this far, if only so I could remind myself that I'd get here again.

"I am not a one-hit wonder," I reminded myself.

"I never thought you were," Chris said, making me scream and drop my things. "Sorry, I didn't mean to sneak up on you."

"I'll be out of here soon." I bent over to pick up the papers I'd dropped, conscious of the fact that I'd overstayed my welcome in his world.

"Stay and spend the night with me," Chris replied.

I stood up, staring at him, utterly shocked. "Are you seriously hitting on me right now?"

Chris laughed, a full-belly, whole-body laugh. "If I was putting moves on you, you wouldn't have to ask." He smirked. "Plus, I'd never encroach on Drew's territory."

"I... What? You... Uh!" Confusion and irritation rose in me, making it hard to find words.

"So eloquent. I see why you're a writer." Chris shook his head.

"I am not Drew's territory, and I am not sticking around so you can laugh at me."

"You're so dramatic," Chris complained. "Is that a queer thing?"

"God, I really want to punch you in the face right now."

"Do it." Chris jutted out his chin. "It's insured."

"Your face is insured?" I asked, incredulous.

"Of course." He tapped a finger to his chin. "So punch away, if it will make you feel better."

I was tempted, very tempted, but I restrained myself and went back to packing up my things. "You're insufferable."

"Not as insufferable as the drive to Arcadia this time of day," Chris said. "Stay and have dinner with me."

"I can't just sit here and pretend like everything is okay." My voice cracked as new tears formed. "The film is over and my dreams are gone. I just want to go home and cry."

"There's that drama again." Chris shook his head.

"And there's that desire to punch you again," I replied.

"You can punch me if it would help. You can pack up and run away if you'd like. But I think I have a better option."

"And what is that?" I asked.

"You'll see," he said, a mischievous smile on his face as he turned and walked out of the screening room.

"And you call me dramatic!" I shouted after him. I wanted to grab my things and go, to pack up and never see Chris Stanson's face again, even onscreen. Yet, despite my trepidation and resentment, I couldn't stop my curiosity from following the sound of his voice into the kitchen.

"Buona sera, signorina," Chris sang along with Louis Prima as he spread dough out on the counter. While I had been crying in the screening room, Chris had apparently been busy in the kitchen. Bowls of chopped garlic, torn basil, and lumps of mozzarella were laid out before me, a decanter of wine sitting next to them.

"This is your solution?" I said, looking at Chris. "Food?"

"Food is always the solution." Chris tossed the dough into the air with artful skill.

"For once we agree on something." I settled myself on a bar stool and silently watched him work his magic, tossing the dough into the air a few more times before placing it on a wooden plank and covering it with just the right amount of toppings. Simón Barboza had been right; Chris knew his way around a kitchen.

"Follow me"—Chris carried the plank of raw ingredients outside—"and bring the wine."

He led me toward a wood-fired oven that I'd never noticed before and gently placed the pizza inside.

"Now we wait." He grabbed the decanter from where I'd placed it on a table and poured us both a glass of wine.

"Chris, about the—" I started.

"Food first," he interrupted, "then business."

I sighed, walking over to the edge of his backyard, sipping my wine as I looked out onto the L.A. basin and a sliver of the ocean beyond, the view obstructed by fog and smog but still beautiful. I remembered sitting here enjoying it with Janelle all those months ago. So much had happened since then and now; so much of our lives had changed. I just hoped it was for the better.

A few minutes later, Chris called me over to a set table, placing a perfectly toasted pizza in the middle before cutting it with a rolling knife, then handing me a slice on a white porcelain plate. "Don't worry, it's gluten-free for your delicate little tummy."

I smiled in thanks as I sat down. Chris topped off our wine glasses and held his up. "Saluti."

"Saluti." I clinked my glass against his.

My stomach growled as I grabbed a slice of pizza from the middle of the table and took my first bite. It was salty, sweet, crunchy, and gooey all at once, a total masterpiece.

"Chris, this is amazing," I exclaimed.

"Don't look so shocked." He lifted his own slice to his mouth. "I told you I could cook."

"What's shocking is that you're actually eating carbs."

"I'm tired of denying myself the things that bring me joy." Chris's voice was sad, and I wondered what else this man who had everything could be missing from his life.

"Are we just talking about pizza here?"

"Pasta, too," he replied, smirking.

"You poor, deprived soul." I rolled my eyes, taking another slice.

"I once spent a month in Italy studying under a pizzaiolo, learning to make dough from the masters." Chris sounded wistful and nostalgic. "And I didn't eat any of it."

"That is quite tragic," I replied honestly, taking a big bite of my pizza and savoring every carb-filled flavor.

"I couldn't afford to get fat."

"Yes, because being fat is the worst thing someone could be."

"It's fine for other people," he claimed, "but I would lose everything if I got fat: my career, my money, my lifestyle. That's why this production company matters to me. I don't want to lose everything when I lose my looks."

"That actually makes me really sad for you," I confessed.

"Do you know what I think about when I'm lying in bed alone at night?" Chris asked.

"No, and I'm not sure I want to," I replied.

Chris continued, ignoring my snide remark. "I dream of standing on stage with a little golden man in my hands. I dream of placing him on the shelf I had made for awards in my office, a shelf that has stayed frustratingly empty since I had it built five years ago. The minute I read your script, I knew it was going to help me finally fill that shelf."

"You believe that much in my film?" I asked.

"Why else would I have agreed to take it on?" Chris replied.

"I figured Drew convinced you into it."

"Trips to Vegas, drunken putt-putt golf, charity auctions, those are the kind of things Drew and I convince each other into. Business deals, movies—we take them on only after consulting lawyers, agents, and accountants. This movie is a good bet, but you're still a gamble. One I'm not willing to lose."

"Is that why you agreed to let me go?" Anger and betrayal boiled back up in me. "Because you care more about filling your narcissistic shelf than you care about me and this film?"

"You have a shit contract," Chris replied.

"It's the best my agent could get."

"Probably true," Chris considered, "although we might need to get you a new agent if she's willing to have you sign contracts like that one."

"I get it, I have a shit contract," I growled. "You don't need to rub salt in my wounds."

"I, on the other hand, have a great agent," Chris continued. "One of the best in the business actually, with a full team of lawyers behind him. I don't sign shit contracts."

"Congratulations," I retorted. "You have a great contract, and I'm fucked."

"Except you're not, even if I think you probably need to be." Chris winked. "You know, I have Silvia's assistant's number, if you want it."

"I'm leaving." I stood up, tired of his bullshit and hating myself for falling for the "good guy making pizza" routine.

"Sit down, Diana. I'm just getting to the good part."

"Make it quick, or I'm going to pour the rest of this bottle of wine on your head."

"That's a Tenute Silvio Nardi 1995 Brunello di Montalcino," Chris bragged. "One of a few left in the world."

"And?"

"And you shouldn't waste such a special, celebratory bottle by pouring it over my head," he answered.

"What exactly are we celebrating?" My patience was waning.

"Like I told you"—Chris took a sip of his wine—"I have a great contract, one that includes a clause that I can walk away and take this film with me at any point before production starts. A clause I used today when I told Silvia to go fuck herself and bought back the script."

"How the hell did you get that?" I sat back down, stunned.

"It cost me." Chris looked around at his house. "A lot. But it will pay off in the end."

"How do you know?" I asked.

"Because it has to," he replied.

"Why?" I had to know. "Why would you risk everything like that?"

Chris sat back in his chair and stared at his glass of wine for a long time before responding. "The way you kept speaking up for Janelle, not shutting up about it, even when I yelled at you to drop it, even when it could cost you everything. It made me wonder if there were people in my life worth fighting for like that." He took a sip of wine before continuing. "Turns out, there are."

"Well damn." I reclined in my chair and looked at the scene in front of me with new eyes. "It worked."

"What worked?" Chris asked.

"Food." I grabbed the last slice of pizza. "I feel a lot better now."

"Don't forget the wine." Chris lifted his glass.

"How could I forget the wine?" I said, taking a sip. "I can't believe you did this."

"Bought out the studio or made that pizza?"

"Both." I chuckled as I took another bite. "You know, you and Simón Barboza would make a great team."

"What makes you say that?" Chris asked.

"Because this pizza is perfection," I mumbled, my mouth full. "His omelet, your pizza, this view. You could open the most exclusive restaurant in town right here in your kitchen."

"Simón is out of my league," Chris said.

"Probably," I agreed, savoring the last bit of crust, "but damn, I'd love to see what you two could create together."

Chris smiled and got up from the table, returning a few minutes later with a platter of bright red strawberries dipped in dark chocolate. "Do you want dessert?"

"Hell yes, I do." I grabbed a strawberry. "Because fat girl."

"You say that phrase so lovingly. Why?" Chris asked. "Most people are scared to call themselves fat, but you use that word with pride."

"It's something I learned from fat activists," I explained, trying to find a way to express what this phrase meant to me. "It's more than just words. It's a motto and movement all in one. It's a way to embrace the stereotypes and realities of being fat, like breaking a chair I sit in, or eating a basket of fries with cheese, or lying down for a nap after the gym. The kind of things people ridicule fat people for but think it's cute when a thin girl does it.

"But it's also about more important things, too," I continued. "Like not being taken seriously by a doctor because of my weight, getting passed up for jobs because of my size, not being able to find clothes that fit, and not being taken seriously when sexually assaulted, because who would want to sleep with a fatty? Situations that have happened to me and my fat friends.

"For me, saying 'because fat girl' is both a reclamation of the term *fat* and a rallying cry for the better treatment of fat people," I stated. "It encompasses the good, the bad, the everything of life as a fat feminine person in this world."

"Because fat girl." Chris nodded.

"Because fat girl," I said, taking another strawberry.

"That should be your company name," Chris proposed. "Because Fat Girl."

"Why do I need a company name?" I questioned.

"First off, you need a company to cover your assets," Chris lectured. "I can't believe you don't have one yet. You really need a new agent."

"Please stop bagging on my agent," I said.

"Second, you need a company name because you'll be producing this film with us."

"I'll be what?" I spat, shocked and confused.

"We're going to need any savings you got. Make your sister get a second mortgage on her house if you have to," Chris replied. "And in exchange, you'll get production credits."

"Holy shit," I exclaimed, thinking about the nest egg I'd saved for just this moment. "I'm going to be a producer."

"Cheers." Chris lifted his glass to mine. "To Because Fat Girl Productions."

"Because Fat Girl Media," I corrected. "I like the expansiveness of that."

"Should we call Drew and tell him the news together?" Chris asked.

At the sound of Drew's name, my heart fluttered. I'd been so wrapped up in Focus and the film, I'd forgotten about Drew, and all the complicated feelings that accompanied him came rushing back. Before I could come up with a plausible reason to object, Chris had already dialed his number.

"Ciao, Chris," a thickly accented voice answered.

"Ciao, Elena." Chris's voice oozed with flirtation. I rolled my eyes. "How's filming?"

"We are delayed, but that just means more time alone with your handsome friend here," Elena cooed.

"Can you put him on, please?" Chris replied.

"He'll need to put some pants on first." Elena giggled as she passed the phone over.

"Hey, Chris, little busy over here. What's up?" Drew sounded rushed and annoyed, the voice of someone who'd been interrupted. I tried not to think about what he was doing with Elena in his trailer with no pants on.

"Elena can wait," Chris asserted. "We need to talk."

"Hold on." Drew went silent for a moment before returning. "Okay, let me hear it."

"Focus is out," Chris said.

Drew exhaled loudly in response.

"We're not going to let that stop us," I added, trying to sound as optimistic as possible.

"Oh, hey, Diana." Drew sounded surprised. "I didn't realize I was on speaker."

"Sorry," I apologized, "should have said something earlier."

"What's next, then?" Drew asked.

"We fundraise," Chris proclaimed. "We were going to have to do that anyways. At least now we own the film."

"What about distribution?" Drew inquired.

"We'll cross that bridge when it comes," Chris responded.

"How'd it go down?" Drew asked.

"Does it matter?" Chris replied.

"I guess it doesn't," Drew said as Elena started saying something in the background. "I gotta go. They're calling us to set."

"I'll have Bradley and Veara arrange a time for us to talk details," Chris said. Drew grunted his agreement and said goodbye.

"Bye," I blurted too late, the line already dead.

Chris picked up his glass of wine and stared at me.

"What?" I asked, very much disliking his scrutinizing gaze.

"All this time, I thought you were just flirting with Drew to get your film made. I couldn't fault you for it—that's how things go in this town, I did the same when I first got started. But now I think it's more than that. Does Drew know?"

"Does Drew know what?" I pulled my wine glass up to my mouth to hide the panic rising in me at this line of questioning.

"I don't think he does." Chris disregarded my feigned ignorance. "Drew's so obviously into you; I've known that since the LACMA party. If he knew you liked him, too, if he thought he had even a sliver of a chance, he'd be on the first plane back here to sweep you off your feet. He's a romantic asshole like that."

"He knows," I said quietly.

"He can't know," Chris insisted. "He wouldn't be pants off in a trailer with Elena if he knew you had feelings for him, too."

"Trust me," I choked up, "he knows."

"Then why is it Elena in his trailer and not you?"

"Because fat girl," I answered.

"Your choice, I'm assuming." Chris's gaze was scrutinizing me. "Drew wouldn't care about that, but you would. You don't want to care, but you do."

"There's no way it would work," I argued.

"You're right. The press would have a heyday with it, the used-to-be-gay fat girl and the used-to-be-fat action star. It even plays into the harmful idea that all lesbians are just waiting for the right dick. I can see why you wouldn't want any of that."

"Thank you!" I threw my hands up in relief. "Finally someone who gets it. Drew keeps saying we'd find a way to work it out, but how? How do you overcome that kind of press?"

"I don't know," Chris replied, his tone serious. "I don't think you can."

"You can't."

"I'm sorry." Chris placed his hand over mine. "For both of you."

"Me, too." I nodded.

"Look at us." Chris took his hand off of mine and leaned back in his chair. "You're not the frigid bitch I thought you were. I'm not the cold asshole you thought I was. We're learning so much about each other tonight."

I chuckled and finished off the last of my wine.

"So"—Chris continued—"we just heard how he's moving on. What are you going to do to put this behind you?"

"I'm going to finish this film," I said. "That's all I need."

"Wow, that's pathetic."

"Not all of us can be notorious playboys like you," I retorted. "Some of us care about things other than sex."

"I am so sorry to hear there are people like that in the world." He placed his hand dramatically to his chest. "I don't care if it's sex or tennis, you need to let off some steam. It won't do us any good if you keep exploding from how wound up you are."

He had a point. My whole body ached from lack of sleep, my mind was fried, my nerves frazzled—and we weren't even in production yet.

"Kali is having a party," Chris said. "It's more like a trip. A long weekend excursion on her yacht."

"Intriguing." I thought about it, torn between the excitement of being on a famous lesbian's boat and the fear of being in the middle of the ocean with someone publicly struggling with addiction right now. "You want me to go on a yacht with Kali?"

"Oh god no," Chris exclaimed.

"You don't have to be quite so repulsed at the idea of me in a bikini," I replied.

"What I meant is that you'd hate it," Chris explained. "Kali's parties are always a glamorous shit show, pretty much everything you despise and full of everyone you complain about the most."

"I don't complain," I interjected. "I critique."

"You complain," he confirmed. "And trust me, you'd be miserable at this event."

"So how is this supposed to help me?" I asked, utterly confused by this man in front of me.

"I said no at first—our whole weekend was booked with meetings. But I think this trip is just what we both need."

"How does you partying on a yacht help me?"

"I'd be gone"—Chris spread his arms around—"and you would have free range of my house. The screening room, the pool, the gym, and a whole staff of people to clean up after you. You could call up some lady and scissor all night."

"You know most of us don't really scissor, right?" I said. "It's way more complicated and overrated than porn makes it out to be."

"Then do whatever you do then. Throw a giant party and invite every queer person in town. Get stoned and fuck in every room," Chris added, "except for mine."

"I take it back," I said. "I'm going to scissor directly on your pillow."

"If that's what it takes to get you to let loose, fine. I'll be sure to have Rosalie change the sheets before I return."

I looked around at his place. "You've got nice things here; I'd be too worried to throw a giant party."

"I'll send my security guys over to keep everyone from going upstairs," Chris replied. "The rest is replaceable."

"I don't even like giant parties."

"Then throw a small one."

"I've got a house of my own, you know."

"In Arcadia. Full of kids. That's no place to let off steam."

"I like those kids." I couldn't deny I was enjoying my time away from being a co-parent, but I did miss pancakes and painting.

"Then have your sister pack up the brats and come stay here. Lounge in my pool during the day and watch movies at night."

"You're serious?" I gawked.

"As serious as your need to get laid." He lifted his glass. "We both could use a weekend off to relax."

"And then what?" I wondered. "What do we do after that?"

Chris leaned his head back, drinking down the last of his wine. Then he looked me directly in the eyes, his tone as serious as I'd ever seen it. "After that, we find a way to make this film. Our way with our people. Focus be damned."

Chapter Twenty-Four

The sun had barely risen, and already Cecily, Ellis, and Reggie were pounding on the door, demanding to be let in.

"The kids were so excited to go swimming that they woke me up extra early," Cecily said, looking as exhausted as I felt. Her arms were full of everything they needed to spend the day here, plus a bag of clothes for me.

Chris and I had stayed up late last night talking about logistics, debating whether or not Kali would make a good Laura and agreeing that Janelle would make a great DP. I ended up crashing in his guest bedroom, too tired to make the drive home, and asked Cecily to bring me a few days' worth of outfits when I invited her and the kids over. Before he left in the morning, Chris showed me the lay of the land and suggested I start keeping a change of clothes, both casual and professional, here in case we had future late-night work sessions. I was too stunned by the suggestion to do anything but nod.

"This place is awesome!" Ellis ran from room to room, Reggie following after them.

"I can't believe we're in Chris Stanson's home." Cecily gawked as I led her to the coffee bar. "This place is surreal."

Surreal but nice, I thought, remembering the LACMA party and my first awkward interactions with Drew in this place. Now, I was spending the night in Chris's guest bedroom and hosting family and friends at his house. Surreal indeed.

"Would you like some tea?" I pointed to Chris's new Breville specialty tea maker. "This thing is so fancy. You tell it what kind of tea you're making and the kettle automatically steeps it at the exact right temperature for the exact right time."

"That is hella bougie," Cecily agreed, eyeing the appliance. "I need one."

I'd been touched last night when Chris showed off the kettle and the large selection of high-end teas he'd gotten just for me, making a point to highlight that the tea was from an Asian-American queer-owned tea company out of San Diego named PARU. Apparently he'd told Bradley to stock up on options for me after finding out I didn't drink coffee. It was a simple gesture, mostly carried out by Bradley, but combined with everything Chris had done and said these past twenty-four hours, I was beginning to feel an immense fondness for him, so much so that I hugged him tightly before he left. He told me to stop being so emotional and let him go, but I could see the smile on his lips.

"Black tea okay?" I asked my sister.

"Yes, please, caffeine." Cecily sidled up to the coffee bar while the kids cannonballed into the pool outside. Chris's big windows and open-floor plan made it easy to watch them from anywhere in the house. "So where are you hiding Andy?"

"What?" I asked, filling the kettle with purified water.

"Come on, late-night production meeting is totally code for 'I'm getting laid,'" Cecily coaxed. "And I know it wasn't Chris you were sleeping with."

"How do you know I'm not sleeping with Chris?"

Cecily laughed in reply.

"It could happen," I insisted.

"There is no world in which you and Chris Stanson could happen," Cecily assured.

"Look around you," I said. "Chris Stanson and I are happening."

"Oh my god." Cecily leaned in and whispered, "Are you really screwing Chris Stanson?"

"Of course not! He's so not my type"—I laughed at the idea—"but the guy is growing on me."

"I can see why." Cecily motioned around the house.

"Have I finally made it up to you for missing the kids' recital?" I asked.

"You're getting there," Cecily allowed. "Introduce me to Chris Stanson and we'll forget it ever happened."

"One day." I handed her a mug. "Here, try this."

Cecily took a sip and smiled. "Chris Stanson has very good taste in tea. I like him even more."

"Chris hates tea," I said, leading us both outside. "He bought this especially for me."

"You sure you're not sleeping together?" Cecily asked, sitting down by the pool.

"He wishes he could get this." I slapped my ass before lying back dramatically on a lounge chair.

"That's a lot of stuff you had me bring," Cecily pointed out. "Are you planning on moving in?"

"Chris suggested I keep some clothes here, and I agree. It could be good for me to be closer to the headquarters of our film."

"I'm sure none of your decision has to do with the fact that your headquarters are located in a movie star's mansion in Beverly Hills."

"It sure doesn't hurt." I smiled, staring out at the view.

"How long do you think you'll be here?" Cecily asked.

"I have no idea." I got up to push a button on the wall that opened an automatic shade for us. "Chris comes back Monday, and I'm going to stay until then."

"Wait, if Chris comes back Monday, we're spending the night, too!" Cecily sat up. "Gotta take advantage of this place."

"Sorry, he said only day guests," I lied. I loved Cecily and the kids, but I needed space to think.

"I get it." Cecily's tone told me she absolutely did not get it. "Us simple folk aren't fancy enough to stay here with you."

"I'm a guest in this place, just like you," I reminded her. "I'll be kicked out soon, don't you worry."

"Well, thanks for inviting us over while you could." Cecily smiled.

We lay there in silence, side by side on lounge chairs, enjoying the view, watching the kids splash around playing mermaid, just like we used to do as kids. Cecily would be Ariel, the princess, and I would be Ursula, the sea witch trying to steal her voice. Ursula was my favorite, the only Disney character I related to as a kid. Sure, she was technically a villain, but she was also a fat, queer woman of color who had her throne stolen by a muscular old white man. The little feminist in me loved Ursula and wanted her to win in the end, which she did when I played her.

Sometimes Henry would be King Triton, and I would steal my throne back from him, and sometimes he would be Flounder, trying to save Cecily from me. Once he'd been Scuttle, but when he jumped in to swim with us, Cecily chided him, saying seagulls can't swim, so he quit and became a shark, chasing us around the sunken ship instead.

We'd spent hours in the pool, our skin turning into prunes. My mother would threaten or bribe us to get out for dinner, but we'd always jump back in, continuing our games. Cecily and Henry tried out for the swim team in high school, but by then I wanted nothing to do with pools and the revealing swimsuits associated with them. I was in my twenties before I felt comfortable in a bikini again, and even then I was on edge, waiting for someone to laugh and call me Shamu.

The day Henry died, I jumped fully clothed into my parents' pool, sinking to the bottom, never wanting to emerge again. Since then, pools had been therapy for me, the weightlessness of water relieving the burden of grief.

"You want to get in?" I asked Cecily.

"Not yet. I'm enjoying being lazy."

"There's a window down here!" Reggie said, popping up out of the water. "I can see into the house!"

"It's so you can watch people swim from inside if you want," I told her, hearing myself as I said it. "This place is a bit ridiculous, isn't it?"

"It's no Arcadia." Cecily sighed, putting her hands behind her head. "But it'll do."

I was about to climb into the pool when a chime in the bushes signaled someone was at the front gate. I walked inside and let Janelle in.

"Hey," I said, opening the big black slab of wood.

"Hey." She smiled awkwardly as she walked in.

"Thanks for coming."

"I couldn't pass up snooping around Chris's house," Janelle replied, taking in her surroundings.

"It is quite impressive," I agreed, still feeling the tension between us. "Cecily and the kids are outside by the pool. Can we talk a bit?"

"Sure." Janelle followed me into Chris's living room, both of us sitting down on his white sofa.

I took a deep breath and started the apology I'd practiced many times in my head this morning. "I'm sorry I didn't stand up for you more vigorously earlier on. I tried, I really did, but I didn't try hard enough. I got wrapped up in my own shit and was afraid I'd lose this job if I rocked the boat too much. But you're important to me, and this dream isn't complete without you in it."

"Thank you for saying that," Janelle replied.

"I'm also sorry about showing up at your place unannounced. I've been your best friend for over a decade. I should have known you'd have a girl hanging around on a weekend night. I'm sorry if I ruined your orgasm."

Janelle chuckled at that. "Crystal did take some convincing that you weren't a hookup. But don't worry. She came around."

"I'm sure she did." I wiggled my eyebrows.

"A warning would have been nice, though," Janelle admitted, "but you know I'm not mad at you for coming to my house, right?"

"I know," I conceded.

"I'm not even mad at you about being off the film," she continued. "Hell yes, I'm mad at the situation. It sucks, but studios pull this shit all the time. That part isn't your fault.

What is your fault, what I am pissed off about, is that you lied to me for so long. Making me think we were still in this together. Equals. It's the fakeness that bothers me."

"I thought I could convince Focus to change their minds," I explained.

"You can't change Hollywood, Diana. I've been telling you that for years."

"That doesn't mean we can't keep trying."

"I'm not going to stop trying," Janelle said. "I just need to be realistic in my expectations."

"This is why we need our own production company," I said.

"Hold up, let me go get a lottery ticket," Janelle teased.

"Actually, I was thinking more like using this house." I looked around me.

"What, you're going to steal Chris's shit now and sell it?" Janelle asked. "Because if so, I want that Warhol."

"Good idea, but no." I leaned forward. "It just so happens that Chris Stanson is a decent human being. Or at least he's trying to be one."

"I'll believe it when I see it." Janelle rolled her eyes.

"I didn't believe it, either, but I saw it with my own eyes yesterday. We went to Focus with a list of people we wanted on this film. You were on it. Focus said no to all of them. So Chris told them to fuck off."

"I bet they did not like that." Janelle scoffed.

"No, they did not like that at all." I wish I had been there to see the look on Silvia's face. "Chris has a buy-back clause in his contract. When he told Focus to go fuck themselves, he cut ties with them, initiating that clause and buying back the film rights. He had to get a second mortgage on this house to do it, but he did. And now it's ours. Which means—"

"Which means you get to pick your team," Janelle interrupted, realization dawning on her.

"I get to pick my team," I confirmed.

"So let me get this straight," Janelle continued tentatively. "We get to make this movie together after all?"

"We get to make this movie together after all," I affirmed, a giant smile on my face.

"Damn, Diana, way to bury the lede." Janelle fell back onto the sofa. "Being your friend is a roller-coaster."

"In a good way?" I asked, wondering where our friendship stood.

"Depends on the day." Janelle smiled. "But yeah, in general, I love being your friend."

"And I love being yours." I nudged her with my shoulder.

"Any other surprises hanging out up your sleeve?" Janelle asked, pointing to a wet bar in the corner. "Because I'm gonna be drunk off of Chris's most expensive booze later, so get 'em all out now."

"I…" I hesitated. Now would be a good time to tell her about Drew. "No."

Janelle sat back up. "What? What was that? So help me god, if you tell me I'm second DP or something, I'm going to lose it."

"No, it's nothing like that," I assured her. "It's just… Okay, don't freak out, but I kind of kissed someone the other night. Before coming to your house."

"My girl finally got some!" Janelle cheered, doing a little dance. "Tell me all about her."

"Him," I corrected, looking at Janelle's face to judge her reaction.

"A trans guy?" Janelle cocked her head. "I can get behind that."

"Not trans," I said.

"Genderqueer?" she asked.

"*Cis. Het.*" I emphasized both words.

"Damn." Janelle dropped back onto the sofa. "Now that's some big news. How did that even happen?"

"It was cold outside. We cuddled under a blanket. One thing led to another... I stopped it early, but it still happened."

"When were you even out with a dude?" Janelle asked. "You only hang out with queer people and Cecily. You don't even know cishet men, except... Holy shit, was it Chris Stanson?"

"Absolutely not," I replied emphatically.

"Thank god," Janelle sighed. "I could not handle you going out with some famous bro type."

My face cringed involuntarily, the impact of Janelle's words rolling through me, the fear of losing my queer community if this got out turning my stomach to knots.

"Oh god, Diana." Realization dawned on Janelle's face. "Tell me you didn't."

"It just happened," I admitted.

"This could go very badly," Janelle said. "For you, for me, for him, for this whole film."

"I know!" I protested. "That's why I stopped it."

"I can't say I'm surprised," Janelle said. "The way he looks at you."

"Wait, how does he look at me?" I asked.

"I just didn't think you'd go for that nice-guy act," Janelle continued without answering me.

"It's not an act," I responded.

"You actually like him?" Janelle was looking at me like I said I'd been abducted by aliens.

"Yes. No. I don't know." I fell back onto the sofa with an

exasperated sigh. "Drew's great, but I could never date him. If people found out about us, then that's it. I'm forever changed in everyone's eyes, and so is this film."

"You know who you sound like?" Janelle asked.

"Who?"

"You, freshman year of college, when you were trying to figure out how to tell your parents that Kate was your girlfriend."

I laughed. "I haven't felt this closeted since college. You'd think it would be easier, saying you're falling for a guy. That's what women are 'supposed' to do, right? Fall for men like Drew Williams. But I can't stop thinking about what my friends and family would say if they knew."

"If you like the guy and he's good to you, who fucking cares?" Janelle asserted.

"I care," I said, emotion rising in me. "I wish I didn't, but I do. I see how we treat bisexuals in society, and it's not good. I've been guilty of it myself. Punishing women who end up with men because of the privilege they gain. Their queerness seemingly erased because of their relationship."

"That's some biphobic bullshit," Janelle spat.

"It is bullshit, but that doesn't mean it's not real," I cried. "I don't want to give up my place in the queer community. I don't want to be ostracized by my friends. I don't want to be some fodder for newspapers about the has-been dyke fatty dating the famous bro dude. I just… I can't. I want to not care, but I do."

"Screw them!" my best friend yelled. "If you want to date Drew, you should do it. I'm not going to judge."

"You already did," I reminded her.

Janelle and I sat in silence a bit, letting my words sink in.

"I'm sorry," she said finally. "I thought it was just a silly crush."

"I wish it were that simple." I sighed. "Then I could just fuck him and get it out of my system."

"Just like you tried with Kate in college." Janelle laughed.

I laughed with her. "And we all know how well that worked out."

"So what are you going to do about Drew?"

"I'm going to push down my feelings until either this movie is done or I explode, whichever comes first."

"Sounds like a horrible plan"—Janelle reached out her hand and clasped mine—"but I'll be here by your side as it inevitably fails."

"Thank you." I squeezed. "You know, I never would have done the film without you, right? I would have found a way to have you as my DP. I will never stop bidding on your dreams, too."

Janelle smiled, returning my grasp. "I will never stop bidding on my dreams, either."

I laughed. "Good."

"Now, if you're done being all touchy-feely"—Janelle stood—"I've got a house to explore."

"Let me know if you find anything salacious," I said, standing after her.

"I'm keeping all blackmail material to myself." Janelle walked toward the stairs. "Mama needs her own production company."

"Hey..." I caught her before she walked away. "Don't tell anyone about Drew, okay? No one else knows, not even Cecily."

Janelle pantomimed locking her lips shut as the buzzer on the wall rang. When I looked to see who was here, Shamaya smiled back at me from inside a matte-pink Porsche Roadster. She zoomed up the driveway and parked right by the front door, unloading multiple bags of food from our favorite deli, Joan's on Third.

"Oh my god, you're the best," I declared, enlisting Janelle to help us unload it all. There were omelets, quiches, bacon, hash browns, and, of course, orange juice and champagne.

"Did you buy the whole menu?" Janelle joked.

"Two of everything, actually," Shamaya said, closing her car door.

"This is why I love you." I hugged her, then carried the food out to the pool area.

"Shamaya brought Joan's!" I shouted, laying the containers out on the table under the shade.

"You're my new best friend," Cecily said, grabbing a bit of crisped prosciutto.

The food was fabulous, and even picky-eater Reggie found something she liked, hogging all of the hash browns and refusing to share.

"That was so amazing I kind of want to cry now that it's gone." Cecily stared down at the empty containers.

"No need for tears. I'm having Tres deliver us lunch in a few hours," Shamaya boasted.

"Will you marry me?" Cecily asked.

"Absolutely," Shamaya replied, "just as soon as Chris Stanson and I divorce."

"Careful there," I warned. "Cecily will fight you for him."

"And I took one Tae Bo class in the nineties, so watch out." Cecily put up her fists.

"What's it like, working with him?" Shamaya asked.

"Most of the time he's an entitled, egotistical prick, and I have to sit on my hands to not punch him in the face," I said. "But sometimes, he completely surprises me and his heart shines through. Like last night, when we found out Focus pulled its funding—"

"Focus pulled out?" Cecily interrupted. "I can't believe you didn't tell us this sooner."

"I didn't want to ruin our fun," I said, explaining the situation to them.

"What's your plan now?" Shamaya asked when I was done. "How can we help?"

"You can't," I said, feeling defeated. "Unless you happen to have five million dollars and a distribution company that can get our film in theaters."

"Sorry, all out." Janelle pretended to empty her pockets.

"Darn," Cecily joined, snapping her fingers. "Used up my last million a week ago."

"Actually," Shamaya said, leaning forward and smiling mischievously.

Chapter Twenty-Five

The doorbell rang, and Chris yelled that he'd get it.

"He acts like answering his own door is doing us all a huge favor." I rolled my eyes.

"It's a miracle you've lasted this long without punching him," Shamaya said.

Over the last six weeks, Chris's house had become headquarters for *Home Bound*, and we'd become something closer than colleagues, maybe even on our way to friends. I was beginning to realize that underneath all of the masculine playboy bravado was a tender, feminine energy I felt lucky to get to see. Just the same, he still infuriated me most days.

"Did you know his face is insured?" I told her.

"Really?" she replied.

"I know, it's totally ridiculous, I mean, really, who—" I stopped mid-sentence, catching sight of a tall, broad figure standing in the doorway. I knew Drew was on his way, understood that he would be here at any moment, but still, seeing him there took my breath away. We'd texted and emailed a bit, mostly about the production, but not a night had gone by when I hadn't thought about him, wondering what he and Elena were up to on set together and hating myself for caring.

"Hi," he said.

"Hi." I tried to smile but ended up in some kind of lopsided smirk.

Drew looked good. *Real* good. His hair was a little overgrown, slightly floppy, but I liked it that way. He was wearing a simple T-shirt-and-jeans combo with slip-on shoes and a hesitant grin.

"You look tan." I blurted out the first thing I could think of to fill the awkward silence.

"Sixteen-hour days on set in Hawaii will do that to you," he said as he walked toward me.

"Let me officially introduce you to Shamaya." I pointed to my friend, trying to distract myself from staring at Drew.

"It's an honor to meet you in person." He shook Shamaya's hand. "I admire your father's work, and I'm excited to see your own style of producing emerge. I'm looking forward to getting to know you better."

"And I, you." Shamaya shook his hand. "Diana has told me so much about you already."

"She has?" Drew looked over at me inquisitively.

"Shamaya has heard all about how we met and the production plight so far," I answered, hoping he would understand that was code for *Shamaya knows nothing about what happened between us, and I'd like to keep it that way.*

"Time for a little celebration." Chris emerged back into the room and handed us each a champagne flute. "Before we get shoved into our fashionable but horribly uncomfortable clothes, I wanted a little time alone together for a toast."

Chris popped a bottle of champagne and poured us each a glass. He lifted his, and we all followed, standing there waiting with our arms in the air.

"Are you going to give a speech?" I asked. "Or are we just going to hold these up like idiots all night?"

"I'm thinking," Chris stalled.

"Don't hurt yourself," I joked.

Chris rolled his eyes, took a deep breath, and began, "Shamaya, I don't know you well, but I know this film means as much to you as it does to the rest of us. Tonight, we are announcing to the world the partnership between Jackie Boy Productions, Because Fat Girl Media, and Kapoorico Entertainment. It's a coming-out of sorts, and we're all the debutantes."

"I knew I should have chosen the white dress," Drew quipped.

"Tonight, this house will be full of some of the most famous and powerful people in Hollywood," Chris continued, ignoring Drew. "But no one matters as much as us four right here."

"I can't tell if that's the most egotistical thing you've ever said or the sweetest," I said.

"I'm trying to have a special moment here." Chris flopped his hand down to his side in defeat, spilling champagne.

"I'm sorry." I put on the most serious face I could muster.

"What I'm trying to say is that tonight is our night," Chris tried again, lifting his glass back up for a toast. "So who cares what those bastards out there say? This movie is going to be a success, and together we are going to change Hollywood for the better."

"I'll drink to that." I clinked my glass against Chris's.

"Screw everyone else," Shamaya added, our glasses toasting each other. "Tonight is about showing Hollywood how fancy and fashionable we are."

"And here I thought it was about the movie." I laughed.

"Fine, that, too." Shamaya smirked.

"To us and this script!" I said as we all clinked our glasses once more and drank our champagne.

Normally, a new collaboration like ours would simply have an intimate dinner with stakeholders to mark the start of our project together, but Shamaya had insisted on an extravagant affair, offering to pay for the whole thing as long as Chris hosted.

"My house is fabulous, but this view screams success," she'd said during our first meeting together on Chris's back porch. "I want everyone in this town to know I've arrived, and I plan on staying at the top."

At first I had tried to reel her in, but once Chris got on board, I had no choice but to sit back and watch the extravaganza unfold. Shamaya's budget was bigger than my annual salary, and she brought a team of people in to make sure everything looked perfect, including us. She wanted the whole thing to be a blend of her three homes—Jodhpur, Los Angeles, and Guanajuato—and she'd enlisted Emmy to create our looks for the event. The men sported Jodhpuri-style suits, Shamaya wore a modern silk sari, and I had a gown that played on the motif of a huipil, all of our outfits dark navy with Mexican Otomi-style embroidery accents hand-stitched into them. The effect was stunning, and together, we presented a unified front, a cohesive team.

I looked around as the four of us got ready together. In a few short minutes, I would be walking down Chris Stanson's stairs into a crowd of the who's who of Hollywood players, Mexican powerhouses, and Indian film stars, some of them flown in just for this event by Shamaya's father. It was the kind of party I'd dreamed about as a teen, a room full of the rich and famous all there to hear about my film. My adult brain could not fathom it all. "Is this really happening?"

"It better be happening," Shamaya said as she adjusted her undergarments. "I didn't yank myself into this Yitty shapewear for nothing."

"Ready?" Chris asked, coming up to us.

"I believe we have a few more touches to add." Emmy looked over at Shamaya.

"Oh yes!" Shamaya exclaimed, opening her bag and pulling out four dark green velvet pouches, handing one to each of us. "A little something special to commemorate tonight."

I opened my drawstring and peeked inside, gasping as I pulled out a stunning pair of sapphire-and-diamond studs with a navy-and-white floral-patterned enamel teardrop falling from them. "Shamaya, you shouldn't have!"

"I absolutely should have," she dismissed, pulling her own massive sapphire-and-gold earrings out of her bag. "Can't think of a better way to spend my father's money than on this movie and this night."

"Cheers to that," Chris said as Emmy helped him with his new cufflinks.

"Thank you, Shamaya." Drew adjusted his own set. "These are perfect."

"Of course they are." Shamaya smiled. "I picked them out."

"With a little help," Emmy nudged.

"With a lot of help," Shamaya corrected, smiling at Emmy. Now that I was retired as a personal shopper, the two of them had been spending a lot of time together at Roussard's. "You've got my vote for costume designer."

"Hey, we don't play favorites around here"—Drew tucked his shirt in, then winked at Emmy—"but yes, mine, too."

"You have all of our votes," I said, and Chris nodded in agreement.

"Thank you. I look forward to showing you my character sketches." Emmy's face was as stoic as always, but her voice showed a hint of excitement and pride.

"Can we go now?" Chris implored. "We have a house full of people waiting for us."

"One more thing!" Shamaya insisted, and Chris groaned. She took out her phone, pulled us all in together—Emmy included—and snapped a candid shot, posting it immediately to social media.

"That's it," Shamaya declared. "Now we can go."

As soon as we took our first step out of the hallway, people cheered and photos started popping off. *I belong here*, I reminded myself with each step down the stairs, thankfully reaching the bottom without tripping.

Chris and Drew immediately set off to mingle, leaving me standing there with Shamaya, unsure where to go. In an hour or so, we'd be back on the stairs for our formal announcement, but until then I was expected to go out into this crowd of famous people and network, something I had no idea how to do.

"Just go up to people and start talking," Chris had advised me, like it was as easy for the rest of us to talk to the rich and famous as it was for him.

"I don't think I can do this." I turned to Shamaya, nerves making me want to run back upstairs and hide in the closet.

"The hard part's already done," she encouraged, looping her arm in mine. "Now, let's go enjoy being famous."

With Shamaya leading the way, I wove through the elaborate decorations and packed crowd, congratulations following us as we went. We found a glowing Janelle talking with Yalitza Aparicio and Lupita Nyong'o, and Shamaya introduced us both to Deepika Padukone and Ranveer Singh. We eventually stopped at an older man in a shining metallic gold-and-black tuxedo who greeted Shamaya with a bear hug.

"Papa, I'd like you to meet Diana." Shamaya beamed at both of us. "Diana, meet my father, Sanjay Kapoor."

"It's an honor," I said truthfully. The man was a legend, an activist in his time, helping to change Indian cinema like I was hoping to change Hollywood. He was handsome, too, charisma and charm oozing off him like it did his daughter. "I see where Shamaya gets her looks."

"It's all her mum, may she rest in peace," Mr. Kapoor replied, looking at his daughter fondly. "Mama would be so proud of you tonight."

"Papa, stop." Shamaya placed a finger gently under her eye where tears were starting to form. "You're going to ruin my makeup."

"Then I will pay someone to fix it." He pulled Shamaya toward him and kissed her on the forehead.

I thought of my own father, mostly absent, always drunk, and a pang of jealousy rose in me. I shook it away, focusing instead on looking for the one supportive family member that was still around in my life.

I left Shamaya with her dad and found Cecily near the door, just having made it inside the house. "I'm sorry I missed your big entrance," she said, giving me a congratulatory hug. "I tried to cut the line, but no one believed me when I said I was your sister."

"I told them not to let you in," I joked as we wove our way through the crowd. "Guess we need new bouncers."

"Then I better make the most of my time here before I get kicked out." Cecily rubbed her hands together. "Now, which famous person should I try to make out with first?"

Cecily had been out of her mind excited when I told her about the party, running around the house screaming and asking me incessantly to repeat the guests' names to her. I'd finally just given her the list we made for security, and she'd put *O*s next to the celebrities she wanted to sleep with and *X*s next to the ones she wanted to marry. Chris and Drew both had multiple *X*s and *O*s. Her enthusiasm had gone from cute to annoying to worrisome very quickly, made worse by the fact that she still didn't know Andy was Drew. I'd meant to tell her, but it never seemed to be the right time, and now here we were with no time left to hesitate.

"Cecily, I need to tell you something," I began, but before I could get anything else out, Janelle came running up to us.

"Oh my god, Lizzo is here!" she screeched, pulling my attention away from the matter at hand.

"Holy shit!" My mouth dropped. "I knew we'd invited her, but damn, I didn't think she'd show."

"Lizzo is at your party!" Janelle beamed.

"Lizzo is at my party!" I repeated in way too high of a pitch for someone who had just been judging her sister for her celebrity crushes.

"Go talk to her," Cecily insisted, pushing me forward.

"I can't!" I turned back around. "What would I say to Lizzo?"

"How about, 'Hi, I'm Diana, welcome to my party'?" Janelle offered.

"I can't just walk up to Lizzo and start a conversation," I insisted. "Plus, this isn't my party."

"It absolutely is your party," Drew said, coming up behind us.

"Do you always creep up on people at parties?" Janelle asked.

"Only ones at Chris's house." Drew laughed.

"At least this time he has food," Janelle teased, grabbing a taco off a server walking by.

"Ohmagawd, you're Drew Williams!" Cecily squealed, mouth agape.

"And you must be Cecily." Drew reached his hand out to my sister.

"Drew Williams knows my name." Cecily comically pumped his hand up and down. "How does Drew Williams know my name?"

"She talks about you all the time." Drew smiled at her as he nodded toward me.

"How do you know Drew Williams?" Cecily asked, finally letting go of Drew's hand and turning to me.

"Cecily, meet *Andy*," I said. "Also known as Drew Williams, producer of my movie and co-owner of Jackie Boy Productions."

Realization dawned on Cecily's face. "You're Andy."

"I am." Drew glanced at both of us in confusion, but before I could come up with an explanation, Chris was by Drew's side.

"Kali's here," he said as an introduction.

"And?" Drew sounded annoyed.

"And..." Chris continued, "you said you would talk to her about the movie."

"Tonight is definitely not the night," Drew objected.

"What better night than tonight?" Chris replied.

"You're Chris Stanson," Cecily interrupted their debate.

"I am," Chris affirmed, turning away from Drew and plastering that famous smile on with seasoned practice. "And who may I have the pleasure of meeting?"

"Chris, meet Cecily," I said.

"Oh, yes, the sister." Chris pulled her into a hug. "I hope you and your kids enjoyed my home the other weekend. I was sad to not get to meet you before you left, but Diana said you had to get back home."

"Diana told me that you didn't want guests here," Cecily said, shaking his hand but looking at me.

"Oh." Chris also turned his gaze to meet mine. "Perhaps I did. You never know with me. Mercurial, I've been called."

"Oh no, I'm sure it was Diana's mistake." Cecily's voice was dripping with anger.

"Come on, guys," Janelle chimed in, grabbing Drew and Chris by the arm, "let's let them talk."

Janelle gave me an apologetic look, and Drew squeezed my shoulder as they walked away, leaving Cecily and me alone.

"Why did you lie to me?" Cecily demanded, her voice ringing out.

"Keep it down," I said, leading her away from the party and down a hallway. "And stop glaring at me."

"Stop lying to me, then." She wrenched her arm from my hand. "I figured you were sleeping with this Andy person and didn't want me to know, but I never in a million years would have figured that you would keep something as huge as you sleeping with Drew Williams from me!"

"We're not sleeping together. We're just friends."

Cecily rolled her eyes at this, like she didn't believe me.

"I was going to tell you, but I never found the right moment."

"And you thought that tonight was the right moment? Did you want me to look like an idiot when he introduced himself to me?"

"I didn't expect him to come over and say hi to you."

"Of course not. Why would he? I'm just your boring old sister."

"That's not what I meant," I said.

"And you told me that Chris Stanson didn't want us around, but he just said he wanted to meet me," she continued loudly. "Am I some big embarrassment to you?"

"Right now you're just embarrassing yourself," I said, looking around to see if anyone heard her. "This is why I didn't tell you. I knew you'd lose your shit like this. You can't handle celebrities."

"Maybe I can't," Cecily responded. "But you didn't even give me a chance."

"I gave you a chance tonight," I rebutted, "and you freaked out, just like I thought you would."

"You're right," Cecily said, her voice cracking, "I did. But not because Drew Williams and Chris Stanson are fucking famous. I freaked out because my sister, my *sister*, my best friend, my life partner, my roommate has been lying to me for months. Hiding me. Ashamed of me. How am I supposed to act, knowing that I don't matter in your life anymore?"

"Of course you still matter to me!" I protested.

"I don't, though." Cecily wiped tears from her eyes. "If I mattered to you, if I really mattered to you—not because of blood but because you actually care—you wouldn't have hidden me, lied to me, and put me in this embarrassing position tonight."

"I didn't know how to tell you without you freaking out."

"I get it." Cecily sniffled. "You don't want your uncool suburban sister around your new fancy friends."

"Cecily, that's not what I'm trying to say," I said, reaching for her.

"It's fine." She ignored my outreached hand. "I'll leave. Have fun at your party. I'm sure it will be great."

I watched as Cecily pushed her way through the crowd, part of me longing to run after her and the other part glad to see her go. I leaned against the wall, taking long, deep, stabilizing breaths. This was why I hadn't told my sister who Andy really was. This was why I wasn't even sure I should invite her tonight. I didn't know how to let her into this part of my life.

You wouldn't even be here tonight if not for your sister, a voice in my head reminded me. It was right. Cecily had saved me more times than I could count. She was my person. She belonged by my side. I started to run after my sister to apologize, but someone grabbed my shoulder, and I turned, shock stopping me in my tracks.

Chapter Twenty-Six

"Diana, right?" a voice I knew so well said to me. I turned away from where my sister had gone and came face-to-face with my childhood idol.

"I'm Kali," she introduced herself, as if that were needed.

I shook her hand, dumbstruck.

"Can we talk in private?"

"Sure," I replied, forgetting all about my sister and following Kali to a little alcove off the main room. At first, I wondered how she knew where to go, then I remembered she was one of Chris's best friends. Of course she knew her way around his house.

"This is probably the best we'll get." Kali turned toward me in the too-tight space.

"What's up?" I tried to play it cool and not think about how my childhood crush's body was so close to mine.

"I want to be a part of this movie," she began.

Ah, of course. That's what this was about, I thought.

"I'm not sure you're right for Laura," I replied honestly. As much as I'd loved Kali growing up, she was too thin now to play the role, not to mention she'd just had top surgery and was now presenting more masculine. I knew Chris desperately wanted her on the team, but she just wasn't right for this role. I was prepared to fight on this matter, until I noticed Kali was nodding her head in agreement.

"I know," Kali admitted, "but I don't want to act in your movie. I want to score it."

"You want to what?" I was confused.

"I want to write the music for your film," she explained. "All of it. Like Aimee Mann did for *Magnolia* and Kendrick Lamar did for *Black Panther.* Original Oscar-worthy songs."

"Can you even compose?" My awkwardness around my childhood crush faded as my business brain and instinct to protect this film kicked in.

"I can. I used to be really good at it."

"What changed?" I dared ask, even though I already knew the answer.

Kali chuckled. "You know what changed. Everyone knows what changed. Between the diet pills and nonstop touring, I wasn't able to write for years."

"And now?" I probed.

"And now, I'm trying. I'm really trying. Every day, I wake up and I try. I'm writing again. And it's good. Really good. Nothing like that overly produced bullshit the studio has had me doing for the past decade. This is like my old stuff. Real stuff. I think it would be perfect for this film."

"You don't even know my film."

"I read the script," Kali admitted. "It's good. Relatable. I want to help make it *great*."

"Why you? There are hundreds of singer-songwriters in L.A. What makes you the right fit for this film?"

"Because I'm gay, and I've been fat, just like Laura." She took a deep breath and sighed. "And because, like the brother in the script, I have cancer. That's where I've been lately, not rehab, not a bender, but the cancer ward. I let everyone think I'd gone off the deep end again because I didn't want them to know the truth."

"How do I know you're not lying?" I challenged.

"Who would lie about having cancer?" Kali sounded appalled.

"I've had addicts lie about worse to me." I thought about my parents and all the lies I'd grown up with, lies they still tried to sell me.

"I can get a doctor's note, if that will make you feel better."

I looked her up and down, trying to find the signs. Her hair was cut short, which I'd assumed was a fashion statement but could also be like someone growing it out from chemo. Dark bags settled under her eyes, but that could be from the drug use. "Show me your PICC," I finally said.

Rolling her eyes, Kali unbuttoned her shirt, and there it was, the cancer patient's best friend, a tube protruding from her chest, a direct line to her heart. She was telling the truth. "Want to see the mastectomy scars, too? Everyone thinks I had top surgery, and that's easier to face than the truth. Years of not wanting my tits, and now cancer took them away for me."

Her revelation was shocking but made sense, now that I knew Chris and Drew more. Those two might live in the public eye, but they held their privacy dear. Considering she was their best friend, I'm sure this was about as private as it got. And it shed a whole new light onto the fights the men had over Kali being on this film as Laura.

"What do Chris and Drew think?" I asked.

Kali sighed and ran a hand through her hair. "Drew wants me to rest. Chris thinks I need something to live for."

"Do you?" I probed.

"Honestly," Kali said, looking me directly in the eyes, "Yes. I've been fighting this for a long time, and I'm getting tired."

"I'm sorry." I shook my head. "I'm not being very empathetic. You just surprised me, and I'm protective of this film."

"I get it." Kali smiled. "We've done a very good job of pointing the tabloids toward drugs."

"Why not just tell them the truth?" I wondered.

"I'd rather have their judgment over something that never happened than their pity over something that did."

I couldn't pretend to get it, but I also didn't grow up in the spotlight like Kali, Drew, and Chris had, their every move documented for the world to see. Still, I understood that fierce desire to hold private their most vulnerable parts. I did the same when Henry was diagnosed.

"Why are you telling me all of this?" I asked. "I'm just a stranger to you."

Kali shrugged. "Chris likes you. He cares what you think. That's rare. Rarer than you would think. So you must be one of the good ones."

"And what if I'm not?" I thought back to my fight with Cecily. "What if I'm a bad one pretending to be good?"

"Then you'll fit in perfectly with the rest of us." Kali chuckled and slapped me on the back.

"We're a team. All of us have to sign off on it, including Drew," I said, and Kali's face fell in disappointment. "But I'll take it to them and see where it goes."

Kali's face lit back up with tentative hope. "That's all I can ask for."

"Should we, like, hug this out or something?" I asked, my awkwardness returning. "I feel like we just had a moment."

"Sure, let's hug it out." Kali laughed as we embraced.

Together, we left the alcove and headed back out into the sea of people. My heart soared when Kali introduced me to Lilly Singh, another queer idol of mine, and I forgot all about Cecily when Priyanka Chopra joined in our conversation.

"There you are," Chris said, coming up next to us. "It's time."

"Time for what?" I asked.

"Our official announcement," he reminded me, leading the way through the crowd toward the staircase now lit up like a stage. Shamaya and Drew were already in position. They greeted me with large, confident smiles that showed none of the nervousness I felt. Janelle and Jaqueline stood together at the base of the stairs, both giving me encouraging smiles as I climbed up into position.

"Thank you all for coming to our intimate little party," Chris started, making the audience laugh. "We're honored to have you here to celebrate the new partnership between Kapoorico Entertainment, Jackie Boy Productions, and Because Fat Girl Media."

Chris continued to welcome people in his professional movie star voice, one that was congenial yet commanding. As he held the attention of hundreds of gathered elites, I understood why he was a star. Earlier, he'd been awkward, lacking eloquence giving his toast to our little group, but here, in front of hundreds of people, he was poised and polished; he captured everyone's attention. You couldn't fake that kind of presence in front of a crowd. You were either born with it or you weren't.

Too bad I wasn't born with it, I lamented for the thousandth time since moving to L.A. Still, I was learning to appreciate my own unique assets, separate from what Hollywood deemed valuable.

Shamaya got on the microphone after Chris, giving a hilarious and heartfelt speech, talking about bridging the USA, India, and Mexico tonight, and joking that I needed to write in a big dance number now, just so she could see Chris and Drew try to learn the choreography. She encouraged everyone to eat, drink, and be merry, then just like we had practiced, we put our arms around each other and posed for pictures like one big happy family. It was a dream come true, an absolutely magical moment. If only my sister were here to share it with me.

Chapter Twenty-Seven

The last stragglers of the night were saying their goodbyes when Jaqueline cozied up next to me on the patio outside, throwing the arm not holding her cane around my shoulders.

"Listen, darling, you know I love you, right?" Her speech was slurred slightly from the evening's free-pouring champagne, and she had a goofy smile on her face.

"I do now." I smiled back, leaning into her embrace.

"So then you know it comes from a place of love when I tell you this." She turned me to face her fully. "Either shit or get off the pot."

"Excuse me?" I laughed, wondering what the hell she was babbling on about.

"You've spent the whole night making sad puppy eyes." She nodded toward her son, who was helping the caterers pick up discarded champagne flutes. "So either do something about it, or get over it. Because this moping-around-at-your-own-party thing is just a waste of a good outfit."

"I wasn't moping around," I objected.

"You weren't living it up, either," Jaqueline countered. "You two have played this dance long enough. I think it's high time you do something about it."

"Even if that were true—" I began.

"Which it is," Jaqueline interrupted.

"*If* it were true," I continued, "that's not why I'm sad tonight."

"Then why, pray tell, are you sad tonight?"

I sighed, sitting down on the outdoor sofa.

"Oh, we're sitting then, are we?" Jaqueline said, making her way down next to me. "Oh yes, that's much better. Now, tell me everything."

I tried to explain my fight with Cecily the best I could, without delving into decades of family history and sisterly competition. Jaqueline was a great listener, nodding along with me and responding when needed. It felt good to talk to her, like a no-nonsense therapist who put everything in perspective in the most empathetic way possible. Even tipsy, she was kinder and more insightful than either of my parents had been. Jaqueline was in the middle of giving me some sage advice when Kali walked up.

"I'm heading out, Jaq." Kali bent over to give Jaqueline a hug.

"Kali, dear, have you met Diana?" Jaqueline asked.

"We met earlier," Kali confirmed, smiling at me. "Great party."

"It was all Shamaya and Chris," I admitted.

"It was all Veara and Bradley," Kali corrected.

"Too true." I laughed. Chris and Drew would both be lost

without their assistants.

"Kali, dear, sit for a bit." Jaqueline patted the sofa next to her. The pop star smiled and did as she was told. "Now, tell me who was that gorgeously tall woman with the fabulous style I saw you talking with tonight."

Kali laughed, a deep belly laugh. "God, I've missed you."

"You're evading the question," Jaqueline said.

Kali looked at me, then down at her hands, then back up at Jaqueline, her face flushed. "Her name is Emmy."

I perked up at the name. What were the chances of two tall, fashionable women named Emmy being at this party?

"Oh dear." Jaqueline patted Kali on the hand. "So you're back together, then?"

"Back together?" I asked, surprised.

"Oh yes, they've been in love for years," Jaqueline drunkenly confided in me. "All you young kids and your tormented on-and-off-again love. Just fuck each other already, like we did in the seventies."

Kali and I exchanged glances and both cracked up laughing, Jaqueline joining in.

"I am hungry!" Jaqueline stopped laughing to yell at the remainder of the guests in the backyard. "Who else is hungry?"

"Mother, why are you shouting?" Drew questioned as he walked over to us.

"Because how else will I get you to listen?" Jaqueline replied, smiling as she held her hand out. Drew took it and helped Jaqueline lift herself off the sofa. "I have a plan."

"Oh, this ought to be good," Drew quipped.

"Shush, you." Jaqueline swatted at him. "Now, where is that lovely blond who owns this place?"

As if summoned by her words, Chris appeared in the

doorway and started heading toward us, Simón Barboza—who had overseen the catering—following close behind. "Jaqueline, did I hear you yelling?"

"How else is a lady supposed to get any attention around here?"

"You're no lady." Chris stepped back as Jaqueline playfully swiped at him with her cane. "What did you want?"

"For you to put all of those culinary classes to good use and make us a picnic to eat out here." Jaqueline pointed upward. "My stars dining together under the stars."

Not eager for this evening to end, I offered to help Chris and Simón in the kitchen while Jaqueline, Kali, and Emmy searched the house for blankets to sit on. Janelle, Shamaya, Bradley, and Veara joined us, and we snacked, chatted, and laughed, the lights of Hollywood sprawled out before us.

It wasn't a cold night, but there was a chill in the air, and I cozied up to Drew, enjoying his body pressed against mine without the pressure of wondering where our touching would go. Jaqueline gave us a pointed look when he wrapped his arms around me, and Shamaya raised her eyebrows seductively when Drew wasn't looking, but I appreciated that no one said anything. Not that anyone had a right to talk; Emmy and Kali were snuggled in one corner, and I swear Chris and Simón were holding hands under a blanket at one point. Even Shamaya and Janelle were platonically snuggling with Bradley and Veara. It was just that kind of night.

"All good things must come to an end." Jaqueline sighed as the sun began to rise on the horizon.

Yawning, we said our goodbyes, and all of us headed out except Simón, who apparently was crashing at Chris's house tonight. Not for the first time, I wondered if Chris wasn't as straight as his media persona wanted everyone to believe. We were starting to be good friends (shockingly), and I knew if I asked he would be honest with me, but I figured if he did sleep with men, he would tell me when he was ready. Besides, I didn't have any room to pry, seeing as Drew and I were holding hands as we walked out of the party.

"You know, my house is closer than Arcadia." Drew pulled me into him. "I'd hate for you to fall asleep driving out there."

"I should go home." I sighed, really wishing I could throw myself into Drew's bed right now and forget that my actions had consequences.

"You could stay in the guest bedroom," he offered. "My mother can be our chaperone."

"She's doing a great job so far." I pointed to Jaqueline, who was standing with Shamaya and Janelle, all of them making loud kissing noises at us.

"My mother is so mature sometimes." Drew chuckled.

"I enjoy her very much."

"She's a pain in the ass." Drew smiled. "But she's a great mom."

"As much as I'd love to spend more time with both of you, I have to go home and take care of some things in my own family."

"Everything okay with Cecily?" Drew asked. "I noticed she left early."

"It will be," I said, hoping I was right.

I gave Drew a hug good night, kissed Jaqueline and Shamaya on the cheeks, said goodbye to Kali and Emmy, and thanked Veara and Bradley for all of their hard work making tonight perfect. Dropping Janelle off at her house, I wondered if I was actually too tired to drive home, and if I should just stay at her place and think about my sister later, but I knew the longer this fight festered, the worse it would get.

It was fully morning by the time I got home, and Cecily's music was playing loudly from inside her garage-turned-studio. Hesitantly, I opened the door and peered inside. My sister was painting furiously, working on an abstract piece that was mixed chunks of our brother's face. When she'd started it, she said she wanted to cut him up to bring him back to life, like the doctors had tried to do. His face was mangled and mutilated, barely recognizable, but the eyes were unmistakably Henry's. Her hands worked rapidly, mixing and treating paint, throwing it up on the canvas, angry brush strokes attempting to recreate our brother. My throat caught as I realized Cecily was listening to the mix we'd made for his funeral. She was deep in it today, and I wondered if it would be better to just leave her alone.

My hand was on the knob, about to leave, when she spoke. "Am I that big of an embarrassment to you that you have to hide me?"

"You're not an embarrassment."

"So then why did you hide me?" she asked, turning around and looking at me.

"I don't know, I just..." I tried to figure out how to succinctly explain the complicated reasons why I didn't want Cecily near Drew or Chris. "Everyone always loves you."

"That is not true," she denied.

"You don't see it, because you're you." I motioned up and down her body. "Thin, beautiful, artsy. Perfect hair, fashionable clothes, just the right amount of wild. You're that twee ingenue everyone dreams of being or dating."

"Only assholes want to date me."

"No, everyone wants to date you," I argued. "You just

choose the assholes."

"Glad you think so highly of me." She folded her arms tightly in front of her.

"I think the world of you. I wish you'd think better of yourself and stop settling for dickheads who treat you like shit."

"So you hid me from Drew Williams because he's an asshole?"

"No, Drew's actually a really great guy."

"If he's a great guy, wouldn't you want me to meet him? Isn't he exactly the kind of guy you keep insisting I need to go out and find?"

She was right. If I set up a profile of the guy I wanted for my sister, Drew would fit it perfectly. He was a total catch, the whole package: friendly, socially conscious, rich, famous, and good-looking. Drew was perfect for Cecily. Problem was, I wanted him for myself.

"He's not right for you," I insisted.

"If you don't think I'm good enough to meet Drew Williams, that's fine. He's a famous movie star who is too busy to meet people like me. I get it," Cecily said in a tone that told me she did not actually get it. "But what I don't understand is why you hid his existence in your life from me. I thought we got over this kind of lying and playing games years ago."

I couldn't answer her. I didn't know how I'd let my relationship with her get so backward again. When I was a kid, I used to keep everything from everyone, especially my popular sister. I hid my body, I hid my sexuality, and I hid my marks of self-harm, until I was so caught up in my own web of lies that I couldn't breathe. The school psychologist had called them panic attacks, but my parents insisted it was asthma, pulling me out of counseling and handing me an inhaler instead.

In college, I finally found someone to talk to, a therapist who was also queer and fat like me, someone who got it.

"What truth are you holding back?" she would ask me when I was on the verge of jumping headfirst into the depths of despair, my heart racing and breath impossible to catch. Answering that question was the key to my survival.

It was time to tell Cecily the truth.

"I didn't..." I started, my throat catching. I reminded myself that I was safe with Cecily, that we'd been through worse than jealousy and a crush. "I didn't tell you who Andy really was, because I knew you'd insist on meeting him. And after you met him, I knew I'd lose it all."

"What do you mean, 'lose it all'?" Cecily implored.

"You know what I mean." I glared at her, pain and shame rising in me. "Please don't make me spell it out for you."

"Unfortunately, you're going to have to," she said, annoyance in her voice, "because I have no idea what you are talking about."

"You know how hard it is for me, standing next to you," I started, and tears began streaming down my face. "You know how hard it is to be the fat sister, the weirdo who is queer in every sense of the word. What did that asshole in high school say? We're like 'beauty being related to the beast.'"

"Maybe he meant you were the beauty," she countered. "Ever think about that?"

"You know damn well I'm the beast," I spat.

"I'm sorry he said that, but that's not my fault," Cecily argued.

"Please, you purposely made that gap even wider between us. You loved boys' attention and flaunted your body any time you could."

"You think it's fun for me, hearing people tell me all the time how smart and talented you are?" she retaliated. "Everyone had high hopes for you, the drama nerd who would go off to Hollywood after high school. But me, all I was good for was arm decoration for football players."

"At least you were safe from their taunting," I shot back. "The guys you dated were some of my worst bullies, and you just sat back and let them do it, safe in your thin, straight privilege."

"Yeah, I was really safe with their groping hands and lack of consent."

"At least you were deemed fuckable!" I yelled, instantly regretting my words, wishing I could take them back.

Shit. Shit, shit, shit, shit. Why the hell had I said that? Why did I always have to jump so far over the line? Was I so insecure that I had to throw away basic human decency just to one-up my sister? God, what had I become?

"I am so, so sorry," I apologized, coming over to Cecily, grabbing her hand. "That was a horrible thing to say."

"Yes, it was." She pulled her hand away from mine, pain and disgust on her face. "You need to leave this house, now."

"You want me to move out?" I'd really crossed the line this time, and I didn't blame her for wanting me out of her house, but I wasn't ready to leave, especially not like this.

"I've told you since you moved in that this is your home, too," Cecily said coldly. "I can't kick you out of your home."

"You could tell me to go and I would have to," I replied. "Your name is on the mortgage. Your things fill the rooms. Your life is permanently here. I was always just a temporary lodger."

"I won't," she said matter-of-factly. "The kids will be back from their father's on Wednesday. Be home in time to kiss them good night."

"Okay." I stood up and walked out, knowing the least I could do was give my sister the space she asked for.

"And, Diana," Cecily called after me as I reached the door. I turned around to face her, daggers glaring out of her eyes. "Don't ever fucking say something like that to me again."

Chapter Twenty-Eight

Janelle let me crash at her house Sunday night, not asking any questions, just trusting me when I said I'd royally fucked up. I tossed and turned on her sofa bed, trying to come up with a way to fix this situation.

Early Monday morning, my phone pinged, and I grabbed it quickly, hoping it was Cecily, only to find a text from my ex.

Saw you on Kali's feed last night, Sam wrote. So cool you got to meet her! Hope all is well.

Immediately, I opened social media to see what Sam was talking about, and there was a photo of Kali, Jaqueline, and me lying together on a blanket under the stars in Chris's backyard. She'd captioned it, "Make new friends, but keep the old, one is silver and the other gold."

Kali had publicly said I was her friend! The little queer teenager in me was freaking out. Of course Sam wrote me when she saw it. We'd gone to two Kali concerts together and listened to her albums on repeat.

I ignored the fact that I hadn't heard from Sam in years, that she'd been horrible to me when we broke up, and that Cecily and Janelle forbade me from interacting with her since it always sent me into a downward spiral of self-loathing. Instead, I spent the next hour lying on Janelle's sofa, secretly sending texts to Sam that got increasingly flirty and somehow ended in me agreeing to meet up with her for dinner Tuesday night in West Hollywood.

Telling Janelle I was taking myself out to a movie, I drove to meet up with my ex, feeling guilty that I was lying to my best friend and wondering if Sam would notice that I'd gained weight since we last hung out. Before I could turn around and back out, I was pulling into a spot right in front of the restaurant. I took it as a sign that Asphalta, the goddess of parking, wanted me to do this, even if everyone else in my life would think it was a horrible idea.

I texted Sam to say I'd arrived, and she responded that she was stuck in traffic, so I decided to wait in my car instead of awkwardly standing on the sidewalk. My phone pinged with a text from Drew, or Fry Guy as he was listed in my phone, and my heart dropped, like I'd been caught cheating. I pushed it aside, reminding myself that we were just friends.

Any plans tonight? he wrote. I'm going to make popcorn and watch a movie, wanna join? Catch up on what I've missed?

That sounds like fun, but I can't.

Big plans with the wife and kids?

I paused, wondering how much to tell Drew, and decided honesty was the best policy. Actually, I'm meeting my ex-girlfriend for dinner. It might be a date? I don't know.

I watched as the little text bubble popped up and down, up

and down, my stomach lurching with it. After a full minute of no response, I started panicking.

Should I not have told you that? I wrote.

It's fine. Friends tell each other these things, after all. I hope you have a good time.

They do, I agreed. Another night then? Maybe Friday?

I leave tomorrow for post-production voice-overs, he responded

I thought you weren't leaving until Friday.

The team moved it up a couple days.

Shouldn't you be packing or practicing your lines or something? I asked.

All packed. Lines learned long ago, he wrote as a text came through from Sam saying she'd finally arrived.

GTG now, but have fun on your trip, I told Drew.

Good luck, he responded. Don't kill Chris while I'm gone.

No promises, I wrote, smiling as I silenced my phone. Maybe Drew and I could do this friend thing after all.

I stepped out of the car and rearranged my skirt, now wrinkled from sitting so long. I checked my lipstick in the side mirror and fluffed my hair. I'd always felt insecure around Sam, who was obsessed with "health" and had been a closeted professional athlete until she wrenched her knee, forcing her to quit sports. But things had been going well for me lately, despite the fight with Cecily. I'd truly gotten to a place of loving my body, even if some days I still didn't like it. Which meant I was able to walk into the restaurant with more confidence than I'd felt in our whole relationship.

I tentatively approached a tall, lanky blonde standing with her back to me. It looked like Sam, but her hair had been dyed black when we dated, and she was a lot thinner now. "Sam?"

"Diana," she greeted, turning around and reaching her hand out for mine. We shook hands, hers calloused as they'd always been, and the whole process felt weirdly formal, considering we'd dated for almost two years. "Sorry I'm late, traffic and all."

"It's okay," I reassured Sam as she gave our name to the hostess.

"Are you hungry?" she asked when we sat down.

"I'm starving!" I admitted, opening the menu.

"Oh, you shouldn't do that to your body," Sam warned, very serious. "It's bad for your digestion to get hungry. You should eat small meals all day."

I wouldn't be so hungry if you weren't an hour late, I thought but decided to be nice and focus on reading the menu instead. A server came to take our drink order, and I requested a bourbon, neat.

"We don't serve alcohol, but we have a delicious sugar-free lemonade with chia seeds," the server recommended, like that was a proper substitute for whiskey.

Only in L.A., I thought as I perused the "Thirst" part of the menu. The whole thing was green juices and infused waters, all of it organic, raw, grain-free, sugar-free, and vegan. My stomach growled in protest.

"I'll try the lemonade," I decided.

"I'll have a turmeric-infused ginger juice," Sam ordered. When the server walked away, she added, "I quit drinking a year ago—it's so bad for your liver. They make the best detoxifying juices here. The food is amazing, too, all locally sourced. It's gotten loads of write-ups on blogs and foodie websites. This really is the place to be seen right now."

"I'm sure it's great," I said, remembering why I hated eating with Sam. I was pretty open-minded when it came to food, but this place was pushing my limits with entrees like "Relaxed"—locally sourced kelp noodles with a spirulina pesto—and desserts like "Abundant"—maca root macaroons that boasted zero grams of sugar.

We ordered our meals—her the avocado whipped mousse on quinoa cakes, me a peanut zucchini noodle dish—and then sat awkwardly in silence for a bit until I asked Sam what else was new in her life.

"I'm really into spinning these days," she said excitedly.

"Ooh, like, in a circle?" I quipped. "My niblings and I love doing that."

"No, like on a bike. At the gym." She stared at me like she was trying to figure out if I'd been joking or not. I lived in L.A., and I knew Sam's obsession with fitness, so of course I knew she meant indoor cycling. I just couldn't take her seriously anymore.

"What kind of cardio are you into these days?" she continued.

"The kind that doesn't make you get off the sofa," I joked, and she looked at me with that old hint of judgment. Sam had never really gotten my sarcastic and often deprecating humor. She didn't understand that I needed it to cope with her annoying interrogations into my diet and exercise regime. Even now, years later.

I tried changing the subject. "So how else do you spend your time, when you're not, you know, spinning in circles?"

"Spinning has nothing to do with circles," Sam said, annoyed.

"The wheels are circles," I rebutted, and the look on Sam's face showed she wasn't as amused with me as I was with myself. Luckily our food saved us from having to continue this painful thread of a conversation.

My peanut zucchini noodles tasted surprisingly good

considering it was basically a lightly dressed salad, but the portions were tiny, and I was still hungry once it was gone. I peered up and noticed Sam had only taken a few bites.

"Don't like it?" I asked.

"Oh, no, it's delicious," she said. "It's just really filling."

My stomach and I both sat in hunger-induced incredulity as she asked the server for a to-go box for her tiny quinoa cakes.

"Can you excuse me for a second?" I said, then headed toward the bathroom.

As soon as I got in the stall, I texted Drew. My ex took me to a raw vegan restaurant and said she was full after five bites. Meanwhile I'm in the bathroom about to eat the toilet paper I'm so hungry!

That should be illegal! Fry Guy responded immediately. Pretend to be sick and leave!

I can't! I wrote, even though I desperately wanted to. That would be so rude.

Not any ruder than taking someone to a raw vegan restaurant without warning! he replied. What's the name of the place? I'll call and say there's an emergency.

It's called "Appreciate." *eye roll* But don't do that. The "friend calling with an emergency" thing is too cliché.

It's Appreciate?! Even I can't eat at that place. It's worse than I thought. You must be saved!

It's too late for me. Save yourself! Go eat bacon and fries with cheese for those of us who can't!

I will do it for you! he said.

Such a selfless martyr, I wrote. Okay, I've really gotta go back now or she'll think this food is giving me the shits.

It probably will!

At least then I could go home, I wrote, washing my hands

and leaving the restroom.

I made my way back to our table, where Sam was looking more thrilled to see me than I was to see her. "Did you see the inspirational messages on the doors of the stalls?"

I nodded, even though I had been too busy texting Drew to notice.

"I just love this place," she continued. "I hear lots of celebrities come here, too!" She glowed, looking out the window, like Ellen and Portia would show up at any minute and invite her to sit at their table.

In that moment, sitting there starving at a restaurant she'd chosen, watching her gush over the possibility of seeing a celebrity, I felt grateful for the first time since our breakup that Sam had the strength to end it when I didn't. She'd said I was abusive, unstable, and even insane. And sure, I had been, but she'd been, too. Sam just happened to be a more socially acceptable form of unhealthy. Together, we were fodder for each other's insecurities. But where I had actively worked through my issues in the years since we parted, she seemed to have gotten even more obsessive.

"Would you like some dessert?" the server asked.

"Oh no, I'm way too full," Sam insisted, patting her stomach.

"I'll take two." I pointed to the carob cake and the coconut milk ice cream. Sam looked at me with skepticism, but I didn't care. I was over starving myself for anyone else's comfort.

Halfway through my flourless chocolate cake—which was actually pretty good considering one of the listed ingredients was kale—a commotion outside got Sam's attention.

"Someone famous must be here!" she said as people held up their cell phone cameras toward the entrance. "Told you this was a place to see and be seen."

I didn't look up, more interested in my coconut milk ice cream than celebrities, but Sam stared openly, craning her neck to get a better view. "OMG," she said, "I think that's Drew Williams."

That made my head snap up from my dessert. Sure enough, there was Drew, smiling at a gawking passerby as he entered the restaurant holding a giant insulated bag in his hands. He said something to the hostess, looked around, and headed straight to our table. Without saying a word, he opened the bag, placed a tray of still-warm fries with cheese in front of me, turned around, and walked out.

"What just happened?" Sam asked as the whole restaurant stared at us.

"I have no idea," I lied, picking up a cheesy chunk of fries.

"You're not actually going to eat that, are you?" my ex asked incredulously.

"Every last molecule." I smiled as I popped the fried cheesiness into my mouth.

Chapter Twenty-Nine

It took me a few wrong turns and a couple dead-end streets, but eventually I found the deceptively simple white house with the cactus-lined driveway that I was looking for. I pressed the buzzer and smiled up at the camera.

"Fancy meeting you here," Drew greeted me at his front door. "How did the rest of your date go?"

"This large brute of a man came and crashed it," I complained, pushing him away and walking directly through the living room, past the first kitchen, and into the second one where I knew the food was kept.

"I can't believe someone would do that," he said as I started rummaging through his fridge.

"I know, so rude." I opened the crisper drawer. "But he brought me fries with cheese, so I forgive him."

"What are you looking for?" Drew asked as I searched through the various containers of meals Serena had prepped for him.

"Meat!" I said, pushing aside labeled containers.

"I've got just the thing." Drew moved me over and opened the bottom drawer. Inside were multiple white packages of butcher paper. He grabbed the one marked "bacon" and put it on the counter next to me.

"My hero!" I cried, throwing my arms around his neck and standing on my tippy toes to give him a peck on the cheek. Drew wrapped his arms around my waist and turned me toward him.

"You know, I would never take you to a raw vegan restaurant," he said.

"I know," I replied, his lips dangerously close to mine.

When our meal was over, I'd said goodbye to Sam and wished her well, knowing I would probably never see her again in my life. That version of me was over. I no longer associated with people who wanted me to shrink. As I drove away from my ex, I thought about my future...and Drew. He'd never asked me to be something I wasn't. He'd never wanted me to be smaller, quieter, less than. He was surrounded by boisterous, larger-than-life women, and he reveled in it. Loved them for it. All the things Sam had tried to change about me, Drew had embraced. And so instead of heading back to Janelle's house after my date, I headed toward his.

"We should make this bacon before I waste away," I said, pulling back from Drew. I reached up for the griddle above his head, stretching and grunting and failing to come even close to getting it. Drew chuckled, easily handing it to me.

"Show off." I scoffed, turning on the gas stove, then placing the griddle over it. "Not all of us are as vertically blessed as you are."

"It's a curse." Drew grabbed some maple syrup out of the fridge. "Are you staying to watch a movie or just using me for my bacon?"

"I'm a wham bam, bacon ma'am," I sang, flipping the strips. "In and out as soon as the bacon is gone."

"So if I keep supplying you with bacon you'll stay here forever?" Drew asked.

"Basically."

"I feel used." Drew placed a hand over his heart.

"At least I'm not using you for sex."

"At least there's that," he responded, plopping down on a kitchen stool.

We sat in heavy silence, listening to the bacon pop on the griddle as I weighed the pros and cons of what staying here would mean. Back in WeHo, I'd been so certain that the time was right. I'd finished my fries with cheese and ran to my car, ready to give in to my desire for Drew. But now that I was here, I found myself completely lost in the logistics of it all.

"Penny for your thoughts?" Drew brought me back to the present.

"They're going to cost you a lot more than that," I countered. "Haven't you heard? I'm a very important screenwriter now, with lots of interesting things to say."

"You're absolutely right, excuse me," Drew said as he flipped over the bacon. "Slice of bacon for your thoughts?"

"That's more like it." I placed paper towels down on a plate to soak up some of the grease.

Drew sat back down, looking at me, waiting patiently to hear what I was thinking. He was a handsome man, there was no denying that, and I wondered, not for the first time, what it would be like to have his naked body pressed against mine, even if he had a whole different set of equipment than I was used to.

But it wasn't his looks that pulled me in. There were plenty of beautiful humans in L.A., and none of them had made me feel as seen as Drew did right in that moment. He'd pulled me out of a crowd, offered me his support, and had been there for me even when I turned him down. He'd taken me to putt-putt, introduced me to his family, and brought me into his life. The person sitting in front of me right now was not famous action star Drew Williams, but Andy, the person who had become my friend over the past five months, the man who, against all odds, had made me rethink what I knew about love, desire, and identity. As crude as the saying was, Jaqueline had been right: it was time to shit or get off the pot.

Gathering all the courage and confidence I could muster, I walked over to Drew and took his hands in mine. "I was thinking that I would like to kiss you right now. If you'll let me."

Drew lifted his hand and placed it on the side of my face. With nervous excitement, I closed my eyes and moved my lips close to his, not yet touching, giving him the option he'd given me right here in this same kitchen: lean in or pull away.

Drew stood up quickly, and I prepared to feel his lips on mine, only to have him abruptly push me away. My heart stopped, shame and rejection filling my body as Drew hurried to put distance between us. I felt so stupid, completely misreading the situation and assuming he'd felt about me like I'd felt about him. Full of apprehension and remorse, I opened my eyes to see where he'd gone and saw a kitchen full of smoke and Drew rapidly moving the bacon off the griddle and onto a plate.

"I think some of it is still salvageable." Drew waved a hot pad in the air to help dissipate the smoke. "Especially if we pour maple syrup on them."

"I love maple syrup on bacon," I replied, trying not to show how dejected I felt. "Cecily thinks it's disgusting, but it really is the best."

"Cecily is absolutely wrong." Drew grabbed a bottle from the cupboard and handed it to me. "Maple syrup and bacon are the ultimate duo."

"Agreed."

While Drew turned on the fan and opened the kitchen doors, I headed over to the pile of bacon to see what could be saved and stared at it a little too long, avoiding having to look up and meet Drew's eyes.

"I'm sorry," he said from the doorway.

"It's okay." I patted the burned bacon with a paper towel.

"Would you believe me if I told you I'm nervous?"

"About cooking bacon?" I turned around to look at him. "I can see why."

Drew chuckled and stepped closer. "I do seem to be off my game tonight."

"What if there is no game?" I closed the gap between us. "What if we just hang out, eat bacon, watch a movie, and see where the night takes us?"

Drew reached out and touched his fingers to mine, entwining them just slightly enough to send shivers up my arm. "That sounds great." He squeezed my hand once before dropping it and heading over to the refrigerator. "How about some BLTs?"

"Brilliant!"

Drew got out a loaf of gluten-free bread, a head of lettuce, and some beefsteak tomatoes for open-faced BLTs, complete with homemade aioli.

"So I was thinking tonight I could make you finally watch the original *Total Destruction*," Drew said, compiling the sandwiches.

"Oh, were you?" I mocked. "What makes you think I'd like

a movie like that?"

"*Entertainment Weekly* said it was action-packed fun," he defended. "And *Maxim* called it a total panty-dropper with great eye candy."

"Elena Marino isn't really my type, and I hear that Drew Williams guy is a dick." I winked at him while I grabbed a glass for water.

"You're just biased against action stars," Drew said. "I see the way you hate on Chris, too."

"Not true!" I protested. "I love The Rock."

"The Rock, huh?" Drew gave me an appraising look.

"Absolutely. You know how married straight women make lists of men they have a pass to fuck? Me and my vagina have that same agreement. Dwayne Johnson is number one on my list."

"I'm a little jealous," Drew said, grabbing our plates, and we headed to the living room.

"Don't worry, it's just a fantasy," I reassured him, carrying the extra plate of maple bacon with me. "I'd never actually hang out with a famously buff action star."

"Because fat girl?" Drew asked, placing our plates on the coffee table.

"You do listen when I talk!" I cheered, plopping down on the sofa.

"You're so loud, it's hard not to." He ducked as the pillow I threw sailed past him. "You have lousy aim."

"Yeah, the sporty dyke gene seemed to skip me," I admitted, settling into his sofa.

The original *Total Destruction* was about what you'd expect from a high-budget action flick. Lots of explosions and gratuitous shots of Drew and his costar shirtless. He was great eye candy, *Maxim* had been right about that, but I wasn't the type to swoon over defined abs. Sure, flat abs could be sexy, but I was a sucker for a panza, that soft, comfortable paunch of fat between hips. I liked to lay my head on it, to listen to what it had to say.

I wondered what Drew's stomach would murmur to me. I figured a stomach that defined would deem me unworthy of speaking to. That was the problem with rock-hard bodies; they usually didn't pair well with soft ones like mine. They opted instead for bodies like Elena Marino, Drew's co-star.

"What's she like?" I asked as Drew and Elena jumped over turnstiles and skidded into a New York subway train just minutes before it closed, leaving their pursuers standing on the platform.

"She's actually really cool. Studied mathematics at Oxford and planned to quit acting once she was done with her degree. Then she landed that big rom-com she was in, *Lovely Rita*, and it propelled her career. But she still does math for fun."

"Who does math for fun?" I scoffed.

"She's a special one, that's for sure." Drew chuckled, endearment in his voice.

"Sounds like you like her." I bit into my sandwich, trying not to sound too jealous.

"I do," Drew said. "We got close on set."

"Did you two, you know?" I made a humping motion in the air. Drew laughed and blushed. "You did, didn't you? I'm glad you're giving pretty, thin girls a chance. They really have a hard time getting laid."

"It happens sometimes on sets. Long hours. Late nights," Drew explained.

"So I've read in the tabloids." I took a bite and dropped a

chunk of aioli on my shirt. "Dammit."

"Ooh!" Drew jumped with way more excitement than the situation warranted. "I've got something for you."

He disappeared into his house, leaving me sitting alone on the floor with food all over my shirt. I looked up at the screen and watched Elena Marino running toward Drew in impossibly tall heels, her short black dress exposing her cellulite-free, long legs.

"What are you doing here?" on-screen Drew asked as he wrapped Elena in his arms.

I could ask myself the same question, I thought, wrapping my own arms around my suddenly insecure waist.

Chapter Thirty

I expected Drew to come back with a super fancy designer Spray 'n Wash or something, but he showed up with a folded bundle of black-and-pink fabric and handed it to me. Delicately, I unwrapped it, exposing a set of designer silk pajamas.

"Watching you and Janelle walk around here the other night in my old shirts and sweats made me realize I needed pajamas for my guests," he explained.

"Do you often have women randomly spend the night?" I asked, taking the pair from him.

"Not nearly often enough." Drew smirked at me as I made my way to the bathroom to change.

The pajamas were XL, but I could tell from looking at them they weren't going to fit. Still, I gave it a try, not wanting to disappoint Drew. I pulled on the shirt, maneuvering my large breasts around to get in the tight, unmoving silk. The only way I could fit in the shirt was if one breast pointed up and the other pointed down and hung out of the bottom. I laughed at the ridiculousness of my reflection and took the shirt off. Or at least I tried to, but the silk had no stretch, and I got stuck inside of it, arms flailing in the air. Try as I might, I could not get the damn thing off.

"Um, Drew?" I cried through muffled silk, claustrophobia growing, as I couldn't move my arms. When I got no answer, I yelled louder. "Drew!"

"Coming!" he yelled from the other room. I could hear his footsteps getting closer until he was on the other side of the door. "What's up?"

"Can you come in here, please? I need your help," I pleaded, wiggling in a futile final attempt to free myself. I choked down tears as I heard him open the door, fully aware that he had an unflattering view of my tits and fat rolls. "Please don't laugh."

"I wouldn't dare," he promised, coming over and grabbing the shirt. With a few hard tugs, my arms were freed and I stood there in nothing but the see-through lace underwear I'd put on earlier that night to try to feel sexy for my date with Sam. I wrapped my arms around my body, feeling vulnerable and exposed. I knew the tears would be coming soon with no way of stopping them, and I desperately wanted Drew to leave, but he just stood there, handing me back the silk shirt.

I reached for my shirt instead, which was wet and soaking in the sink. "I'll just put this back on."

"Do you want one of mine?" Drew asked.

"I think I just need a moment alone." I willed my tears of insecurity to stay in my head just a little bit longer.

"Yes, of course." Drew headed out and closed the door behind him.

Embarrassed, I put my head in my hands and let the

waterworks start to flow.

"For what it's worth," Drew added, his voice muffled through the door, "I like what I saw."

I wasn't sure how it was possible to blush, smile, and sob at once, but I did just that as I heard Drew walk back down the hallway. A moment later, his footsteps returned, paused in front of the bathroom door, and then left again. Curious, I dried my eyes, threw a towel around me, and opened the door, stepping onto his Guns N' Roses shirt, folded neatly there on the floor. I picked it up and put it on.

Drew beamed at me as I came out in just my lace underwear and his cotton shirt. I'd thought about keeping my bra on so my boobs wouldn't flop everywhere, but I figured he'd seen me practically naked stuck inside silk pajamas. Sagging boobs inside a cotton tee were nothing now.

"I like you in that outfit," Drew confessed as I slid onto the sofa next to him.

"Better than the predicament you saw me in earlier?"

"I liked that, too." He smiled and pressed play again on the movie.

As on-screen Drew and Elena wove in and out of traffic on mopeds, I slid my hand over to his, weaving our fingers together.

"You should know that we're just friends," Drew said.

"Oh." I unlaced our hands, feeling rejected.

"I meant Elena Marino." He returned my hand to his. "She and I are just friends. I'm not seeing anyone right now. Except you."

"But aren't we just friends, too?" I asked.

"Sure." He nodded, intertwining his fingers with mine. "Whatever you say, *friend*."

"Is it ever weird for you?" I asked as Drew and Elena tore

each other's clothes off on screen. "Watching yourself during a sex scene?"

"Always," he admitted. "It kind of feels like I'm masturbating in front of you right now."

"Hot." I lifted my eyebrows a few times, making him smile and pull me closer.

I had to give Drew credit; he was very sexy in this movie, especially when he was pushing a moaning Elena up against the wall, holding her arms above her head with one hand as the other made its way down her body. I was sure I wasn't the first woman to imagine herself as Elena watching this scene, but I was in the unique situation to actually have the chance to recreate it with him. The thought of that made my whole body shiver.

"Are you cold?" Drew asked, pulling me closer.

"Actually, I'm quite hot right now," I said, running my finger up his arm.

"See, total panty-dropper." Drew smirked at me.

"I bet you bring all the gals home and show them this scene."

"The only time I've seen this movie with other people was in a theater sitting next to my mom, full of press."

"I'm sure this bit was awkward." I nodded to Drew naked on top of on-screen Elena.

"Oh god, yes," Drew confessed. "When the sex scene was over, my mom patted me on the arm and said, 'Good job, honey; she looks like she enjoyed it.'"

"She did not!" I guffawed.

"She did. Made the press around us laugh so hard they printed it in their review."

"Oh, Jaqueline." I sighed. "I love her so."

"She adores you," Drew said. "Do you know that?"

"She has told me that a few times, yeah."

"She doesn't like most people," he added.

"I'm honored, but can we stop talking about your mom and go back to the beginning?"

"Absolutely," he agreed, rewinding the scene.

I scooted closer, and Drew pulled me into him. It felt good being held. My whole being lit up as he gently ran his fingers up and down my arm. With work and life in the suburbs, sex had been nonexistent lately, and my body shivered, reminding me how much it craved being touched.

Hesitantly, Drew moved his hand a little lower, resting it right above the swell of my chest. I lifted my body, giving him permission to continue, and continue he did, cupping my breast and gently caressing my nipple with his thumb. I let out a little moan as his hand reached across me and pulled us down on the sofa, both of his arms now wrapped around me.

We fit there perfectly, spooning and purring, his hands exploring my curves as he kissed the back of my neck, his hardness pressing into my back. I rubbed my hips into him, and soon we were moving together, one solid motion, our breathing heavy, our moans deep, our longing palpable. Somewhere in my brain, that old warning signal was telling me to put up walls and pull away, but I ignored it, closing my eyes and surrendering to this glorious sensation instead.

His right hand made its way to my belly, cupping it like he did my breast, lovingly and longingly. He brushed a ticklish spot on my inner hip, and I giggled, my laughter turning into a whimper as his fingers skimmed over the thin lace of my underwear, teasing me mercilessly.

"Please," I whispered.

"Please what?" he demanded, swiping his finger over my clit.

"Oh my god, please." I was fully begging now.

"Tell me what you want, Diana," he whispered in my ear.

"You," I whimpered, turning my body toward him. "I want you, Drew."

Our mouths met as his fingers pushed my underwear aside and plunged into me, my body wet with longing, his body hard against mine. It felt so good to kiss him, to lean into lust, to let myself be held and kissed and fucked by this person that I'd desired for so long.

"More," I panted, trying to get Drew deeper inside of me.

"We need a better angle," he said, flipping me over until my back was pressed against him again. "How's that?" he asked, placing his palm against my clit and three fingers inside of me.

"Here," I moaned, moving my hips and his arm until he was in just the right place. We began rocking together, and I let out a loud, guttural moan as pleasure coursed through me. "Oh my god, yes, there!"

I grabbed his other hand and began sucking on Drew's fingers, need building up inside of me. I felt him harden even more behind me as I sucked and he fucked and we rolled together on the sofa, one fluid motion.

"More," I pleaded, still sucking on his fingers, and Drew put a fourth finger in me and pressed his thumb against my clit. I let out a cry as he filled me up, lifting my hips even higher, sucking harder, wanting him deeper inside of me. With each thrust I moaned his name—Andy, not Drew—until I could take it no longer and rolled over the edge, screaming in pleasure, my voice muffled by his fingers.

He didn't stop, just held on to me as my body spasmed and came again, going over the edge three times before I declared enough, lying spent, wasted, and soaking wet in his arms.

Breathing heavily, I closed my eyes, and when I opened them again, the movie had ended and Drew was kissing my shoulder, saying my name.

"Sorry to wake you up," he said, "but my arm is painfully asleep."

I apologized, groggily sitting up and noticing a pile of drool I'd left on his forearm. *Real sexy, Diana*, I thought as Drew shook his arm out.

"Sorry about drooling on you." I couldn't look him in the eyes, suddenly very aware of the scent of my arousal in the air.

"You snored and mumbled, too," he jested. "Just so you know all of your sleeping quirks."

Quirks. That's a polite way of putting it.

As Drew massaged out his arm, I curled into myself on the couch, feeling self-conscious about what we had just done together. It had felt good, really good, but what was supposed to happen next? Did I stay, or did I go? Would we return to being friends once that was out of our system, or had we made friendship impossible now? If we weren't friends, what were we? Realistically, where could we go after this?

"I should head home," I said, breaking the silence.

"Do you want to head home?" Drew asked.

"Do you want me to head home?" I replied. I was swimming in a tempest of emotions, drowning in the dark, desperate for some kind of solid ground.

"No." He reached his hand out for mine, offering me a lifeline. I took it, and he pulled me up off the sofa. "Come on."

Drew led me out of the living room and down the hall, passing the guest room I'd stayed in before and heading into the master suite.

"Make yourself comfortable." He ran his finger down the

side of my face, lingering at my lips. I kissed his hand, smelling myself on him, then pulled him toward me, our lips meeting. The kiss was tender, sweet, and way too short.

"I'll be right back." He pulled away, then headed back toward the main part of the house.

I slipped into Drew's bed, feeling the cool cotton against my bare legs, relishing the smoothness of high-thread-count sheets. His bed was huge, larger than a normal king, and I was swimming around it when Drew returned with two glasses of water, placing one on each side of the bed: his and mine.

Taking off everything but his boxers, Drew crawled into bed and we lay there, staring at each other from opposite sides, a large field of space between us. I wondered if this was how it would be from now on, a gap we were constantly trying to bridge.

After a moment's hesitation, we found our way to each other again, navigating across the distance in the dark, his arms engulfing me, pulling me into his hard body, reminding me of my softness, of the way it made me fragile, of how much I had to lose. I heard his heart beat under my ear, fast and expectant. I peered up at his eyes and saw fear there.

What could a man who has everything fear? I wondered as I curled against his chest. His fingers traced up my arm, finding the ridged scar along my wrist.

"What's this from?" he asked.

"A very bad day," I confessed.

I uncurled myself from him, trying to get a glimpse of Drew to sense what he was thinking, but it was too dark to see his expression, so I pressed my hand to his face.

Drew laughed as my fingertips explored his skin. "What are you doing?"

"Reading you," I replied.

"Reading me?" he asked, skeptical.

"Yes, reading you." I continued my exploration.

"Like a book?"

"Not like a book. Like, I don't know, like a human."

"You're reading me like a human?" He chuckled. His laughing made me self-conscious, and I pulled my hand away from him.

"No, don't stop." He placed my hand back on his face. "I want to know how the story ends."

"I once tried seducing a woman by naming all of her body parts in Italian," I admitted, my hand exploring his body.

"Oh yeah? How'd that turn out?"

"She broke my heart," I said, "but the sex was great."

"Are you really sharing ex stories right now?"

"I'm pretty bad at this whole seduction thing, aren't I?"

"'Are you trying to seduce me, Mrs. Robinson?'" Drew quoted.

"It's actually 'Mrs. Robinson, you're trying to seduce me. Aren't you?'" I corrected. "If you're going to quote a classic, you better make sure you—" The rest of my sentence was lost in Drew's mouth as it pressed against mine. He tasted of bacon and longing, and as his arms pulled me even closer to him, I felt his attraction for me growing.

The way I saw it, I only had two options in that moment: make a cautious escape back to my own world or recklessly propel myself into his. I chose the latter, taking off the Guns N' Roses shirt, leaving nothing but underwear between us, knowing that would soon be gone, too.

The truth was I'd made this decision long ago, probably as far back as Rapunzel's castle on the putt-putt course. I came here tonight sure I would sleep with him if given the chance, knowing I'd wanted this for months now. As I drove up to his house, I told myself that when Drew inevitably left me in a pile of confused emotions and broken promises, at least I'd know that I was brave enough to have given us a try. And if he stayed, if somehow beyond reason and logic we made this thing work, well then, that would bring its whole own set of issues, and I'd cross that bridge when it came.

At first, I tried to make myself detach, to think of this as nothing but a physical need being met, but Drew made that hard, kissing me like a lover and whispering sweet nothings in my ear. I had no choice but to surrender, to give in, to let myself be engulfed by this man. I grabbed and squeezed him, kissing and licking and drinking in my fill.

He smelled amazing. How did he always smell so good? I started to get self-conscious about my sweaty pits, but I didn't have time to linger on the thought as Drew's teeth nibbled on my nipples, making me crane my head back and moan in painful ecstasy.

I pulled him up to kiss me and ran my hand from his neck to the tuft of his manscaped pubes, tugging them playfully. He nipped at my lip in response. His chuckle turned into a deep-throated moan as I wrapped my hand around him, gently guiding my fingers up and down, feeling him get even harder beneath me.

"Andy," I whispered.

"Diana," he moaned.

"Do you have condoms?" I asked and felt him perk up against me.

"Are you sure?" He kissed my neck, stuttering as I continued to stroke him. "You know you don't have to—"

"I want to," I said, tugging on him. "Where are they?"

As Drew leaned over and pulled a box out of a drawer in his bedside table, I shimmied out of my underwear and threw them on the floor. I turned back to Drew and grabbed a packet, prepping to tear it open when he stopped me.

"Wait." He paused, putting the condoms to the side and grabbing a dental dam out of the drawer. He laid me back on the bed and began kissing me on the neck, then breast, then stomach, moving his way down my body until he was at my hips, plunging his tongue in between my thighs, licking and kissing me through the thin latex, filling me with pleasure until I loudly went up and over the edge once more.

Drew kissed his way back up my body until we were eye to eye again. "I've been dying to be between your legs for months," he admitted, making me wet all over again.

I handed him the wrapper that was still in my hand and tried to remember all the tips I'd learned in high school for properly applying a condom. I felt like a virgin again, eager but unsure of what to do next. Luckily Drew took the lead, pinching the tip and rolling it down. He positioned himself next to me, an adorably eager smile on his lips.

"I just suddenly got really nervous," I blurted out.

"We can stop right here," Drew reassured me, pausing where he was.

"Please don't." I pulled him on top of me.

"Are you sure?" he asked as he settled between my legs.

"Very." I reached down and guided him in, both of us moaning loudly as he entered me.

It felt amazing, having Drew on top of me, inside of me, kissing me, and looking down at me with a tenderness and longing so intense I had to close my eyes or I would start crying with the overwhelming emotions of it all.

We moved around, indulging in each other's bodies all night, kissing and laughing the whole time. Drew held me as I cried, and I kissed him as he came. We talked until the sun came up about everything and nothing, and I marveled at the ease with which we spoke, like best friends who had known each other decades, not months. By the time we started dozing off, Drew little spoon this time, my body felt sore and satiated. It had been a long time since I'd had sex, and even longer since I'd made love.

Because like it or not, that's what existed between Andy and me: love. We were more than colleagues and so much more than just friends. We were lovers now, and as my eyelids got too heavy to hold open, I prayed that this feeling could hold up under the scrutiny of the light of day.

Chapter Thirty-One

Drew was stroking my hair when his alarm went off, and he quickly reached over to silence it, thinking I was asleep. With one last kiss to the forehead, he pulled away from me and quietly crawled out of bed. I listened as he turned on the tap and briefly thought about joining him in that glass shower, both of us exposed for the world to see, but my confidence was waning quickly. Drew might have enjoyed the softness of my body against his at night, but it was another thing to see the way I folded in on myself in the light of day, every roll, bulge, and insecurity exposed.

As quietly as I could, I jumped out of bed and grabbed his Guns N' Roses shirt and my underwear from where I'd thrown them the night before. I contemplated finding the outfit I'd arrived here in, but I didn't know where it was in the house and who I'd run into trying to find it. I was sure the housekeeper and gardener were used to seeing half-naked women in Drew's home in the morning. I just couldn't handle anyone seeing me here like this.

I heard Drew turn off the water, and I quickly hopped back into bed, hiding underneath the covers. Part of me wanted him to just leave without saying goodbye, to go and let last night be what it was, no strings attached. Another part of me wanted him to come in here, wrap me in his arms again, and promise that everything would be okay.

"Good morning," Drew said, walking into the room wearing nothing but a towel. A primal part of me longed to rip it off and have another go before he left, but uncertainty had hold of me, and I turned my head so he kissed my cheek.

"Morning breath," I explained as my excuse.

"I don't care." He tried to kiss me again.

"Just one second." I hopped out of bed and headed to the guest bathroom, buying myself some time to think. I found the toothbrush and paste that Drew kept for guests and took my time cleaning myself up, brushing my hair and washing my pits and bits, "the double-p shower" as Cecily called it. When I got back, a set of luggage was ready near the door and Drew was sitting in the sun on the patio just off his room. I'd completely forgotten that Drew had to leave for post-production pickup scenes today.

"You packed quickly," I said, squinting against the Southern California sun as I joined him outside.

"I packed yesterday," Drew reminded me, scooting over to make room. "Just had to throw in some last-minute things."

I joined him on the sofa, and he went for my hand. I flinched a bit when he touched it, making him pull away.

"I'm sorry," I apologized, seeing the look of hurt in his eyes.

"No, no, it's okay." Drew shook his head. "I get it."

"It's just, um…" I glanced around at him, his house, his world. Everything was perfect, except for me. "It's a lot to process."

"I get it."

"Do you though?" I asked. "Do you get what it means for someone else to wake up in this house?"

"What's the quote Julia Roberts says in *Notting Hill*? 'People go to bed with *Gilda* and wake up with me?'"

"Yeah, except I went to bed with Andy and woke up with Drew Williams."

"How is that different?" he asked.

"The part that attracts most people to you is the part that repels me," I explained.

"Nice to know I repel you."

I could tell I'd hurt him and hated myself for it.

"I didn't mean it like that," I promised, touching him reassuringly. "I meant that I really like the you that I get to see—my friend Andy, the one who gets me fries with cheese and plays putt-putt. But I'm not sure what it means to be intimate with the famous Drew Williams."

"'You know all that fame stuff means nothing. At the end of the day, I'm just a boy standing in front of a girl, asking her to love him.'"

"You're really gonna pull that line on me right now?" I laughed.

"I'm going to double down on it, too," he avowed, moving closer to me. "'I have to leave today, but I thought, if I didn't, I was wondering if I could see you a little. Or a lot.'"

"Quoting *Notting Hill* won't make me like you more," I protested, but I leaned in toward him anyway, our lips touching.

"Won't it?" Drew pulled me on top of him, our bodies entwined. He tasted like peppermint and smelled of expensive soap, and I wondered how long we had until his driver came to take him to the airport, how far we could go on like this before life interrupted us.

I twirled my hands through Drew's hair and pressed down into his lap, feeling his eagerness poking into me, my own excitement seeping through my lace-thin underwear. His mouth left mine and hungrily found my right breast, licking and sucking my nipple as his free hand made its way down to my thighs. My head lolled back in ecstasy, and I felt my body vibrate with anticipation.

No, wait, that wasn't coming from my body. It was coming from Drew's pocket.

"Someone's calling you," I moaned.

"Whoever it is can wait." Drew pressed his finger against my clit, stroking it through my underwear.

"You're going to miss your flight," I reminded him, my breathing growing heavy.

"That's the glory of flying private," he said, his fingers pushing aside the lace. "They don't leave without you."

I let out a cry as Drew entered me with one hand, his other reaching around and pulling a condom out of his pocket.

"That's rather presumptuous of you." I smirked as he unwrapped the foil.

"Call me an optimist," Drew said, rolling the condom over himself. "Come here."

"Gladly." I threw off my clothes and climbed on top of him, insecurities be damned. I grabbed his shirt in my hands and tore it off, too, needing to feel our skin touch again.

"God, you're so fucking sexy," Drew said before his mouth engulfed my breast, his tongue flicking my nipple, sending shocks of pleasure through my body.

His phone vibrated again, but we ignored it as I rode him hard, our bodies smashing into each other, seeking release. Drew's hands were on my ass, pushing himself deeper into me.

"I'm so close," he cried, our eyes meeting.

"Me, too," I breathed, reaching my hand down in between my legs to rub my clit.

"I want you to come with me," he moaned, moving one hand up to my face. "Oh, Diana, please come with me."

"Yes." I gasped. "Yes, Drew, yes."

We pushed into each other harder and harder, both on the verge of exploding as his phone rang again and again.

"Shouldn't you get it?" I said breathlessly, my orgasm coming. Drew didn't answer me, his mouth too busy sucking hard on my nipple. I could feel that rising tide within me, a tsunami about to break. Just a few more strokes.

"Drew?" a high-pitched voice yelled from inside his house. "Drew Williams, where are you?"

"Fuck," Drew swore, his mouth leaving my breast.

"Should we stop?" I whined.

"God no." Drew pulled me into him, kissing me hard as he thrust into me, taking us both over the edge, his mouth absorbing my scream.

"Drew Williams!" the high-pitched voice repeated, this time on the other side of his bedroom door.

"I'm coming!" he yelled back.

"I'm sure you are," the voice nagged, "but tell whatever hussy you've got in there that you've got a publicity shoot before the voice-overs and you cannot be late for this."

"Did he just call me a hussy?" I growled, climbing off Drew and heading back toward his room, searching for my clothes.

"Diana, wait," Drew said, running after me, trying to pull

the condom off and his pants on at the same time.

"Is it normal for you to keep your team waiting while you fuck girls on your patio?" I asked, pulling his Guns N' Roses shirt over my head.

"I hear you," the voice yelled.

"Who is that asshole?" I pointed toward the door.

"Gary, my manager," Drew explained, throwing on his shirt. "He prides himself on the promptness of his clients."

"How did he even get in?" I wrapped myself in Drew's blanket, not wanting to have Gary see me half-naked.

"I havc no idea," Drew said, loading his arms with luggage. "But I'm going to fire my security team."

"Drew Williams!" Gary yelled.

"Dammit, Gary." Drew flung open his bedroom door. "Just give me a minute!"

"One minute," Gary agreed, taking Drew's luggage and giving me a judgment-filled side-eye.

Drew looked at me apologetically. "I've gotta go."

"I know," I said.

"Can I call you when I land?"

"I don't know. Can you?"

"Actually, I can't." Drew sighed. "We go straight into shooting. But I can call you tonight."

Soon, Drew would be in Hawaii filming promo shots and pickup scenes with his gorgeous sidekick, Elena. Meanwhile, I'd be back here in L.A., going full speed ahead on pre-production with Chris. We'd worked it all out as a team weeks ago, and every detail was accounted for.

Every detail except us sleeping together.

"Last night was great," I said. "Can't we leave it at just that?"

"I don't think I can, Diana." Drew lifted his hand to cup my face. "I've waited too long to kiss you. Now that I have you, I don't want to let you go."

"What if I need to be let go?" I asked. "What if I can't handle this?"

"Then I'll walk away knowing I at least got to taste you for a night." Drew lowered his lips to mine. Our kiss felt desperate, wild, the primal longing in it drawing us together. Drew broke away first, leaving my body needing more.

"And what happens if I want to stay?" I wondered, standing there, feeling like my whole self was laid bare by that kiss.

"You can stay as long as you want." Drew hugged me tightly.

"Careful, I'm a queer woman," I quipped. "I might pull up here in a U-Haul with all my stuff."

"I'll move the Tesla over so it can fit." Drew laughed, then kissed my forehead one last time before releasing me. "No one will be around today, so the house is yours. Just press two fingers on the door to lock it when you leave."

"I'll head out soon," I promised, wrapping the blanket around me as Gary began walking back toward us. "I should get home. Cecily and I need to have a chat."

"I hate leaving you like this." Drew pulled me toward him again.

"I'm fine." I stiffened.

"When a woman says she's fine, she never is," Drew stated, stroking my face with his hands.

"You should go," I urged, overwhelmed by this whole situation.

"I'm going to be pretty booked, but I'll find a time to call you," Drew promised, letting go of me. "Please pick up when I do."

"I'll try," I replied, unsure of what else I could do.

"I'll see you soon," Drew said before heading down the hallway toward a loudly chattering Gary.

I closed the door and turned to look at my surroundings. Last night, there had been a moment when I found the perfect crook in Drew's arm and laid myself in it, my whole body fitting into his like a missing puzzle piece. Now, standing in his bedroom alone, I felt completely out of place, unsure of where to go or what to do.

I wanted to cry, but tears wouldn't come. I wanted to shout, but I couldn't find it in me to scream. What I really wanted most of all was to lift this weight of fear and insecurity off of me, so I could think. Realizing exactly what I needed, I walked out of Drew's bedroom and directly into his pool, Guns N' Roses shirt and all.

In an hour, I'd leave this mansion in the hills and drive back to Arcadia to try to mend things with Cecily. In a week, all of the cast and crew contracts would be solidified. And in a little under a month, I'd be expected to direct a full-length feature film. All while trying to figure out what it meant to be falling in love with one of my producers, a cishet man to boot. The pressure of it all could crush me alive, if I let it. But right there, in Drew's pool, I felt weightless. Right then, with Drew's smell still on me, I felt like I could fly.

Chapter Thirty-Two

When I got back to Arcadia that evening, I heard Cecily down the hall reading *The House on the Cerulean Sea* to the kids. I crawled into bed with Ellis and listened in. It felt soothing, losing myself in someone else's story, Ellis's little body dramatically clinging to mine. They loved playing up their reactions. Exaggeration was their specialty. When Cecily reached the end of the chapter, she closed the book and asked us all to say what we were grateful for that day, her usual bedtime ritual with the kids.

"I'm grateful that it was my special helper day at school." Reggie beamed with pride. She loved special helper day because it allowed her to be two of her favorite things: in charge and of use.

"I'm grateful that I sold a new canvas today," Cecily said.

This was news to me. I was excited for her and sad that she hadn't texted earlier to tell me about it. Usually that was the kind of information she couldn't wait to share.

"I'm grateful that I got to see Aunt Didi tonight." Ellis looked up at me. "We never get to see you anymore."

"I'm grateful," I said as Ellis snuggled against me, "that you all are being very patient and understanding with me as I follow my dreams and get this movie made. And I'm sorry I don't get to see you as often as before, but I'm very grateful I got to be here to tuck you in tonight."

Ellis cuddled closer to me as their mom and I sang "I've Got Rhythm," one of our favorite bedtime songs, then we tucked them in, turned on the night light, and headed back to the living room.

"I was thinking maybe we could pour some wine and talk on the back porch," I suggested.

Cecily agreed, and we headed outside, me with two glasses in my hands, her with a half-empty bottle she'd opened at some point while I was gone. Cecily poured the wine, looking at me expectantly.

"I am so sorry," I began. "So, so, sorry. For lying to you about Drew, and especially for what I said."

"I just don't know how we got back here," Cecily replied, her voice hitching. "I thought we were past the anger, lies, and bitterness, past the fighting we did as kids. I thought we were adults in sync now, working together toward a common goal of building a home and raising these kids."

"That's the problem, though. This was never my goal." I pointed around me. "This house, those kids, they're your dream, not mine. I like this home. I love those kids. But two kids and a house in Arcadia is not the life I want to live."

"You think this is the life I wanted?" Cecily challenged, her voice rising. "I moved to L.A. to make something of myself, too, you know. But life happens and we can't all just wait around for our dreams to come true. Some of us have to grow up and support our families."

"It may not be the life you wanted," I countered, "but it is the life you chose. Marrying, having kids, moving here. These are all your decisions. I didn't make you give up on your dreams, you did that on your own."

"You chose it, too, when you moved in here," Cecily reminded me. "I didn't drag you out to Arcadia—you came willingly."

"You're right. I chose to come help you out after your divorce, and I chose to stay so I could save money," I agreed. "But I never gave up on my dreams. This was always supposed to be temporary for me. I was always going to leave."

"I knew you'd move out someday." Cecily's eyes were now swollen with tears. "But I thought we were in this life together after Henry died. I thought you'd always be here for me."

"I am."

"Are you?" Cecily sobbed. "Because you're all I have left of family, and I feel like I'm losing you, too. You hiding me from Drew and Chris, it just reminded me that my sister is going places and I'm not. Every day I feel like I'm falling further and further behind in life and you don't even care that you're on a rocket ship and I'm being left in the dust."

"I live in a city I don't like, surrounded by people I don't have anything in common with, in a home full of things I didn't buy, with kids I didn't have. What more do you want me to sacrifice for you?"

"You can't put this all on me and the kids," Cecily protested. "You moved here to save money for your movie, too."

"I could have saved money other ways." I could feel my temper rising, the years of resentment coming to a head. "I never would have chosen this life for myself. I came here to help you because you couldn't raise your kids on your own, and now I feel trapped in a life you chose, bogged down by decisions you made, decisions society praised you for while ridiculing me for being a queer, independent, childless woman. So yes, I want to get the hell out of here as fast as I can, and I'm sorry if you feel left behind, but it's not my fault you can't keep up." I sucked in air, lungs empty from my tirade.

Cecily didn't look at me but stared at the almost-empty glass of wine in her hands. She then raised it to her lips, chugged the last of the liquid, and stormed inside.

Dammit! I grabbed my glass and the empty bottle of wine and followed after her, wishing I knew how to have a hard conversation with my sister without it ending in us attacking each other. Cecily was standing in front of the sink, loudly doing dishes. She turned, and for a split second I thought she was going to hit me, but she grabbed the wine glass out of my hand instead and thrust it into the soapy water, so forcefully it burst.

She cussed loudly as the sink started filling with blood. I quickly grabbed a dish towel and went to wrap it around her hand, but she shooed me away, taking a paper towel from the rack and pressing it against her skin. I ran to the hall closet and grabbed antiseptic cream and bandages, returning to find Cecily on the floor, crying while holding a now-red paper towel to her chest.

I sat down next to her, gently prying her hand out toward me. She hesitated at first, pulling her injury closer to her and snapping at me like a hurt dog, but eventually she let me inspect it. The cut was short but deep, and I removed a small shard of glass out of it with the first-aid-kit tweezers.

"I knew you were unhappy," Cecily admitted as I applied

antiseptic cream to her hand and wrapped it in a *Star Wars* bandage. "But I didn't realize how much you hate it here. How much you hate your life with us."

"I love you and the kids, really, I do," I promised, giving back her hand. She examined my work and adjusted the bandage. Always the perfectionist. "I just don't want this life for myself anymore."

"I'm sorry I trapped you here." She squeezed my hand with her unhurt one. "I'm trying to get stronger and more independent. I am doing better. You've helped me get better."

"You've helped me, too." I choked up. "And so have those kids of yours."

"You've made all of our lives better, living here." She leaned her head against mine.

"And my life has been made better living here." I leaned back into her.

"So then why are we fighting right now?" Cecily asked.

"Because Mom and Dad taught us to handle our emotions by getting drunk and screaming at each other."

Cecily laughed. "True."

"We got here because I lied to you about Drew Williams," I admitted.

"Did this all really start over a guy?" Cecily asked. "Am I really sitting here with a bleeding hand because we are fighting like schoolgirls over a boy?"

"We are not fighting over a boy," I insisted. She raised an eyebrow at me. "Okay, fine, we're fighting over a boy."

"Do you love him?" she asked.

"What? No," I sputtered. "That's a stupid question."

"So you love him, then," she said, and this time it wasn't a question.

"I can't love him," I responded.

"I didn't ask if you could," Cecily pointed out. "I asked if you did."

"But I can't," I maintained.

"Why not?"

"Because fat girl," I cried. "Because even if I was thin and pretty and felt worthy of a sexy superstar, I'm still gay, and I have no idea what to do with a man."

"You've slept with trans men and even cis men before, back in the day," Cecily pointed out. "Riding a dick is like riding a bike; it'll come back to you real quick."

"Yes, I know the logistics of sex." I laughed as Cecily did a ridiculous imitation of a bike rider. "What I don't know is how to date a man. The heterosexual mating ritual is so far from anything we queers do. Straight girls suddenly get so helpless that men have to open their doors. Men's egos are so fragile they fall apart at the tiniest suggestion that their dicks aren't the center of the world. Masculinity is so damn toxic. I worry that I hate men too much to date one."

"God, you're such a gay girl stereotype." Cecily rolled her eyes.

"Except that whole 'I'm in love with a dude' thing."

"Except that," she agreed, smiling warmly at me. "If you're going to fall for a guy, Drew Williams is a good one to choose. He's famous, rich, hot as hell. What's not to love?"

"The bashing I'll get by the media," I answered honestly.

"I'll hide all the newspapers from you, then," Cecily promised.

"No one reads newspapers anymore. It's all on the internet now."

"Fine. I'll hide the internet from you."

I laughed. "Even if that were possible, I don't even know if he likes me. I mean, I know he likes me, but does he *like me*, like me?"

"Oh my god, you're being such a child right now." Cecily huffed, standing up. "Seriously, Diana, you sound like Reggie."

"I feel like a teenager with my moods all over the place!" I whined, getting up and following Cecily into the living room where we both plopped on the sofa. "I have no idea what to do with all of these emotions. Boys make me feel insane."

"Love makes you feel that way," Cecily rebutted. "You act this way every time you fall for someone, regardless of their gender. You go into this downward spiral of insecurity until you've convinced yourself there's no way this person could like you. Or if they like you, then there has to be something wrong with them. Just stop it already."

"Easy for you to say. Your brain doesn't work like mine."

"Oh really?" Cecily cocked her head at me. "Didn't this whole fight we're having start because you were afraid I couldn't keep my cool around famous men? Aren't you always telling me that I'm great until a man comes along? You can't hate on me for my lack of boundaries around relationships and then act like it's all so much harder for you."

"It is so much harder for me!" I insisted. "Dating is so much harder when you're queer and fat."

"Sometimes I think you make it harder on yourself."

"Says the straight, thin one."

"Life's hard for me, too, Diana."

"Life's hard for everyone, but some of us have it harder. You will never know what it's like being a fat, queer woman. And neither will Drew."

"So you're just going to dismiss everyone with more

privilege than you?"

"No, I'm just not going to have sex with you," I said.

"That's good, because I'm your sister," Cecily mocked.

"You know what I mean."

"What I do know is that I haven't seen you light up like this over someone in a long time. Not since Sam."

"And we both know how that turned out," I said, rubbing my finger along the white scar on my wrist.

"You've come a long way since then."

"Have I, really?" I asked. "Or have I just not had to put it to the test?"

"I like to think that you wouldn't try that again, now that you have us."

"I had you before, and that didn't stop me," I admitted.

"I need to believe that you won't do that again, now that Henry is gone." Cecily reached for my hand. "I don't know what I'd do if I lost you, too."

"I don't know what I'd do if I lost you, either," I cried, taking her offered hand. "I can't promise that those thoughts won't ever come back, because I know they will, but I can promise you that when depression hits, I will use all the tools I have to stay here, alive, with you."

"Thank you." Cecily squeezed my hand.

"I saw Sam yesterday," I confessed.

"Where?" Cecily asked.

I told her the whole story, stopping at the fries with cheese delivery, not quite ready to tell her about last night with Drew.

"Sam was always nice on the surface, and in theory you looked great together, but those underlying insecurities were making you both unstable," Cecily said. "I'm glad you got that closure."

"Me, too," I admitted, thinking about my night with Drew, the ultimate closure for getting over Sam.

"So, like what, you've got a crush on Drew Williams now?"

"Oh god, you're going to be insufferable about this, aren't you?" I threw my hands in the air.

"Do you, like, want to put his poster on your wall?" she joked. "I could cut up some magazine pictures and tape them to your locker."

"I hate you right now," I moaned, a contradictory laugh leaving my lips.

"You should totally ask him to the Sadie Hawkins dance." Cecily's voice was pitched like a teenager. "Then, like, maybe you two could officially 'go around.' After school you could, like, walk to the corner store, and he could buy you a pop or something."

"You're enjoying yourself right now, aren't you?"

"A little bit." she chuckled. "But, seriously, if you like him, what's holding you back? He's Drew Williams, for fuck's sake!"

"There is no way this doesn't end up in me being screwed," I said.

"I mean, isn't getting screwed kind of the point?" Cecily nudged me with her elbow.

"You know what I mean." I pushed her back playfully. "There's no world where someone like me can date someone like him and not get the shit end of the stick. We're just too different to make this work, so I might as well save myself the heartache."

"This is going to sound cheesy, but celebrities are just like us," Cecily said. "Maybe Drew Williams has been looking his whole life for someone as amazing as you. Maybe you need to stop coming up with all the reasons this won't work, and finally allow love back into your heart."

"You're right, that does sound cheesy," I replied.

"Good thing you love cheese." Cecily smiled.

"Especially on fries," I agreed.

"I know men can be assholes, especially famous ones, but he seemed cool. Down to earth. And totally into you. I saw the way he looked at you that night. Like he wanted to kiss you, hold you, and never let you go. I know it's been a while since you've been attracted to a man, and that's scary for reasons I won't get as a straight woman, but if you're going to start exploring men again, Drew Williams is a great choice. I bet he'd be great in bed too, actually caring about your pleasure unlike most of the men I've dated."

"That last part I can verify." I blushed.

"What?!" Cecily said, scandalized. "When did you sleep with Drew Williams?!"

"Last night." I blushed even deeper. "And again this morning."

"Tell. Me. Everything!" Cecily accentuated every word. "Wait, no, hold up."

She ran to the kitchen, made two cups of tea, then came back to the sofa, handing me one. "Okay, now we're ready. Spill it."

I laughed and told Cecily everything I'd held back all these months: the LACMA party, putt-putt, that night in the kitchen, kissing at Jaqueline's, last night at his house, this morning, and all the worries and fears I'd had along the way. It felt great to sit together on the sofa and finally talk with her about this. I always felt stronger with my sister by my side.

"And now I don't know what comes next," I said.

"You work in Hollywood. You should know how this goes,"

Cecily replied. "You fall in love with him, he falls in love with you, and you both live happily ever after."

"You of all people should know that the fairy tale ends. Eventually, love dies, and your relationship rots."

"Such a romantic." Cecily rolled her eyes.

"Don't get me wrong, I believe in love. I'm surrounded by love: you, the kids, Janelle. Amazing people who cherish and adore me, and I cherish and adore them." I insisted. "But what is that saying we always heard growing up? Sin dinero, el amor sale por la ventana. Love can't last without a practical foundation based in reality."

"This coming from one of the most impractical people I've ever met." Cecily smiled.

"Am not!" I protested.

"Am too!" Cecily stressed. "You're always running around telling people to 'bet on your dreams,' refusing to believe that you can't make it in Hollywood despite everyone else telling you otherwise. Who else do you know could walk into a party full of famous people and snag the fucking prince of the ball?"

"Lots of people," I said.

"Name one."

"You want a name?" I smiled. "Cinder-fuckin'-rella."

"You quote rom-coms way too much to be so cynical about love," Cecily said. "I don't think you give yourself enough credit for how lovable you are."

"Sure, I'm the lovable, fat sidekick," I bemoaned.

"You're more than that," Cecily insisted. "If people can't see your beauty, they don't deserve you."

"That's just something thin girls say to make fat girls feel better."

"Does it help?" Cecily asked.

"Nope," I said.

"What would help?"

"Society changing to accept fat bodies as equal and seeing sexuality and gender as fluid," I responded.

"I'll work on that. Until then, how about some more tea?" Cecily got up from the sofa and walked toward the kitchen, not waiting for me to answer.

"I think we're going to need something stronger," I said, joining her.

"Whiskey?"

"Even stronger." I opened the freezer and pulled out a bag of tater tots.

Cecily laughed. "Who needs a man when you've got fried potato products?"

"Amen!" I poured the tots out onto a cookie sheet. "Hey, I heard you tell the kids that you sold a new canvas today. Congrats."

"Thanks." Cecily smiled. "It was just a small one, really nothing."

"Every sale is something," I interjected. "You're out here betting on your dreams, too, you know."

"Thanks for that reminder," Cecily said as she turned on the oven. "I love being an artist, I really do. I just wish it would pay better. I don't know how I'm going to afford this place when you move out."

"Maybe I'll just get mega-rich and buy us all a giant house in Hollywood Hills, and we can ship the kids off to boarding school in Switzerland when they're moody teenagers."

"Can I go with them?" Cecily begged. "I've always wanted to see the Alps."

"Sure. I'll buy us a chateau, and we can visit anytime."

"I like this plan." Cecily nodded.

"Me, too," I agreed, pouring some ketchup on a small plate.

"And where does Drew fit into this fantasy of yours?" Cecily asked when the tater tots were done.

"Oh, those feelings are just tucked away and ignored forever until I get over them easily and never feel heartbreak again."

Cecily laughed. "That sounds about as realistic as us owning a chateau in the Swiss Alps."

"I don't know what to do," I admitted as Cecily placed the hot pan of tots between us. "This whole scenario with the movie is far beyond my wildest dreams. I feel like I should just be happy with what I've been given and not throw love into the mix."

"That sounds so sad," Cecily lamented, picking up a tater tot and blowing on it.

"I know I sound pathetic."

"You sound like someone who was told her whole life that girls like her don't get a happy ending," Cecily corrected. "But isn't that exactly what you're trying to do with this movie, change the script?"

"God, I hate when you're right." I ignored the smug look on my sister's face. "I don't know how I'm going to do any of this. Make a movie. Date a guy. I'm alone in new territory without a map, and you know how horrible I am with directions."

"I have no idea how you're going to make it all work," Cecily said, "but I do know one thing."

"What?" I asked, picking up a tater tot.

"You don't have to do it alone," she reminded me, grabbing the tot out of my hand and popping it in her mouth.

Chapter Thirty-Three

The morning of our first table read, I found Chris muttering to himself as he obsessively made changes to the platters of food he'd prepared for the event, moving it all around, trying to make it look perfect, sprinkling salt on top, then taking some of it off.

"I find it best in moments like this to just let him do his thing," Bradley said to Cecily when I approached them standing in the doorway, watching.

After our late-night conversation over tater tots a couple weeks ago, I'd talked with Shamaya, Chris, and Drew about Cecily being a production assistant for the film, giving her a much-needed boost in income and allowing me to have my sister by my side along for the ride. They'd agreed to bring her on, and we put Cecily to work immediately, organizing the mounds of paperwork producing a film required. She soon became an integral part of the team, working hand in hand with Chris's assistant, Bradley, to keep all of us organized, calm, and ready to go.

"I think the hummus needs more tahini," Chris announced.

"It's fine," Cecily assured him. "Now, go get the rest." Chris sighed and headed back to the kitchen with Bradley.

"We're lucky it's a small cast." Janelle maneuvered her way around the tightly packed room and placed the name card for "Laura (played by Marie Austin)" on a chair. Marie was one of the few fat actresses on television these days and a hilarious comedian, who brought a levity to the script that I hadn't known it needed. She also had a huge online following—which Chris loved—and posted often about body positivity and intersectional feminism—which I loved. I was happy to have her on the project, even if I was still a bit sad to not be playing the role myself.

"Hola, hola, hola!" Shamaya sauntered into the room, wearing a silk-and-velvet suit that screamed power and money.

"You look fierce as hell," I said, kissing Shamaya on both cheeks.

"Of course I do. Got this from 11 Honoré." Shamaya twirled around. She turned her gaze to me and my striped jumpsuit paired with white flats. "You look cute, too. I love that comfy, chic look."

"Anyone else and that remark would feel snide, but I'm going to take it as the compliment I'm sure you meant it to be."

"Oh, honey, yes. You should know by now that I'm never snide. Or sarcastic. I just tell it as it is."

"And we love you for that," Janelle added, reaching in to hug Shamaya hello.

"Don't wrinkle the suit!" Shamaya pulled back quickly and kissed her on the cheek instead.

"You're ridiculous." Janelle shook her head.

"You love it." Shamaya twirled around once more.

We were out of pens, so I ran upstairs, ignoring Chris's yells that he needed my help in the kitchen. We'd used up all the supplies from his office, so I went to rummage through the guest bedroom when I walked in and saw Drew sitting in a chair, reading.

"I didn't realize you were here already," I said, closing the door behind me.

"I came over early this morning." He was nervous, more nervous than I'd ever seen him, and I wondered if it was producer nerves like Chris or something more. Something like me.

"I'm sorry we haven't been able to really talk lately," I said. "Things have been so hectic around here."

"I figured you were avoiding me," he said.

"Maybe a little," I admitted, then smiled up at him. "But I'm glad you're here now."

"Me, too." He smiled back at me. "Did you need something?"

"Oh yeah." I walked over to the desk and retrieved pens out of the top drawer. "These."

"Never enough pens."

"Not the way Chris marks up a script," I said, looking around. "I can head out, if you'd like. You looked busy."

"I was working on memorizing my lines." Drew picked his script up off the table. "Don't want to get into any more trouble with my director."

"Who said you're in trouble with me?"

"When you sleep with a woman and she doesn't call you back, it's a good assumption you're in trouble," Drew pointed out.

"What if I'm the trouble, not you?" I replied.

"Oh, you're definitely trouble." Drew moved closer to me.

"That makes us quite a pair, then, doesn't it?" I laughed nervously as Drew's finger touched mine.

"So we're a pair now?" Drew asked, closing the gap between our bodies.

"I meant…" I started, but Drew's lips were on mine before I could finish my sentence. He kissed me like a long-lost lover, his want mirroring my own, our bodies pressed into each other, desperate to close any remnant of the gap that had been between us.

"I dreamed of you every night," Drew confessed, pulling away to look at me, running his hand down my face.

"Freud would have a field day with that," I joked, leaning into his touch. "I love dreams. They tell you so much about a person."

"What do your dreams say about us?" Drew asked.

"I've always dreamed of making movies. Big ones, the kind that premiere on screens all around the world. I dream of walking red carpets in fabulous avant-garde outfits, waving at the paparazzi and my adoring fans. But not once, not a single time, did that dream include someone walking next to me." I dabbed my now tear-filled eyes, trying to prevent mascara from smearing all over my face. "My whole life I've been told that you can't have it all, so I've chosen my career over a relationship. I don't know how to make this movie and date you. I don't know how to dream that big."

"I have bigger dreams than just this one movie," Drew said, pulling me closer to him.

"Big dreams like two movies?" I quipped.

"Like us running off together to Italy. Or joining the circus and traveling around performing as acrobats."

I laughed. "Will there be lions and tigers and bears, oh my?"

"Absolutely not," Drew said. "That's animal cruelty. But there will be pasta."

"Gluten-free, of course," I added.

"Of course." He smiled.

"I like this bigger dream." I picked up the script where Drew had dropped it. "But we've gotta get through this one first."

"I love you, Diana," Drew let out, taking my hand instead of the script I was offering him. My heart stopped as he wrapped his fingers around mine. "And that love is not going anywhere. I'm going to do everything I can to help this dream of yours come true, but I want you to know you deserve a bigger dream, one that's not so lonely. It doesn't have to include me if I'm not who you want, but it absolutely should include love."

"I would like it to include you," I said, my voice cracking as the want filled me. "I would very much like it to include you."

"Then it will." Drew hugged me tightly. "I'm not going anywhere."

We stood there, his arms around me, my head pressed into his chest, until the doorbell rang, reminding us that there was a whole cast and crew of people filing in downstairs.

"What do we do now?" I wondered, looking up at him.

Drew kissed the top of my head, then let me go. "Right now, you go downstairs and greet your team while I stay up here and learn my lines so my director doesn't fire me."

I laughed. "Okay, and then later?"

"We'll deal with later later," Drew said.

I nodded and walked to the door, turning around to watch him silently mouth his lines. He looked up at me, smiled, and shooed me away. I smiled, too, and closed the door, sighing heavily.

Que será, será, I sang to myself, walking down the hall. I had no idea what was going to happen with Drew, where this love would take us, and what it meant for my life and career. I did know, however, that worrying about tomorrow wouldn't help me today, so I pushed my fears aside and focused instead on this dream that was coming true right now.

With a giddy smile, I made my way downstairs and was greeted by a room full of cast and crew, all excitedly chatting with each other in the small spaces between chairs. I stood in the doorway for a while, watching people interact, appreciating the ensemble we'd gathered together. Francine was talking with our new lead, Marie. Miel and Shamaya were in the middle of the room, laughing at something Janelle had just said. Even though she wasn't needed this early in the process, Kali was there to meet everyone, sitting off to the side on Chris's sofa, her head sporting a super-cute neon beanie, Emmy sitting next to her, holding her hand.

Drew came down to join us, and we all took our assigned seats, with me in the middle of a horseshoe arrangement of cast and crew. It was a varying display of skin tones, abilities, identities, and presentations, and I was honored that they'd all gathered together for this little story of mine. I looked out onto the room, everyone holding a copy of my script in their hands, staring up at me expectantly with excited anticipation on their faces.

It was exactly how I'd always imagined it.

"Ready, everyone?" I asked, looking first to Cecily on my right, then Janelle on my left. Shamaya beamed at me while Chris nodded. I looked up at Drew, and he winked at me, mouthing the words, "You've got this," with a big grin on his face.

"All right, then." I smiled at my new team, my new family. "Let's begin."

Epilogue

Some girls spend their childhoods dreaming of their wedding day. I spent mine planning for the Oscars.

They called it Hollywood's biggest night, but really, it's a whole season, one full of screenings and junkets, interviews and appearances. It took months just to plan my outfit, mostly because no one would dress me. Turned out designers still hated fat people, even famous ones. Luckily, Christian Siriano loved working with women of all shapes, colors, and sizes, and he happily took on the group of us.

My dress was long and dark red, with rose-like petals of silk adorning the bodice and continuing down the skirt like they were falling in the breeze. I wore dark flats, because screw heels, and massive chandelier earrings. Janelle glowed in a bright orange pantsuit with a matching cape, and Cecily was stunning in a white gown with silver stars down the front. Together we'd be an elegant walking ad for Christian Siriano, which felt right, a diverse group of stars wearing a designer known for dressing diversity.

I'd always thought tonight would be the catalyst for change, that I'd step onto the red carpet and into my true self, a confident creator and artist who was proud of her work, her body, her life, herself. But when the Oscars finally arrived, I realized that change happened long before tonight.

It happened in my college classes and on dance floors in gay bars. It happened at protests and rallies for the rights of myself, my friends, and all LGBTQIA+ people.

It happened when Henry died and I moved in with Cecily, our whole worlds crumbling. It happened when we worked together to climb out of the ruins.

It happened with every awkward person I helped feel confident at Roussard's, and every time I dressed myself, defiant of fashion's boxy clothing and "flattering" looks meant to hide my fat body.

It happened when I showed up to that LACMA party like I belonged there. It happened when I refused to settle while making this movie. It happened on set as we all came together and poured in our hearts and souls.

I'd found my community, a group of people who loved and accepted me as I was. That was what I'd been searching for my whole life. That was making it.

Don't get me wrong, I still wanted an Oscar, I'd always chase that little golden man and the prestige winning would give me in my career, but I didn't need him as a shield anymore. I was surrounded by the protection of the people I loved.

People like the ones gathered around me tonight, who were all in a tizzy because the limo had arrived. Suddenly, everything felt real, and I jumped up and down shouting, "Aaaahhh," getting all of my nervous jitters out while I could. When I was done, I picked up my purse and headed for the door.

"Wait!" Janelle grabbed my hand and pulled me toward the hotel suite's full-length mirror.

"What?" I asked, worried I'd forgotten something important.

"We're fine as hell," she started, a huge smile on her face.

"And sexy as fuck," I continued, my smile matching hers. I *had* forgotten something important, the most important thing of all.

"People are lucky to share space with us," Janelle added, tears forming in her eyes.

"They should pay us to be in their presence." I felt myself getting teary-eyed as well.

"Damn right," Janelle finished as we pulled each other into a tight embrace.

"Damn right!" Cecily joined us.

"I friggin' love y'all," I said as we squeezed together for a group hug—done carefully so as to not mess up our hair or outfits—then headed out of the suite followed by an entourage of assistants.

Hotel security led us through the back halls to avoid paparazzi, and we met our chauffeur at the loading dock, which smelled like trash and urine. It wasn't the most glamorous start to our evening, but it was a lot better than dealing with the hordes of people who waited outside the hotels on Oscar night, hoping to catch a glimpse of the celebrities attending. It still shocked me to know that now included me.

Limos weren't in style anymore. These days people opted for Rolls-Royces or Escalades, depending on their image, but I'd always imagined arriving at the Oscars in a classic black limo with Cecily and Janelle by my side, so that's what I ordered. Or

I should say, that's what Suzanne ordered, the new publicist I'd gotten through Drew.

Drew… The thought of him made my heart skip. He'd been nothing but professional publicly, respecting my wish to keep our relationship out of the press so it didn't take away from the film. But privately, he'd been one of the most devoted lovers I'd ever had, making me fall for him again and again. It wasn't all romance and roses; we'd had many heated conversations working through our differences—topics like queer identity, non-monogamy, childhood trauma, privilege, and birth control came up a lot—but there was something special and long-lasting between us that had me even more excited about tonight. Two years ago, sitting on Jaqueline's back porch, I'd made a promise to Drew that if I won an Oscar for this movie, he could have me right there in front of everyone, and tonight I planned to make good on that promise, whether I won or not. Because my love for Drew wasn't something I wanted or needed to hide anymore.

I was a fat, queer woman from a small farming town who overcame grief and crippling depression to make a movie full of queers, sex workers, and people of color with a mostly woman and non-binary crew. That movie had been nominated for multiple Academy Awards and made millions of dollars at the box office. More than any of that, it had changed lives for the better, making a massive positive impact in this world. If people wanted to talk shit about me dating Drew Williams, they could have at it. I'd already done what I came to Hollywood to do.

"Ready?" Janelle asked as we approached the front of the line of cars.

"No," I said, tears filling my eyes. "I've spent my whole life impatiently waiting for this moment to come, and now that it's here, I want to stop time."

"Do not start getting all mushy and make us cry!" Cecily insisted. "I refuse to have us photographed by thousands of cameras with red eyes and smeared mascara."

I laughed as I patted my eyes dry using the handkerchief Jaqueline had embroidered for me, with red roses to match my outfit and my initials on the corner. Chaz, the one stylist we'd been able to fit in the car with us, gave me a look over, touched up my lipstick, and then spritzed me with some kind of freshener that smelled like the ocean.

"You're ready," Chaz declared.

Squeezing Janelle and Cecily's hands one last time, I knocked to tell the driver it was time.

He opened the door, and the immediate barrage of lights and screaming was overpowering, a tidal wave of sensory overload. I had no idea how I was supposed to exit the limo gracefully when I could barely see or hear. I wanted to climb back into the depths of our car, let the others go first and pave the way, but Suzanne had given us strict instructions on the order we exited, insisting I be first.

"We'll be right behind you," Cecily said, easing my worries. One minute of posing for the cameras by myself, then Janelle would join me, followed by Cecily. I wouldn't be alone for long. I could do this. I took the chauffeur's hand and entered the fray.

The sound of it all was deafening. Smiling journalists and large television cameras lined the wide red carpet, with paparazzi behind them flashing away. Above it all, rows of bleachers held screaming fans, and I was shocked to hear my name on some of their lips. Before I could take any of it in, someone grabbed my hand. I glanced up to see Shamaya beaming next to me.

"I heard I was only a couple cars ahead of you, so I made them wait," she said, posing for photos like she'd been born for this, which, I realized, she had. She squeezed my fingers reassuringly and added, "We're in this together."

"We're in this together." I squeezed back, smiling while I scanned the crowd. There was a group of obviously queer teenagers taking up a corner of the bleachers closest to the street, and I led our entourage over to them, taking selfies and signing autographs despite security's insistence that we go back to the photo line.

This is why I made this movie, I thought as a genderqueer kid gushed about how much the film had meant to them. *Remember this moment. This is why you're here.*

Our hearts swollen with pride, we made our way back to the main runway, ready to tackle the press. Shamaya and I took the interviews together, a well-rehearsed pair stepping up to cameras and microphones in an act we'd been doing for months on the road. Cecily and Janelle stood back, both preferring to stay out of the spotlight, and watched the rush of celebrities going past them.

"Diana, I see you've got your sister here with you tonight," one reporter said, calling Cecily over. "What was it like, watching yourself portrayed on the screen?"

"As Diana always says, 'surreal, but nice.'" Cecily smiled awkwardly into the camera.

The reporter turned to Janelle. "What would you tell young girls out there wanting to make it in film?"

"Be the kind of person who bids on your own dreams," Janelle said. "Everyone thought Diana and I were being unreasonable and unrealistic in film school when we set out to make movies with a diverse cast and crew. Nobody believed it could work, but now we're here, and we did that by sticking together. So bid on your own dreams and find yourself a crew to go all in with you."

"Great advice from Janelle Zenon, who is nominated tonight for Best Cinematography," the reporter said, turning back to the viewers at home as we were ushered away from her and into the theater.

"I have no idea how I'm going to do it, but I desperately need to pee," I said, looking around for a restroom.

"You helped me with my wedding dress. I'll help you with this." Cecily pointed to a WOMEN sign in the corner.

It was quite a job, but working together to lift our layers, one at a time, Cecily and I were both able to relieve our bladders. Giggling, we made our way to the mirror to wash our hands and touch up our makeup, when I noticed a familiar older woman with white-blonde hair next to me at the sink.

I couldn't breathe. I couldn't speak. I just smiled and nodded when she said hello, drying her hands and walking out with the kind of grace that made her a star.

"OH MY GOD!" I shouted once she'd left. "That was Meryl Streep! I shared a bathroom with Meryl Streep! At the Oscars!"

I screamed. I couldn't help it. I screamed and grabbed Cecily, and we jumped up and down, not caring if I was supposed to act composed and professional.

"I could die happy," I said as I leaned against the bathroom wall.

"No more dying in this family," Cecily insisted, handing me my lipstick out of her purse. Even at the Oscars, she was the mom, holding everyone's stuff, keeping us in our place.

"I love you," I said, staring at this amazing woman who did so much for so many. She smiled and handed me another Jaqueline-embroidered hankie from her purse to wipe my tears.

As we headed toward our seats, there was so much

happening that it was hard to take it all in. Later I'd only remember it in bursts, walking down the aisle, people I admired shaking my hand, strangers congratulating me on my film and its nominations. It was all a blur until I caught the familiar faces of Chris and Jaqueline smiling at me from a row that was shockingly close to the stage.

"There she is, the belle of the ball." Chris drew me into a hug.

"If I'm Belle, would that make you Beast?" I asked, smirking.

"I believe Drew has claimed that role." Jaqueline nodded at her son, who was walking toward us.

"Happy Oscars." Drew kissed everyone on the cheek, lingering a bit longer against my face to whisper, "God, you look amazing," in my ear, which sent shivers down my whole body. I almost grabbed and kissed him right then and there, but Chaz would kill me if I ruined my lipstick this early in the night.

"What am I supposed to do?" I asked as we took our seats, the show about to begin.

"Just watch and play along," Drew said.

"And smile," Chris reminded me, showing a perfect row of newly whitened teeth. "No matter what happens, smile."

And then we were live, streamed to millions of homes around the world, homes like mine where I'd watched the Academy Awards every year, dreaming of the day I was there. I watched, smiled, and laughed along through opening numbers that poked fun at actors in attendance and introduced the stars that night—including me!

I sighed in disappointment when Emmy lost the Best Costumes category but screamed wildly when Janelle won for Best Cinematography.

"This is for all the little Black girls out there, trying to find their light," she said, keeping it short and simple, but still making the whole audience tear up.

We cried even more at the In Memoriam section of the evening, honoring all those lost over the past year, hating seeing Kali's face in the mix. Chris had picked out her photo, one taken that night we had our picnic under the stars, and she smiled down at all of us from the screen. She'd fended off cancer just long enough to finish the score for our movie, which was nominated for Best Original Song tonight—Chris and Drew singing a heartfelt version of it live in her stead. Her funeral had been a celebration of life, making me both grateful I'd gotten to know her before she was gone and devastated I didn't have more time with my new friend.

Everyone was bawling in her memory, and I wanted to pull our whole crying group into a big hug, but the show had to go on. Soon it was time for Best Screenplay, and I smiled and waved as Daniel Kaluuya said my name. The camera pointed at me, and I tried to remind myself that no matter what happened next, tonight I was already a winner.

"And the Oscar goes to," Daniel said, lifting the flap and pulling out an envelope.

"Diana Smith for *Home Bound*!" he revealed, and I froze, my whole body in shock.

"Diana, go!" Chris shouted at me from down the row of chairs, and Cecily helped push me on stage as I shook with nervous excitement. Dazed, I made my way to the podium, taking the little golden statue and staring at it a long time before Daniel poked me in the side, reminding me we were live.

"Oh, yes, my speech!" I remembered, making the audience laugh.

I had written something, of course, a short but thoughtful piece thanking everyone who had made this possible, but once I was up there, I decided to just go with what my heart wanted to say.

"When I was a little girl, a stranger asked me what I wanted to be when I grew up, and I told him I wanted to make movies," I started, my voice growing stronger with each word. "The old man laughed, patted my stomach, and told me I'd have to lose about twenty pounds to make that dream come true. I was twelve, and he was the first of many who said this moment would always be impossible for me to reach, whether because of my weight, my gender, or my sexuality. I'm much larger than I was then, both in size and stature, and it was only by embracing my grandeur that I was able to make it here to this stage.

"This Oscar is mine, yes, but it also belongs to every fat girl out there. It belongs to all the queers, the kids of color, the ones struggling with their mental health, the outcasts, and the misfits. To anyone who has ever been told you were too much, I beg you to stand tall in your greatness. I beg you to expand and grow. I beg you to never shrink away."

The crowd stood and cheered as I followed Daniel Kaluuya and a model a tenth of my size off the stage. They led me to a staging area where I posed for photos, tears still running down my face. When we were done, Chaz was brought around to retouch my makeup while an assistant held me in place, waiting for a commercial break to let me go to my seat. While I stood backstage, they announced Best Supporting Actor and sadly Drew lost. He looked happy for Ncuti Gatwa when the cameras panned to him, but I knew he had really wanted to win.

As soon as the assistant gave the go-ahead, I ran back to my seat, where everyone was waiting with excitement to congratulate me. I grabbed Cecily and hugged her first, tears ruining the makeup I'd just had retouched. We passed my new little man around between us, and Emmy came over to congratulate me with a large smile on her face, the happiest I'd seen her since Kali passed. The assistants hushed us, prepping to go back on air, and I sat down in my seat between Cecily and Drew.

"You won an Oscar!" he said, grabbing my hand and squeezing it.

"I won an Oscar!" I screamed, getting shushing noises from the cameraman next to me. "I'm sorry you didn't win," I whispered to him.

"It's not over yet." He smiled.

Next up was Best Supporting Actress, and we all applauded and screamed when Miel won. Her acceptance speech was a manifesto of sex workers' rights, and I cried again, thinking about how much I needed speeches like ours as a kid watching the Oscars every year, how much I still needed them as an adult. When she started praising the relationship I had with Cecily and the way our crew made her feel like she had a family again after hers disowned her for being gay, I completely lost it, resigning myself to being that girl the internet made into emotional memes.

I thought the shock would subside each time we won, but it just amplified as *Home Bound* raked in the awards, including Marie for Best Actress and Kali for Best Original Song, which Jaqueline accepted in her honor. It hadn't been lost on me, my team, or the press that I was passed over for best director, even though my movie had more nominations in other categories than any other film. The Academy rarely acknowledged women directors as equal to men. Hollywood had made progress in my lifetime, but it still had a long way to go.

The disappointment in not having my name read for Best Director was abated a bit, though, when Chris won Best Actor and said, "None of this would be possible without a feisty little coffee girl named Diana Smith."

Then, in what felt like an eternity and a millisecond all at once, it was time for Best Picture. Everyone in our group linked hands, from Chris down to Miel, who reached back for Emmy's hand, which was clasped together with Jaqueline's. Mindy Kaling was announcing the nominees, and seeing her up on stage, I remembered the LACMA party at Chris's house, Janelle and I watching her walk by with our mouths agape. It seemed like a whole lifetime ago that we were all strangers, this mismatched group of misfits I now considered family.

"And the Oscar goes to…" Mindy said, opening the envelope and smiling, "Chris Stanson, Shamaya Kapoor, Drew Williams, and Diana Smith for *Home Bound*!"

I crumpled to the floor, bawling. That was it, then. I'd done it. I'd made an Academy Award–winning film. All the sacrifices, all the energy, all the classes and books on craft, all the years of waiting and working on my script and waiting some more. It all finally paid off.

I thought of Henry, how much I wished he could be there with Cecily and me, how much I owed the drive in my life to the loss of his. And I swore I felt him squeeze my shoulder, right there at the base of my neck, the way he used to do when he'd hug me. I swore I heard him whisper in my ear how proud he was of us.

Cecily was standing above me, yelling at me to get off the floor, but someone else reached down to help me up, large, strong hands that were gently lifting me off the ground. I turned to see Drew with tears in his eyes and the largest smile I'd ever seen on his face. Without hesitation, I jumped up into his arms and kissed him. It was a long, deep, full-mouth kiss, the kind that left nothing open for interpretation. I heard the audience's applause grow louder as he wrapped his arms around me, pulling me into his embrace. I didn't care who was watching, and I didn't care if my lipstick was smeared all over his face. All I cared about was showing Drew how much I loved him, how much I appreciated all he'd done to help get me here to this moment.

"Get it together, you two. You're on national television," Chris hissed, walking past us and up the stage.

Drew stepped away from me, laughing as the people around us hooted. I blushed as I took Drew's hand in my right and Shamaya's hand in my left, and together we walked up to accept our award. The Best Picture Oscar technically went to only the producers, but we'd decided long ago that this was a group effort and, if we won, we all deserved to be up there together, so the whole cast and crew came with us.

For so long, I'd focused on getting onto this stage that I hadn't put much thought into what would happen after I got there. Chris and Shamaya would give the acceptance speeches for all of us, we'd arranged that much, and then we'd pose for photos and go to parties where we'd be congratulated by everyone, the belles of the ball as Chris had said. I'd critique outfits with Shamaya, dance wildly with Cecily, and watch Janelle try to become best friends with Lena Waithe. I'd probably sneak away with Drew to make out like teenagers at prom, and I would definitely make him help me find Meryl Streep and convince her to have tea with me.

At some point we'd go home, and I'd hug Reggie and Ellis,

letting them play with my Oscar whenever they wanted because, really, if you thought about it, it was just a golden doll and they deserved to hold it as much as I did. I'd officially move into Drew's house–I spent most nights there anyways–but I'd make sure to go back to Arcadia for pancakes and painting as often as I could.

I'd befriend all the famous queers, now that I was one of them, and I would kiss Drew whenever I wanted, knowing my sexuality was mine alone to define. As soon as this was over, I would crawl into his arms and not leave for days, Serena making us breakfast in bed. I would let him take us all on a vacation to Italy—Cecily, the kids, and Jaqueline, too—like he'd been saying he wanted to for over a year now. We would eat so many gluten-free carbs and I would never again care who saw us together.

I would celebrate every little second of this with everyone I loved, with Cecily and the kids, Drew, Jaqueline, Janelle, Shamaya, Chris—everyone who helped make this all possible. I would party and dance and relish every single moment of this dream coming true.

And then, when I felt well-rested and full of love, I'd do it all again. I'd make another movie. I'd tell another story. Because my happy ending didn't come when I got a man, little golden one or tall human one. My happy ending came every time I had the guts to stand up and declare that my story was worth telling.

Acknowledgments

In 2017, Dwayne Johnson asked me out, and I turned him down. I loved him, but I couldn't handle the hateful comments I would get for being the fat queer girl dating The Rock. I woke up from that dream and wrote *Because Fat Girl*. So first off, I'd like to thank Dwayne "The Rock" Johnson, for inspiring this book, and for showing the world that masculinity can be gentle, kind, and caring.

I was living in Mexico City at the time, and while I was writing the first draft, we experienced a catastrophic earthquake. Muchas gracias to the strangers and friends who saved me that day and made me feel safe enough to be creative again, including Laura, Ana Luisa, toda la familia de Tere, and the people of Coyoacán.

This book would have stayed a dream without the constant support and cheerleading of its biggest fan, Kylee Singh. Thank you for never letting me give up, even when all seemed lost.

I am forever grateful for the input of my beta readers Rachel Brethauer, Claire Palzer, Jenny Kindschy, Mars Pacelli, Lauren (Finn) Lofton, and my fellow students at the UCLA Writers Program and Esalen Writers Camp. Thanks to Matt Kugelman for showing me it can be done, Jenn Leyva for being my writing dominatrix, Nicté Trujillo for checking my Spanish, and Taneet Grewal for adding depth and accuracy to Shamaya and her family. I've had some spectacular writing coaches while working on this book, including Suzy Vitello, Lynn Hightower, Steve Almond, Camille Dungy, Lydia Yuknavitch, Samantha Dunn, Lynell George, Cheryl Strayed, Pam Houston, and the divinely magical Steph Jagger–thank you for making me a better writer and human.

Elise Capron, your publishing advice has been great and your friendship even greater. Thank you for your invaluable insights and constant support, personally and professionally.

Huge thanks to the whole Entangled Publishing team, especially Jessica Turner, for matching my excitement and eagerness to take risks and try something new. Thank you to my agent Jill Marsal for introducing us. So much thanks to my editor, Yezanira Venecia, for truly understanding this story and making it better. To Lizzy, Curtis, Justine, Angela, Elizabeth, Bree, Heather, Lauren, Meredith, Ashley, Madison, and Liz, thank you for putting your heart and sweat into making this dream come true.

San Diego is the book capital of the world because of the kind, talented, and accomplished authors that I'm lucky to be in community with here. So much gratitude for my write-or-dies Sarina Dahlan and Caroline Fowler Davis, who got me through the last big pushes of this book. Thanks to everyone in the SD Writers Group and at the *Off the Record* days for your invaluable insight and camaraderie, and Lani Gobaleza, Amy

Truong, Emily Deady and the whole team at PARU teahouse for the Spare Pen Club that kept me inspired and the matcha that kept me awake. We're able to support such a thriving and diverse literary community here because of the wonderful bookstores we have. I'm grateful for all of them, but a special thanks to Mysterious Galaxy, Meet Cute, Verbatim, Libélula, and the downtown library for your support along my journey.

Thank you to every queer, poly, kinky, genderqueer, trans, neurodiverse, chronically ill, and fat activist and artist who came before me so I could legally and safely share my stories. In everything I do, I hope to pave the way for others as you did for me.

I am honored to work with some of the greatest humans in the world through my company, School for Writers®. Thank you especially to Jess Elianet Pupo, Mars Pacelli, and all the WYFBAES who have helped me grow Write Your Friggin' Book Already® into the impactful, diverse, and supportive program it is today. I am so grateful for the ongoing support and advice of Kaitlyn Clark, Laura Eigel, Pam Covarrubias, Ekta Kaul, and my Biz Besties, Max MacKellar, Indigo Blue, and Katie Treggiden.

Thank you to my Befri, Cariwyl Hebert, who keeps me grounded, dorky, and sometimes drunk, and my Befri-In-Law, Kevin Smokler, who encourages our shenanigans. I'm not sure how I would have survived the past decade without Crys Harris and Ronise Zenon, and I'm so grateful to you two and the rest of our leather family, Shelli, KL, Kelli, and SaBrina Elliot, for feeding my belly and soul. Thank you to everyone at DESIRE who infused this book with kinky magic, especially Morgan Hart. And to M, you expanded my capacity for pleasure and brought light back into a darkened part of my life. Thank you for answering my call.

Creativity was fostered in my early years thanks to my first patrons, Gramma and Poppo, and I'm so grateful to the whole Fleming and Austin families for always showing up at my performances and supporting my work. To Liz, thanks for being a loving second sister and having the best laugh in the world. To Ally, Ryan, Icoris and Leena, follow your passions and get a little wild knowing your Aunt Yolo will always be proud (and there with bail money). To Brandon and Andrew, I miss you both so much. I hope you're playing baseball together somewhere over the rainbow.

Mom and Dad, you've always supported my love of the arts, from driving me to theater rehearsals to sending me to film school. I'm able to take giant leaps of faith because I know you'll give me a place to crash if things don't work out. I'm so grateful for all you've given me. From the bottom of my heart, thank you.

And to my sister, Michelle. I'm beyond lucky to have you as my life partner, even if it creeps people out when we say that. Thanks for giving me a reason to live when I thought all hope was lost, and for making me pee my pants laughing more times than I care to admit. Poop fart butt vagina (that means I love you).

Last, but so very far from least, to you, the reader. From the beginning, *Because Fat Girl* has been about diverse communities coming together to tell our stories on our own terms. My biggest hope for this book is that it inspires you to go out there and write your own. Get a group of friends and make a movie on your phone. Start a podcast. Produce a play in your community. Kickstart a web series. Bet on your dreams.

Because the world needs your story now more than ever.

Don't miss the exciting new books Entangled has to offer.

Follow us!

@EntangledPublishing

@Entangled_Publishing

@EntangledPub

AMARA
an imprint of Entangled Publishing LLC